To Russell Frederick Roth
with borrowed regret

# Contents

## ACKNOWLEDGMENT

To Mr. William Lester McKnight and Mr. Walter N. Trenerry of the McKnight Foundation of St. Paul, Minnesota, go my sincere thanks for providing me with funds while I wrote this novel.

. . . When you are actually *in* America, America hurts, because it has a powerful disintegrative influence upon the white psyche. It is full of grinning, unappeased aboriginal demons, too, ghosts, and it persecutes the white men like some Eumenides, until the white men give up their absolute whiteness. America is tense with latent violence and resistance. The very common sense of white Americans has a tinge of helplessness in it, and deep fear of what might be if they were not commonsensical.

Yet one day the demons of America must be placated, the ghosts must be appeased, the Spirit of Place atoned for. Then the true passionate love for American Soil will appear. . . .

—D. H. Lawrence
*Studies in Classic American Literature*

# PART
## ONE

# The Torment

# 1

No Name waited until it was dark. Then he threw a white robe over his shoulders and stooped out through the door and quietly made his way toward his sweetheart's lodge.

It was the Moon of Scarlet Plums. An autumn wind stirred the heavy leaves of the cottonwoods behind the Yankton village and ruffled the waters of the River of the Double Bend. The low murmur of Falling Water waved on the brisk wind. High above, a frost of stars sparkled all across the skies. The evening fires made the pointed tepees glow like soft lanterns. A good fire jumped in the council lodge in the center of the village, and every now and then the silhouette of a warrior moved huge and flitting across its parchment skin.

Narrowing his eyes, No Name could just make out the level black horizon of the prairies to the east. He moved slowly, stepping like a bird, toe down first, then the heel, wary of where favorite ponies might be staked out for the night. The skunktails tied to his heels, which he wore only on special occasions, fluffed across the grass. Other night-walkers moved about too, hoping to catch some maiden out on a late night errand. Mothers soothed their babies with lullabies. Fathers told stories. And in a far tepee, Moon Dreamer, his mother's brother and the tribe's holy man, sang in a hoarse voice over Wondering Man, his ailing grandfather.

No Name was a Yankton Sioux of seventeen winters. He was slim, with high wide shoulders, lean arms and legs, and hands as sure-fingered as a squirrel's. His skin was a deep rose-brown, which at night looked almost black. His eyes were a brooding velvet brown. His lips were full, sensuous, somewhat tremulous at the corners. He was both very much in love and very sad at heart.

"Tonight," No Name said to himself, "tonight I will ask Leaf to elope with me. We will fly across the prairies and visit my uncle Red Hail. He will protect us. Then after a time we will come back and her father and mother will forgive us."

Leaf's tepee stood under a single towering cottonwood at the open end of the camp circle. The fire in it had sunk to embers and he could barely make it out. Her father Owl Above was one of those who always went to bed early. Some months before, a raiding party of Pawnees had stolen all his horses and killed his son Burnt Thigh. Owl Above had been downcast ever since. His youngest wife had even left him because he had neither work nor food for her.

No Name stopped. He fumbled under his white buffalo robe for his flute. He placed his fingers over the four holes on top and his thumb over the hole on the underside and blew gently into the flat mouthpiece. A soft whooo trembled on the wind. Leaf would know what he meant. "I am here," his flute said. "I am ready for you." He blew again, gently. "It is cold. Come. I have something to tell you. Come quickly."

He waited in the dark. The north wind threshed through the cottonwood leaves above him. Then the wind fell slowly away. The fires in the tepees dimmed. People still out doing late chores, old women securing ponies, warriors heading for the council lodge, brushed past him. He stood outside her lodge, rooted, patient as a tree.

A mare whinnied behind his father Redbird's lodge. Far across the prairies where the night herder had hobbled his father's many horses a stallion answered with a great shrilling. A falling star streaked in a wide arc across the skies.

Stepping closer, No Name blew his flute again, this time very softly. "Come," his flute said, "I have something to tell you."

He waited. In the lull the smells of the camp wafted by him: meat drying behind Leaf's tepee, a buffalo hide curing on a rack, a pipe spuming kinnikinick, sweetgrass and sage burning in the council lodge where someone was being initiated into a warrior society.

He moved up until he stood beside the door flap of her tepee. "I hear you," his flute said, "my ears are as keen as a robin's and I hear you breathing. You are there. Come. The rustling tree whispers above."

He waited. A dog howled at the far end, setting off a long series of answering yowls from dogs all over the village. Moon Dreamer had taken to beating his medicine drum, slowly, t-thum, t-thum, still exorcising in a high chant over Grandfather Wondering Man. Nearby another nightwalker blew love notes on a flute.

A hand touched his elbow. It was Leaf. Her wide smile flashed up at him in the dark. She stood in the slanting door, her feet still inside the tepee, her thighs and body outside. Her head came up to his chin. In a loving manner he threw his white robe around her. They nestled together inside the fur.

"I have come to you," he said.

"Have you?"

He stroked her arms from the shoulder down to the wrist. He had slim eloquent fingers and he caressed her again and again. Her snowy doeskin dress made soft ruffling noises under his fingertips. She slipped an arm around his middle. The musk smell of the robe enclosed them.

"There are many moccasin tracks before your door," he said.

She smiled up at him. Her face was like a gently smiling brown moon. Her slanting eyes glinted like a pair of willow leaves.

"I have seen a young girl who looks so beautiful to me," he said, "I feel sick when I think about her."

She slipped her other arm around him. "Tomorrow you will sing about me and call out my Name for the others to laugh at me. And I will feel ashamed and will hide."

"Have I called your name before?"

She rested her head against his chest. She said, "A maiden does not talk to her lover until he has married her."

He groaned over her. The perfume of coneflowers rose from her hair. There was also in her braids the smell of a tepee fire. "I am without a wife," he said. "I am naked."

"Your father has many horses," she said.

With soft downward strokes he rubbed her firm well-muscled arms. He was sick. Her father and mother wanted many horses in payment for her. Yet he had no horses. And, until a vision had been given him by the gods, he could not ask his own father and mother for horses.

No Name sighed. Three times he had gone to a high hill in lonely fast to receive his vision, and three times nothing had happened, no protective spirit animal, no spirit wolf or spirit bear, had appeared to him to become his helper in war and peace. There had been only hunger, and very lonely nights, and much weakness after.

His father Redbird had said nothing, though it could be seen in Redbird's manner that he was disappointed in his son. Redbird was very old and afraid he would die before his son received his vision of life and performed a deed of valor. The village knew this, and wondered, and that was why some of the younger braves, taunting, had taken to calling his son No Name. The older warriors meanwhile shied from asking his son along on their war parties or inviting him to join their warrior societies.

No Name sighed for a second time, deeply. He held Leaf close.

Leaf guessed his thoughts. She looked up at his hair where he should have been wearing an honor feather. She asked, "Is not the fourth time the sacred time?"

"But my god will not come," he cried.

"My father is restless," she said. "Already he eats from the hand of Circling Hawk."

"Ai! Then it is Circling Hawk's footsteps I see in the dust before your tepee."

"Circling Hawk's breath stinks," she said. "I do not favor him. Also he chews loudly."

"He is a brave man. He has a coup feather."

"He eats before my father has finished smoking the pipe. Also his face is rough. Like a toad's back."

"What does your mother say?"

"She looks in the pot and sees that it is empty."

No Name stroked her arms, lovingly. "What should I do?" he cried.

"Have you spoken to your uncle Moon Dreamer?"

He felt the touch of her hands. Her palms were like pads of leather. She was a hard worker and would make a good wife. He said, "My father does not much favor him."

"Your father is perhaps afraid of his brother-in-law's medicine."

No Name trailed his slim fingertips over her wrists. "Oh, let us run away to my uncle Red Hail. Let us elope. Come." He tugged at the fringes of her white tunic.

She hid her eyes. "My father must have the horses first. The Pawnees have stolen his horses and he remains a poor man."

"Come. Let us run away. My uncle Red Hail will be kind to us."

"Also my brother Burnt Thigh is dead." She wept a moment in memory. "We loved him very much, yet he was killed by the Pawnees when they stole our horses."

"I have seen a maiden who is very beautiful," he said winningly, "and I feel sick when I think about her."

"And I see a young maiden crying alone on the prairies, bitterly. Her heart is broken because her lover has used her and then has thrown her away."

He tugged at her under his robe. "Come. Let us fly to my uncle Red Hail. He is a kind man."

She said archly, "My father says when a young man has known a woman too soon his god will shun him."

"What must I do?"

"I wish to keep that which no man has yet touched."

"Has not Circling Hawk touched it?"

"No man."

He saw stars reflected in her black eyes. He was almost beside himself. His nostrils flared on each breath. His shoulders, already high, lifted as if he were about to pounce. "What must I do?"

She touched his hands. "When you return with the center feather of an eagle in your hair I will dance and make a song for you."

He brushed her arms downward, with free-flowing loving fingers. "Tonight, after your father and mother are asleep, I will come in the dark, silently, and slide under the back of the lodge and lie under the robe with you."

Her white teeth laughed at him. "My mother and father know very well how to bind their daughter so she cannot move."

"My father taught me how to loosen the tightest knots, silently, so that no one can hear."

"Have you stolen a favorite horse from a Pawnee chief then?"

"Also my father told me that when one desires a maiden very much it is good to cut the ropes with a knife."

She laughed. "I have a lover who sounds very clever. Yet he has no honor feather."

He groaned.

Abruptly his white buffalo robe was jerked away and the head of an old woman appeared between them. It was Leaf's mother Full Kettle. "Daughter," Full Kettle said, holding her face averted to No Name, "your father cannot sleep. There is too much talk near his tepee."

Without a word, crestfallen, No Name slipped away in the dark. The skunktails on his heels fluffed across the grass, erasing his trail.

# 2

When he returned to his father's lodge the fire in the center had fallen to pink embers. He stole around to the right, careful not to step between his father and the fire, and in the back of the tepee settled on his knees beside his fur bed. He slipped off his buckskin shirt and leggings and breechclout. He stretched out, feet to the fire, then snuggled under his sleeping robe, pulling it up to his chin. The buffalo fur comforted his naked skin. The grass under the fur bedding made the earth feel soft.

"Son?" It was his mother Star That Does Not Move calling him. He could hear her stir beside his father Redbird. "Son?"

"I have come."

The pink coals fell in upon themselves with soft sounds. His father's favorite hunting pony, Swift As Wind, stomped in sleep outside. The wind rose again and moaned low in the smokehole above.

He lay waiting for sleep.

Hard fingers touched his throat. "Little Bird?"

It was his father's other wife, Loves Roots. Loves Roots was one of those who fancied skunk meat because she had noticed skunks ate many roots. She was calling him by his baby name, Little Bird, the one his uncle Moon Dreamer had given him at birth. No Name wished Loves Roots would leave him alone. She was always seeking to ensnare him in a love embrace.

"Little Bird?" Her calloused fingers stroked his high nose.

He lay very still.

"Little Bird?" Her fingers moved down under his robe and touched his thigh.

"I am known as No Name," he said bitterly. But even as he spoke desire moved warmly in his limbs. His body could not help itself. He pushed her away, gently, because he did not want her to be angry with him. An angry second mother was even worse than an angry father.

Her hand touched him again and she tried to slip under his sleeping robe. She too was naked. "I am still young."

"I cannot defile my father's house."

Her hand stroked him. "They are old and will not hear us."

"Go. I love my father."

"Your father is old and sometimes neglects his wives."

"Go." No Name's flesh burned for her. It would be an easy thing to wive her. "My father is a great chief." Again he pushed her away, this time more firmly.

"Son?" It was Star That Does Not Move calling suspiciously from beside Redbird. "Son?"

"I am trying to sleep, my mother."

Loves Roots slid back to her bed. She lay across the lodge from Redbird.

No Name sighed. Tomorrow Loves Roots would give him covert glances while pretending affection for his father.

The moon came up outdoors. Its rays slowly began to bend into the smokehole. Gradually they filled the cowhide lodge with silver light. He could make out the meat curing over the fire. A stone ax hung caught behind a lodge pole. His father's medicine bag and war gear dangled from a tripod just inside the door. Two forked sticks beside the fire held his father's redstone pipe. Kettles and baggage and parfleches of food stood against the wall behind the inner tepee lining. He could even make out the muffled forms of his father and mother, and Loves Roots, under their sleeping robes, feet to the fire and heads away, like petals of a coneflower radiating from a common center.

Presently the moon became as bright as a little sun. It shone with such dazzling silver inside the tepee that the quillwork on the parfleches and saddlebags began to glow in warm luminous colors: red, yellow, white, blue.

Bright moonlight also fell on his father's copper-tipped spear standing against the tripod. No Name's eyes fixed on it. As always he saw it as a magic thing. It was wakan. Watching it, he saw the copper tip begin to glow like a long golden tooth.

He had once seen the copper tip give off little sparks after his father had rubbed it some. His father explained why this was. Long ago when Redbird was a young man he had been told by the Thunders in a vision that he should go to the Porcupine Mountains far in the Chippewa country. There under a certain pine on the north side of the Lake of the Clouds he would find a round green ball. He was to take this green ball and return home with it and polish it until the copper shone through and then hammer it into a lance tip. The Thunders told him that as long as the copper tip was kept shiny, the Yankton Sioux would thrive. When it was not, the Yankton would wither away as the red leaves of autumn. The Thunders told him they favored shining copper because it gave off little sparks in imitation of their great sparks.

No Name knew it as a truth that the Thunders liked the copper tip. Once, as he and his father and mother were eating their evening meal, a big thunderstorm came up. Suddenly there was a sound of "Thun!" and lightning came through the smokehole and struck the fire, scattering ashes and firebrands all around. Everyone sat in shock for a moment, then began to spit and vomit. When they looked at the copper-tipped lance standing against the tripod, they saw a ball of glowing green fire hovering over it. The green fireball hung there until heavy rain, coming in through the smokehole, caused it to fade away.

No Name watched the moon move up the sky. Soon a shaft of silver touched him. It came straight at him from the Old Woman In The Moon herself. Her haunting eyes were fixed sharply on him. He hoped it meant she was going to give him a dream and tell him he would soon have his vision.

He waited. The moon's rays made his eyes glow like a wildcat's. Then, remembering a remark of his father's that too long a look at the moon-being might addle his soul and make a woman of him, he turned his head aside and closed his eyes.

He stirred on the soft musky bedding. His flesh was still aroused from Loves Roots' visit. He thought of Leaf. He considered stealing across to her tepee. He had heard his mother say that Full Kettle not only bound Leaf up for the night but also tied her to some stakes driven in the ground. Full Kettle was making doubly sure that Leaf would remain a virgin until she had been safely married. A young virgin was worth ten good ponies.

Of a sudden No Name thought of his older brother, a brother he had never seen. His mother often talked about him. The telling always made her weep, and afterward she would be extra kind to No Name, giving him special treats from the parfleches of dried fruit she was saving for winter.

His older brother's Name was Pretty Rock and he had come to Redbird and Star within a year after they were married. Pretty Rock was born lively, mischievous, loving, and Redbird had high hopes for him. Redbird indulged the boy, and early gave him a toy bow to shoot at mice and small birds. When Pretty Rock was eleven he asked to go along with a war party against the Omaha to the south. His mother, however, said he was too young. When Pretty Rock was twelve he asked to go along on a horse raid against the Pawnee to the southwest. Again his mother said no. When he was thirteen he asked to go against the Ree to the west. Once again his mother said he was too young.

When Pretty Rock was fourteen he at last had his vision and was ready to go to the warpath. But before he could leave, the village moved to the place where the sacred pipestone was quarried. Redbird thought his son needed better horses for the raid and so had decided first to make a few redstone peace pipes and offer them in trade to their tribal cousins the Teton Sioux. The Tetons were known to have the swiftest of all horses.

So they went to the Place of the Pipestone where the flesh of their ancestors had been hardened into stone. They pitched their camp near a patch of red kinnikinick, west of the quarry. Across the stream were the Two Maidens and the Rock Split By Thunder. Redbird, Moon Dreamer, Owl Above, and certain other braves who had refrained from intercourse and were worthy, took the sweat bath, rubbed their limbs with silver sage, offered an incense of burnt sweetgrass to Wakantanka, and then, purified, delved into the earth. The other braves, meanwhile, hunted buffalo, and the women cut and dried the meat.

It was very early in the spring. The fresh tips of new grass were still a pointed yellow, like sharp gopher teeth, and the wild crocus had just come to bud. The tall bluestem, red and musty from long winter drying, clogged the feet. Robins scurried for worms on the warm hills to the north.

The Yankton bird, the meadowlark, cried to them: "Spring is here! cheer up! Spring is here! cheer up!" The meadowlark's whistling was irresistible and presently the maidens answered it, singing, "The meadowlark is my brother, friend! The voice of fidelity is in the air."

The lynx-eyed boys, Pretty Rock among them, played games. They found some dried rose hips and pelted a fleeing cottontail with them. They went to Leaping Rock and dared each other to make the jump across the chasm. It was Pretty Rock who finally tried it and made it. He stuck an arrow into a crack of the red rock, then teased the others, saying he was now a true brave while they were but cowards, and when they still didn't jump, leaped back to show them he was twice brave. Next the boys played at the foot of the double Falls of Winnewissa. Here all the boys dared to leap across the chasm and show their valor. Next Pretty Rock picked up a piece of defective pipestone and dared the boys to touch their lips to it. All knew that even the bad piece of pipestone was wakan because it was the flesh of their ancestors turned to stone. No one took him up.

Next the boys went across the meadow and dared each other to touch the Rock Split By Thunder, the place where a Sioux brave had been struck down because he refused to offer the usual sacrifice of tobacco before pitching his tepee. The place was so wakan, however, that even Pretty Rock was afraid.

Then they went to play near the Two Maidens, or the Place of Six Strange Boulders. Here Pretty Rock was once again daring. He challenged the others to play follow-the-leader and climb with him onto the cluster of mysterious mossy granite rocks and see if they could keep off the ground by leaping from one rock to the other.

At this Pretty Rock's friends became very frightened. They knew the six boulders were greatly wakan. Under them, in a hole, lived the Two Maidens who like to catch young boys. "Something will happen," they cried.

Pretty Rock laughed. "Cowards!" He leaped from the largest moss-green boulder on the east end to the one with the wide lips, then to a small boulder, to another small one, to yet another small one, and finally to the big boulder on the west end. "See," he cried, "they do not harm me."

His friends backed away into the tall grass, their eyes rolling in fear. "Come down, come down! Something will happen!"

Pretty Rock only laughed more. "The Two Maidens won't hurt me. They like me. See?" He leaped across the little boulders again, all three, and then up on the Boulder With Wide Lips. "Besides, if the Two Maidens don't like it, I'll marry one of them."

His friends clapped hand to mouth and looked from side to side in fright. "Aiii!"

Just then Pretty Rock's moccasin slipped on green moss, and the wide lips below grabbed his foot. Scared, he scrambled to jerk free. But the Two Maidens had heard him and they caused the Boulder With Wide Lips to keep a tight hold.

His friends ran crying to his mother Star. "Aiii!" they cried, "the Two Maidens have grabbed Pretty Rock."

Star came quickly. She saw that her son had been caught around the ankle. Trembling, for she was very much afraid of the medicine of the Two Maidens, she ran to get a travois pole. Standing on her toes, she tried to push him off.

Finally, poking desperately, she managed to pry him out of the grip of the Two Maidens, and he rolled to the ground. Still shaking all over, Star picked him up in loving tender arms and carried him home to bed.

He became very sick. All night he saw balls of fire come streaking across from the Two Maidens to his brain. And at dawn he died.

His mother wept, and gashed her breasts and legs. His father covered his head with ashes, and chopped off a finger. Next his father and mother gave away all their possessions. And they placed the body of Pretty Rock on a tree scaffold beside the six strange boulders under which the Two Maidens lived. "Because," they said, "he had made a promise to marry the Two Maidens and belonged to them." Later, when his bones fell out of the scaffold, they buried his remains under the Boulder With Big Lips.

Recalling it all, No Name stirred restlessly under his sleeping robe. Sometimes he dreamed about his brother. In these dreams Pretty Rock always managed to beat him to his mother's breast. Sometimes No Name fought like a wildcat with him for her breast. Yet always he lost.

No Name groaned. He knew his father expected him to take the place of Pretty Rock. At the time of Pretty Rock's death Redbird and Star had given up all hope of having another child. There had been only one in fourteen years and it looked as though that was all they were destined to have. Twice Redbird married likely maidens with Star's consent, in the hope that another wife might bring him a son. When no son was born he sent the maidens back to their parents. It was when he took Loves Roots as his fourth wife, because she was so lively, that at last Wakantanka looked down upon them in favor. But it was Star who conceived, miraculously, not Loves Roots, and No Name was born.

No Name's place awaited him. He needed but the proper vision.

Otherwise, failing, his cousin Circling Hawk would become the tribal chief. Circling Hawk had not only had his vision, but already had placed his coup stick on sleeping Omaha braves on three different occasions without waking them, had conducted two successful horse raids, had slain four Pawnees. Because of these exploits Circling Hawk had the right to wear nine eagle feathers in his hair. Worse yet, when he became chief, Circling Hawk would have the power to compel Owl Above to accept ponies for Leaf.

The Yanktons were eager to have No Name become a valiant one. They liked him. Circling Hawk they respected, and were glad he was on their side, but they were worried that he would someday lead them into doing something rash.

The Yanktons were proud of their Name among the Dakotah Sioux. They were known as the peaceful keepers of the sacred Place of the Pipestone, a Shining People. They were also proud to be known as They-who-live-in-the-center-of-the-world, in proof of which they had only to point to a place just a day's journey to the north where all the rivers began: the River of the Double Bend, the River With Red Blood, the River of Milky Water.

The moonlight became dim in the smokehole. Gradually the lodge darkened. And at last No Name fell asleep.

And, sleeping, he dreamed. In his dream he too had been caught by the Boulder With Wide Lips. The Two Maidens would not let him go. The one named Loves Boys was especially eager to keep him. When at last his mother Star came and poked him free with his father's copper-tipped lance, he also fell sick on the ground. All night he lay dying on his sleeping robe. Streaks of fire came burning across from Loves Boys, touching him in two places on his chest. The streaks of fire were like long burning thongs tied to thorns thrust through his skin. He pulled, and hung back on them, and danced against them, but they would not let him go. He screamed in pain.

"Son?" Someone was shaking him. "Son?"

Slowly he broke out of the grip of the terrible dream, bathed in sweat.

"Son?"

At first he was afraid it was Loves Roots again. She sometimes called him "son" too. But then his breath returned to him, and he smelled, and he knew it was his father. Also, the hand was soft.

"Son?"

He could just make out his father's high shoulders against the smokehole. "I dreamed, my father."

"Ai! And what did they of the other life have to say?"

"I cannot remember, my father."

"Was it an evil shadow?"

"It was, my father."

"Sleep again, my son. The next dream will be a happy one."

"I will try, my father."

He was glad it had been Redbird who had shaken him awake. When he was a boy of seven he had sometimes run crying to his father's bed after a bad dream. "Father, let me lie under your folded robe." And always his father had taken him in his arms and held him until morning. His father was always warm, his arms always strong. His father smelled of a windy day on a high dusty hill. This was because his father was one of those who worshiped the Thunders and often sat on a high place waiting for them to come.

# 3

In the morning he was awakened by the soft scuffing of moccasins on the beaten grass floor. He opened an eye a crack. It was his mother Star stirring the ashes. He watched her, unmoving.

She found a live ember deep in the gray ash. She pressed down a tuft of grass and blew softly. On the fourth breath a flame like a puppy's tongue licked up. Yellowish smoke wisped about and slowly lifted to the opening above. She threw on a few twigs, then a dozen small branches, placing them in a circle with the small ends up like the poles of a tepee.

Watching his mother between barely parted lashes, No Name felt compassion for her. She was as faithful as the morning sun. She was always the first to get up and start the day with a fire. He saw how gray her braids had become, how wrinkled her cheeks, how thin and pursed her lips. Whitish films had lately grown across the black pupils of her eyes so that she had trouble seeing. She said she saw best now at twilight. Her doeskin tunic, new and freshly decorated with red and yellow and blue quill-work as became the wife of the richest man in the village, failed to hide her wasting body. She was still strong, could still set up a tepee as quickly as any woman in the band, but she did it now with an effort of will rather than out of the vigor of hardy flesh.

No Name loved her. He wished she would come around to his side of the fire and stroke his nose and think to awaken him.

The smells of burning oak and of steaming meat had just

begun to sweeten the air in the tepee, when Thunder Close By, the village herald, let go a roar outside, calling the people to get up. "Ha-ho! It is time to renew the body with water! Get up! Water is your body!" Thunder Close By had such a powerful voice he sometimes had to cover his own ears to keep from hurting them.

Redbird stretched under his sleeping robes, then sat up. His fur-wrapped braids slid forward and hung down his chest. He turned his great eagle nose and looked at where Star was tending the steaming pot. "Woman," he said quietly, with a sweet gentle air, "where is my water?"

Without a word Star stepped outside and got a clay pot of water.

As he washed his face and arms, Redbird looked over at where No Name still lay pretending sleep. "Get up, my son. Go down to the river and renew your body. It is time to bathe again."

No Name sat up. "Yes, my father."

Looking at his father's naked body, No Name hoped he would be as well preserved when he reached the great age of sixty winters. Only over the elbows and around the neck were there any wrinkles. Redbird's long slender arms were still full and smoothly muscular, his bronze chest with its two sun dance scars still rose out of his belly in fine swelling power, his eyes were still piercing black. He carried himself with grave high-headed dignity. His manners were those of a well-born one, exquisite, leisurely, sure.

No Name looked next at his father's left hand with its missing forefinger, the finger chopped off in memory of Pretty Rock. Staring at it, he hoped he someday would have the manhood to show such devotion.

Redbird glanced at No Name again. "Do not forget the feather, my son. That of the goose tickles best."

"I know, my father."

"Good, my son."

No Name smiled warmly at Star. "Good morning, my mother. And how is the day?"

"It is without wind, my son."

"Then it will be a good day."

"Ae, but the ducks are already coming down from where it is always white."

No Name noticed that Loves Roots' bed was empty.

Star caught his look. "The time of the moon came upon her in the night."

No Name brightened at the news. With Loves Roots gone, he could have his father and mother to himself. Loves Roots would have to stay in a menstrual hut at the end of the village seven days and would not be allowed to return until after the old women had given her a sweat bath. No one but the old women could come near her. They would feed her while she sorrowed. She would not be allowed to touch anything with her hands. She could not even scratch herself.

"My mother, will we have meat boiled with dried plums for breakfast? It is my favorite dish."

"You must eat what the pot gives up, my son."

No Name got up. Throwing a white robe over his brown shoulders, picking up a goose feather, he stepped through the door flap.

Dawn had just broken, a misty pink, over the east prairies. All of the tepees in the village circle, the old smoked-up ones as well as the newer white ones, stood bathed in the reddish light. Smoke had just begun to wisp out of the nearest lodges. Children and dogs were already whining for food. There was no wind and the cottonwood leaves hung like the ear lobes of old men. Outside, the rushing noise of Falling Water was louder too. A mist rose off the sliding river, both at the foot of the splashing falls and up on the streaming cataracts. The jagged red rock gave added depth to the pink morning.

No Name threw a quick look at Leaf's lodge under the cottonwood. Her lodge had just begun to puff smoke too. Gray wisps were curling off the pointed ends of the poles in the smokehole. The gray smoke slowly dispersed into a dull buckskin sky. In a few moments Leaf and all the other camp maidens would go down to bathe in their private place near the willows.

He was the first of the young men to reach Falling

Water. The roar hurt his ears almost as much as Thunder Close By's cry. No Name watched the pale limpid waters tumble over the worn red rocks, watched them spill into the swirling pool below. Behind the braiding waters lived the Buffalo Woman, the tribal guardian spirit who always sent them plenty of meat in the hunting season. She always remained hidden, yet was ever alert to their needs. She was one of the reasons they continued to dwell on the rolling prairies between Falling Water and the Place of the Pipestone, slowly chevying from one to the other, depending on the season.

Climbing a jagged wall to the right of the falls, he emerged above on the cataracts where the young men had their own bathing place. Here the River of the Double Bend, sliding slowly down from higher ground, spilled across staggered slabs of rock in a thousand tiny streams. Eons of flowing water, grit-laden, had honed the red quartzite down to so fine a polish that it resembled the smooth silken flesh of quartered beef. Throwing aside his robe, he kneeled and drank a great quantity of water. Then, after a little wait to make sure the stomach was well cleansed, he carefully thrust his goose feather deep into the back of his throat. He tickled until he broke into a violent cough; kept tickling until the cough exploded into a vomit.

Next he found himself a small swirling pool a foot deep. Slowly he let himself down into the cold water. "Ai! it is truly cold this day." He rubbed his dark brown body briskly. As he bathed in the pink morning, shivering, spilling water down his goose-pimpled skin, he sang the rising song:

> "Friend, rise,
> Wash away the night,
> Cleanse away the gall,
> Make the blood quick,
> Friend, rise,
> Water is your body."

Off in an eddy lay a curl of reddish sand. He gathered up a dripping handful, took a deep breath, then, shivering, began rubbing down his entire body, around the neck under the braids, around and over his high wide shoulders, down his slim belly and hips, down his legs, scouring until his rose-brown body slowly pinkened over.

Other young men came straggling up, sleepy-eyed, shivering under their robes.

"The morning is good," No Name called out cheerfully as he put on his white robe again. "Hurry. It will be a good day."

The foremost among them returned the greeting, smiling, white teeth gleaming in the morning light. A few gave him a dour look.

No Name was proud of the young men in his band. The Yanktons were a tall slim people, runners, with broad deep chest and sinewy legs and arms. Most had naturally large feet which, placed parallel upon the ground, enabled them to walk as sure-footed as bears. Compared to the dark Teton Dakotah, the Yanktons had glowing rose-brown bodies. All had luxuriant night-black hair which, when left unbraided, hung down as straight as horsetails. Some had hair so black a red sheen glinted over it. The faces were usually oval, with strong cheekbones and high arched noses, with the inner angle of the eye slanted down. Their bodies were hairless, they had little or no beard, and like the women had very little pubic hair. A few of the young men, those who had counted coup, had sun dance scars and tattoos on their chests.

No Name spotted his cousin Circling Hawk coming down the path. Despite the chill in the air, Circling Hawk scorned the use of a robe and had on but a narrow breech-clout and a red-tipped feather in his hair.

Circling Hawk hailed him. "Is the morning good, friend?"

"It is quickening, friend."

Circling Hawk was very tall, had great muscular bulk, and big hands. His face was as Leaf said—rough, like the back of a toad. It was also huge, more round than oval, with rolling flashing eyes. There was an air about him suggesting that on the least provocation he was ready to go down

the violent path with one. Circling Hawk danced energeti-
cally in the dust of the path. "Well, well." Circling Hawk
had a way of talking all over, with his face and hands, with
even the muscles of his body. "Ha, how is it that one who is
last to dream is always first to bathe?"

No Name tried to hold up to Circling Hawk's eyes;
found he was not quite up to it. "My father laughs when I
tell him what you say."

Circling Hawk's feet stilled. His eyes began to glow in
his great head. "Your father laughs at what Circling Hawk
says?"

"Ae. He says the Thunders are preparing a special vision
for his son."

Circling Hawk's hair rose like bristles on a wild boar.
"Must No Name always wait for his father's words? Has he
no words of his own to speak?"

No Name could see that Circling Hawk longed to call
him a coward to his face but didn't quite dare. Circling
Hawk knew that No Name could be brave when necessary.
No Name had once swum the Great Smoky Water when it
was raging full of ice. Somehow Redbird's favorite buffalo
pony had got across before spring breakup and when No
Name saw tears in his father's eyes at its possible loss he
plunged in without a word. He swam across, caught the
horse, swam back again, steering the horse ahead of him by
its tail, calmly braving the driving cakes of ice and all the
lashing whirlpools.

Circling Hawk glanced scornfully at No Name's body;
then touched a pair of white sun dance scars on his own
chest. "I see you still have the body of a woman. When will
you torment yourself?"

Disdain rose in No Name. Circling Hawk was a crude
man. For a brave who dreamed of replacing Redbird as
chief of the band, Circling Hawk had little of the reserve
and dignity that went with such an office.

"The day waits for me," No Name said then, and
brusquely left Circling Hawk standing alone.

Coming through the horns of the camp, the opening to
the east, No Name found the women up and about. All

were lighting cooking fires outside their lodges. The various plumes of smoke around the camp circle rose straight up into the windless air, then, at about tree height flattened off into a vague cloud. The sun was at last fully up, above the mist on the land, illuminating the smoke plumes with a hue as softly purple as the inside of a clam shell. The old women opened up the food parfleches and immediately all the dogs and children crowded in. The slim-legged fierce dogs became so daring the women had to club them away. One yellowish-gray dog, with the flashing green eyes of a wolf, was hit both front and back, and ran hobbling off on only a front paw and a hind leg, yelping pitifully. The old women called up the little girls to get more water for the cooking. Presently the young women returned from their bathing. Some took to combing their hair in the sun, decking their cheeks and the parts in their hair with vermilion. Others got out the master's spear and shield and medicine pouch and hung them in the sun high out of reach on the tripod. Soon too the old men got up and poked their heads out of the door flaps and looked at the morning sun. A yell from some of the boys told of how they'd been caught stealing meat from a drying rack. At this the old men smiled. Stealth learned early made for bold raiders. It would come in handy when they went on horse raids later on.

Looking around, No Name finally spotted Leaf sitting on a high red rock at the edge of the camp circle, combing her hair. Her face was hidden behind a long lash of hair. Her hair glowed with a touch of rust, like a raven's wings in springtime. He whistled and she looked up. She gave him a wide fulsome smile, then went back to her grooming.

Redbird's lodge stood opposite the horns of the camp circle, west of the council lodge. In the bright sun the painted emblems on the lodge stood out very clearly. The upper half of it, including the smoke flaps, had been painted a deep black. This signified that Redbird had once been given a vision by the Thunders. The panel to the right of the door featured a running horse. It was done in red ocher, and was so spirited in detail that No Name sometimes had to look twice to make sure it wasn't their spotted horse Swift As Wind. It signified that Redbird had once dreamed of a horse of a certain swiftness. The imprint of a bloody hand decorated the panel to the left. It signified that Redbird had once killed a man barehanded.

The most decorated tepee in camp belonged to his bachelor uncle Moon Dreamer. It stood next to Redbird's lodge. Moon Dreamer the holy man had once heard in a revealed vision the White Woman In The Moon singing a majestic song. To commemorate the great event he had painted a rising white ball at the top of his tepee. Thirteen rays shot out from the ball. One of the rays became a long curving line and pointed at a picture of the Sioux bird, the singing meadowlark. Moon Dreamer had also spoken in dream with the Ancient Of Clouds as well as the Ancient of Darkness and so had worked out the design of a dark cloud moving across an empty land, with below a band of deepest black from which reared the dark head of a buffalo.

No Name stooped through the door of his father's lodge. "I am here."

"When you come I am glad," his mother said. "The meat is ready."

No Name sat down before the steaming earthenware pot with his father. Cross-legged, knives in hand, they each speared up a piece of dripping buffalo meat, the fat on it globular and grayish. They chewed solemnly together, with smacks of satisfaction. No Name consciously tried to imitate his father's delicate way of turning his knife around as he ate. Star brought them both a chip of baked prairie beans. She served the bread on a wide piece of cottonwood bark. Then she sat back, folding her arms inside her loose wing sleeves.

"My mother, the bread is very good," No Name said.

"I am glad." Star sat in the woman's way, knees and feet to one side. Her hair and braids shone from combing. The part down the middle, from the forehead back to the nape of the neck, had been neatly painted with vermilion. Copper earrings dangled from her ear lobes.

"The bread is very light, mother. It is like the lungs of a dog."

"Eat, my son. You are very thin."

Finished, both men stabbed their knives into the sandy earth to clean off the fat. They washed their hands in a jar of water.

Next they prepared the toilet for the day. No Name loosened his two fat braids, as well as the finely plaited scalp lock in back, and combed them out with the rough side of a dried buffalo tongue. Tangles he cut through with his knife. He found a few lice, as well as nits, and killed them by placing them on a flat smooth stone and whacking them with the handle of his knife. The larger lice made a light pop of a sound when hit just right. Redbird reclined on his willow back-rest and held up his long hair to the light of the smokehole, looking for gray hairs. When he found one he jerked it out with a quick, deft snap of fingers.

Again Thunder Close By, the crier, made the rounds of the camp, roaring out more orders for the day. "Clean up! Our helper the sun is here again. Clean up!" Almost immediately Star along with all the other women in camp bustled about, dragging out the sleeping robes to give them an airing and sweeping the grass floors with rush brooms. They rooted out the mice and their nests, with eager yipping dogs killing as many as the women. The women next rolled up the leather bottoms of the tepees a foot to let the air pass through and freshen the interior. Mothers also checked over the little children, examining them for lice, redoing their braids, looking for dirt in the ears. All the while Thunder Close By kept up his roaring, making the rounds four times to make sure all the laggards had been routed out. "Clean up! Our helper the sun has come again. Clean up!"

At last Redbird looked at No Name. "My son, the horses wait and the night herder wishes to be relieved. Take Swift As Wind and bring her to the best grass with the other horses. Let her have water where it runs cool and clear."

"I will go, my father."

While Star packed his lunch in a heartskin, No Name drew on his clothes: clout and leggings and buckskin shirt and fresh moccasins. He tested the string on his bow, culled out the better arrows, slung bow and quiver over his back.

Just then there was a cry outside. The cry was of such a nature that No Name, Redbird, Star, all three, started. Their eyes became suddenly the glittering eyes of alert wolves.

Redbird rose up from his back-rest with a rush, poked his head out through the doorflap.

"What is it, my father? What do you see?"

After a moment Redbird heaved a huge sigh and withdrew his head. He gave his son a sad twisted look.

No Name looked for himself.

There, from behind the council lodge in the center of the camp, came Circling Hawk's fat mother, Soft Berry, leading a string of ten handsome ponies, some black, some red, a few spotted. Nose high, puffed up with haughty pride, casting a scornful look in No Name's direction, she paraded by. A troop of handsome young men followed her, trailing elegant elkhorn quirts, fluttering, chuckling, favoring the ladies with sheep's eyes. All came from Circling Hawk's warrior society. She waddled up to Leaf's tepee and with a stone hammer pounded a stake into the ground near the door. She picketed all ten of the horses to it and then spoke into the door. "We put our kindness before you so that you will remember it. We have a son who wishes to marry your daughter. We are poor, humble, therefore we have but ten horses. We know the value of your daughter and would, had we the wealth of a great chief, give a hundred horses for her. Remember us. I have said." Then, with a final look of haughty triumph in No Name's direction, she walked back to the tepee.

No Name was sick. Ten ponies! Leaf's father and mother would surely accept the offer of marriage.

No Name turned. Quickly grabbing up his lunch, he ran around behind the tepee, loosened the picket rope, and leaped bareback on Swift As Wind. The red-spotted pony needed but a touch of the heel and they were off with a gathering clatter of hooves.

# 4

He sat alone on a high hill. It was noon, and as warm as summer again. Below him, in the bend of the river, the ponies grazed, some two hundred of them, sleek blacks, sun-burnished bays, lively sorrels, here and there a gray, with only a dozen or so of the most prized of all, spotted horses. Further along the bluff, northwest, sat another Yankton lad, No Name's friend White Fingernail. He too sat watching a herd of horses. All the horses had just had their fill of water and were back to cropping grass in the meadow.

Far off to the north, where the River of the Double Bend made its last big turn before finally heading south to the Great Smoky Water, stood their camp. No Name could just barely make out the smoke-blackened tops of the tepees, all tilted slightly to the west the better to slip the prevailing winds. There was a shimmer in the hazy air, and sometimes the whole camp seemed to shift back and forth, as if the earth beneath were quaking. Sometimes too he could make out the children playing in the streaming red cataracts.

Like a wild animal ever alert for signs of danger, he watched on all sides. The Pawnees were known to make raids even in broad daylight. They were experts in picking exactly the right moment in which to sweep off a band of horses. He savored each bird call in his ear to make sure it was a true bird call. He studied every puff of wind in the tall grass. He examined with close attention the whistling of the gopher and the soft rustling passage of the rattlesnake.

After a while he felt sleepy. His lunch lay heavy on his

stomach. He waved to his friend White Fingernail to watch both herds while he took a nap.

No Name placed his bow and quiver near to hand and lay on his belly on the hard ground. Eyes focusing up close, he spotted a red ant trying to drag the husk of a beetle four times its size through a clump of short grass. No Name watched the red ant for a while, finally decided it was stupid. A little to the right or the left and it could have had a clear path.

The shimmer of a fragile web next caught his eye. It hung just above where the red ant struggled in the clump of grass. He decided a spider was probably lurking nearby, set to pounce. He ran his eye up and down each blade of grass, finally spotted it. The spider had drawn itself up into a tiny ball in imitation of a head of seed.

He waited. He watched through half-closed eyelids. The spider stirred once, its movement resembling the twitching of an opening seed bud. He waited. And waiting, fell asleep.

A sound coming by way of the ground gradually woke him. Something was wrong. His eyes opened on the shimmering spider web, now but the length of a finger from his nose. Slowly he rolled over, pretending to be lazy, like a puppy casually lolling in the sun. He picked up his bow, strung it, took an arrow from his quiver, got set to leap to his feet. His eyes flicked from side to side, then all around.

He saw nothing. His friend White Fingernail still sat in stony repose on the far hill, intent upon the horses in the valley below. The pony Swift As Wind was also at ease, cropping quietly in a coulee immediately below.

He sat up, quickly threw a look at the swale south of the hill, then around at all the horizons. The only thing different was the sky. The haze was gone. The wind had gone around to the north and all objects were now clear and sharp to the eye. His mother had been right to say that ducks southing meant cold was coming. He got to his feet, catching his quiver over his shoulder.

He waved to White Fingernail, received a wave in reply. He wasn't satisfied. Something was still wrong. He walked a few steps back and forth, eyes glittering, examining everything closely, even the still things. The twoleggeds and the fourleggeds and the wingeds were easy to account for. It was the still things that were sometimes treacherous.

A meadowlark cheered from the twig of a small ash in the swale behind him. "Wake up! there is much to see." He was about to imitate it for use as a secret call when out spying, when it struck him that the whistling was not quite the true meadowlark call. Ae! that was it. He stepped toward the swale some twenty paces, then called out, "Come up, my father. You are there under the little tree."

No answer.

He studied the swale closely, blade for blade, watching the north wind stream through the grass. He also studied the stones to see if there might not be one that resembled a humped back. This was to be another of his father's lessons and he was eager to show him how good he was at reading signs.

He considered. It was a good hour's walk from camp. His father would hardly walk that far, not as long as he had a good riding horse in the corral behind the willows. That was it. Find the mare, Red Moon, and he would find where Redbird lay hidden.

His eye followed the swale down to where it fell away into a ravine. The ravine in turn slowly curved east into the river. He decided his father had come in from the east, slipping into the ravine without being seen by White Fingernail and picketing his horse out of sight in the deepest part. Redbird was probably right now peering at him through the tall grass where water from the swale first trickled down into the ravine.

No Name smiled. He fitted an arrow to his bow and drew it back almost to its full length even as he aimed it.

Precisely at that moment Redbird rose in full view, a smile on his face. Redbird waved a hand to indicate the game was off. He stepped back into the ravine, vanishing completely for a moment, then reappeared astride the mare Red Moon, copper-tipped lance held high. A rawhide lariat rolled on his arm. Redbird rode up swiftly. He had not rebraided his hair that day and it streamed behind him as he came on. His black hair and bronzed chest and the black mane and the burnished bay of the horse glowed brightly in the lemon light of the afternoon. The black and bronze of the man and burnished bay of the horse moved as one harmonious aspect of a single creature.

Redbird charged until he was almost on No Name; then, with a quick hauling up of the reins, drew Red Moon in, so sharply that the mare reared, kicking gravel and dust over No Name's leggings.

No Name jumped back.

Redbird laughed down at his son. "Oho! So a certain son was asleep on his watch, ae?"

No Name laughed back at him. "Ho! So a certain father thought to surprise his son, ae? Yet his son heard him. It was the earth who told of his father's coming."

"Ha! I see a certain son has become such a nightwalker that he needs sleep in the day."

"The meadowlark I heard sang very well."

"Perhaps this son was seeking a vision while he napped."

At that No Name's face clouded over. A vision, ae. And a nightwalker, ae. By now Leaf's mother and father had probably already accepted Soft Berry's offer of ten ponies. Perhaps also by now, at the very moment even, Leaf lay in Circling Hawk's sleeping robes, cowed and a wife.

No Name did not dare search his father's face for some hint of what might have happened back at camp. Instead he looked across to where White Fingernail sat watching the horses.

Redbird glanced up at the clear blue sky. "It was here that they came."

"Who, my father?"

"The Thunders. One day a black cloud came. I went out to meet it, holding up my pipe to it. When I came to this high place, lightning jumped down. I fell on my face, hearing the Thunders roll a great stone across the sky. Then the Thunders spoke to me, telling me to get the great ball from the Porcupine Mountains and make a copper tip of it for my lance. It happened in the spring after my sixteenth winter and ever since I have been eager to smoke the pipe with them again."

"They will not come today."

"I am old. My bones make breaking noises when I run. The Thunders will come some day soon and call on me again. Then they will take me with them."

"Do not go yet, my father."

Redbird slipped to the ground with a slow easy motion. He brushed horse hair from his crotch. "Thou art a good horse," he said, petting Red Moon. The mare arched her head around and nipped playfully at the buckskin fringes of his leggings. Redbird laughed. Redbird loved the bay mare almost as much as he did Swift As Wind. From Red Moon he already had three fine colts, two bays and a black. Redbird's only regret was she hadn't dropped him spotted colts instead.

"My son," Redbird said, right hand toying with the loose ends of his hair, "in the spring when the season of growing comes again, we will trade with our cousins the Teton Dakotas for a white stallion at the fair. We will give them good walnut bows and some redstone pipes for such a white one. The dark gray we have now has not helped much."

"But such a white one is sacred, my father."

"We will ask for a white stallion with a black mane. It is the white stallion with a burning mane that one must fear. Such a one is wakan. And with the red eyes."

No Name fell silent.

Redbird pointed. "White Fingernail's father has come. Good. Now we will hold a race to see if the slitting of the nose has helped the gelding named Lizard." Redbird waved across to where White Fingernail and his father Speaks Once stood conversing. They waved back and after a moment began walking toward them.

Redbird had noticed that a certain flashy black gelding got off to a quicker start in a race than any other horse in his bunch. But then, after a couple of hundred yards, the gelding always faded. Redbird had thought much about why such a fine runner could not hold up. He had even consulted holy man Moon Dreamer on the matter. It was when he'd made a close-up inspection that he discovered the cause: the holes in the gelding's nose were too small. Redbird was handy with the knife both in castration and in skinning, and out of his experience an idea came to him. He ordered the gelding hobbled and dropped on the ground, had him tied securely, and then operated on him, slitting the nostrils open and cutting away the excess flesh and cartilage and skin. He treated the bleeding wounds with an herb ointment. The gelding cried during the operation, much as he'd done when castrated. Afterwards, looking down at the raw nose, No Name had named the gelding Lizard.

White Fingernail and his father, Speaks Once, came striding up. Speaks Once said, "We have come. Has the nose healed?" Speaks Once was a heavy-hipped man with a broad face and thick lips. It was said of both Speaks Once and his son that they resembled the Chippewa, they of the thick lips. Also both he and his son, like Redbird, had the white scars of the sun dance on their chests.

Redbird handed his coiled lariat to No Name. "My son, get the gelding from the herd."

White Fingernail pointed down at the grazing Swift As Wind. "Who will ride her against Lizard? Shall I?" White Fingernail had often begged for a chance to ride Redbird's favorite mare.

Redbird smiled. "Come, we will cross the river and hold the race in the meadow below." He looked at No Name again. "Well, my son, will you catch the gelding you named Lizard?"

No Name stripped down to his clout, tied his braids tight around his head, slung the lariat over his shoulder. Picking a handful of fresh red clover, he walked on silent moccasins toward the herd. He headed into the wind in such a way that the hobbled bell-mare, a gray named Old Wise One, was the first to catch his scent. She smelled him, lifted her head, snuffed again, finally lowered her head, satisfied. Keeping his lariat out of sight, No Name stepped softly on. He pinched the red clover leaves lightly. Almost immediately a sweet scent rose from his fingers. He held the sweet leaves out toward Lizard. A few of the nearer horses lifted their heads quizzically, ears working back and forth. They snuffed, snorted, came forward a few steps, stopped. They stared at him. But Lizard was cagey. He seemed to sense it was he they wanted. The operation on his nose, plus the castration, had made him wary of human beings. Ears down, he snaked out of sight behind the others.

No Name saw his father gesture in sign language. "Whistle his call, my son. He has his certain call. Like the gopher's."

But No Name for once had his own idea on how to catch Lizard. He went softly through the herd, careful not to make any quick moves. He whispered his horse-catching song, one he had yet not told his father about:

> "Horse, you are mine.
> I sing over you.
> Friend, stand still.
> My song is clever
> And my hand is sure.
> Horse, see,
> I have you at the end of my rope."

The black gelding continued to avoid him, sliding out of sight behind a roan gelding, then a pair of dun-gray colts, then a painted mare. Close around No Name reared staring hammer-heads. Nostrils fluttered. Tails like falling fountains wavered and trembled above him.

No Name continued to pinch the handful of red clover lightly. In a winning way he repeated his song. Still Lizard kept slipping away, keeping the bunch between himself and his pursuer.

No Name stopped and considered. It was easy to see the horse was wild again. They had let him run too long after the operation.

Out of the corner of his eye he saw Redbird still gesturing from the edge of the meadow. "Use his whistle. Like the gopher's."

No Name ignored his father again. He stood very still in

the midst of the herd. In the bright sun iridescent shimmers glinted over the sleek coats of the blacks and bays. There was also such a luster of brightness on the fresh green grass that No Name had to narrow his eyes to slits against it.

After their first smell of him, the horses slyly grazed away from him, cropping once here, cropping once there, each time a bit farther along, so that at last he was finally left standing alone in a wide empty circle. A couple of the farther horses with seeming casualness stopped a moment to water. The smell of horse urine was soon strong in the grass.

Again he pinched the sweet clover leaves, pinched until his brown fingers were stained with green juice. And gradually, as the scent of the sweetness sharpened and luxuriated away from him on the soft wind, very slowly, hobbled Old Wise One crow-hopped toward him. She was used to getting tidbit treats from his father.

She came close, her old black gristle nose reaching for the clover, snuffing loud. He let her have one leaf. She tasted, then hopped up to nibble the rest out of his hand. He toyed with her rubbery lips, withholding the leaves, whispering his horse song, "Horse, you are mine." All the while he slyly watched where Lizard drifted, trying to hold the crushed clover leaves in such a way that the wind would carry their scent in his direction. The other ponies followed the old mare's lead and gradually came up close too, slowly filling the circle again, until at last they all were massed tight around him, blacks, grays, sorrels, duns. His black braids were of one piece with the great tumbling of raised black tails and erect black manes.

Finally Lizard, not to be left out, drew near too, though with his ears down and his head still snaky.

Looking past the round red rump of a bay, No Name had a good look at Lizard's new nose. The scar was healed over. A pair of gray-black patches lay where once nostrils trembled. The two long gaps gave the black gelding's nose the curious look of a pair of halved willow flutes.

Suddenly, as he softly whispered his incantation, "My song is clever and my hand is sure," No Name let fly with

the lariat. The rawhide rope uncoiled neatly. The loop circled once around, slowly, like a hoop about to fall, and then
like a long arm it caught Lizard around the neck before he
could rear back. Instantly, very swiftly, No Name whipped
his end of the rope half around his body and leaned back,
sideways, anchoring himself on the ground. Horses exploded away from him as if he had suddenly turned into a
raging grizzly. There was a bouncing of round rumps and a
thudding of hooves. Tails popped. There were wild snorts
and quick screams.

Lizard bounded backwards too, high on his rear legs,
front hooves pawing the skies; then he came down and let
fly at the skies with his rear hooves. He broke wind, then
darted to one side. No Name hung on, leaning back almost
to the ground. His feet slid through the thick lush grass.
Twice his feet hit piles of horseballs and exploded them in
an arc. Then his heels caught in a gopher hole. Quickly anchoring himself in it and leaning back, he held.

Lizard shook his head back and forth, so furiously his
neck cracked. He shuddered from stem to stern. Suddenly
he rolled completely over on the ground and came up
bounding in a great lifting spring. Then he backed again, all
four legs working, like a dog trying desperately to back out
of a hole, choking on the rope. Each jerk only made the
slipknot grip him tighter. A low frenzied wheezing gurgled
in his throat.

Horse and man hung balanced. The rawhide rope
hummed between them. Lizard's tail stood out straight. His
eyes burned balls of hate at No Name. His new nose-holes
pulsed with a sobbing noise so that he resembled a huge
catfish thrown up on land.

No Name sung his song, quietly, soothingly.

Lizard broke sideways with a wonderful leaping bound.
He ran around No Name tight on the lariat. But the lasso at
his throat slowly gripped him tighter and tighter. It cut his
breath until he again had to stand still. Then, shaking his
long black mane a last time, looking sadly at all the others
in the herd who stood around him at a distance with heads

and tails lifted in wondering sympathy, he suddenly let down. The rope fell slack and No Name eased up.

After a wait, No Name began to work slowly hand over hand up the rope. He grunted deep from his chest, making powerful horse medicine talk. "Hroh. Hroh. Hroh." He rolled his shoulders and head in a slow hunching rhythm. He fixed the black horse with half-lidded magnetic eyes. Still sobbing for breath, Lizard stood as one charmed, rooted. Hand over hand No Name moved up. Gradually his monotone "hroh, hroh, hroh," changed to a low sibilant "shih, shih, shih."

Finally he touched the horse's mouth. He let Lizard smell his fingers a moment. Then, leaning forward, he breathed a few deep breaths into the open nares. Lizard still stood as one caught in a trance. In another moment, with a sure turn of his wrist, No Name flipped part of the lariat around Lizard's lower jaw and had the horse in control. He sprang on Lizard, bareback, leaned ahead to ease up the choking loop, then, whistling low, touched his heels to the horse's flanks. Lizard responded, docile.

No Name rode up to his father, smiling.

Redbird smiled too. "I see my son has forgotten how to whistle like a gopher."

"I taught him a new song instead, my father."

Speaks Once turned to his stub of a son. "You see? Here is a child who has first listened to his father and then has gone and done it his own way."

White Fingernail's lips bubbered. His eyes flickered with envy. Then his eyes steadied and his glance shifted to No Name's chest. "There are some I know who have not yet cried in torment."

"Enough," Redbird said. "We will now have the race. Will White Fingernail ride Swift As Wind?"

At that a smile flashed over White Fingernail's face. "I will."

While they waited for Lizard to catch his breath, Speaks Once and Redbird fell into a talk about horseflesh. Speaks Once was envious of Redbird's big herd. He had but fifty to Redbird's two hundred, though the fifty made him the second most wealthy man in the band. Speaks Once secretly hoped that his son would prove to be a brave and lucky horse-raider so that he could build up his herd. Speaks Once was often heard urging his son to go out on raiding parties. He also secretly hoped that No Name would continue to be without a vision, at least until he and his son had built up a wealth comparable to Redbird's.

Speaks Once asked Redbird if he had any horses to trade.

"What have you to give?" Redbird asked mildly, looking aloft.

"In my lodge lies folded a buffalo hide. It has white hair. It is wakan. I will give it for Swift As Wind."

Redbird considered a moment; finally, as if with reluctance, shook his head.

"With the white hide tied around his belly the gray stallion will breed many war horses invulnerable in battle."

Again, as if with reluctance, Redbird declined it.

"The white hide will help the gray stallion father many spotted colts."

Redbird pushed out his lips to show he didn't think much of the notion.

There had been an argument in the council over the white skin. It was the custom of the Yanktons to offer the skin of a white buffalo to Wakantanka. It was considered a bad thing to keep such a wakan hide as a private possession. Many in camp believed it was due to this sacrilegious act on the part of Speaks Once that so few spotted colts had been born to the Yankton mares the past year. The Yanktons desired paints, because, besides being showy, they blended leopard-like into the landscape.

Speaks Once next pointed to a lively sorrel grazing nearby. "I have this to give for a thin mare."

Redbird looked; considered; shook his head.

"The sorrel holds his head very high. He throws his feet forward as he walks."

"But his tail is too broad. Also his veins are coarse."

"He has a white spot in his left eye."

"But his hooves are also white and soft. And his withers have sores."

"Sores?" Speaks Once cried. His thick-lipped face dark-

ened over. He was always one to bristle when it was suggested he was cruel to his horses. Yet it was true. He had
more than once out of whim deliberately ridden a horse to
death. Further, he had little mercy for horses who devel-
oped saddle sores. "It is the sores of the fly that bites deep
that you see. Many horses have them."

Redbird looked back at his own herd, and fell silent. It
was easy to see that the deep-biting flies were partial to the
flesh of one certain herd.

Speaks Once caught the look. To emphasize what he said
he kicked over a pile of buffalo droppings lying underfoot.
"Bull dung does not lie. It is as I have said."

Redbird still held silent.

Then Speaks Once turned to his son. "Hold the race
horses for us until we return. I wish to show the chief and
his son a certain thing."

White Fingernail took hold of the reins of both Swift As
Wind and Lizard. "I will, my father."

Speaks Once led the way, Redbird and No Name following. Speaks Once walked with a heavy rolling tread, quite
pigeon-toed like a woman. Redbird and No Name walked
lightly, toes straight ahead. They circled a village of prairie
dogs. They stepped across a swale, using toggly hummocks
as stepping stones. They skirted a rocky ledge covered with
coils of pricklepear cactus.

As they approached the herd of Speaks Once, the nearer
horses shied off. A few snorted danger. The hobbled bell-
mare, a bay with many scars over her back, began to
crowhop away.

"Whoa now, whoa now," Speaks Once called in a coax-
ing voice.

At this the bell-mare took fright and began to two-hop as
fast as she could. The others moved off with her.

"Friends, stop!" Speaks Once roared. "Respect your
master!"

The horses continued to hurry away, cropping quick
here, catching a tuft of grass quick there, always away from
Speaks Once.

Redbird paused, hand to his chin, reflecting.

This only angered Speaks Once the more. He began to bellow in a loud hoarse voice. His face blackened over. White flecks gathered at the corners of his heavy lips. "Hold up, you low-bellied dogs! Come here! Respect your master!"

Redbird said, "Friend, perhaps we should call White Fingernail and let him catch them." Redbird turned to No Name. "My son, return. Watch the racers."

"Friend, wait," Speaks Once said, choking down his pride. "Hold up. We will let them get used to our smell. Perhaps we are strange to them today."

The three men stood.

Then, as they waited, proof of Redbird's claim appeared before their very eyes. A fine upstanding gray gelding, some fifteen hands high, came running through the herd, head down. Bluish-green magpies chased after the gelding in slow graceful flight, long tails dipping, wings flashing white. They came crying raucously. The gelding saw the men and stopped. Before he could slide away to one side, the harrying magpies settled on his back and began pecking at his saddle sores. The young gelding lifted his head to the skies, sideways, and screamed. Then all of a sudden he leaped straight up, all four hooves leaving the ground, with the rear legs highest and lashing up at the flapping magpies. Long black tails fluttering, squawking, the magpies merely rose a circle higher, just out of reach. Then, the moment he hit earth, they resettled on his back, digging in with their stout claws. The gelding shuddered. His skin rippled long slides of hair. But the magpies were dug in deep and weathered the shaking. Once more the gelding screamed. Then he tried rolling over on his back, and finally and at last succeeded in brushing off even the most dogged of the magpies. Released from the harrying long-tailed furies, he wriggled back and forth on his spine, scraping himself hard on the ground, feet up like a playing puppy, crying with pleasure at the relief, eyes turned up so far into his head the orbs showed white. All the while, however, the bluish-green magpies waited above him, hovering, cawing in displeasure. At last he struggled to his feet. He had barely shaken off the dust, rippling his skin fore and aft, when with screams of delight the magpies dropped on him again, digging in with their claws pecking at tatters of gray-purplish flesh, gorging.

Redbird looked at No Name and No Name looked at Redbird. "This is what happens when saddle sores are left untended," their eyes said.

Speaks Once hated them for their look.

Redbird said quietly, "It is said that if such sores are covered with the paunch of a buffalo and then sprinkled with ashes, the magpies will leave."

Before Speaks Once could react to the remark, there was a whistle from White Fingernail across the meadow, sudden, shrill, full of warning. It was a whistle in imitation of the jaybird and it meant, "I see the Pawnee!"

Instantly all three whirled. Without question they headed on the dead run for White Fingernail.

No Name, running with an easy lightness, was by far the swiftest and was the first to reach White Fingernail.

"Where are they?" No Name grabbed for his bow and quickly strung it. He tossed his quiver over his back. "Where, friend?"

White Fingernail pointed to the ravine east of them, the same one Redbird had crept up earlier. Even as No Name looked, four Indians with horn-like scalp locks and mounted on painted red ponies, erupted from the ravine. In an instant they were splashing through the river and heading for Redbird's horses. They shrilled cupped yells. "Ohow-ow-ow!" Then out from behind their backs fluttered dark buffalo robes.

No Name leaped on Lizard. He grabbed the reins from White Fingernail and wheeled Lizard around. "Take Swift As Wind, friend!" he cried. "We must head off the enemy before they stampede the herds."

White Fingernail hesitated. "But Swift As Wind is your father's favorite horse."

"My father will not care. Hokay-hey! Let us hurry. The sun shines."

White Fingernail vaulted aboard Swift As Wind in one bound.

"Come, friend!" No Name cried over his shoulder. "We are good-looking, we are young, we are of the right age to die! Our fathers will cry wonderfully over our dead bodies!" He touched heel to flank. Lizard leaped forward.

Lizard seemed to know exactly what was wanted of him and headed for the gap between the rushing Pawnees and the two herds, veering slightly to the left as he went. No Name plucked an arrow from over his shoulder, fitted it to the bowstring, aimed and fired all in one motion at the nearest Pawnee. The Pawnee ducked; from nowhere came up with a bullhide shield. The Pawnee managed to get his shield set slantwise just as the arrow hit. The arrow glanced off and tumbled harmlessly end for end to the ground. Before the Pawnee could bring around his own bow and arrow, No Name fitted on another arrow and let fly. Then as rapidly as possible, one after the other, like a milkweed pod suddenly spitting winged seed all in one burst, he shot off a half dozen more arrows. Each time the Pawnee, riding his bounding pony with perfect ease, warded off the arrows with his shield. The Pawnee laughed big white teeth at him.

No Name raged. He became a wolf on a horse. He kicked Lizard hard in the flanks. "Horse," he cried, "charge them! You have a new nose. It is good. It is wakan. We are safe from the arrow. Run."

Lizard dug in. His flexing back quarters almost touched ground on each jump.

The Pawnee let fly a line of arrows in turn. They came at No Name like grass spears shot by a whirlwind. They came straight for him at first, then at the last moment, miraculously, he and the horse passed ahead of them.

"Hi-hi-hi!" No Name cried. "Charge!"

Another surge and Lizard carried him almost on top of the Pawnee. The Pawnee, seeing them loom up, ducked down and slid around to the off-side of his pony. Only a heel and an elbow showed. The two horses bounded along furiously. Their hooves thudded hard on the grassy turf. Lizard ran in a fury, black mane snapping. The red pony ran in terror of its life, an eagle plume decoration fluttering in its tail.

At last No Name could see the ducking Pawnee's scalp lock. He fitted yet another arrow to his bow and let fly. The arrow flashed down, swift as a sun mote. It stuck into the Pawnee's neck. The Pawnee stiffened, held yet a moment, then, falling, hit the ground. He rolled, back over belly and belly over back, legs flopping grotesquely, a moccasin flying off. And suddenly doubling up, he lay still. It was No Name's first kill.

"Yi-yi-yi!" No Name shrilled. "It is good to die young! I must think of the children and the helpers at home!" He waved his bow high. "Charge!" he cried. "Hokay-hey! There are many more!"

With his knee he turned his horse for the next Pawnee. As he did so, fitting arrow to bow, he saw White Fingernail haul up short, leap off, and touch the dead Pawnee with his bow and scalp him. "Ai!" No Name cried, "my friend has made the first coup! Well, he already has had his vision and it is his right."

Lizard began to rage like a wolf himself. With his strange nose and his bared flashing teeth, he looked more like a demon alligator than a galloping horse. Four great leaps and they were on top of the second Pawnee. So ferocious was their charge that the Pawnee quailed, closing his eyes in fear. The Pawnee's arrow slipped from his bow and with a choked yip, he bent down and tugged his horse around and away. The Pawnee had thought to make his red horse impervious to enemy arrows with wakan yellow paint spots. But the yellow spots only made his horse easier to follow in the whirling rush of dust and tails. Quartering across, No Name found himself directly over the humped-up back. No Name let fly. His arrow passed completely through the Pawnee.

"Yeh-he-toe!" No Name cried. "It is good to die before one is old and good for nothing."

Again No Name saw White Fingernail pause, get off, count the first coup on a fallen Pawnee and scalp him.

The remaining Pawnees had enough. They folded away

their stampeding robes and quickly veered off to the south, across the River of the Double Bend and beyond over the blue prairies.

No Name reined up. He looked back. The yelling and waving of the robes had just barely started the two horse herds in motion. They were trotting, wild heads up, tails lifted. No Name quickly turned his horse to head them off on the right. He saw White Fingernail whirl around behind him to head them off on the river side. Riding swiftly, singing low soothing words, they soon had the herds in control.

Redbird and Speaks Once came stalking up. Their wild black eyes burned with excitement.

"You have done well, my sons!" Redbird cried, lifting his hands in blessing.

"Ai! The Pawnees are cowards this day," Speaks Once said. "They have even left their dead behind."

"My sons, the Yanktons are a great people today."

After some more excited talk, Speaks Once had a question to ask. "Ae," he said, "but who gets the pawnee ponies?" Nearby stood two red ponies, heads down, reins caught underfoot.

"Your son shall have them both," Redbird said. "White Fingernail struck the first coup twice."

White Fingernail beamed from the back of Swift As Wind.

"You have ridden well, my son," Redbird said, taking hold of Swift As Wind's bridle. The mare still stood puffing from the hard run. She was streaked with sweat.

"She was well trained, my father," White Fingernail said.

Redbird looked from Swift As Wind to Lizard and back again. Then he clapped hand to mouth. "Ai!" he cried, "see, Lizard hardly breathes. Yet Swift As Wind is winded."

It was true. No Name had already noted it. The slitting of the nose had been a good thing.

# 5

No Name did not learn what had happened to Circling Hawk's offer of ten ponies until sometime after he returned to his father's lodge. No Name was painting his face for the victory dance at the edge of the camp, when he suddenly heard loud talk in Owl Above's tepee.

"You want to be rich," Full Kettle cried, "you want many horses. Well, a great man's mother comes with an offer of many horses, as many as the fingers on your hands, enough to begin the new herd you want, and yet you choose to remain as poor as the grasshopper."

"My daughter has told me that she does not fancy Circling Hawk," Owl Above said quietly. Owl Above was one of those who thought it disgraceful for a husband to fight with his wife. "I have said."

"Hah! And what does she know about what is good for her?"

"My daughter has told me that he has warts all over his face."

"Warts all over his face?" Full Kettle cried. "Then what you have all over your behind are the rotten sit sores of a lazy dog!"

"My daughter says she does not want Circling Hawk."

"A brave man who will keep the pot full of meat in our old age," Full Kettle cried, "and he is chased away."

"My daughter does not want Circling Hawk."

"Who will fill the pot?"

"We must think of how our daughter feels about him."

"Hah! this is what comes of having a poor stud of a man for a husband. Hah! if a bull moose were to lose his road

and come and stand before you in the path, he would have
to fall over dead for you to kill him."

At last Owl Above had enough. He sprang up roaring.
"Where is my warclub? I see that someone who lives with
me must be beaten again!"

With that No Name quickly ducked out of sight behind a
red rock.


That night the Yanktons celebrated. There were kill talks
all over the camp.

Two bloody scalps dangled from a pole beside a big
jumping bonfire. All the women took turns reviling them.
The wrinkled old women were especially violent. Shrill
with exultation and terror both, they yowled obscene oaths,
cried down the wrath of the Dark Ones upon the mothers of
the dead, called upon the sun and the moon to utterly destroy the Pawnee people.

But it was when the bodies of the two dead Pawnees
were dragged into camp that the wild gloating of the withered hags hit its highest peak. They mutilated the bloody
dusty carcasses, disemboweling them, cutting off the fingers and toes, dismembering the arms and legs. Hard
Bones, widowed daughter of grandfather Wondering Man
and sister of Redbird, inflicted the ultimate insult. She cut
off the privates of the dead men, spat upon them, watered
over them in public, roasted them to a crisp in the fire, then
tossed them into outer darkness for the coyotes to fight
over.

Around and around the women danced, the old ones, the
young maidens, the little girls. The braves meanwhile stood
watching them, smiling, awaiting their turn to take over the
stage. The little boys, watching their fathers, also stood
back and looked on with smiles.

No Name's eyes were on Leaf. He was pleased to see
that compared to the others, especially his aunt Hard
Bones, she danced and sang with decorum. Dressed in her
best, soft white doeskin glistening with quillwork, she
moved shy and birdlike on the outer edge of the hopping
dancers. She avoided his look, smiling a little to herself.

Off to one side, scowling on a red boulder together, were Leaf's father and mother, Owl Above and Full Kettle. They and Circling Hawk, who also sat glowering to one side, seemed to be the only Yanktons in camp not enjoying the victory dance.

No Name became gradually aware of a hand slipping in under his robe. The hand was warm. It was his father's.

"Yes, my father," he said, turning, "what is it?"

"It is an old thing. It grieves me that my son has not been given his new name."

"I also grieve, my father."

Redbird spoke in a gently chiding manner. "And yet my son is brave enough to kill two Pawnees."

"The horses were there to be saved, my father. Your son did not first prepare himself to be brave."

"Many there are who first prepare themselves to be brave but who afterwards discover they are cowards."

"My father, surely you know that one cannot trust a leader who has not yet had a vision?"

Redbird's voice sharpened a little. "My son, this night Speaks Once will be a proud father. It will be because his son struck first coup on an enemy that another killed for him. Speaks Once will give his son a new name."

"But, my father, surely you jest. Killing does not count for much. It is the coup that comes first. White Fingernail has had his vision and therefore it is his right to count coup."

Again Redbird spoke with a taunting edge in his voice. "I see that White Fingernail still has all of his arrows."

"My father, it is good for the band that such deeds are celebrated by someone. The band needs the glory."

"Well spoken. Yet I know one who would give his son a new Name also."

"What is there to be done, my father?"

Redbird sighed, and at last his hand slipped off No Name's arm.

Presently the camp singers and drummers came out of the shadows. One of them hit a big drum, once, loud. The boom instantly silenced the gyrating yelling women.

Painted faces streaked with sweat and dust, looking well
pleased with themselves, they withdrew to the edge of the
circle.

Speaks Once, dressed only in a clout, with honor feathers
in his hair and rattles on his moccasins, walked up carrying
the skull of a dog. With solemn ceremony, he placed it at
the foot of the scalp pole, its chalky nose pointed toward the
east. Then he stepped back, held up his hand, and called out
in a loud voice, "My son was a brave man today. It is because of this that the council of elders has voted to give him
two honor feathers. I am glad. I see that everyone has
painted his face. I see that some of the mothers have gone to
cook a dog for the feast. I see the old chiefs have cut the tobacco and mixed it. It is good. Let us have a big dance and
then the feast in honor of my son. I have said."

"Houw! Houw!"

The big drum boomed again, this time twice, very
quickly. A voice rose, more in cry than in song, and instantly the center of the camp began to bristle with feathers
and lances. Half-naked painted bodies moved en masse
around the great bonfire. Elkhorn whips lashed about.
Shields, gaily painted and hung with dyed feathers, revolved around and around. The braves were all bronze
birds. They danced lightly. Their feet lifted on the beat.
They pranced, hovered, hardly touched ground. They
floated. Their shadows flitted across the tops of the glowing
tepees in the background. Some cried like crows, some
howled like wolves, some bellowed like bulls, some
shrilled like eagles. Huge round feather suns turned on their
buttocks. Shooting rays glowed around their heads. Dust
swirled up in the red light. The red fire and the red dust and
the red bodies became as one. Rattles buzzed like mad-
dened diamondbacks. Singers yowled like hoarse magpies.
Certain of the old women stood in a chorus off to one side
trilling old war songs in falling quavering accents.

Stubby White Fingernail was in his glory. His face was
daubed with the black paint of triumph. A bustle of magpie
tail feathers, his medicine, hung from his seat, so that, waggling with each move he made, he resembled a squat bird

hopping from carcass to carcass. He danced solo. He danced with such fury, became so pent up, he at last even danced in his blackened face. His head bobbed convulsively, his startled eyes bulged in and out, his nostrils opened and closed in steady spasms, his thick lips writhed rhythmically.

At last, coming out of it, he told of the great deed. He danced up to No Name, pointing at him four times, and then in pantomime recounted No Name's battle with the Pawnee, how No Name rode his horse Lizard, how he bent his bow, how his arrows found their mark.

White Fingernail next danced up to the white skull of the dog at the foot of the scalp pole. Three times he danced up to it and made as if to strike it with his lance, with the drummers and singers building up a crescendo of sound each time, and then, the fourth time, did strike it. Instantly silence fell over the camp. Only the fire talked and the river laughed.

White Fingernail's chest swelled with a great breath. Then, touching the topmost scalp hanging from the pole with his lance, he pronounced, "I have overcome this one."

It was a true claim and no one spoke up to deny it.

White Fingernail touched the second scalp with his lance. "I have overcome this one."

It was also a true claim and again no one spoke up to deny it.

White Fingernail next told how he had been the first to spot the Pawnee raiders, how he had whistled the bluejay call across the meadow to warn Chief Redbird and his father Speaks Once and his friend No Name, how No Name came running, how No Name gave chase, how No Name killed two of the enemy, how he, White Fingernail, came riding after and struck the first coups.

Lifting his face to the darkness overhead, he sang his song:

> "Hohe! have you seen the Pawnee?
> Friend, they have gone.
> They were afraid of our arrows.

Hohe! have you seen the enemy?
Friend, they are cowards.
They have left their dead behind."

"Houw! houw!"

He sang his song a second time, with the drummers and singers joining in, and the chorus of old women singing the tremolo in falling wavering accents.

Then Speaks Once stepped forward, thick lips screwed up proud, bustling, clam shell ornaments jingling, skunk-tails fluffing at his heels. He too struck the white skull of the dog with his lance four times. Again, except for the crackling bonfire and the laughing river, there was solemn silence.

"Friends," Speaks Once said, "you have heard my son. You have heard his story. You have heard his song. Is there anyone to deny it? Others can speak. I will listen. I have said."

The silence continued, full, intent. Black eyes glittered in the glowing firelight. Bronze forms stood enstatued in the red quartzite basin.

"No one steps forward to deny it. It is good."

Speaks Once turned to Redbird sitting at the edge of the crowd and beckoned him to come forward. "Father," Speaks Once said, "we ask this. Our son needs a new name. Will you give it?"

Redbird got to his feet and stepped up. With a grave air, he drew two feathers of the golden eagle from his belt. He held them up in the light for all to see. The bottom portion of both feathers were white, and the top brown, with the points tipped with the red down of a woodpecker. He turned each slowly. They glistened in the dusty red light.

"My son," Redbird said, and he touched White Fingernail on the shoulder with one of the feathers.

White Fingernail knelt in the dust at the foot of the scalp pole. His hair, purposely left unbraided, flowed in two black streams down his back.

"My son," Redbird said, "today you have made the Yankton people a great nation."

"Houw, houw!"

"It is because you have done this for us that we now give you these." Redbird thrust the two feathers into the youth's hair at the back, setting them in a horizontal position. Then slowly, solemnly, he turned to the assembled tribe. "Friends, hear me. Our son has earned a new name. Today he struck first coup twice." Redbird turned and looked down at the kneeling youth again. "My son, take courage. Your Name is now Strikes Twice. Arise. Stand on your feet. I have said. Yelo."

The great drum boomed twice, deep.

"Houw, houw, houw!"

Singers awakened. Again the drum beat swiftly. Dancers revolved around the fire. Involuntary yells burst on the night air. Rattles buzzed. Clam shells tinkled.

The drummers beat in an ecstasy of exultation. The drum was a hollowed out cottonwood butt with a piece of stretched bullhide for membrane and every time the drummer's stick fell on it the cottonwoods along the river seemed to thresh their leaves in an agony of joy. Through the beating drum the cottonwoods at last had heartbeat. The drumbeat became the heartbeat of all living things: the rooteds and the wingeds, the twoleggeds and the four-leggeds. The drum beat the tempo of their common origin.

All the while the marshalls kept order. The marshall's symbol of authority was a willow wand some four arm-lengths long, forked at the small end, peeled and dried. The tips of the forks were ornamented with quills from the golden eagle. All the marshalls wore a black stripe from the outer corner of the eye to the lower edge of the jaw. People feared them and always fell silent when they came near.

Presently a sudden whoop sounded from the council lodge. Out of the darkness bounded seven naked dancers, all of them tall, handsome, and members of the Foreskin Society. Each had a naturally long foreskin, from which dangled a red feather tied on with a buckskin thong. On each chest was painted the rampant figure of a buffalo bull. They were all known as brave fighters and were held in high esteem. The other dancers made respectful room for them in the circle. Only the little boys sitting along the edge giggled at the sight. All the women and the old chiefs, however, looked on with solemn gravity. These men were wakan. They had been born with a certain mark which set them apart.

The seven naked stalwarts had barely made two turns around the fire, dancing and singing their society songs, when another shout sounded from the dark. This time four more naked braves, members of the rival No Foreskin Society, sprang dancing into the circle of light. Each carried a crook; each had bared his part to show he had a natural right to his membership; each had painted his nose a bold red. The little boys tittered at the red noses, but again the women and the chiefs looked on with gravity. They were brave men who also had been born wakan.

Later, when No Name looked around for Leaf, he discovered that both she and her parents had vanished. One look at their tepee under the cottonwood near the horns of the camp and he knew that they had gone to bed. The door flap was lashed down for the night.

"Ae, their tepee is asleep," he said to himself. "It is easy to see that Full Kettle did not like the celebrating."

Their withdrawal made him melancholy. Brooding, he wandered away from the dance. He let his toes find a way. They took him west down a trail and climbed him onto a high rock overlooking the village.

He heard the guards on the hills behind him whistling bird calls to each other that all was well. Once a coyote yowled a falling cry. One of the guards immediately imitated it so clearly, so cleverly, that for a moment No Name had trouble making out it wasn't a true call. A star fell. It streaked across the eastern skies like a giant firefly. "Ae," he thought, "another of the Old Ones has fallen from his appointed place in the Other Life." Cold settled down on him like a strong draft. The night was extraordinarily clear. The stars above and the fires below burned sharply. He snuggled against the fur inside his white robe. He watched the river wrinkling in the light reflected from the bonfire.

The sound of Falling Water was faint. An owl hoo-hooed in the trees down river.

It was well after midnight before the dancing Yanktons finally went to bed. The bonfire slowly died away. It became still out. The low sounds of the night on the prairie, mysterious irregular footsteps, spirits laughing and whispering and chuckling overhead, moved around No Name.

Thinking that his father and mother might be wondering about him, he climbed down from the rock and slowly headed back to camp.

No Name brooded as he followed the path. Strikes Twice was now a full man. Ae. It was certain the gods did not favor the son of Redbird. Otherwise one of them would long ago have visited him in a vision and told him what he was to do in life. Standing at the door of his father's lodge, in the dark, he could not find it in himself to go to bed. He felt lonesome. He had a need to be stroked. Not by his father and mother, but by someone else.

Abruptly he turned about. Slowly and softly he toed across the grass toward Leaf's tepee. She would be asleep by now, bound to stakes for the night, with coils of rawhide around her thighs so no sly nightwalker could come creeping in and seduce her. He smiled to himself.

He stopped behind her tepee. Reaching up, he picked a few pieces of meat off their drying rack. These he fed to Full Kettle's four dogs, making friends with them. Then, hanging his robe on the racks, he got down on his bare belly at the back of the tepee and quietly lifted its cowhide side and slid in. He listened. Full Kettle and Owl Above were snoring loudly. He hunched along like a measuring worm, in a looping manner. His hand touched a parfleche. He pinched it, felt giving pemmican inside. He crept on. He touched a leather case of clothes.

Then his fingers came upon a row of stub stakes. Cords rose from each one, and following them, he felt Leaf's arm. He listened. She was breathing slowly, evenly, asleep. Peering intently across the lodge he tried to make out where Owl Above and Full Kettle snored. But the fire was almost out. Its center threw out but a vague light, pinkish. He touched Leaf's shoulder, her neck, her bosom. His fingers moved gently, hardly touching her. As he expected, her belly and thighs were crisscrossed with rawhide thongs.

She stirred, restless, against the thongs.

He pitied her. It was not a good thing to sleep all night long bound against the earth in one position, with only the head free. He fumbled with the knots. He found them too intricate. He could not make them out in the dark.

No Name ran a finger along the cutting edge of his stone knife. It was sharp, like catfish teeth. Very slowly, yet with some pressure, he began sawing at one of the thongs over her thighs. It parted slowly under the rasping edge of his knife, finally snapped with a loud pop. Afraid that the sudden sound might have awakened her father and mother, he pressed his belly tight against the grass floor, hiding his head behind her hips. He listened. To his relief Owl Above and Full Kettle snored on soundly.

Then he noticed the rhythm of Leaf's breathing had changed. Ai! she was awake.

He leaned close and whispered in her ear. "Someone you know has come."

She lay still.

"He has a great ache in his heart."

She took a slow deep breath.

"I have seen a maiden who looks so wonderful to me I feel sick when I think about her."

Slowly she turned her head. Hardly audible she whispered in his ear. "My mother will hear."

"I ache and feel sick for you."

"Tomorrow you will sing about me that you have wived me without giving the horses. You will call out my Name for the others to laugh at."

"I am without one to comfort me in the night."

"Shh!"

"Even the horses when they feel lonesome at night stroke each other with their noses."

"Shh."

He slid his hand down to the next thong over her thighs. Pressing hard, sawing, he was suddenly through it. There was a loud snap and the end of the thong slapped him in the eye. He jerked back, and hit his head against a slanting lodge pole. A piece of smoked meat hanging from the lodge pole began to swing back and forth in the dark above him. He listened, hearing the smoked meat creak on its string. Presently something dropped from the swaying meat, falling exactly in the middle of the pink embers. There was a soft sizzle. Suddenly a single flame leaped up, white-yellow, lighting up the whole interior. A piece of fat had broken off and fallen into the live embers.

Leaf gave him a wild look. He returned the look. Then he ducked down, began sliding backwards. His buckskin leggings made a soft ruckling noise on the grass floor.

Full Kettle rolled over under her sleeping robe. She lay listening a moment. Then she gave Owl Above a bump in the ribs. "Old man, wake up. Someone is in the lodge."

No Name flattened himself in Leaf's shadow.

Again Full Kettle gave her husband a poke in the ribs. "Old man, wake up. Someone is in the lodge."

"Waugh?" Owl Above whoofed, sitting up suddenly, long braids falling forward. "Who is here?"

Leaf pretended her father's cry had awakened her. "What is it, my father?"

Owl Above stared at Leaf; rubbed his sleep-bleared eyes; stared some more. "There is someone with you, my daughter?"

"I have been sleeping, my father. Also I am bound to the earth."

At that Full Kettle sat up, suspicious. Looking sharply, she saw the severed thongs. "Old man," she cried, "someone has cut the ropes. See, the ends are freshly cut. Get up!"

Owl Above peered intently. "Ae, it is one of the night-walkers again." Groaning, stark naked, he reared his old bones out of his sleeping robes and staggered over to where Leaf lay. The flame of the spitting fat glowed a brilliant yellow. Hands hanging open at his bronze thighs, he glared down at her. "Who was it? Tell your father."

"My father, I was asleep."

"The thongs are cut, my daughter."

"Perhaps it was Circling Hawk come to steal what I would not let him purchase."

Full Kettle snorted from her bed. "Hah! I say it is that No Name. He thinks to take a thing for nothing."

Owl Above knelt beside Leaf. He examined the parted ends of the thongs. "This has been cut, my daughter. Did you not feel his knife?"

"My father, I dreamed and did not know if it was real."

Suddenly Owl Above spotted No Name's eyes glittering in Leaf's shadow. He let out a roar. "Hi-yu-po! Where is my lance? Where is my bow? Old woman, give me my warclub!"

Full Kettle leaped to her feet, eyes wild, braids tousled. "Where is he? Where is he?"

"Woman, my warclub!"

The four dogs outside came alive, roaring. In a moment all the dogs in camp were howling with them.

Like a brown cricket springing backwards, No Name flipped himself under through the leather side of the tepee and then up on his feet. But it was too late. Even as he turned to run for his father's lodge, he found himself surrounded by what seemed a thousand dogs, all of them snarling mad. He clawed up and around, trying to find the meat racks, thinking that a few handfuls of dried beef might shut them up. Just then Owl Above came flying out the tepee door, warclub in hand. Behind him came Full Kettle. Full Kettle quickly threw a piece of buffalo fat into the live embers of the cooking fire outside the door. A flame shot up like a leaping red fox, lighting up both horns of the encampment. No Name saw instantly that the best thing for him to do was to scramble up on the meat racks. He made it in one flying leap. He grabbed up his white robe that he'd hung on the racks earlier and caught it around his shoulders. The meat racks swayed under his sudden weight. Crouched, looking up, he saw a cottonwood limb hanging just above him. Quickly standing erect, he got a good hold on the limb, chinned himself on it, swung a leg up and over, and in a flash vanished into the leaves above. The dogs below, frustrated, sat down on their haunches and yowled up after him.

Owl Above appeared in the midst of the dogs, still naked, angrily waggling his maple knurl. He saw where the dogs looked. He too stared up into the cottonwood. Light from the flickering fat flames gave his eyes the glowing sharpness of a bobcat.

Full Kettle ran up. "Where is he?" she cried. "Where is this thief who would rob a maiden of her trading goods?"

Braided heads began to poke out of the door flaps all around the camp circle. "What is it?" some cried. Most eyes were pink with sleep. Some looked on with open mouths.

Full Kettle saw them. "There is a hymen thief in the tree!" she shrilled. "He tried to steal our daughter's price!"

"Woman, hold thy tongue!" Owl Above commanded. "There is already enough shame in our lodge."

Full Kettle looked at a certain tepee on the west end of the camp circle. "I see that our old chief sleeps through all the noise. Perhaps he is very tired from having given a new Name to the son of Speaks Once."

Owl Above roared. "Woman, hold thy tongue! Dogs, be silent! Someone is in the tree, yet how can he be heard in all the noise?"

Just then the fat in the fire gave out, and darkness, more intense than before, swooped in again.

"Ai!" Full Kettle wailed. "Now he will get away."

Owl Above cursed. "Woman, back to thy bed. I will bind our daughter again. I will tie the dogs to the tree to hold the thief safe until morning. Go." And grumbling, throwing aside his warclub, he lashed the four dogs to the roots of the cottonwood. Upon that all the doors around the camp circle flapped shut again.

No Name sat very still in the tree. He trembled like a squirrel waiting for a hunter's arrow to find him.

The dogs slowly quieted down. Presently No Name heard the mutter of low talk in the tepee below. He guessed it was Owl Above busy repairing the cut thongs and retying Leaf to the stakes.

He heard Leaf protesting. There was a low sibilant reply. Then Leaf said, loud and clear, "My mother, my father will not let me go outside and sit a moment."

At that Owl Above let out a roar again. "Woman, stay in thy bed! Daughter, wait until morning! I have said."

Silence.

No Name sat crouched inside his fur robe. His thoughts were as black as the night. In the morning the lynx-eyed boys would help Owl Above spot him in the leaves. What laughter there'd be. The whole camp would go into a laughing fit over this son of a great chief who as yet had no Name and who was foolish enough to get caught in a tree. Ae, and the loudest to laugh would be Circling Hawk.

He sat very still in the rustling tree. A wind moved down from the north bluffs. It stirred the outer leaves, finally touched his brow. There was the smell of a far-off place in it, of ice and snow. The white giant of the north was at last awakening out of his long summer sleep. Slowly No Name stiffened up. Gradually he fell into a stupor.

Just before dawn, suddenly, as if startled in sleep by a bad dream, a certain she-dog gave an agonized yelp. The yelp awoke her and she broke into a prolonged yowling cry. The cry then awoke the other dogs around the camp circle, and before the echo of it came back from the hills, they joined in, one by one, soulful, piercing. It was a crying from a dark time, all of it discordant. It rose to such a pitch that No Name's ears began to bellow with it. It roused him out of his stupor.

After a moment, blinking, shivering, he decided he ought to take advantage of the horrible clamor and do something about getting down out of the tree.

Carefully, somewhat stiffly, he crept along the limb. Bark broke off in his hand. Once a soft-center twig snapped in two.

He came to the main trunk, a massive corrugated bulk. He felt around it for another limb higher up. In so doing his hand came upon a thick grapevine. It was only then that he remembered how late in the Moon of Ripe Corn he and his friend Strikes Twice had climbed the cottonwood to pick wild grapes. The vine reached almost to the top of the tree. Quickly, while the yowling still owhed and owhed in echoing waves below him, he climbed the gnarled vine until he found where it divided in two. He broke off the smaller of the two branches, jerked it free of the bark and twigs, then going out on a limb on the west side, away from the four dogs, fastened one end to the limb and let the other down to the ground. He knotted the robe around his waist, then eased himself off the limb, catching at the dangling vine with his legs. He let himself slide down, slowly, surely, letting his toes, then his hands, find their own way. Hand over hand he lowered himself down through the rustling leaves, down into the howling darkness.

The moment his toes touched ground he ran leaping for his father's lodge.

The old she-dog was the first to quit howling. In a moment, the other dogs fell out after her, one by one. The raucous concert gradually died away. A strange unearthly silence followed.

# 6

The next morning when No Name saw Leaf and her mother heading down the valley with baskets on their arms, he painted two red circles around his eyes and stole after them. The two women followed the path by the River of the Double Bend. The path curved north away from Falling Water, went through a thicket of red willows, climbed a bench of grassy land, and descended into a narrow ravine coming down out of the north bluffs. The ravine was the place where many fat rosebuds grew.

No Name followed them into the tangled bushes. The two women sometimes had to creep on hands and knees to get through, going down tiny narrow paths made by grouse and gophers. Full Kettle glanced back several times, but on each occasion No Name managed to duck out of sight in time, once in a washout and another behind a red stone.

The two women picked along, talking. Every now and then their talk erupted into laughter. No Name knew what they were laughing about. And he understood why Full Kettle might make merry about his undignified flight up the tree in the dark cold night, but not Leaf.

He stole after them, eyes glittering.

The sun rose slowly.

He heard Leaf exclaim about something. Carefully he parted the tangled brush, pushing until the furzy pricks stung him through the buckskin shirt.

Leaf was holding up a turtle by its stub tail. It was about the size of a man's full hand. The turtle's knob head kept poking around while its feet clawed air.

"It will make good soup," Full Kettle said. "Owl Above will like it."

Leaf laughed at its antics.

"Why do you laugh, my daughter?"

"It reminds one of how men are, my mother."

Full Kettle looked down at the turtle a moment, then laughed too, her face wrinkling on either side of her pocked nose. "My daughter knows too many things for a maiden."

Leaf gave her mother a wise look. "Thy daughter was given eyes to see with, my mother."

"My daughter, remember, we are a family which has not yet had one bad woman in it."

"I have that which no man has yet touched."

"No man?"

"My mother, man has yet to put pestle to my mortar."

"It is good. Come, the sun rises. Owl Above will be hungry if we do not work. Fill your basket and then we will return."

"My mother, it is your basket that needs filling."

No Name watched Leaf's slim tough fingers search along the vines. Swiftly they caught up handfuls of rose hips. He admired her nimble fingers. She worked with her back to him and all he could see of her was the painted part of her black hair and her moving plucking fingers. Watching her, his eyes filled with involuntary tears. He loved the round back of her head.

At high noon Full Kettle said she was tired. "Let us eat a little of the pemmican we took with us."

"Father waits, my mother."

"We have picked many rose berries. Also, sometimes your father says I am a lazy squaw. Well, then I shall be a lazy squaw this once."

They sat against a pink boulder. The sun shone on them. It was suddenly warm after the frosty night. They nibbled at the pemmican. They brushed sweat from their brows. After a time Leaf loosened the thongs across her chest and drew her dress down over her shoulders and arms, exposing her breasts to the sun.

Full Kettle sighed. "Me. Water. I wish."

"I will get you some," Leaf said, springing up. "Also, I will take my bath for the day."

"Do that. I will sleep a little sleep."

No Name watched her slip light-footed down the slope toward the river. No Name smiled to himself. At last his time had come. He followed her silently down the other side of the ravine.

He hid behind a fringe of wild plum trees. A few late plums hung dotted among the yellowing leaves. He watched her step out of her clothes on the golden beach. He had stroked her with her clothes on many times and knew her to be as lovely as mourning doves, but watching her now poised on her toes in the bright sunlight he knew her to be as lovely as tufted redbirds. Where the sun struck her thighs her flesh was exactly the hue of polished pipestone. Her tufty loins resembled a blackbird about to lift into flight. A torment of passion smoked in him. He watched her cup water over her redbird breasts. He watched the water stream down her belly.

He slipped out of his clothes. He picked two of the dark ripe plums and tiptoed toward her. He held his fingers to his lips to warn her not to cry out. He was halfway across the soft sand when a pebble squeaked under his big toe. She flashed a look up and around. "Oo-ee!" she cried, low. Then she saw his fingers pressed to his lips and quickly clapped palm to mouth.

He paused, ear cocked for the wild rosebushes above them, waiting to see if the little cry had awakened her mother. Both stood listening, he still on tiptoe on the pink-gold sand, she in water up to her knees. When no sound came from above, their eyes opened warmly on each other.

He threw her one of the plums. She caught it and blushed a dusky red.

He ate his plum. She ate hers.

He desired her, openly. She wondered at his manliness, openly. The sun was warm upon them. He toed to the edge of the flowing water. "Are you looking for pretty clams?"

She looked at the circles of vermilion painted around his

eyes. She pretended the circles made him look very fierce. "Swimming in the river will wash them away."

"Looking at the maiden I want as my wife has made me forgetful."

She looked at him full again and then looked down. "I speak with my face the other way."

He took a step toward her. Water ran cold over his toes. "Your mother will sleep long. We have the whole day yet."

She stepped away from him into the water, until it rose doubling over her thighs, hiding her. "Remember, I have that which no man has yet touched."

He smiled thickly. "You have used sorcery on me. I cannot help myself. You have taken part of me and eaten me and now I desire to have myself back. I cannot help myself. I have said."

"Tomorrow you will sing about me."

He stepped deeper into the water, until a doubling wave also washed over his hips. "I have come to you."

"Have you?"

"I have seen a young maiden who looks so beautiful to me I feel sick when I think about her."

"Do you?" She stood with her feet straight and close together, her palms pressed tightly against her thighs. "Have you brought ten horses?" She pretended to look for them up on the bank. "My father says he cannot let me go until he has seen ten horses before his door."

"But I cannot have my father's horses until my guardian spirit has come to me in a vision."

A smile moved across her brown moon face. The pink of her lips was exactly the pink of her fingernails. "You will tire of me soon and put me aside. Thus I want some property for the day when you do."

He stepped closer. Gliding threads of water tickled the inside of his legs. "Marry me. When father dies we will have many horses."

"You will marry without a vision?"

He placed his hands on her welling hips. Under the water her skin was as smooth as waterworn stone. "Come."

She laughed at him. "My lover has wings." She trembled

under his hand. The urging water pushed them together. "My lover flies into the rustling tree like a crow when danger approaches."

"I suffer patiently until my anger goes off."

She leaned away from him, still laughing. "Did you find a place to sleep in a bird nest?"

"It is sometimes good to rest in the great space between heaven and earth."

He trembled in love for her. Her breasts slept on her chest like curled-up squirrels. She turned her head. Her braids swung with it and settled over her breasts, partially hiding them. The brown eye of each breast peeked out at him. "You will tire of me soon."

"Come, let us fly to my uncle Red Hail. He will be kind to us."

"Where is your feather?"

"Come, let me use you like a good wife. I wish it. Come."

"Where is your new name?"

He groaned.

"Sometimes I am glad when I see you. But not always." She glanced at his naked chest. "When will you torment yourself?"

He groaned. "The torment I have is already great."

"Afterwards my father will say to me, 'Go, sleep again in the holes of the young unmarried men. My daughter, you are not worth an old horse now.'"

He looked at the glowing rust of her hair where the sun shone on it. Vermilion lay a deep dusty red down the parting. The smell of wood smoke still lingered in her braids. His right hand stroked her smooth hollow back while his left hand spilled water over her belly. He groaned. "Come. I am naked. I need a wife."

"My father says that a man should suffer and see a vision first before he lies with a woman. Otherwise he will not become a great man. When he remains a virgin he smells good to the gods. When a man has used a woman he smells bad to the gods."

"But my guardian spirit will not come to me!" he cried.

"Perhaps your god does not like it that you have the Name of No Name."

"Come, let us fly!"

"Perhaps your god does not like it that you desire me as a husband desires a wife."

He placed his left hand where no man had touched her before. "Come. I only want a sign from you that you are in earnest that you love me."

"Ooee!" she cried, startled. Then, with a wild little laugh, she cupped her hands full of water and splashed him in the face. Turning, she dove for the deepest part of the channel. Her black hair lashed back and forth in the water. He stood momentarily blinded; then dove after her. Both swam swiftly. She saw him coming and headed for the other shore. They reached it at the same time and emerged with water spraying golden to all sides. Some of the vermilion around his eyes had washed off. She ran up the bank, shrilling a low wild laugh, one hand over her mouth. He bounded after her, one hand reaching for the wet tail of her hair. She sped for a thicket of red willows higher on the bank. She flew into them. The red withes parted before her as if by magic. He was but a step behind and the red twigs whipped his red belly as they swung back into place. The red willows deepened and thickened. Her skin blended with the red bark. He watched the tail of her rust-black hair lash back and forth through the yellowing leaves. He caught her by the hair just as the willows opened on a bare patch of glistening pink sand. "Ooee!" she cried, laughing, falling back against him. She quivered when she felt his urgent pressing. "I have you!" he cried. Together they fell to the earth. They tumbled over each other a moment. Then he rose over her and pushed his knee between her legs and held her very tenderly. He saw her eyes softening under him. Gleams of black velvet laughter slowly changed to a look of soft red-brown love. Her thighs gave way. Her eyes half closed. Blood rushed to his head. He hardened to the game of love. He thrust at her. "Ooee!" she cried. Her head turned from side to side. She tried to double up under him. Then, again giving way, she abruptly joined with him in a rolling rhythmic rocking. He remembered her holding the small land turtle and his eyes closed and he began to swim under ebbing blood.

Sitting on the pink sand, she said, "Now you will sing about me."

He turned away from her. He gouged his heels in the sand. "I must go."

"Will you give my father the ten horses after you return from the vision?"

"I must go." He wondered why it was he now felt sudden disinterest, even disgust, for her. The fathers had never told of this.

She covered her face with her palms. "You have deceived me," she cried. "You will never bring the ten horses. Oo, oo, I am lost."

"I have already given you something. I have given you some of my strength. Part of my soul has passed into you. We have passed through one another and I am weak."

She wept. "I will dream of snakes. They will devour me."

"Well," he said at last, getting to his feet, turning his back on her, "I must try to be a brave man and take things as they come. I cannot weep."

"You will always smell bad to the people of the spirit world."

He began to walk away.

"I have nothing to live for," she cried after him. "I will take my own life and give it to the wolves. They will like it."

"I must take things as they come."

The red willows parted and he was gone.

That evening there was a sudden wild cry in the lodge of Owl Above.

"Aii! my daughter has lost a horseshoe! Aii! my daughter has lost a horseshoe!"

The whole camp was awakened by it. Redbird got up from his bed, put on his chieftain's robe, picked up his copper-tipped spear, and went out to have a look.

Presently he came back and rejoined his wife Star in their sleeping robes.

"What is it?" Star asked.

"Full Kettle says Leaf did not return."

"Ai!"

"She looked for her but found nothing but her clothes on the river's bank."

She sat up in the darkness. "She has taken her own life."

"Well, they cannot find her picked bones."

"She has taken her own life."

"Full Kettle believes the Pawnees have captured her. She thinks they still lurk near the river. To please her I have sent out extra guards. In the morning when it is light we will send out a searching party."

"She has taken her own life. Oo, oo."

"But why, my wife?"

"Leaf did not like Circling Hawk. She liked our son. But our son cannot get the vision. Ai, she has taken her own life. The Yankton women are proud."

There was a long silence. Finally Redbird murmured, "There is nothing we can do, my wife. Either the Pawnees have taken her or she has taken her own life as you say. Besides, it is they of the other world who decide these things."

Star slowly lay down again. "Ae, there is nothing we can do. Tomorrow I will join Full Kettle in her lament. It is a sad thing to lose one's last child. First, the boy, Burnt Thigh. Now the girl, Leaf."

Redbird and Star rustled together in their sleeping robes. After a time Redbird began to snore, and then Star also.

No Name lay quietly, his eyes glittering up at the smoke-hole.

The next morning No Name joined the searching party. The men circled the camp four times. No Name also led them as far as the pink sand across the river. They found no trace of her. Nor did they find any trace of Pawnees lurking near.

Leaf had disappeared without leaving so much as a foot-print.

# 7

The next afternoon his father thrust his lean head through the door and said, beckoning, "Come with me, my son."

"Yes, my father."

Together they stepped across the circle toward the horns of the camp. The cottonwood towering over Leaf's tepee had turned into a pillar of gold in one day and the sky was like a bluebird and the red rocks under Falling Water glistened in the sinking sunlight. Yet there was sadness in the village and the children were out of sight and the women were quiet in the lodges.

No Name was sure his father was going to show him the body of Leaf. With the new day love for her had warmed him again and he felt sick about her. No Name did not dare ask how she had come to her end.

He was greatly surprised, however, when Redbird passed by Owl Above's lodge and instead stopped in front of Grandfather Wondering Man's lodge. Only then did he notice that Moon Dreamer was no longer beating his medicine drum for the ancient man.

Redbird coughed lightly in warning to give those within time to prepare for visitors, then stepped inside, No Name following, their two quick shadows darkening the interior. They stooped around behind those near the fire and found themselves a seat in the place of honor opposite the door.

No Name crossed his legs at the ankles, knees out. Gradually his eyes adjusted to the dusk inside. Hard Bones, his widowed aunt, sat with her head bowed on the women's side. The top of her head was covered with gray ashes. Her braids were undone and hung like writhing snakes down her neck. Grandfather Wondering Man's lance and bow and quiver hung in their accustomed place on the tripod.

No Name heard rustling on his left. Flicking a look, he saw his uncle Moon Dreamer. Moon Dreamer also sat with his gray old head bowed. Except for clout and buffalo mask, he was naked. Around him lay the contents of his ceremonial bundle—a small age-blackened drum, a rattle made out of a buffalo bull's scrotum, a parfleche of wakan herbs, a bag of bone powders, a sacred crook decked with red feathers, a suction tube to draw out evil spirits. Moon Dreamer was not as well preserved as Redbird. He was quite wrinkled over the belly, and the skin over his thighs had the parched look of old age.

No Name and his father sat very still, eyes fixed ahead. The fire burned quietly under the smokehole.

As No Name's eyes continued to clear, he finally made out the form of his grandfather. Grandfather was lying on his side, partially curled up on his sleeping robe. Even where he sat, in semi-dark, No Name could see gray specks swarming in the roots of his grandfather's snowy hair. No Name remembered his mother saying that when people became very old, lice stirred to life under their skin and came out on them. Grandfather's skin was almost black and the veins over the backs of his hands were sun-empurpled, as if smoke-dried for a century. And his sunken cheeks and shriveled temples made his great nose seem larger than ever. No Name recalled the time when as a little boy he had asked Grandfather how he got such a big one. Sitting back in dignity, Grandfather looked past his nose and said that every night after all had gone to bed he used to go to the fat pot and rub his nose with grease. That's why it got so fat. No Name remembered the last time he had seen Grandfather out in the sun. He was bent over, leaning on two sticks, big nose sniffing the air, resembling a dog more than a man. Ae. It was a bad thing to think such a thought about one's own grandfather. But how could one help it? Grandfather had always seemed more of a relic to him than a relative. Grandfather had rarely shown any interest in him, had sat out his old days in the sun, passive and wordless, seemingly paying little attention to either his family or his tribe.

No Name was presently startled to see his grandfather stirring. No Name clapped hand to mouth. "Ai, he still lives," he whispered to his father.

"Yes, my son." Redbird spoke in a low grave voice. "He asked to see you. His wishes to speak to you for a last time."

No Name sat straight up. His eyes began to glow. Truly it was a strange thing that his grandfather should finally wish to see him.

Wondering Man moved again. A stalk of a hand fumbled with his great nose, then fumbled with his eyebrows. His skin cracked.

No Name waited.

The ancient's mouth opened, wide and ghastly. A hoarse whisper came out of it. "Is there not someone here who will hold open my eyes? I wish to see my grandson for a last time."

Redbird went over, and kneeling, gently drew back his old father's eyelids with his thumbs. "There, Grandfather. Can you see?"

Wondering Man's eyes rolled slowly, at last came together and focused on No Name. "My grandson."

"Yes, my grandfather."

"Grandson, you have not yet had the vision?"

"No, my grandfather."

"Have patience, my grandson."

"Yes, my grandfather."

"I look upon you and remember my youth. I am very old. I will die at last. Well, it is a good thing. My back aches. The little children walk on my spine but it does not help. I am without teeth and must be fed like a baby again at a mother's breast. My age has at last made me helpless. I have been rendered womanish by my many winters. It is time to go on. Moon Dreamer your uncle has tried his medicine and it does not help. He has sung all his songs and they do not help. The people of the other world want me to come. Well, I shall go to them."

Moon Dreamer lifted his head. His mouth was drawn from all the chanting. "Our grandfather's body is of the earth," he said, voice cracked and dry. "No one lives long in this world. Even for such an ancient one as your old grandfather it is very short. I am sorry for this."

Hard Bones the widowed daughter broke into a low wail. She began to tear her hair.

Wondering Man went on while Redbird held open his eyes. "It was my hope that I might see the issue of my thighs a brave man before I went on to that other place. I wished to see the sign of torment on my grandson's breast. I wished to see his secret medicine help him bear himself as a man. I hoped for this very much because I did not wish to see Soft Berry's son become the chief of our band."

"But my guardian spirit will not come to me!" No Name cried.

"Have you prayed, my son?"

"I have prayed, my grandfather, until I was dead for a little time."

A harsh sigh escaped Wondering Man. Gray lice began to move out of his white hair onto Redbird's bronze thumbs.

"Grandson, I have yet one wish."

"Speak, my grandfather."

"Carry me to the big red rock behind the camp that I may see the sun go down one more time."

"Yes, my grandfather."

No Name went over and picked up the fragile old man. Holding him as if he were a baby just born, he carried him out through the round door and across the camp circle. Redbird and Hard Bones and Moon Dreamer followed behind, single file. All the people sat silent in their tepees. No Name went up the pink path and at last came to the big red rock. It was the same one he liked to sit on. Gently he leaned his grandfather against the rock.

"Open my eyes," Wondering Man whispered. "I wish to see."

No Name lifted the dry eyelids with his thumbs.

Wondering Man's eyes slowly focused. Black pupils

emerged out of gray milky deeps. Gradually his eyes came to glittering life.

They waited. The sun sank very slowly. They waited.

At last, after another long wait, the sun touched the long low horizon and then sank behind it.

Wondering Man sighed. "I have yet one more wish."

"Speak, my grandfather."

"Bring me something to drink from the Great Smoky Water. It is wakan and full of medicine. It will give me strength for the long journey ahead."

"But the Great Smoky Water is a distance from here, my grandfather."

Redbird stepped forward. "We have some saved in a bladder, my son. I will get it."

Wondering Man took a little of the water. He savored it, making the noise of one chewing snow.

Then, after he had gazed yet again upon the place where the sun went down, he sighed and said, "Let my eyes fall shut. Now I can die."

# PART
## TWO

# The Vision

# 1

Early the next spring, in the Moon of New Grass, a strange thing occurred. Not a single spotted colt was born to the Yankton mares. This was a grave disappointment to Redbird.

No Name knew why. He decided to tell his father. He found Redbird meditating beside his fire.

"My father, I have come."

"When you come I am glad."

They passed the pipe and sat smoking in silence for a time.

"My father, I am miserable. My heart is cut into strings."

"Speak, my son. My ears are open and they listen."

"Leaf still does not return. She is dead. It is I who have caused her death."

"It is as the gods wish, my son."

"My father, I am sick. I took Leaf as a man takes his wife. She did not wish it. Afterwards she ran away. A Yankton woman is proud and often takes her life with her own hand."

"Ai!"

"My father, thus I am no longer a virgin and will never dream. It is done. I walk at random. I wander without a purpose."

A louse moved along a single black hair across Redbird's bronze brow. It touched his skin. Redbird felt it, caught it, and cracked it between his thumbnails. "Have you had a medicine dream?"

"No. My mind is in the manner of a hard knot. It will not loosen."

"There is nothing we can do. We must wait."

"My father, it is my blame there are no spotted colts this spring."

"We need a new medicine for the mares."

"The gods are angry with me, my father," No Name groaned. "I will go with the head down."

Redbird sat silent. He looked gravely at the fire. Presently Star came in and picked up a few dry twigs and mounted them over the red embers. Gray smoke gradually changed to tiny flames. She waited until the flame began to whip about like little wild mare's tails. Then she put on the water for the meat and withdrew.

"My father, the old ones tell us that a gifted man has powerful dreams. I am never given dreams. My father, your son is numbered among the dumb."

Redbird looked at the wrinkles over his old knuckles. "You must have patience, my son. Perhaps the gods are testing you."

"But I am too old to play with stick horses. Where is my guardian spirit?"

Redbird pulled his heavy buffalo robe over his shoulders. "My son, the Yanktons do not wish to hear much said on the same thing. Let us wait until the gods change their minds." Then Redbird looked up through the smokehole and addressed the skies. "Oh sun, make this boy strong and brave. May he die in a raiding party and not from old age and sickness. It is good to die young."

# 2

Four mornings later, as he was about to awaken, No Name had a terrible dream. Supine in his sleeping robes, he dreamed he began to play with Loves Roots, his father's other wife. He threw her a light thing; she threw it back. When he threw it, the thing was a stick horse. When she threw it the thing was a grass doll. Back and forth. Stick horse and grass doll. This was fun. He laughed. She laughed. They were very far apart and could not touch each other. Suddenly a feeling of doom hung over them. It came creeping in through the tepee door. It hovered over the fire. After a while, mingling with the gray smoke it turned into the head of a white mare. It had terrible teeth, like those of a grizzly. It had terrible eyes, like those of a madman. Then it was given two hands, calloused like a woman's. It went over to the women's side and picked up his mother's butchering knife. Quickly he crossed his arms over his chest. He placed his hands in such a way that his fingertips protected his mouth hole and his nose holes and his ear holes. Suddenly the white mare began to rush around. She changed into a fox and ran straight across the tepee for him and stabbed at him. The point of the knife struck his wrist, into the bone, making a slicing noise. He tried to awaken and could not. He choked. He was fixed upon the ground on his back. He screamed.

A warm hand touched him. It shook him. It was his father.

Slowly he awakened. He lay gasping. His heart galloped like a wild horse, trying to get out of his chest. Cold sweat filmed him from head to foot. His hands and feet lay still, as if dead.

"My son, what is it?"

No Name spoke as one awakening from a seizure. "I—dreamed—of—a—white—mare—my—father."

"Ai! And what did she say?"

"She—tried—to—kill—me."

"Were you afraid?"

"She—took—our—mother's—butchering—knife."

Redbird placed a hand on No Name's brow. "Son, you are cold." He slipped in beside him under the sleeping robe. "Come, I will warm you. You are very cold." He held him in his arms as in the old time. The tobacco smell in his father's hair was comforting.

When No Name had warmed up some, he said, "Is the white mare my guardian spirit, my father? Has my protector come at last?"

"No, my son. It did not come to you after a fast. It was a nightmare."

"Did it come to tell me a thing?"

Redbird got up. He dropped a twig on the sleeping embers. A little flame licked up, giving off a vague blue light. Redbird next mixed some tobacco on his chopping board. Solemnly he lit up. Then with a glance at the sleeping forms of his wives Star and Loves Roots, he said, "My son, tell me the dream. What was it?"

No Name told him.

"It is as I thought." Redbird puffed on his pipe a moment. "The gods have at last decided on a good thing. Tomorrow you must take a gift and a pipe to Moon Dreamer, our holy man. He will tell you what to do."

No Name suddenly felt very good. He sat up. "They will send me a vision?"

Redbird held out the pipe to his son. "Smoke, my son. We will know in the morning."

After breakfast, after Redbird had sent the horses to the hills, Star and Loves Roots prepared a gift. The day before No Name had killed a juicy buffalo cow. The two women took its fresh tongue as well as the leaves of well-cured tobacco and wrapped them up separately in corn husks and placed them in a handsomely decorated parfleche. Redbird meanwhile unrolled a leather pack and got out his best pipe. The pipe had been cut from the purest red pipestone, carved to represent a wolf chasing a buffalo, with the wolf serving as a handhold and the buffalo's mouth as the bowl. Redbird used the pipe only on special occasions.

Redbird said, "Carry this pipe to Moon Dreamer. He is a wise and good man. He will speak true. His tongue is not split like a snake's."

No Name took the gift in his left hand and the pipe in his right hand.

"You have taken the morning bath, my son?"

"I was the first again today, my father."

"Good. Now go. We will await your return."

No Name stepped across to Moon Dreamer's lodge next door. The skunktails on his heels erased the trail behind. He held his shoulders high under his white robe. He looked straight ahead. Boys playing stick horse stopped to stare at him. Women working on hides clapped hand to mouth. The eyes of old men sitting in the sun narrowed to black gleams.

No Name stopped before the door of Moon Dreamer's lodge. He looked a moment at the painted symbols on the outside, the rising white ball and its thirteen rays. Then he coughed politely to let his uncle know that company had come and stooped through the doorhole. "I have come," he said. He stood a moment in front of the fireplace.

Moon Dreamer sat huddled under a robe. A small fire smoked in the center. The lodge smelled of old people, of sour sweat and urine-stained clouts. It did not seem to help much that Star sometimes came in to clean up and cook for her brother. In a day or two the bad smells were back.

Still stooping, No Name moved around toward Moon Dreamer. He placed the gift of tongue meat and tobacco at the holy man's feet. Then he held out the pipe and said, "Obey the pipe."

Moon Dreamer turned his face away.

Again No Name held it out. "Obey the pipe!"

Moon Dreamer held up his hand against it.

"Obey the pipe!"

Moon Dreamer refused yet again.

"Obey the pipe!"

It was the fourth time and Moon Dreamer could no longer deny him. He accepted the pipe and said, "Sit, my son."

No Name took a seat on a folded robe to the left of Moon Dreamer. Wisps of smoke curled upward out of the fire.

In patient ceremony Moon Dreamer opened the packet of tobacco. He filled the pipe and lighted up with a hot coal from the fire. He presented the pipe in turn to the powers of the sky and earth and the four great directions. He puffed gravely a moment to himself. Then he handed the pipe to No Name.

No Name also presented the pipe to the great powers and puffed solemnly to himself.

When they finished the pipe, Moon Dreamer stood up. He slipped off his buffalo robe and put on a buckskin shirt worked with many porcupine quills. Tufts of sweetgrass protruded from holes in his shirt front. The smell of the old dried grass was suddenly sweet in the lodge. Moon Dreamer next put on his ceremonial buffalo-head mask.

"Father, the old ones tell us that a gifted man has powerful dreams. I am never given dreams. Father, I am numbered among the dumb."

"You must have patience."

"Father, I have seen that one must have a true vision first before one can be well-to-do. I shall be poor because I have not had such a vision."

"It is for the gods to decide."

"Father, in the night I dreamed of a white mare. My father tells me it was only the nightmare. My father sends me to you."

"Ai! And did the nightmare speak to you?"

"No. She tried to take my life."

"Ahh."

No Name then told him the dream.

Moon Dreamer's dark eyes burned in the eyeholes of his buffalo-head mask. Then, looking down at the bare ground between his knees, Moon Dreamer said, "Oh earth, hear. This son has had a strange dream. What shall he do?" Moon Dreamer held his head to one side, listening attentively as if to some far voice.

No Name held himself in rigid check.

Moon Dreamer next looked up at the darkened smokehole above. "O Moon, hear. This son has had a strange dream. What shall he do?" Again Moon Dreamer held his head to one side, listening.

No Name waited.

At last Moon Dreamer said, "My son, this is what the dream means." Moon Dreamer's voice was grave, even awesome, inside the buffalo mask. "In your dream a certain spirit mare wished to speak to you alone. You would not listen. You played childish games with one who was neither your true mother nor your sister. Also, you took a thing from a young girl which she wished to keep. You would not listen. Therefore the white mare became angry with you. That is why she took your mother's butchering knife and stabbed you. The white mare loves you and wishes to tell you something. Therefore it is at last time for you to go to a high hill. There you must fast and await the true vision."

"Do you see the high hill? Where is it?"

"When the moon spoke to me I heard the sound of great thunder."

"Houw!"

"Your father is one of those who has seen the Thunders." With a twig Moon Dreamer drew a picture of a great two-legged thunderbird in the dust between his knees. "Therefore you must go to the far hill where the Thunders like to come."

No Name's eyes lighted up. "I have heard my father speak of such a hill. It is very high and is known as the Butte of Thunders. It is beyond the country of the terrible Rees. I shall ask my father to tell me the way."

"Are you afraid?"

"Father, it is only the vision I lack, not the bravery."

"Good. Go there. You will be given the revelation of your calling. Now listen to me."

No Name bowed his head and listened.

"When you are there, do not swallow any rain water that may fall. Do not eat. Lie very still and await patiently the thing that will happen. Otherwise you will have to wait yet another year."

No Name trembled with joy. "Hoppo! At last I shall be as strong as the grizzly. Ae, and as swift as the deer and as majestic as the eagle and as cunning as the fox. I shall be a great man."

"Ae."

"After my father has departed, I shall be a bold leader, a good and valiant man. I shall be a firm wise father to my people."

"May it be true."

"My people shall be known to all, to friend and enemy alike, as the Great and Shining People, keepers of the Place of the Pipestone. We shall be a people of glory, as many as the stars."

"The moon is our mother. She does not lie."

"And I shall be given a new name."

"My son, it is time for the vapor bath. You have wived with a woman and must be purified in a sweat lodge."

"I am ready, father."

"Also, you must choose a companion who shall go with you to the Butte of Thunders."

"Shall it be my friend Strikes Twice?"

"His Name shall be given you in the purification."

Moon Dreamer then went out and called Redbird. Together the two old men went down to the river and cut fourteen willow branches, each no thicker than the butt of a thumb and no longer than a war lance. Selecting a bare spot behind the village, they drove the branches into the ground in a circle, then bent them down and tied them together into a round frame. They covered the frame with buffalo hides, leaving an opening for a door on the east side. They dug a pit in the center of the floor to the depth of two hands and to the width of three hands and took the loose earth from the pit and piled it in a little mound four steps from the door. They also spread a little of the loose dirt in the path from the door to the little mound. The little mound stood for the earth; the path for the good road. Moon Dreamer got a weathered buffalo skull from his lodge and set it on the little mound, facing it toward the door. The buffalo skull stood for the great herds of buffalo which Wakantanka sent them each year so that they might have plenty to eat and a long life.

A crowd gathered to watch the ceremony: rosy naked boys and wondering little girls and idling braves and grave-eyed maidens and solemn old folks. Most sat in a circle on the ground; a few climbed up on the red rocks above the sweat lodge.

After scattering fresh tufts of aromatic wild sage on the ground between the little mound and the door, Moon Dreamer next selected four young virgins and sent them to the hills to collect twelve stones, each stone to be no larger than two fists placed together. He instructed them to bring only those that had the mark of volcanic firing in them. Moon Dreamer next told the four virgins to find a cotton-wood sapling of about the thickness of a man's wrist. They were to chop it down carefully, removing the branches and sharpening the butt to a good point. This became the sacrifice pole which he thrust into the ground near the door. Redbird brought out four brilliant redbird tail feathers, a package of fresh tobacco, a ball of treasured horsetail hair, and tied them to the pole as a sacrifice to the sun. From among the young men in the crowd Moon Dreamer chose two to be his helpers: thick-lipped Strikes Twice and scowling Circling Hawk, the first representing friendship and the second rivalry. The two were sent out to get fire-wood from the cottonwood grove down the river.

When all was ready, Moon Dreamer placed four lengths of wood side by side on the ground, pointing them east and west, then put on a layer of kindling, then four more lengths of wood, crosswise. He took up the twelve stones one by one and set them on top in neat rows. More fire-wood was placed around the sides, starting on the east side and going around with the sun. From his own lodge he got a red coal. Then in hushed silence he started a fire on the east side.

While everyone watched, quiet, grave as wondering gophers, Moon Dreamer let the fire burn fiercely until the stones were white hot. Then, giving a signal, he ordered No Name to strip down and enter the sweat lodge. No Name threw off his shirt and leggings and moccasins and stooped inside. Turning left with the sun, he crept on hands and knees along the wall of the sweat lodge until he came around again to the door. He sat down. Moon Dreamer stripped down to his clout too and stooped inside, taking a seat as leader just within the door and across from No Name. Moon Dreamer took up a pinch of tobacco and offered it to the six powers, took a second pinch and placed it in the pit. After a short pause, Strikes Twice handed in a smoking coal which Moon Dreamer placed in the pit too. Again Strikes Twice reached in, this time a handful of dried sweetgrass, which Moon Dreamer carefully placed on the red coal. A pleasant odor swept through the lodge. Very gravely and slowly, Moon Dancer rubbed his arms and body with the wafting sacred smoke. The red pipe was next handed in. It too was purified in the sacred smoke. Murmuring low words to himself, Moon Dreamer filled the pipe, lighted it, offered it to the six powers. Then he and No Name smoked together. When the pipe was empty, Moon Dreamer carefully emptied out the ashes and placed the pipe on a chip of buffalo dung.

Moon Dreamer clapped his hands and Strikes Twice and Circling Hawk took up their forked sticks and immediately began bringing in the hot stones. With a forked stick of his own Moon Dreamer placed them in the pit one by one, saying as he did so, "The first stone represents Wakantanka, the Great Mysterious One, who lies at the center of everything. The second stone represents the earth, the mother of all, who lies under all things." The twelve stones filled the pit exactly. They were so hot they gave off an eerie pink-gray light.

A leather bucket of water was next handed in. Both took a short drink, then doused their heads. Moon Dreamer barked a command and Circling Hawk closed the door tight from the outside. The vague light from the seething stones became a trembling pink.

Moon Dreamer said, "My son, you know why we are here. This small lodge is now the womb of our mother earth, this darkness in which we sit is the ignorance of our minds, these burning stones are the coming of a new life. Remember this and keep it near your heart."

"I will, my father."

Moon Dreamer took up the bucket and splashed some water on the stones. There was an explosion like the sound of a boulder breaking open in deep winter frost. The low tight hut became pitch black with choking steam.

No Name gasped for air. For a second he was terrified. "Aii!" Sweat burst out all over on him.

"My son, this hissing steam is a good thing. It is a sign that the place from which all the seeds come is still alive. Take comfort from this."

"Hi-ye! I will, father."

"Is it very hot?"

"It is! Thank you, thank you."

"Do you feel the purification at work?"

No Name was ready to faint in the choking heat. "Yes, father. It feels very good. It is very good for me."

Moon Dreamer poured water on the seething stones four times. Steam whistled up like great drafts of wind. The glowing stones slowly faded, from intense pink to ugly red to dull orange to old brown. Yet the heat increased, the steam thickened.

Sweat burned in No Name's eyes. His lungs labored. Darkness pressed down on his mind.

"Breathe near the ground, my son."

"I will, father."

The stones cracked and hummed in the pit. Steam continued to whoof up in harsh explosions.

"Thank you, thank you. I am being purified."

Just when No Name thought he could stand no more,

Moon Dreamer called out and Strikes Twice raised the cover from the door. Light poured in, as well as blessed fresh air, and the scent of wild sage.

"Hi-ye!" No Name cried. "It is good. I am glad to be alive. It is a good day."

"My son, the opening of the door to the east is the dawning of wisdom in men. Take heed and remember it."

"Yes, father. Yes, yes. Hoppo."

More water was handed in and the door closed a second time. Darkness and whistling steam filled the tight hut once more. No Name suffered it.

"My son, the sweat lodge makes brave men."

"Ai, father. I will be brave. Hokah."

The lodge was darkened four times. Each time the heat increased, the steam thickened. Had it not been for his wetted hair No Name would long ago have fainted.

Moon Dreamer lifted his voice in chant, more in sigh than in song:

> "Father, see, we are here.
> We have smoked the pipe.
> We have heated the fire stones.
> We have raised the sacred steam.
> Your son has suffered much.
> Have pity on him
> And let him be purified."

"Hi-ye!" No Name cried. "Thank you for the steam. I am being purified. Hi-hi-hi."

Then Moon Dreamer called out, loud, "What do you see, my son?"

"I see myself going on a long journey. Also my hair is wild and left unbraided."

"What else do you see, my son?"

"I see my rival Circling Hawk."

"Aii! You have chosen Circling Hawk. He will be your companion on the road to the Butte of Thunders. It is good. Come." And with that Moon Dreamer whipped open the door and stepped out.

No Name followed, leaping out in one great spring. His skin shone, roasted to a deep livid red. "Hoppo!" he cried. "I am purified." He leaped about in a circle, frenzied, full of exaltation. "Thank you, thank you."

"Take of the sage, my son," Moon Dreamer commanded, loudly. "Rub your body with the sacred sage."

No Name grabbed up handfuls of the aromatic sweetness and rubbed himself harshly. Bits of the silver leaves stuck to his rosy skin. He rubbed and rubbed.

The crowd pressed close. Hands reached out to touch him. The people cried and cheered. Redbird in joy began to dance. Star and Loves Roots sang the tremolo, tears streaming down their faces.

"Come, my son," Moon Dreamer called, "to the river. Run."

With a wild cry, No Name sprang down the path to Falling Water. He ran like one released from a burning stake. Then with yet another cry he leaped off a high rock and dove into the boiling water under the falls. There was no shock. Only bliss. The tumbling water rolled him over and around and over. He was a spirit. He was beyond flesh, ennobled, ready to soar with spirit eagles.

"Aii! I am purified. Thank you, thank you, Hi-ye!"

Moon Dreamer stood nearby in shallow water. With old veined hands he cupped water over his belly, cooling himself. Then he raised his hands and said, "My son, have the new life. It is given you. You have performed the ceremony in the true manner. Feel right, think right, be happy."

# 3

It took three sleeps to reach the Great Smoky Water. The first day they arrived at the farther end of their own land, the second day they rode across the land of their cousins the Teton Sioux, the third day they moved into the land of the terrible Rees.

They traveled light: a red pipe, a bow and quiver of arrows, a light pad saddle, a rawhide war bridle with a long lead rope, a parfleche of dried meat. For the rest both man and horse lived off the country. They traveled along the sides of hills, avoiding high ground as well as wide barren river bottoms. They paced their horses, driving them an hour, then walking them an hour, with two hours to rest at noon. No Name rode the gelding Lizard, Circling Hawk rode a dun gelding named Dusty.

The second day out it became plain the two horses got on better than did their masters. The two horses kept edging toward each other. When let out to graze they nuzzled each other between bites. The budding friendship embarrassed No Name and Circling Hawk and each in his sly way tried to keep the horses apart.

On the evening of the third day, just after sunset, the soft gray-green earth suddenly dropped away into a wide shadowed valley. No Name, up ahead in a narrow descending ravine, reined in his horse. He signaled for Circling Hawk to stop. He peered past the ears of the horse. A breeze coming up the ravine lifted both his hair and the horse's mane. Far below, beyond a thick fringe of cottonwoods, streamed the Great Smoky Water. Sheets of silver raced up and down the tan waters. A spring-green meadow lay on this side of the river, a steep bluff with fired rocks rose beyond it. No Name let his eyes drift to the left, following the water, and saw far to the south, on a lesser hill, small balls of moving black.

"Buffalo," No Name said, pointing.

Circling Hawk sniffed. When irritated, or when unhappy about something, Circling Hawk had a habit of clearing his nose with a quick intake of air.

"There may be Ree out to hunt them," No Name added.

Circling Hawk's wolfish eyes danced. His pocked face glowed like pitted pipestone in the rosy dusk. He stared intently at the moving balls. Finally he held his hand in front of his chest, palm down, then swept it forward, palm up. It was the gesture of no.

No Name considered. The Rees had villages both to the north and south of them, an hour's ride apart. Small parties were sure to be visiting back and forth on such a fine spring day.

A tiny winged speck appeared high above them against the darkening blue sky. It bounced in the air, strangely. Then, folding up into a ball, it abruptly dove at them. Enlarging slightly, it came down so swiftly its flight set up a low whistling hum.

"Ai!" No Name cried, instinctively ducking, pushing his nose into Lizard's dusty mane, "it is a spirit. It will strike us."

Circling Hawk flashed up a look, then he too ducked down.

When it was almost upon them, its wings suddenly opened, long and angular, showing white markings, then with a low boom it swooped up and away, rising easily and gracefully into the dark blue sky above.

"Nighthawk!" No Name exclaimed, sitting erect again. "There was an arrow of white under its throat."

"Unh! He means to warn us."

The gray-green bird once again resumed its strange erratic bouncing flight high above them. At the top of each fluttering spurt it let go a cry, more an anguished bleat than a song.

"Look," No Name said, "attend."

"A thing will happen to us," Circling Hawk said.

Again, after a moment of weird fluttering, the nighthawk closed its wings and dove at them. It came on like a falling star. Then, when it was almost upon them, its angular wings once more opened and with a light boom it was up and away.

"Ae, a thing will happen to us," Circling Hawk said.

No Name glanced back at his companion. "Circling Hawk is not afraid of a little nighthawk, is he?"

"A thing will happen. The winged one is wakan and means to warn us."

No Name laughed. "Friend, it is only playing. My father has told me about them. After they catch a bug they like to play."

Circling Hawk grunted. "Unh. The bugs are still asleep in the earth."

Twice more the bird dove at them and opened its wings with a booming sound and soared up and away. And then it vanished.

"See," Circling Hawk said, "four times it told us of a thing that will happen. It looks very bad. Perhaps we should return and come another time."

No Name shook his head. For himself he considered the sudden appearance of a nighthawk a good omen, not a bad one. It meant there were no Rees lurking about. Otherwise the bird would never have played so carefree. "Come," he said, "tomorrow night I wish to sleep in preparation at the foot of the Butte of Thunders. We will cross over in the dark. I have said."

Again Circling Hawk sniffed in irritation.

"Come. It is safe to go on."

No Name touched heel to flank and they moved down the ravine.

Night came on rapidly. Every now and then the hooves of the horses started small avalanches of stones. The scent of newly budded buffalo-bean flowers rose from the ground. The choke-cherries and plums were in bloom and showed up as small clouds of subdued white on the walls of the draw. Their scent lay heavy and sweet in the ravine. Both man and horse rode along drunken with it. The ravine gradually flattened out and became part of the valley. Soft grasses deadened the footfalls. They moved under great rustling trees. Darkness deepened. They rode between tree trunks as big as three buffalo bulls standing together. The earth underfoot softened. There was little sound of their going.

Suddenly ahead lay a wide sloping sandbar and beyond it a rippling expanse of water on which starlight twinkled. The two braves reined in, stopping just inside the dark shadow of the cottonwoods. They sat silent a long time, listening, slowly looking from right to left, then behind. The horses looked too, ears flicking back and forth.

An owl hooted immediately overhead. Both man and horse started.

"It is too near not to be a true call," No Name whispered.

"Ae. But it will be as the nighthawk said. A thing will happen."

No Name considered. For all his crude ways, Circling Hawk was as crafty and as daring as any Yankton. These things had been proven many times, on horse-raiding parties as well as on buffalo hunts.

No Name said, "Come, let us sit on the ground a while. I hear a cricket under us. It is one of those who know how to point the way. I will catch it and ask it how we should go."

Both dismounted, letting their horses crop in tall grass.

No Name sat very still, as did Circling Hawk. The cricket, which had fallen silent when they stepped down, presently started up again, chirking lively cheer at No Name's feet. No Name's eyes narrowed, began to glow like a panther's. After a second, he made out the cricket, as much by sight as by sound. Its rubbing wings gave off a tiny radiance. Hollowing his hand, he cupped it up in a darting motion.

"Have you caught it?"

"Ae. But it is frightened. We will let it rest a moment."

The cricket sprang twice, trying to get out of his cupped hand. Each time it tickled him so much he almost laughed

out loud. He held it gently. It sat very still. No Name
breathed with his mouth open and so slowly his breath was
not audible. He waited.

After some moments, the cricket moved, itching No
Name's palm.

"Ah, it is ready to speak." No Name cautiously opened
his hand and looked in. He could barely make out the
cricket against the light skin of his palm. "Little grandfather," he said, "is it safe to cross over this night? We wish
to know."

The cricket twitched this way, that way. It seemed bewildered by the question.

"Tell us. You are the wise one of the night. We wish to
know."

Circling Hawk, squatting near, leaned in close to watch.
His smell was very strong, and No Name was reminded of
Leaf's remark that his face was rough all over like a toad's
back.

The cricket twitched back and forth once more, then suddenly sprang out, straight ahead toward the river.

"Ae," No Name whispered. "It tells us the true way.
Come, let us cross over. We thank you, little grandfather."

Circling Hawk got to his feet slowly. "The medicine of
the cricket is not as great as that of the nighthawk. A thing
will yet happen to us."

"Hoppo! let us charge the river. I am not afraid."

"Also, the other side has steep mud banks. Our horses
will sink under us."

"The water will carry us far." No Name looked across
the wide sheeting water. "I see a place where a small river
enters from the west. There will be sand at its mouth."

They led their horses by the nose toward the river. Both
men had thumb and forefinger ready to pinch off any inquiring whinny. Hooves and moccasins crunched softly in
the giving sand. The sandbar glowed underfoot with a
vague amber light.

The sand began to slope down sharply. They stopped.
Without a word both took off the robe pad saddles, removed their clothes, rolled clothes and arrows inside the

robes, the ends tucked in tight and waterproof, then fastened the packs and also their bows on top of their heads. They urged the horses into the water.

Lizard leaned down to drink.

"Come, brave one," No Name whispered, "you must not drink now or you will founder. Also it is time to cross over. Soon the Nibbled Moon will appear and by then we must be hidden in the woods on the other side."

They moved into the sliding waters. Despite the deep dark, the waters still had a yellowish-brown cast. The waters moved up cold ring by cold ring, stinging, over the knee, up the thigh, searching in the crotch, up the narrow belly, each time making them catch their breath.

Lizard suddenly was of a mind to go back. He snorted; tried to turn in the water. No Name quietly closed off his nostrils and held him to the task. They struggled in the washing waters, snorting, coughing. Then, wrestling, both plunged over the drop-off and the river took hold of them.

No Name gave his horse a final whack on the rump, then slid back along the horse's flank, careful to stay out of reach of the powerful stroking hooves, and latched onto the tip of the horse's tail. He steered Lizard for the far shore. Only the horse's waggling head and his own pack-burdened head showed out of the water. Circling Hawk and his dun horse followed close behind. Dark curling eddies washed off to one side of them. The sound of their swimming was lost in the wash of the rushing current.

The water was burning cold, but the river was not too wild. A moon or so later, during the great spring flood, the waters would roughen into loud boiling whirlpools, with uprooted trees sawing up and down in the waves.

Then, even as the thought of the deadly sawyers passed through his mind, and just as they reached the driving main channel, a thing came sliding out of the north toward them. It was a huge cottonwood with vast sprawling limbs. It came at them roots first, like an octopus half-risen in wrath out of the river. No Name was so startled he cried out, once, gulping water. Then, recovering, he quickly gave Lizard's tail a jerk, trying to steer him downstream and outswim it. But Lizard, who had also started at seeing the suddenly looming thing, was too busy trying to stay upright in the rushing channel. It was then that No Name noticed that the water below moved faster than the water on the surface. He could feel the terrible suck of it beneath him. Again he jerked at Lizard's tail, twisting it viciously, trying to steer him to the left and ahead of the looming terror. But the struggle to stay upright in the racing tan water was all-consuming and both horse and man headed straight for the tree.

Circling Hawk cried out in warning.

They collided. The great cottonwood bore on for a second, then slowly began to revolve in the water. Both man and horse struggled against the turning wheel of roots. Finally one of the huge tentacle roots landed on Lizard's neck and shoved him under. A moment later a second root, snake-smooth, caught No Name under the belly and lifted him clear. The wheel of roots began to turn swiftly. The root under him lifted him so quickly he stroked twice in the air before he could catch himself. When he came to the top of the wheel's revolution, the horse's tail was jerked out of his hand. He grabbed onto the root under his belly with both hands and hung on.

Again Circling Hawk cried behind him. "Ai!"

Down the other side No Name went with the great wheel. He hit neck-first and went under in a wallowing glut of cold muddy water. Instantly buoyant waters pressed him tight against the root, almost squeezing the breath out of him. He felt the air-tight pack of clothes push against his head, then jerk at it. Then something cracked him over the back of his skull, hard. His brain suddenly went hot with it, then numb.

He came back to life lying on his belly. He heard grit sand grinding against his forehead. Someone was bouncing him up and down on the sand. Each time he hit, his forehead and nose worked deeper into a little trench. He heard someone grunt over him as he was lifted yet again.

He stirred, trying to roll over and get his face out of the scouring sand.

The someone, feeling him stir, instantly turned him over. Carefully he sat him up. "Come back, friend, I have you safe."

No Name opened his eyes. He saw a big head and huge shoulders humped over him. The shape reminded him of his dead brother Pretty Rock. He coughed. Water trickled from the corners of his mouth. His eyes cleared. Then he saw that the someone was Circling Hawk. "Friend," he croaked, "I thank you. You are my brother."

"You were very heavy in the water."

Suddenly No Name's bones began to ache with cold. He shook with it. "The tree caught me. Then it hit me."

Circling Hawk covered him with his fur robe. "I saw it. When the tree turned again I wrestled you free."

No Name coughed. Again water trickled down his chin. "Ahh," he gasped in misery, "a part of me has died."

Circling Hawk bundled him warmly in his arms. "Your breath soul left you for a time. But not your shadow soul."

No Name shivered. His teeth began to chatter like a cicada chirring. "You have saved me," he said slowly, hollowly. Again the deep cold in his bones made him shiver. "What shall I give you?"

Circling Hawk shook him roughly in his arms. "Be strong. Tomorrow you go to fast."

"Where is my horse?"

"It stands behind us."

No Name looked. The Nibbled Moon had just come up across the wide river and in its vague light Lizard shone like a wet blackberry. "It is good."

"The nighthawk told true that a thing would happen."

"Ae. And the cricket told false. Perhaps it was frightened."

Circling Hawk shook him again, hard. "Come, we cannot linger here. There may be Ree after all. The nighthawk may have meant to tell us of yet another thing besides the angry water tree."

Still dizzy, No Name struggled to his knees. Long snakes

of black hair lay sopping wet on his neck. "You have saved my life. I shall remember it forever. What shall I give you, my brother?"

Circling Hawk got to his feet. He stood very still for a moment. Then a raw sob escaped him. "Where is Leaf? Where are her bones?"

No Name staggered to his feet. He stood apart, alone. Slowly his whirling mind steadied, slowly his lips became grim and his eyes hardened. Then he said, "We must try to be brave men and take things as they come. We cannot weep."

Circling Hawk stiffened on the sand beside him. "I lay my hand over the mouth. Take up your robe and let us move on."

They slipped into their buckskins again, slung the quiver and the bow over their backs. The bowstrings were wet and hung slack, so both made sure of their knives.

They went barefoot, leading their horses, with Circling Hawk up ahead. They moved cautiously up the river bed of the small stream, staying well in the deep shadow along the south bank. The water was shallow. It rippled gently against the shin. The sand underneath, though harsh, made good footing.

The stream wound back through high land. With each twist and turn the bluffs kept parting to allow them passage. The Nibbled Moon provided for the eyes just enough light to make out the silhouettes of trees and bushes. Occasional bats skimmed erratically across the surface of the water.

They had traveled upstream for about an hour, and were well back into the west hills, when Circling Hawk suddenly held up his hand for silence. Quickly No Name slipped an arm around his horse's nose ready to choke off a whinny. Horse and man stood motionless in the water. No Name's wild black hair still lay in wet strands on his neck and every now and then a drop ran down his back. Also, an eyelash seemed doubled under in the corner of his eye. It itched, almost hurt, each time his eyes moved back and forth, but he dared not lift a hand to rub it.

Then, like Circling Hawk, he saw it. The top of a horned

head slowly came to view over the edge of a large gray boulder on the north side of the stream. Next came a pair of broad bare shoulders, then the heavy torso of a man. No Name instantly recognized the horned head. It was a Ree, one of those who were cousins of the Pawnee. The Ree had probably heard splashing in the water and had come to investigate.

No Name saw Circling Hawk's hand slide slowly up over his shoulder and carefully select an arrow in his quiver.

"The fool," No Name thought, "the bowstring is still wet. It cannot send the arrow."

The same thought must have come to Circling Hawk. His hand paused, held, then slowly fell back and reached for his knife instead.

The Ree's dark torso loomed clearly against the stars. The soft light of the Nibbled Moon gave the Ree's chest the deep hue of walnut. From where they stood hiding in the deep shadow, a good fifty steps away, No Name thought he could make out the slow rolling back and forth of the Ree's eyes, and see his nostrils quiver, opening and closing, trying to get scent of them.

The Ree's right hand rose and also reached over his shoulder for an arrow. He fitted it to his bow. The feather on the arrow glinted for a second as he turned it a little to make it fit perfectly. The Ree drew the arrow all the way back to the point, then let fly. The arrow speared straight for Circling Hawk. No Name's eyes blinked just as the arrow was upon Circling Hawk and for a second he was sure his companion had been hit. But Circling Hawk did not cry out. Nor did his horse jump. Then No Name heard the arrow whack into the clay bank beside them.

The Ree waited, watching to see what effect the arrow might have.

No Name held himself stiffly erect. His thumb and forefinger lay poised over Lizard's nose.

The Ree at last seemed satisfied, and slowly withdrew, the waist first, then the chest, and finally the horned head.

Circling Hawk broke out of his stony stance and let go of

a long soft sigh. He looked over his shoulder at No Name. "The nighthawk was right to warn us."

"Ae, it is true." No Name rubbed the eyelash out of the corner of his eye. He looked up at the moon. "The night departs. Let us go on."

An hour later they found a good place to sleep. It was a turn in the river where young willows grew thick on a low sandy bar. They picketed their horses and trampled down a place for their beds. Rolling themselves up in their robes, with the smell of horse sharp in the fur, they fell asleep side by side.

# 4

Munching jaws awoke him.

Opening his eyes cautiously, No Name saw it was their horses. Lizard and Dusty had found themselves a small patch of spring grass within the willows.

Then he noticed all the birdsong. A goldfinch sang from a twig immediately above him: "See-see-e! Baby-babee!" A cardinal called somewhere behind him, clear, happy: "With with with cheer! with with with cheer!"

No Name smiled. The wingeds were happy this morning. It was good. He nuzzled comfortably against the coarse fur of his robe.

Circling Hawk stirred against him.

No Name called softly. "Day is here, my brother."

Circling Hawk sat up with a rush out of his sleeping robe. "Whaugh!"

For the first time in his life, No Name found himself looking upon Circling Hawk's wolfish features and wild eyes with pleasure. This was now his brother, the brave man who, despite their rivalry, had saved him from drowning and had comforted him in his huge arms.

No Name said, "Shall we kill a rabbit for breakfast?"

"We have a certain quantity of dried meat left. Also a corn cake my mother prepared which I saved."

"I am hungry. It will be good to eat over a fire again."

"Ai, but you have been purified. There will be no fire until you have had a vision."

Sighing, both braves then got up. They made pad saddles out of their buffalo robes again and cinched them around the horses.

As they were about to mount, Circling Hawk suddenly asked, "Friend, tell me, did you wive Leaf by the river? I wish to know."

No Name caught himself just in time. He kept his face passive, expressionless. "She is gone. Why do we speak of her?"

"I wanted her for wife," Circling Hawk said slowly. "I would have given twenty ponies for her. I felt sad that I had but ten. I did not have the second ten ponies."

"I wanted her for wife also. But I did not have any ponies to give."

"Your father has many ponies to give." Circling Hawk burned a fixed unwavering eye upon him.

"I could not ask my father for the ponies. I did not have the vision. Therefore my grief was great."

"Your father is related to many in our village. You have many cousins who could help you with the horses."

"You are also related to my father," No Name said. "Your father is my father's cousin. Why did you not ask my father for the second ten ponies?"

"My father is dead. My mother is not well liked. Also there are those who do not favor me."

No Name held up to Circling Hawk's glaring eyes. "You say well. But my grief is still a great grief."

Circling Hawk sniffed up a quick nervous breath; then expelled it with a blast.

Irritated, No Name did the same.


They rode steadily all day, going up the valley of the little stream as it meandered in from the west. The lofty round bluffs gradually drew together and at last became a narrow canyon. The footing in the stream changed, sometimes treacherous with quicksand, sometimes cruel with sharp rocks.

They came upon a ravine which opened into the canyon from the northwest. A small creek trickled down it. They turned off and went up the creek. The land rose steadily. The ravines became a narrow depression, finally leveled up onto a high plateau. All around lay the slowly sloping horizons of the high plains. The grass became sparse, mostly last year's brittle stalks. In the hot afternoon sun the old grass gleamed a dull brown-gold. Occasional patches of pricklepear cactus came along. Twice the horses shied from green rattlesnakes. Dust puffed up on each throw of the hoof, lingering palely behind and riding slowly off on a soft west wind. Shortly before sunset, as they gained a long rise in the land, the Butte of Thunders reared out of the northwest horizon.

No Name looked at the butte with mingled feelings of joy and awe. As his father had told him, the butte was like unto the sacred power of a great stallion. Holding hand to mouth, long hair streaming on the wind, he cried, "There is the place. I see it. I am happy."

Circling Hawk had also watched the butte rise into view. "There is some brush on the first hump on the south side. It will make a good place to camp and hide the horses."

"It is a good place."

When they came to a yet higher rise in the land, so that the whole of the gray-green butte was sharply etched against a yellow west, he saw why the Thunders liked to come to the place. Its flat top made a good platform halfway between heaven and earth from which to broadcast messages.

No Name reined in his horse and got down on his knees on the ground. He rubbed himself reverently with a handful of silver sage. He held out his hands to the holy hill and began to rejoice. "Thank you, thank you. I am glad I have come. Tomorrow I will climb upon you and talk to the Thunders. They will send me the vision. Hi-ye! I have said." He got to his feet and turned to Circling Hawk. "Friend, lead the way. You have had the vision and thus are my older brother. I am but a suppliant. Instruct me." He remounted Lizard. "May the vision be a true one."

Mares' tails moved across the sky to the north of the butte. The slow high movement of the thin clouds had the effect of making the butte lean some to the west. The sun sank and the shadow on the east side deepened to a greenish black.

Jogging along on his horse, No Name continued to rejoice. "Thank you, thank you." He held his right fist to his chin, forefinger out, in sign for truth. "This is the place my father spoke of and I am happy to come."

"I see a small stream beyond," Circling Hawk said. "It will be a good place to water the horses each day."

No Name made out some rocks strewn down its side. "Look. Attend. See where the Thunders have been angry. It is where they have thrown stones in anger."

Circling Hawk blew his nose clear with a loud blast. He looked down at the grass going by underfoot. "The horses will suffer in this country. One of us will have to get grass."

They were within a mile of it, when suddenly a piece of the rimrock broke off. It fell a ways; then, magically, sprouted wings and flew off in a great curve to the west, slowly mounting the air on great beating wings, rising higher and higher, until finally it was but a tiny speck. Then, between eye blinks, it vanished altogether.

"It was one of the Thunders," No Name said reverently. "He has gone to tell the others that I have come."

Circling Hawk gave his horse a kick in the flank. "It was but an eagle. When the eagle saw we had arrows for him he flew away."

They stopped just below the butte, on the south side, on the hump where part of the rimrock had fallen. Debris lay scattered to all sides. Some of the fallen rocks were larger than horses. Rosebushes and chokecherries grew between the rocks. The valley all around shone with silver sage.

Eyes glowing, thick hair streaming down his shoulders, No Name continued to look up at the towering place of the gods. "Ho-heeh-e-tu! I have come to the holy place of the Thunders at last."

# 5

He was sleeping one moment, the next moment was wide awake. Something stealthy was moving near his head. He heard thick breathing. Someone seemed to be in a terrible rage. His heart began to bubble in his chest.

"It is Circling Hawk," he thought. "Ae, Circling Hawk accepted the mission to come with me, because it was wakan and worthy to do, but he also hated me with all his soul and therefore has decided to kill me. He has found a great stone and now stands ready to drop it on my head."

No Name shivered.

The sound of the thick breathing continued. Yet the stone did not descend. There was no smashing crack on the skull.

No Name finally opened his eyes. There, in the soft weak light of the Nibbled Moon, was a white prairie wolf. The great wolf's eyes were red, and they blinked and burned into him. White bristles twitched on its blackish nose. Its countenance was so close, so full upon him, that for a moment No Name thought he was having a bad dream.

He heard a chewing sound in the chokecherries behind him. Ae, there was yet another wolf in the camp. He remembered his father Redbird saying that wolves like to gnaw bridle ropes because of the human smell in them.

He blinked. And just as quickly the white wolf vanished.

At that No Name sat up. Ghostly shapes with bushy tails, as vague as streamers of mist, slipped across the rock-strewn slopes. No Name stared at them, watching them fade into the dim dark-green distance. Not one shape seemed real. Had it not been for the lingering stink of the white wolf's breath he would have sworn he had dreamed it all.

Shivering in the frosty cold, heaving a long sigh, he lay down again and snuggled inside his sleeping robe. All of a sudden he became very lonesome for his father and mother and for the wonderful smell of their fire and the remembered taste of fat hump. He began to wonder if the ordeal he was about to undergo was worth it after all.

At last dawn broke in the east, a speckled black slowly giving way to a smoky blue.

He waited until a certain bright star overhead faded away, and then, hardening himself to it, got up.

He touched Circling Hawk. "Friend, the morning is good."

Circling Hawk sat up with a start. "Where are they? I dreamed of wolves."

"The great day has come. You must watch as I prepare myself."

Circling Hawk was immediately attentive. He threw back his sleeping robe, got up, stretched, then seated himself on a rock.

No Name removed all his clothes. He gathered a handful of silver sage and rubbed himself briskly, until the air was stuffy with its dusty aromatic smell. He found a crumble of volcanic ash underfoot and carefully painted his face black, well up into the roots of his hair, under his ears and chin, even down his chest some. He combed his wild, straggly hair with the rough side of a buffalo tongue. He unwrapped his red pipe from its case.

He handed Circling Hawk his bow and quiver, and also his knife. "Friend, will you keep these until I return?"

"They shall be as my own until you come."

"Also, will you keep the watch until I return?"

"Do not fear. May the gods hear your prayers."

"Look. Attend. The red of the morning. The sun is almost here. It is my wish to begin the vigil on the mountain top at sunrise. Now I go to climb the hill my father spoke of."

"Are your hands clean? They are not defiled?"

"I have taken the sweat bath. I have traveled a long way to get here. I have rubbed myself with the sacred sage. You have seen. I am ready."

"Go. Depart. Climb to where the eagles like to sit. Receive the vision."

"This is my fourth trip to a high hill. The fourth time is the sacred time. I am ready. Hoppo."

Erect, face up, holding his red pipe in front of him, he walked stiffly around to the east side of the butte and began the ascent. His naked body glowed a dusky red. "O great spirit," he cried, "be merciful to me that my people may live!"

It was cold. A gauze of frost lay over the ground. Under the pink dawn it sparkled like glazed blood. The cold ocher soil burned his bare feet. He let his bronze toes pick the path, around spine cactus, over clumps of sage, around red ant mounds, across shivered shale.

The slope began to tilt up, then to steepen sharply. The morning rose as he climbed. Blackened face lifted, erect, gleams of red flashing down his black hair, he worked upward. The land behind him fell away. A clattering cricket jumped out of the short grass. It opened its wings and became a flying drop of blood. Still the slope steepened. It lengthened. What looked sleek green from a distance, close up was rugged terrain. More and more rocks, fallen from the eroding escarpment above, lay in his path. He skirted them, stepped over them. Some of the rocks had just broken off, their edges a fresh hard gray. Others had lain a millennium and were covered with light green lichen. He puffed. The escarpment began to hang over him like a looming cliff. The smoke-blue sky lowered slowly toward him. He could feel the horizons all around sinking and falling back. He climbed, dark glittering eyes fixed on the rimrock, up, up. The work of it warmed him. His heart struggled loud in his chest. His heart pumped him up the hill.

Immediately below the rimrock lay even greater piles of freshly broken-off rock. There was no grass or moss or lichen to soften the footing. Twice he stepped on stones so sharp they cut his feet. Rich glowing pink surrounded him.

It bathed all things. The sun was about to burst over the horizon. He hurried, holding his red pipe before him.

A sheer wall towered above him. He looked along it to the south for a way up. It was unclimbable in that direction as far as he could see. He looked along the precipice to the north. There, not a dozen steps away, next to a jutting rib, was a large chimney-like opening. He scrambled over and found it to be full of good handholds, even a few step-like projections. Then he spotted some half dozen perfectly shaped round stones on a ledge. "Ae," he thought, "wakan stones. Someone, perhaps my father, has carried them here in a ceremony. I have found the true way. It is good."

He climbed swiftly up the chimney. It narrowed. There was just enough room the last few feet for him to squeeze through. Grunting, lifting himself, his head finally popped out on the flat top above. He heaved up the rest of himself, and then, standing erect, turned to face the east.

At that very moment the red sun began to show over the horizon. For a moment the edge glowed like a distant prairie fire. It shimmered, wavered, increased, at last became a full circle and lay on the far rim of the earth, a huge burning stone. Almost between the wink of an eye the whole of it lifted free and it began to revolve around and around. One furious flush after another raced across its face.

"The sun is my father. I am ready." Pipe stem pointed ahead, he began to look for a clean level place to lie down on. He paced completely around the outer edge of the butte top, now and then glancing down at the prairie far below. He found that the whole top was about as large and as round as their village circle. Most of it was covered with frost-shivered shale and eroding gray rock, with here and there some pockets of soil, a few prickly pear cactus, some clumps of grayish sage, and the pale green tufts of new buffalo grass. There were innumerable ant mounds. The butte top seemed to be a sort of heaven for them. Red ants, some crawling, some flying, swarmed everywhere in the warming sun.

He found a gap, or opening, in the south edge of the rim,

where the rock had tumbled down. It looked upon their night camp. The size of the gap surprised him. It had not seemed that large from below. The gap was at least ten horses wide and four deep. He spotted Circling Hawk below rubbing down the horses. He was so high above them that Circling Hawk resembled a small turtle with hair, while the horses looked like small bloated boudins.

The sun rose. Between him and the oscillating sun lay a vast valley, a pale blue prairie yielding at the horizon to a paler blue sky. He looked at the sun until it seemed to him two coals were slowly searing their way through the bone at the back of his head.

From the sun's position he marked out the four cardinal points. On each point he piled stones in pyramids of seven each. He intoned, in a low soft chant, "Here is the yellow east where the sun always rises. Here is the red west where the sun always sets. Here is the blue north where the source of purity lives. Here is the white south where the source of life lies."

He surveyed it all a last time, finally decided he would lie beside a different pyramid each day until the vision came to him. He chose the east side first. The source of all light might be kind to him on the very first day. He carefully placed his red pipe stem up on a small forked stick. He made a broom of sage stems and removed every living and growing thing from a space on the ground big enough to lie upon. Then, naked, he lay down with his bare feet to the east.

He looked straight up, awaiting the vision.

The rock under him was still cold and damp with night. He held himself against it. He fixed his thoughts on the sun. It would warm him when it came overhead.

"Come, my god. I am ready. I await you."

Looking past the end of his blackened nose, he watched the great ball of fire rise. His back froze while his belly heated. He saw the sun as a vigorous forefather. It spilled fatherhood to all sides. It rose in the morning, it held high during the day, it plunged into the earth at night, and in so doing fathered many peoples.

"Come, my god. Give me my name. I await it." His song was a whisper, a sigh in verse, a soft exclamation sinking at the end.

A single winged ant, a female, lighted on the point of his blackened nose. In the sun its small bulb tail was almost the color of the back of his hand. He watched it. To his amazement he saw its transparent wings were still growing.

He spoke to it, crossing his eyes to get it in focus. "Tell me, little grandmother, have they sent you to give me a message?"

The winged ant lifted his bulb tail and flew off.

The sun lifted and the rock under him gradually warmed. He remembered the instructions to lie very still. Sweat formed between his toes. Hunger began to turn in his belly like a whimpering blind puppy.

At noon he felt drowsy. Afraid he would fall asleep and so miss his god, he held his eyes up to the sun a while, until once again two holes began to burn into the back of his brain. He turned his head from side to side.

His joints began to ache from lying so long in one position. He waited. He sang songs in a low voice, sighing. He sighed, singing. He drifted off into sleep. His body heated in the afternoon sun, his mind raced with fleeting dreams.

Of a sudden he dreamed he had been caught by the Two Maidens. The Boulder With Wide Lips had him fast by the leg. Surprisingly it felt good. The gray lips sought to get a better hold of his leg and he did not prevent them. After a time he even helped them. The granite boulder began to sway from side to side, worrying his leg playfully like a friendly dog. The wide lips smiled at him. Then of a sudden a small sun raced in from the blue north, from where the sun otherwise never went, and it burst directly over his belly and became a golden stream, pouring, pouring. He was joyfully happy. Then he awoke.

"Hi-ye! that was a good dream. It was not a bad one. Therefore I will not have to return." Then he saw what had happened. "But I have defiled myself."

He broke out of his rigid posture and on hands and knees

crawled to a clump of silver-gray sage and taking a handful purified himself with it. Whole again, groaning, he crawled back to his clean place on the rocks and lay down, this time with his head to the east and his feet to the west.

"I will watch my father descend. Perhaps he will look upon me at last when he has seen how attentive I have been."

Late in the afternoon a wind came up from the west. At first it came softly, in irregular breaths. But after a time it began to come in rising gusts. The wild sage began to show first silver then gray. The winged ants flew up in protest and then cowered on the lee side of stones. Bits of dust hit the soles of his feet, tickling him.

"Perhaps he will speak to me out of the dark center of a roaring whirlwind. I am happy. Let him come."

He narrowed his eyes against the wind and flying dust. The wind moaned over him. It chilled. It crooned in the wide gap on the south edge of the rimrock. It whistled shrilly in the chimney on the north edge.

The sun set. The wind died away. No god came to him. No voice from above spoke to him.

The flat top remained warm for a long time after dark. He lay very stiff. He watched a great throw of stars slowly spread across the heavens. He knew the stars to be supernatural people. He watched them move off toward the west. Just before moon-up, a cloud cover swept in from the northeast, hiding the stars and the dark bulky horizon. After a time he could not make out if he were lying high or low. The wind, also coming out of the northeast, whooed in the chimney like a hoarse owl. The whooing reminded him that his mother used to scare him with owl talk, telling him that if he did not behave an owl would come and get him. He whispered to himself the song she used to sing:

"Hi-ye, hear the hooting owls
In the passing of the night.
They sit in the trees
And scare naughty little boys.
Hi-ye! hear them.

Hoooooooting owls
In the passing of the night."

He remembered the time too when he boasted he was too
old to be frightened of her stories. He even laughed at her
when she began telling them. But then one night, as he
laughed, a big ghost leg suddenly came poking in under the
tepee wall. In terror he ran to his mother's arms. "Ai!" she
said then, "see, you have been very naughty and a ghost has
come to take you underground with him." A long time later
he found out that the ghost leg was his father's arm dressed
in a legging and a moccasin.

He lay still. To fight sleep, he filled his mind with stories
his old father used to tell him, stories of bravery, of manly
behavior, of kindly giving. His father in telling the stories
would take up one of the fringes of his sleeve and describe
a certain trail he had taken. When his father picked up a
long thick fringe, the trail told of would be an arduous one,
when he selected a short thin fringe the trail told of would
be an easy one. He also recalled certain brave acts performed before his very eyes. Once his father got rid of a
black headache by digging a black nerve out of his forehead with a knife. Another time his father tied a sinew to
one of his rotted teeth and to the tail of a horse and then
gave the horse a whack on the rump. The horse had to drag
him twice across the camp circle before the bad tooth
would let go. Then there was the awful morning when his
father gashed his thighs, so that a scarlet blanket of blood
slowly trickled down his legs until sunset, because Buffalo
Woman, the protecting goddess of their band who lived behind Falling Water, had in anger drowned two of their most
comely virgins. All these brave things he remembered. It
comforted him to remember them. Thus he endured the
night.

When the sun came up the second day, he rose with it,
uncracking his joints and releasing his stiff back muscles.
He was so happy to see the revolving oval of the warm sun
again that he broke into a dance and chanted a song:

"The sun is my father.
He is my begetter.
He rises a great tree in the morning.
He warms me all day with his loving arms.
He soothes me at twilight with his colors.
As long as he shines I shall not want.
He is my father."

His stomach, rebelling at the fasting, growled inside him like a surly dog. Twice involuntary belches broke from it, so that he had to speak to it. "What, can you not endure a little hunger for the sake of a calling and a given name?"

He found another soft stone dark with fired ash. He re-painted his face carefully, painstakingly, well up into his hair, then down on his chest to the nipples. He also painted a long, black zigzag line down his left side and groin. Then, having prepared himself, carrying his pipe, stem forward, he sought out the pyramid of stones on the north edge of the butte top. With a broom of sage stalks he brushed out a level place, clean of dust and pebbles and insects, exactly diamond square. He knelt and lifted his hands, palms up, toward the sun, saying, "I walk in a remote place. I pray as I cry. I have neither eaten meat nor drunk water. I am poor. Great father, this day bring me the joy of a new Name and the power of a new destiny." He followed the prayer with a passage of hands to the ground, four times. Then he lay down in the square, his feet to the north. He folded his arms over his belly. He worked his tongue, bringing up wetness, so that gradually his hunger subsided.

The sun rose and warmed his right side, from his ear to his toe. There was no wind. It was very quiet. Behind him he heard the winged ants buzzing. He looked past his nose and saw the points of his hipbones and the square mounds of his kneecaps and the tips of his toes. The north sky was very blue. To the right of his toes, through a fault in the rimrock, he could make out very clearly where the yellow-green land touched the sky. He lay outstretched, patient.

At noon he turned on his right side to give his back a

rest. He lay stiff, anklebone resting on hard anklebone, ear and elbow on hard cold rock.

He cried as he prayed. "It is the second day, my father. I am waiting. Send my guardian spirit to me that I may be named and become a brave man. I wish to hear the shouts of the little children when I return from the hunt with meat for the camp."

Then to the right of his nose, close up, he saw a strange thing. Attached to a bending stalk of buffalo grass was a speck like the egg of an insect. His eye caught the hint of movement in it, as if the tiny speck were hatching. At once very wide awake, he watched it. After a few seconds the speck began to crack open at one end. He thought he could hear it opening, like the soft cracking of a milkweed pod in autumn. He forgot himself and his agonies. He watched it enraptured. At last the speck flipped open, in halves. Something glimmered in the opening. A second later a very tiny fly, a toy fly, emerged. It sat on the edge of one of the halves and flexed its fragile wings. The wings gleamed brilliantly in the sun, a strange bluish green. The little fly's wings began to lengthen, and widen, and glow like the tender gossamer of spider webs. And even while this happened, the fly's body also enlarged, the wriggling head becoming a tiny flat shield with a magic design on it, the tail rising and falling like a tiny bloated waterskin in wind. Blinking, watching amazed, he next saw the growing fly, a male, take a few trial flights, from the edge of its egg to the top of the blade of grass, from the blade tip to a small stone, and then, most astonishing of all, to the inside of his right elbow.

"Well," No Name said then, softly. "So it is you they have sent, is it?"

The fly flexed its wings. It balled its belly up and down. It cleaned its pig snout nose with its forefeet.

"Ai, it is the blue fly of death. It wishes to tell me of Leaf."

The fly dipped, took a nip of No Name's skin, and then, in a quick curving blue flight, was gone.

"Ai, she is dead." And exhausted from the close-up watching, he turned slowly on his back again.

Again that afternoon his stomach balked in protest. It not only barked up belches at him but bit him inside. Once it bit him so ferociously he had to press down on it with his fists to subdue it.

His tongue swelled fat in his mouth. He could no longer bring up wetness. He had trouble crying his prayers. His lips cracked. Running the tip of his swollen tongue over the cracks, he pried up flaps of peeling skin. These he chewed, and ate.

He waited, patiently.

Again a strong wind rose late in the afternoon, this time from the south. It soughed up through the gap. The wind blew bits of chipped rock against the top of his head, sprayed them against his toe tips. Sometimes certain of the winged ants flew too high, became too daring, and despite desperately beating wings were blown out over the abyss, coasting away into nothingness.

Again, at sunset, the wind died away. It became very still. The sun sank, a yellow ball falling out of a light blue sky into a yellow-blue horizon. It disappeared like a spirit stone thrown into spirit waters. There were no after-ripples. Night raced out of the east. Stars lowered into sight.

The high rock cooled. Cold air breathed over him, coming straight down from the stars. He opened his mouth and drank of the cold air. He thought it wonderfully sweet, better than spring water. He opened his hands and gathered it up and washed his hot face with it. He felt faint.

"I do not wish to sleep, but dream, so that I can at last have a name and know who I am."

Of a sudden he fell asleep and dreamed. In his dream he saw a light sweep over him. It came from the blue north. Looking very carefully he saw that it was a prairie fire. Its huge flames raced toward him like wild red horses. The flames became as tall as the tallest rustling tree. The prairie fire finally swept up the sides of the butte, its flames so eager they licked over the edge of the rimrock and warmed the soles of his feet. "This is very wonderful!" he mur-

mured in sleep. "I am warm, I am warm. The night is cold
but the fire you have sent me is like a big lodge fire. Give
me a fur robe and I shall sleep well, my mother." Then he
saw that the whole butte was on fire. He heard it melting
under him. Presently it began to incline more than usual to
the south. "Ai! save me, my father. The fires are eating
me." And crying aloud, terrorized, he awoke bathed in
sweat.

Eyes wild, he became even more terror-stricken when he
saw a real light sweep over him. A real fire was actually
burning up the butte. His heart began to jump around in his
chest. It struggled like a terrorized dog trying to get out of a
leather bag.

Then he saw what it was—the Burning Lights. They
were leaping out of the deeps far beyond the north rim of
the earth. Like flying bits of mush ice, they streaked up
from the horizon as if thrown by a high whirlwind. Sometimes the whole sky was full of glittering advances. Occasionally he thought he could hear rustling noises, like
slender icicles gently threshing together, faint, very far off.

His heart calmed down.

After a time the northern lights faded slowly again, sinking back to their sources in the blue north. Stars reappeared.
All was again as it had always been.

Toward morning a cramp settled in his left thigh, deep,
immediately under the black zigzag line he had painted on
himself. It burned him. He suffered it because he fancied
the clutching knot sent warmth through the rest of his body.

The third day the sun rose bright and clear again. He
staggered to his feet. When he tried to dance a greeting to
the sun, his left thigh buckled under him and he fell to the
ground.

"Father," he groaned, "I am very weak. You do not send
me the true dream. When shall it be?"

He got up again. Slowly he stretched his limbs and tried
walking. His thigh held.

He limped along the rim, carrying the red pipe. Looking
down he had the odd feeling that the butte had risen in the

night. Objects on the prairie below seemed smaller than usual. When he came to the gap on the south rim he saw Circling Hawk with the horses. Circling Hawk was now hardly larger than a daisy head and the horses but glossy beetles.

He was glad to see his ugly friend still in attendance. He remembered how Circling Hawk had held him in his arms and warmed him after he had nearly drowned in the Great Smoky Water. He realized at last that Circling Hawk was truly an older brother to him. He wept about it. He swore to reward him for it. He opened his arms as if to embrace what had once been his hated rival. Then, before Circling Hawk could look up, he turned abruptly away. Both Moon Dreamer and his father Redbird had told him to walk in a remote place, crying alone to Wakantanka, neither eating nor drinking, nor holding converse with any man, until the vision came.

After he had blackened his face, he swept a foursquare place near the pyramid of stones on the west side. Perhaps the power on the red side of the world would carry his cries and lamentations to the Thunders. He puffed as he worked. He picked up every loose pebble, plucked away every growing thing. Then, sighing, he lay down, heels almost to the rimrock, face up, arms crossed over his sunken belly.

He waited, patiently.

He no longer felt hunger. His stomach was silent. Nor thirst. His tongue, after the many drinks of cold air, lolled at ease in the back of his throat. He felt dully satisfied.

Dozing off, he dreamed. He had been out hunting with his new brother Circling Hawk. They were very happy with a great killing of buffalo cows. Now the Yankton mothers could make many tepee covers. They placed the bloody humps of meat in a circle on the grass and then lay down to sleep inside the circle. They snored. While they slept, a brownish male snake crept out of the river bottom, and hissing at the red humps of meat, slipped up to where they lay. "Do not eat me," No Name cried. "I am the son of Redbird and my helper has promised me a long life." The snake heard him and smiled. It winked. At that Circling Hawk stiffened. He tried to cry out, but could not. Then the snake entered Circling Hawk's backbone and ate its way up into his skull. Presently it looked out of Circling Hawk's left eye, smiling at No Name, winking, flicking its tongue. Strangely the snake's tongue was not forked, but single, like the nose of a minnow. "Ahh," No Name whispered in his dream, "it is wakan."

Then he awoke. He lay half asleep for a while, full of wonder at the dream he had dreamed.

He turned on his left side. Lidded eyes almost closed, looking vaguely, he saw an arm of brownish flesh pouring slowly toward him across the hard lichen-covered rocks. It did not surprise him to see it. Its skin was flecked over with green, and it moved almost invisibly through the sparse clumps of buffalo grass. Blinking, still caught in the hypnotic hold of his dream, he recognized it as the male rattlesnake that had eaten its way up the backbone of Circling Hawk.

He spoke to it, gently, in a low cracked voice. "What is the message from Circling Hawk? What does he say?"

The brownish snake paused, then its arrow head slithered back, angling almost into a coil. Slowly its head lifted and its red tongue glittered in the sunlight. He saw that its tongue was forked. Only then did he see it was not the snake of his dream.

He was not frightened. Redbird had taught him that snakes were sacred animals, beloved by the Thunders, that they were sometimes even known to speak to men.

"Tell me, old father, what do they of the other world have to say? When will they bring me sight of my helper? My eyes are ready to see him."

The snake blinked its dusty eyes.

"When will Wakantanka speak to me?"

The snake waited a moment, then slowly withdrew, sank from sight in a fissure of rock.

He lay in trance a long while, not quite looking at the sun, staring a little below it. This time it did not burn two holes in the back of his brain, though it filled his eyes with dancing boils of red light.

At last, almost beyond suffering, he raised open palms to the skies and murmured, "Father, I am not blameless, yet take pity on me. Give me a name. Do this and I will give you a scarlet blanket before all the people when I return to camp."

His tongue felt thick. A fat turtle had crawled into his mouth. When he tried to speak the turtle ate up his words.

Moments slipped away as drops in a sliding waterfall. He did not see the sun set. His eyes gradually darkened over. He saw neither moon nor stars. All was black. He struggled to stay awake, yet slept much. He lay with his mouth open.

During the night a thunderhead rose in the west. It coasted in silently. When it was almost upon the butte it began to sprinkle the land with fat, finger-sized drops of rain. The big drops fell in irregular patterns. They moved up the slope and across the top of the butte. They moved to where he lay, drummed on the bones of his chest.

He lay suffering them, not quite aware of what was happening.

The sprinkling thickened into a heavy dropping rush of rain. Water streamed down his face. It fell into his mouth. It gathered in his throat. It was so sweet it made him cough. The cough awakened the turtle. It tried to back out of his mouth. Then he himself awoke some. He swallowed and the turtle became his tongue.

At that he became wide awake. He cried out. "Ai, I have taken water!" He clamped his lips shut, shook his head from side to side in torment. "Now they will not come."

Like a great bumblebee the thunderhead dropped its tail, and let fly a dancing bolt of lightning. It speared into the south rim of the high butte. Dazzling fire seared the rock on all sides. The butte and all the land around rolled under the afterclap.

"Thunders, you have come!" he cried, electrified. "Thank you, thank you." A series of vast rattling echoes raced away across the prairies. Immediately after, even heavier rain fell. It came across the butte top in lashing veils. The sage began to smell very sweet and fresh in the rain.

There were no more bolts of lightning. The great bumblebee cloud had but one sting in its tail. It moved on. Presently the rain let up.

"What have I done?"

A cold wind sprang from the west. It moaned off the prairies below.

"I drank unwitting."

Stars came out. They twinkled brightly above him.

"Father, I am not blameless, yet take pity on me. I will give you a scarlet blanket before all the people when I return to camp. I will torment my body in the sun dance."

The butte cooled under him. He heard water trickling over rocks. He felt a drop of rain trembling in the hollow of his upper lip. He dared not lick his lip for fear of touching the drop.

The stars moved west. The butte moved east.

He reached up and tried to finger the stars. He saw his finger tips move darkly amongst them but they did not quite touch them.

He lay stretched out. The little water he had accidentally swallowed in sleep had awakened desperate thirst in him. One moment his big toe moved, the next his eyeball. He fought off the thirst. He determined not to think of it. He composed himself.

"I await the morning," he murmured. "Tomorrow is the fourth day of my fast. The fourth time is the sacred time. Tomorrow Wakantanka will send someone."

He lay the night through in a dreamy, half-paralyzed state.

# 6

When the sun rose on the fourth morning, he discovered that his shadow soul and his flesh soul had become separated during the night. His shadow soul was happy that the fourth day had come at last. It was very eager to prepare for the coming of his guardian spirit. But when he tried to get up nothing happened. His arms and legs continued to sleep on the cold hard rock. His body lived by itself and no longer obeyed commands.

Then he saw his shadow get up by itself. It stood scowling in disgust at his sluggard body. Finally it turned to the morning sun and stretched itself leisurely in the yellow light. It began to dance in honor of the rising sun. From very far away he heard it sing:

> "A long journey I have made.
> I am quick and strong.
> I am a swift bird ready to fly.
> Yet my flesh is a coward.
> My helper has promised to come.
> Yet my flesh is a coward."

He watched his shadow soul stroll along the edge of the butte top. It looked down on two sides, the yellow east and the blue north, and then came back to the red west side and stood looking down at him. It said, "Arise, take up thy flesh and prepare the place on the south side."

His flesh roused. In a low faint voice it said, "Bring me water. I desire some. Bring me a corn cake from my mother's big pot. I desire some."

"What! would you give up the fast on the fourth day?"

"I am killed. I have to leave you."

A look of sadness moved across the face of his shadow soul. Then a darkness entered his eyes and both fell silent.

He was roused by the sound of threshing winds just above. Gusts of beaten air bruised his face. Dust and sand whelmed up around him.

"It is the black whirlwind," he thought. When the beating gust continued, he said in his mind to the whirlwind, "Go. Where you are going it is bad. Go by yourself."

Instead a heavy weight settled on his chest.

"Ai, it is not the black whirlwind. It is the nightmare again. It comes to choke me." He wept inwardly. "Now I will have to return to my people without the vision. It is crushing me so that I cannot breathe."

The weight moved on him. Digging claws anchored down into his ribcase. Suddenly there was a terrible peck into his belly, then something sharp caught at his navel and tried to rip it up.

Opening his eyes, he saw a great bird perched on his chest. "Aii! it is the Thunderbird!" His wild cry made the great creature let go its bite and turn and look at him. It cocked piercing black eyes at him. Then he saw what it really was.

"Ai, it is a golden eagle. It thinks I am a fallen calf. It has come to rend me and feed its little ones."

Sunlight burned in shivers of gold over the great bird's thick brown feathers. The great bird stood on him larger than any wolf he had ever seen. Again its proud beak turned and it looked down at him. Shifting heavy stalk feet, its black claws took a new hold on his ribcase.

"Are you my helper?" he asked, weakly.

The eagle spread out its wings, ruffled them majestically, resettled them, then looked at him in outraged amazement.

"Are you my guardian spirit?"

The eagle started, blinked, then spread its vast wings again, got set to fly off.

Then No Name's flesh soul awakened. It turned into a wolf within him. It made his eyes blaze. Suddenly his arm sprang up and before the eagle could take off he seized it by the tail. The great bird screamed, harshly, brokenly, with a laugh like that of a maniac. It flapped its great wings, again, again, hard, until air rushed around them as in a whirlwind. The power of its beating wings lifted No Name to a sitting position. Yet his flesh soul hung on grimly.

"Do not go!" he cried. "Are you not my guardian spirit?"

Abruptly the feathers he had hold of parted from the eagle's broad tail, and, released, the great bird shot up into the air.

He watched it go. He looked from the tail feathers in his hand to the bird rising in the sky. He scrambled to his feet and reached out after it, calling, "Come back, come back!" He watched the bird until it became as small as a hawk. It cut a curving line off to the northwest, became a speck in the blue morning sky, then was gone.

Amazed to find himself on his feet again, he cried, "I am not killed. My shadow soul has rejoined my flesh soul. Hi-ye! Thank you, thank you. Something wonderful is about to happen." He danced a short morning salute to the sun.

Wavering, staggering some, carrying the red pipe, he moved to the pyramid of stones beside the gap on the south side. He looked down. He saw the circle of fallen stones below and the rosebushes between them and in the midst of them the two horses Lizard and Dusty, and then, narrowing his eyes, also Circling Hawk. All three seemed to be looking up at him. He gave them the sign that all was well, holding his right hand against his heart, level, then swinging it outward.

He turned. He got down on hands and knees and cleaned off another foursquare place in the midst of loose shale and pebbles. He picked some silver sage stems and brushed away all the stray curdles of dirt. He found a crumbling dark stone and painted his face black a final time. Then he lay down, face up, head to the north and feet to the south.

"I am ready," he said, "let it come."

He dozed down into a vast wide calm. He felt himself arriving in a world where there was nothing but the spirit of all things. He saw it was the true world, the one behind the world of shadows he usually lived in. He now knew more things than he could tell.

A voice spoke. "Watch closely, twolegged one. There is something you shall see. Hey-hey-hey."

He lay floating on a soft cloud.

And then, looking down, he saw it. Below, through the gap in the rimrock, lay a nest lodged in a circle of rocks. It was made of carefully chosen twigs and lined with white horsehair. The white skull and white bones of a buffalo lay in a litter to one side.

"Ha-ho! a mare's nest," he whispered. "I will watch to see if she returns before the nest becomes cold."

He watched. A wise and knowing smile curved his lips. "She is the mother of all the living and I wish to see her."

Suddenly he saw a white mare coming toward him, trotting lightly, shaking her curly mane, whisking her long tail. She was so glistening white he could not look directly at her. She was whiter than sun on snow on a bright winter morning. Also a halo of whiteness hovered about her. The whiteness cast a dazzling sheen on all things near her, the rocks, the rosebushes, the silver sage. She was a holy being, a great and mysterious one, incomprehensible, wakan. She neighed lightly. Gaily she lifted her tail. Watching her closely he saw she had reddish lips and blue eyes. She smiled at him in a secret way.

The hair on his head stiffened. His heart jumped wildly.

The white mare stood over him. Holding her head to one side, she looked down at him. "Are you afraid, my son?"

The moment he heard her voice he felt calm. "I no longer fear."

She smiled. "Why are you here, my son?"

"I have come to fast."

"And why do you fast?"

"To know life and gain strength."

"Your body is very weak."

"I know this. But that standing within me which speaks to me has become strong."

"It is good. What would you do?"

"I wish to know my guardian spirit. Where is he? I wish

to do a great thing for my people. If I can do this perhaps I shall be known."

"It is good. It shall be given to you in time. You shall be a great man. Your people shall be as numerous as the leaves of the rustling tree."

"When will this be?"

"Will you listen to my words?"

"Your words shall be scarred on my heart."

"Your helper shall be a certain white stallion. He will help you. He will be the new medicine your horse breeders need. He will give your people many spotted colts."

"Where is he?"

"Listen carefully, my son. There is much for you to remember. First, you must take a long trail alone, on foot, to the River That Sinks. It is to the south where the Pawnees live. There it will be told you where the white stallion lives."

"Alone? On Foot? I will be afraid."

"It will be given to you to be brave."

"Where will I get the meat? Who will make my clothes? Where will I sleep?"

The glowing white mare smiled down on him indulgently. She shook her head up and down. Bluish fire sparked out of her threshing mane. "Meat and clothes and a place to sleep will be given to you also. Have courage. Be patient unto the day."

"Your words fall on my heart and I will never forget them."

"The white stallion will be very wild and fierce. But after a time you will conquer him. After you have caught him, cut off a piece of the scarlet mane between his eyes, that place where all can be seen by the horse, and place it in a square leather case. This scarlet plume you must put away until your return to the village. After your return, bring the scarlet plume to your intercessor and ask him to perform the proper ceremony over it. Your intercessor will divide the plume into two parts, making twists of them. One twist is to be worn in your hair as your fetish, the other twist is to be hung on your tripod as your medicine. Do you hear me?"

"I hear you, great one."

"In the meantime, to help you catch the stallion, your intercessor will give you a horse chestnut, that strange piece of grayish black gristle growing on the inside of a horse's leg. It is to be your substitute fetish. Your intercessor will tell you to wear it inside the fat braid that hangs behind your left ear so that it may speak quickly to you in time of trouble and advise you. Later, the horse chestnut is to be replaced by the scarlet plume. Do you hear me?"

"I hear you, white one."

"As long as you keep the two twists of the scarlet plume safe, you shall always prevail. With them in your possession you will grow to be an old man without ever becoming feeble or racked with the pains of old age. You will desire maidens until the day you die."

"Then it will be as it is with my father Redbird."

At that the glowing white mare looked down at him oddly, and fell silent.

"What is it? What have I done?"

"My son, the gods do not wish to hear much said on some things. Wait until I have finished telling you all of the message."

"I throw myself on my face on the ground."

The white mare stepped over him with her white front hooves and then leaned down her belly as if to give him suck like a colt. "My son, did you not promise Wakantanka a scarlet blanket?"

"I promised, O great sacred white one."

"It is good. The first part of the vision has now been told you. The second part will be told you after you have given me the scarlet blanket."

"My flesh is very weak. Shall I wait to give the scarlet blanket until the Moon of Fat Horses when the others give themselves in torment in the village sun dance?"

"You must give the scarlet blanket immediately, and alone, when you return to the village. You will not be able to use the power of the vision until after you have performed the sun dance for the people to see. Also, I want the people to see this thing very soon so that they may receive courage therefrom and have the glory of it before summer comes."

"I will return immediately to my father Redbird. He will help me."

Again the white mare looked down at him strangely. "Moon Dreamer will help you. He will be your intercessor."

"When shall I be given my name? To be free one must have a name."

"It will be given you after you have returned from conquering the white stallion. Remember this, my son: life is a simple thing when once it is accepted wholly."

The white mare looked down on him in a sweet way, her red lips smiling tenderly. Then, throwing up her white head, her long glossy tail whisking bluish fire, she slowly walked away from him toward the west. Flakes of white like crystal chalk floated in the air after her passage. When she came to the edge of the rimrock she did not stop, but walked on, stepping stolidly and firmly on air. Gradually she faded away until she became a white star on the western horizon.

He was being shaken, gently. He opened his eyes. He saw Circling Hawk bending over him.

"Have you had the vision?" Circling Hawk asked.

"It has come."

"Have you received your name?"

"It will be given to me after I have returned from conquering a certain wild stallion."

"It is good. Now we will return to our mothers."

Circling Hawk took him up and carried him down from the mountain top. He gave him warm soup and some corn and cool sweet water. He placed him on a thick bed of sweetgrass and covered him with a white robe. He let him sleep in warmth for a long time. When No Name's strength returned some, they began the long journey home.

# 7

Toward evening, about an hour's ride from camp, Circling Hawk spotted lookouts on the bluffs above the Yankton village. He immediately rode up on a small knoll so that the lookouts could see him clearly against the horizon. He made his horse Dusty go through a series of quick-stepping maneuvers to signify that he and No Name were friends and that No Name had survived the fast on the mountain. At that the lookouts signaled for them to approach. The camp awaited them.

Circling Hawk rode beside No Name. "Shall we paint our horses and prepare our faces?"

"I did not receive the full vision. The second part is yet to come. The gods will not like it if we rejoice too soon."

"My brother, it shall be as you say."

The two horses sensed they were near home. They neighed, and threw up their manes and tails, and ran eagerly against tight reins. The trail ropes dragging behind raised low racing snakes of dust.

When No Name saw again the tepees of his people in the valley below, the camp still set in a neat circle like a curved row of catfish teeth, his heart leaped. He wept when he finally made out his father's dark thunder-painted lodge. He cried when he saw the single cottonwood still towering over the lodge where Leaf had once lived.

No Name led the way through the horns of the village, holding his pipe before him. The sun was just down. All the people came out to greet him. Happy black eyes flashed him welcome smiles.

A comely round-faced maiden named Pretty Walker called out, "Have you any new songs?"

No Name shook his head, slowly.

Pretty Walker smiled. "We wish to sing."

No Name smiled too, a little. "Perhaps I will have a song for you tomorrow."

Then Soft Berry came waddling through the crowd. She grabbed hold of the bridle of her son's horse. "Well, my son, and how did it go with you?"

"We have been around on a long journey, my mother, and have now come home."

"Good. The pot is full of meat. Step down. There is rest and a cake of corn for you in your accustomed place."

Still holding his red pipe before him, No Name rode straight for his father's lodge. He saw Redbird standing in the doorway, looking at him with grave impassive eyes. No Name slid to the ground, and handing his horse over to Loves Roots, went immediately inside. He sat in his own place before the fire, across from his father. His mother Star That Does Not Move took off his moccasins and rubbed the soles of his feet. She set warm food and drink before him. He ate ravenously.

Star kept to the shadows. Occasionally she flashed him a wondering searching look. Loves Roots also kept in the background on the woman's side. Her mobile lips remained properly sober.

Redbird got out the pipe as soon as No Name had finished eating. With grave dignity he filled it and lighted it with a coal from the fire. He puffed until he had it going well, then handed it across to No Name.

The taste of his father's wetness on the pipestem affected No Name deeply. He almost burst into tears.

Finally, after they finished smoking, Redbird asked, "My son, tell me, at what place have you stood and seen the good?"

"My father, I have been through an awful hour."

"It makes my heart glad to see you again."

"I have seen dark shades and white manes and strange ghosts."

"Did you fast and receive the vision, my son?"

"My father, a beautiful white mare came to me in dream. The white mare told me to catch a certain white stallion. I must go to the River That Sinks. There it will be told me where the stallion lives. The stallion will be very wild and very fierce."

Redbird started. "Ai, a wild white stallion will give us many spotted colts. It is the power of his wildness that will do this."

"The white mare said that I must go alone."

"Ai!" his father cried. The two women in the shadows gasped and clapped hand to mouth.

"My father, not all of the message was told me. The second part will be told me after I have given a scarlet blanket in a sun-watching dance. I must dance it alone. Also my Name is to be given me after I have returned from catching the wild stallion."

Redbird sat very straight. "When is this sun dance to be?"

"Tomorrow."

Redbird sat in silence a while. Then he sighed and said quietly, "Well, my son, you must go through with it. Both the torment and the journey. I will help you prepare yourself for the sun dance."

No Name looked down at his fingers. "My father, the white mare did not speak of you. Moon Dreamer is to be my intercessor."

Redbird gave No Name an odd searching look. Then his black eyes closed to glimmering slits. He sat musing to himself, looking at the low flickering fire. Shadows stirred behind him. Finally he said, "Let it be as the gods wish."

The next morning No Name went back to fasting. He washed himself harshly in the streaming red rock pools above Falling Water. He purified himself in a vapor bath. He painted his face with white clay, the outline of a mare on his right cheek and the outline of a stallion on his left cheek.

Meanwhile Moon Dreamer instructed Thunder Close By,

the crier, to announce to the camp that the son of Redbird wished to give a scarlet blanket to Wakantanka, that he would do so as a single votary, that Moon Dreamer himself had been sent a special dream on how to conduct the ceremony. The people were instructed to be kind to one another, to prepare gifts, to sing songs, to be happy and live right.

Putting on his buffalo-head mask and decorating himself with a single white feather, Moon Dreamer chose a level grassy place south of the encampment and beside the flowing red cascades. A double ring of cottonwood poles was put up about the grassy place in the shape of a round horseshoe, the open end to the east. Beams were then fastened to the tops of the poles, joining one ring with another, and willow branches were tossed up on the beams until a good green shade was made for the spectators. Moon Dreamer also set up a small leather tepee on the west side of the medicine lodge in which No Name was to wait with his pipe until the ceremony began.

For the sacred place, Moon Dreamer chose a spot in the center of the open grassy place. He removed everything that breathed or grew from a circle four steps wide. He next dug out a square to the depth of one finger. He cleansed the square with wild sage, painted a white cross in it, and sprinkled sweetgrass on a few live coals to one side of it. He set a ceremonial buffalo skull beside it.

He offered the sun dance pipe to the six powers, saying, "I smoke with Wakantanka so that he may give us a blue day." He puffed solemnly to himself with all eyes on him, finally placed the pipe against the buffalo skull. He also cleared a small square east of the sacred place, dug a round hole a yard deep in the center of it, filled the hole with freshly melted buffalo fat.

Selecting four of the young men, he sent them to the river's edge to look for a sapling cottonwood. The young rustling tree was to be as straight as a lodge pole and had to be without blemish. The young men did as instructed and scouted for the tree as though looking for an enemy. When they found a certain slender cottonwood, they counted coup on it and then rushed to tell Moon Dreamer. They were welcomed back by the people with the joy and uproar usually given a victorious war party. They were fed meat dainties, and embraced with love, and cherished with deep marks of gratitude.

Then four virgins were chosen, with Pretty Walker named as leader. The four virgins approached the tree, singing songs. Most of the people followed them. Pretty Walker was given an ax and she made a feint with it as if to strike the tree, then gave the ax to the other virgins, who in turn also made as if to strike it. Finally Pretty Walker took the ax firmly in hand and began chopping it down, cutting it so that it would fall to the south. Great was the shout of victory when the sapling began to sway, then to fall. Twenty young men, marshals especially chosen by Moon Dreamer, each wearing the customary black stripe from the outer corner of the eye to the lower edge of the jaw, leaped to catch it before it hit the ground.

The four virgins sang:

> "A young man we know.
> He wishes to please Wakantanka.
> Therefore he gives his flesh.
> A young tree we seek.
> It must be overcome.
> Therefore we have done this."

Moon Dreamer took the ax and cut off all the branches close to the trunk except the one near the top. Pregnant women scurried around him, eagerly gathering up the trimmings as good luck charms. With leather thongs Moon Dreamer tied a wooden bar to the remaining branch, so that the stripped tree resembled a cross. Moon Dreamer permitted no one to step over the sapling while he worked.

The twenty marshals, two abreast, then took up the pole on their shoulders, the crossbar first, and with Moon Dreamer and the people following, headed for the sacred place in the open center of the circular medicine lodge. No one was permitted to precede the sacred pole. Young braves on horseback raced back and forth behind the procession. Grapevines tied to their horses' tails trailed along the ground.

When the sacred pole was almost in the center of the medicine lodge, Moon Dreamer stopped the procession. He held up his hand and cried in a loud clear voice, all the while shaking his buffalo mask vigorously, "Now is the time to bring an offering or make a wish!"

Immediately the people ran to their lodges and brought out prepared gifts, of tobacco, clothes, food, bags, and presented them to one another. The noise and the joy of giving became so great men could not hear the sound of their own voices. Men and women treated each other on terms of equality, with friendly hilarity.

Suddenly through it all roared the great voice of Thunder Close By. Gradually the hubbub ceased. Old women stood trembling, the children stood solemnly still, the horses looked up alert.

"Look! Attend! Redbird our father wishes it to be known at this time that after the sun-watching dance he will give away certain of his many horses. He will give them away in equal shares. Redbird says a time for giving and rejoicing has come because of what his son is doing. Therefore he wishes to give this to his children, the Shining People. I have said. Hechetu aloh! It is so indeed."

Instantly the women raised the tremolo of joy and rushed up to Redbird and touched him and sang praises in his ear. The men shouted together and went up to him and embraced him one by one.

After suffering their love for a time, Redbird raised his copper-tipped lance. A soft morning breeze ruffled the fringes on his sleeve. The snowy filament of the feathers in his headdress fluffed gently. "My children, listen to me. A great day has come. My son is doing the sun-watching dance so that he may receive the second part of his vision and help make our people a great nation. Therefore my heart is full of joy. My friends, here beside our River of the Double Bend, where our guardian spirit the Buffalo Woman lives under Falling Water, here we shall raise our children and be as little chickens under the mother prairie hen's wing. Behold, I see a good nation walking in a sacred manner in a good land. I have said." And holding his lance before him, he took a seat under the circular brush shelter.

Still praising Redbird for his goodness in forthgiving and sharing, the people also retired under the shelter to await the great thing.

Moon Dreamer then stripped the sun dance pole of its rough ocher bark, painted it with red stripes from the cross-bar down to its base, festooned it with fresh cherry leaves. He fastened a thick foot-long stick with a red-painted knob, representing the human phallus, at the very top of the pole. He hung the effigies of a man, a buffalo, and a moon just below the crossbar. Last he fastened on a long rawhide thong which was separated into two parts at the near end.

Nodding his buffalo head, Moon Dreamer prayed in a low gutteral voice. As he did so, the young marshals began to raise the sun dance pole, catching its thick end into the fat-filled hole. The people watched in respectful silence. There was only the sound of Falling Water, low, murmurous, unending.

The moment the pole stood upright and was firmly tamped into place, the people began to shout ribald remarks at each other. They cried, "They of the other world have two faces. The Obscene God now prevails over us. We cannot help ourselves." Men and women commingled, jesting of sexual things, touching and handling each other in a lewd manner, even pretending vigorous carnal relations. "Kill the Obscene God," they cried. "He has power over us. Help us before all the virgins are taken."

Moon Dreamer pretended to be very angry. He took up a bow and shot an arrow at the red-tipped phallic symbol tied to the top of the sun dance pole. His aim was true and the wooden phallus came tumbling down. Then he took a dried buffalo penis from one of his medicine bags and quickly leaned it against the bottom of the sacred pole. At that the people immediately ceased their ribald behavior and broke into shouts of rejoicing. Some ululated. Some patted their lips with their fingers while uttering a prolonged cry in falsetto key.

They sang a song for the sun dance pole:

> "Friend, behold, sacred I stand.
> At the center of the earth.
> I look around at all of you.
> I see you are my Shining People.
> Behold, sacred I stand."

A woman named Thrush brought her little boy babe forward to have its ears pierced. Beside her stood her husband White Rain. The little one lay gurgling in her arms. It had straight, wispy black hair, reddish skin like the hair of a fresh-born buffalo calf, little fat hands wider than they were long. Its black eyes gazed blankly up at the blue sky. The babe had been very ill during the winter and both parents had made a vow that if Wakantanka would spare its life they would consecrate it to him at the next sun dance ceremony.

Moon Dreamer addressed the parents. "I see you with this child. It is good to see parents who want their child to grow up in the Yankton way. This piercing of his ears shall always be a sign that he is a true Yankton. Let him possess the four Yankton virtues: be brave, give generously, speak with a single tongue, beget many children. I have said."

Moon Dreamer then knelt at the head of the babe, placed the lobe of one ear on a block of wood, and quickly pierced it with a bone awl. He pierced the other ear in a like manner. The father White Rain then inserted copper rings in the holes. Slowly the babe's black eyes filled with amazement. Then he let go with a roar of rage. The people laughed in joy as the mother picked it up to comfort it.

Circling Hawk, following instructions from Moon Dreamer, took up a position a short distance apart from where No Name sat in his little tepee. Circling Hawk feigned discovery of No Name as an enemy. Circling Hawk's great eyes rolled and he whooped the Yankton war cry. Then he rushed upon the tepee and dragged No Name forth and wrestled with him and threw him prone on the ground. Loudly he announced, "Hi-ye! I have captured the enemy! He is ours. Now we shall torment him as the gods prescribe."

Circling Hawk sat No Name up and, still under Moon Dreamer's instructions, painted a red sun high on No Name's chest and a black crescent moon on his back, with twenty-eight stripes of white radiating away from the sun and coming together again on the black moon. "Look. Attend. Here is the man in the sun and here is the woman in the moon." He arranged No Name's hair in a loose fashion and tied a white feather to a lock in back. He hung a whistle made of the wingbone of an eagle around No Name's neck. He outfitted him with a white deerskin apron, fastening it at the waist and extending it below the knees both in front and back.

Dark buffalo head inclined, Moon Dreamer took No Name by the arm, lifted him to his feet, and led him to the sacred pole, facing him to the east. He lit the sun dance pipe with a coal from the sacred square place, held the stem to the sky, the earth, and the four great directions, took a puff himself, held the pipe out to Circling Hawk for a puff, held it to the lips of No Name for a puff, then replaced it on the buffalo skull.

"Behold!" Moon Dreamer cried. Again he approached the waiting No Name. With a bone awl he picked up a point of skin low on No Name's chest, lifting it clear of the flesh, and then, with a quick stroke, cut off the raised portion with a knife, leaving a small raw hole the size of a chokecherry. Blood instantly welled out of the raw hole and began to flow down No Name's belly.

No Name stood perfectly still, suffering it without flinching. "Have pity on me, Wakantanka," No Name said quietly. "Send me the second part of my vision so that I may go on my long journey and then receive my Name upon my return."

Star his mother began to wail in a low tremolo from the sidelines, the notes falling slowly, almost imperceptibly, until at last they could hardly be heard.

Moon Dreamer worked on, calmly, cutting a row of raw

spots from one side of the chest to the other. Presently No Name's belly was sheathed in a moving blanket of blood.

Redbird, Star, Loves Roots, Circling Hawk, Strikes Twice, Owl Above, Full Kettle, Soft Berry, Pretty Walker, the virgins, the twenty marshals, and all the people looked on in silence.

"Have pity on me."

With thumb and forefinger Moon Dreamer next took hold of the flesh above No Name's left nipple, lifted it up, and then, quickly, thrust a sharp ash skewer through it. The flesh gave way with the sound of punctured buckskin. Moon Dreamer also thrust a skewer through the flesh above the right nipple. This too No Name suffered without flinching.

Moon Dreamer grabbed hold of the two ends of the long rawhide thong hanging from the crossbar of the sun dance pole and looped an end around each thorn and fastened them with a tight knot.

Star shuddered. She raised another tremolo, slightly higher in pitch, which also at the end sank away in falling wavering accents.

Moon Dreamer said in a low voice, "My son, do not let food touch your tongue. Do not let water touch your lips. Also, do not touch your body. All will be done by those who intercede for you." Moon Dreamer picked up the eagle-bone whistle from around No Name's neck and placed it between his lips. "Blow upon this from time to time that Wakantanka may know that you are giving him of your most precious possession, your flesh and blood. The eagle is his bird and he will attend to the whistling. Keep your head back and your eyes fixed on him who is our father. It is still morning. The day is still before you. Therefore, be brave as a man would. Let the child in you die and the man in you come forth, as the horse grows out of the tender colt. Follow the blazing one around the pole. May it be given you to follow your father the sun around the circle until the skewers pull out. The circle is sacred. All this is done so that it may be forever scarred on your heart. Ep-e-lo. I have said it."

Strikes Twice sitting at the foot of the sun dance pole hit

the great drum once, deep; then followed it with a series of
very quick one-two beats; then leveled off into a very slow
methodical beat.

Crying aloud, "Have pity on me!" No Name leaned back
on the ends of the thong, hard. Flesh rose off his ribcase in
two places like the small sharp breasts of a young girl. He
fixed his eyes on a point just below the burning sun. His
skull became filled with racing red flames. At the same
time, in slow motion, he began to dance in step with the
drumming, birdlike, toe down first and then the heel.

The people under the circular shade watched in silence,
their black eyes full of reverent wonder, their lips set in the
ancient grimace of sympathy.

Moon Dreamer gathered up on the point of his knife all
the tiny bead-size bits of flesh he had cut from No Name's
chest. Carrying them carefully, walking with a rolling
gaited step, he took a seat on a log a few steps west of the
pole. He turned to the watching Yanktons, and holding
aloft the bits of flesh, cried out, "Look upon your son! Behold the flesh he has given! Behold the scarlet blanket he
has promised. Your son has kept his promise. Soon now the
second part of his vision will be given him and we shall
know what future Wakantanka has in store for him."

No Name concentrated his attention on the dancing
manes of fire in his skull. From time to time he blew on the
wingbone whistle, low, persistent. "I am happy," he whistled. "Soon I shall know."

Moon Dreamer every now and then gave instructions to
the people. "We do this for the young boys so that they can
learn to become men. We do this for the old men so that,
remembering the time when they once were strong and
could endure the torment, they may be restored in spirit."

No Name danced on. He kept his eyes fixed on a spot
just below the sun. Lashing plumes of fire continued to
flower in his brain. "Soon I shall know."

Moon Dreamer then spoke to No Name. "My son, look
upon the noble world. Do you see it? Draw the great power
of it into your breast and be joyful. Be one with Wakantanka. He loves his Shining People and wants them to be

great. We are here in this place, on the red rock beside Falling Water on our River of the Double Bend. The red rock is our all-father. The red rock is the ancestor of all things. We are a part of the earth's body beside the river and this earth is part of our body. We are the breath of the earth. We breathe for her. We are also the breath of Wakantanka. We breathe for him. Remember this and be good. Follow the right path of living."

The people waited patiently. The sun ovaled up the sky. The red rocks beside the river warmed. The small leaves of the willows quivered a fuzzy yellow in the bright light. Falling Water poured glancing golden lights. The horses across the river grazed in peace.

Moon Dreamer stood up. He handed a specially decorated lance and a water dipper to Circling Hawk. He took up a feather-frilled crook for himself. Then, gesturing, he led a slow majestic walk completely around No Name. He held up the crook to the sun and cried, "Let the power flow inward! The people of the other world are greater than you!" Again he made a complete circle around No Name, with Circling Hawk following. "The power of your shadow soul is greater than the power of your flesh soul. Live inward. Grow inward. Be strong. Pass into that place where there is nothing but joy which makes life good."

No Name danced in step with the slow booming pound of the ceremonial drum. The searing little cuts across his chest as well as the terrible pulling gradually became sweet pains.

Moon Dreamer relit the pipe and held its stem out to the six great powers, saying, "Circling I pass to you who dwell with the father." He took a puff himself, allowed No Name to puff. Moon Dreamer said, "The gods walk on the road of man. The road of man is sacred. Be strong. Do not be afraid. Arrive at the place where they are waiting for you. Soon you will know. Endure the sacrifice of flesh. Become a brave man."

Pretty Walker approached. A look of grave compassion was on her young round face. With wisps of sweetgrass she gently wiped off the blood flowing from the wounds made by the thorns. She was careful not to touch any part of the blanket of blood below.

Star sang a song in a low voice to encourage her son:

> "Friends, look upon our son.
> He suffers and we rejoice.
> He says this:
> 'Wakatanka, pity me.
> Henceforth for a long time will I live.'
> He says this."

Moon Dreamer returned to his seat on the log. Shaking his dark buffalo head up and down, he said, "Obey the power. Let it flow two ways. Alone you are weak. Soon you will see with the eye of the heart."

The blanket of blood on No Name's belly and chest gradually congealed. Slowly it turned black. He moved as if encased in hardened mud.

"Wakantanka, pity me," he whistled through the wing-bone, "henceforth for a long time I will live."

Moon Dreamer said, "Wakantanka does not hate. He loves all his creatures, the twoleggeds and the fourleggeds of the earth, the wingeds of the air, and all green things that live."

The sun passed by overhead. No Name followed it around, dancing a circular rut in the red dust.

Even the red babies snug in their cradles on their mother's backs looked with big, solemn bluish eyes at the dancing man. Their little round black heads lolled with every move and shift of their mothers, their eyes always returning to the figure hanging from the rawhide thongs.

During the hot afternoon Circling Hawk and four male singers, with Strikes Twice at the drum, sang four songs for him. The first was sung in slow measure, low, plaintive, the drum and the rattle sounding gently:

> "Behold, hear me crying.
> I cannot escape the thorn.
> I am bound forever
> To the pole of torment.
> Hear me crying."

The second was given in a slightly faster tempo, with bolder tones:

> "Look, friend,
> I dare to look upon
> The face of the sun
> As I make this request:
> 'Grant me the full vision.'
> I dare to look."

The third was rendered in a tight rhythmic unit of sound:

> "The sun is my father.
> On my breast
> I wear his mark.
> The moon is my mother.
> On my back
> I wear her sign.
> They are my friends."

The fourth was sung in loud and joyous tones, the drum and rattle sounding vigorously:

> "Well, a white horse is now here,
> Very wild and fierce.
> I have caught it.
> See, a white horse now is here.
> It wishes to kill me.
> Behold, I have conquered it.
> Wana hiyelo."

Suddenly No Name let the whistle fall from his lips. He cried out, "I see it! I see it! The sky is terrible with a storm of plunging horses. They shake the world with their neighing. Only the Thunders dare to echo back."

At that very moment the horses grazing across the river lifted their heads and whinnied sharply. The sound of it over the low pouring waters was as clear and as pure as the silvery call of meadowlarks.

"He is winning, he is valiant!" the people cried.

"U-hu-hu-hu!" the warriors grunted with intense satisfaction.

"U-wu-wu-wu!" the maidens intoned.

No Name strained against the thorns, leaning back with all his might. He set his feet in the rut in the dust to get better leverage. He hung so heavy that at last the flesh on his chest gave a little, ripping apart in narrow seams. Fresh blood began to flow.

Pretty Walker came up singing a low song of comfort, intending to wipe away the new blood with some sweetgrass.

Moon Dreamer waved her back, imperiously. He shook his dark buffalo head threateningly. "Do not touch him. It is coming." He pointed at the lowering sun in the western sky. "Soon our shining friend will rest with his people in the region under the world. There he will commune with The Great Master Of All Breath. Beware!"

At the mention of the unspeakable name, Pretty Walker shrank away as if struck a blow. The people around the circle fell into a deep stricken silence. Hands covered mouths in shock. To mention Him Who Is Behind All by his big Name was to touch the secret and sacred eternal fire itself.

No Name leaned back in a frenzy. He jerked his body from side to side, violently. He fought against the thong like a wildcat resisting capture. The two-pronged pain in his chest reached all the way up to his skull. A pair of working claws seemed to be mauling his brain.

Struggling, dancing, he kept his eyes on the sun. The world became a place of racing shimmers. Suddenly his eyes seemed to shoot upward into a single terrible blinding whiteness, a massive illumination into which blood and flesh and phallus and memory and love and day and red rock vanished. The eye became the sun and the sun the eye.

Moon Dreamer cried loudly. "Be brave, my son! Endure the torment! Give generously! Speak with one tongue!"

No Name felt a great inrush of power. He leaped up wildly. Then with a great cry he gave one final wrenching backward jerk, and at last the thorns tore out of his flesh, first on the right and then on the left. And losing his balance, staggering, he fell to the ground with a hard thud. The forces of the wild, the dark urges of the universe, had heard his cry and had taken dominion over him.

Circling Hawk and his four singers leaped to their feet and gave the sudden whoop of victory. A shout, a tumultuous roar, broke from the circle of watchers. Redbird's cry was loudest of all.

No Name lay unconscious. The bleeding slits on his chest lay open and swollen as if they had just given birth to puppies. Sweat coursing down his chest caused the painted red sun to run. But the painted mare on his right cheek and the painted stallion on his left cheek remained as vividly white as when first put on. As his face convulsed, the two painted horses struggled to be released so that they might strike each other.

The people crowded in close on all sides, looking down at the prostrate form. Moon Dreamer waved the people back. Slowly, wonderingly, they retreated to their places again under the ring of shade.

Moon Dreamer whispered something in Circling Hawk's ear.

Circling Hawk nodded, big eyes whirling up and around. Then he ran to get a heartskin bucket and filled it with water from the streaming red cascades.

Moon Dreamer took the water and splashed some of it over No Name's face. After a few seconds, when No Name still showed no sign of reviving, Moon Dreamer threw some more over him.

No Name's eyes slowly opened. A grayish purple haze lay over them. The pupils were almost obscured.

"I see you have returned, my son," Moon Dreamer said gravely.

No Name's eyes rolled; finally fastened on Moon Dreamer's buffalo head. He seemed to recognize him.

"I see you have returned, my son," Moon Dreamer repeated.

At last No Name's eyes cleared some and he asked,

"Where is Redbird my father?" No Name's voice was greatly changed.

"He sits in his accustomed place. Why does my son ask?"

"I have been told the second part of the vision. Now I know."

"Ei!" Moon Dreamer cried. His eyes began to glitter in the eyeholes of his dark buffalo head. "And what did they of the other world have to tell you?"

"The gods were reluctant to give me my vision for a reason." No Name rolled his head from side to side. "Now I know."

Moon Dreamer held No Name in his arms, lovingly. He gave him to drink from what was left in the heartskin bucket. "What did they have to tell you, my son?"

No Name's eyes fixed themselves on Moon Dreamer's eyeholes. "Where is my true father?"

"Hi-ye. Did they speak of the fathers?"

For a third time No Name asked, rolling his head from one side to the other, "And my father, where is he? Does he live?"

Moon Dreamer stiffened. He waved Circling Hawk back with the others under the willow shade. Then he removed his buffalo head and placed his ear near No Name's mouth. "Speak, my son. I am your mother's brother and I attend you. We lie alone. What did you see? What did you hear?"

No Name's eyes closed. He whispered, "It was the mare with the silver tail again. She was as white as a snowgoose in the morning sun. Her lips were red. She flashed her sacred tail over me."

"What did she tell you?"

For a fourth time No Name asked, "Where is Redbird my father?"

With a puckering of lips Moon Dreamer pointed in Redbird's direction.

No Name looked at his father a moment, piercingly; looked at the copper-tipped lance shining above him; then looked up at the blue sky overhead. "It is fated," he said sadly.

"Tell us the second part of the vision," Moon Dreamer demanded. "What did the white mare have to tell you?"

"She flashed her tail over me. She said, 'After you have returned with your white horse from the River That Sinks, your true father must die.' " No Name burned a look of anguish into Moon Dreamer's eyes. Black centers had returned to his eyes. "I love my father dearly. I cannot kill him."

Moon Dreamer began to cry. His old face broke up into jerking wrinkles. Tears ran down his face. He hid his face from the watchers. The dark shadow of the late afternoon sun reached across to the sacred place east of the sun dance pole.

"What shall I do?" No Name whispered.

"Nephew, the white mare knows best. Follow her words."

"But I love my father dearly. I do not wish to kill him."

Moon Dreamer groaned. "Follow her words."

"Also, what shall I tell my father? He will wish to know what I have heard today. See, he sits waiting to hear. I do not wish to tell him that he must die at my hand."

With an effort Moon Dreamer recovered his poise. "Nephew, you must go through with it. Terrible punishment awaits those who do not fulfill the vision. The Thunders seek them out and mark them for death. You must go through with it."

No Name sat up. "But I love my father dearly. I love him even more than I love my mother."

"Nephew, follow your helper. Do as she tells you. First go out and conquer the wild horse. Then, when you return in glory, your Name will be given to you and it shall be told you what you must do about the second part."

"But shall I tell my father all this?"

Moon Dreamer considered. At last he said, "Let us wait until you return before we tell your father. It will then be given you what you must do."

"And what shall we tell the people? They also sit waiting to hear."

"My son, if your father who is our chief must wait, the people must wait."

No Name looked around at the people sitting in the shadows under the willow shade. Again his eyes sought out his father and his copper-tipped lance. He forced back tears. After a short struggle his face became impassive. "I must do as the white mare commands. It is fated. There is nothing I can do. I must try to be a brave man and take things as they come. I cannot weep."

The virgin Pretty Walker approached shyly, hesitantly. "Did your helper give you a new song? We wish to sing it."

No Name remembered her request. He smiled at her, slow, grave. With Moon Dreamer and Circling Hawk helping him, he got to his feet. As Strikes Twice struck up the drum, gently, he sang in a low hoarse voice:

> "Friend,
> I come from conquering a horse.
> My horse flies like a bird when it runs.
> It is wild and very fierce.
> It likes to bite.
> Friend, I come. Be careful."

When he sang it a second time, Circling Hawk and his four singers joined in. Over them all, like a skylark drifting gently down, quavered Pretty Walker's virginal voice.

Then Moon Dreamer faced the people. He lifted his hand and proclaimed to all. "Haho! let the people know this. No Name, our son, was valiant and dared to face the sun all day. He conquered the sky-horse before it could sink behind the earth in the west. He was valiant and he conquered. Also, the second part of the vision was given him. It will be told to all the people when he returns from conquering the great white stallion. I have said. Yelo."

The people shouted tumultuously. The men sang wildly. The women's speech became as the happy warblings of birds.

# PART
## THREE

# The Chase

# 1

It was the fourth morning after the sun dance. No Name was ready to leave. He had bathed in the streaming cascades. He had eaten a hearty breakfast of meat boiled with dried plums. He had bound up his braids under a tight wolf cap.

He stood alone with his mother inside their tepee. He watched her look him over to make sure he had everything: leather shirt and leggings, moccasins, bow and arrow and knife, several pairs of extra moccasins tucked under the belt, long rawhide lariat also caught under the belt, light pack over the shoulder stuffed with dried meat, pemmican, pipe and tobacco, awl and sinew thread.

She gave his sleeve a tug. "Son, the sun shines. It looks well for you."

"I have seen, my mother."

She gave his sleeve another tug. "Son, the thing you seek lives in a far place. It is good. Go to it. Do not turn around after you have gone part way, but go as far as you were going and then come back." Her old waxy eyes looked at him in love. "If you are to be killed, be killed in open air so that the wingeds can eat your flesh and the wind can breathe on you and blow over your bones. Also, be killed on a high hill. Your father believes it is not manly to be killed in a hollow."

No Name waited. The long black lashes over his eyes held still.

"Son, keep this thought in your heart. The man who loafs in his lodge will never be great. No. It is the man who is tired from taking the trail who becomes great, the one who sweats, who works."

"I listen, my mother."

"Do not be afraid of the Pawnee. Some day you will be the head chief of the Shining People."

"I will remember."

Again she tugged at his sleeve. "My son, have you told your father the second part of the vision?"

No Name stirred. "I cannot. Also, our uncle Moon Dreamer says to wait until I return."

"It is good. We do not wish to know it. Yet speak to your father of something before you go."

"He waits at the red ford to walk with me for a short way."

"It is good." She reached up and with both hands stroked him, from his shoulder down to his wrist. "Go, my son. Be valiant. Earn your name."

"I hear you, my mother."

He ducked out through the door.

From behind the drying racks stepped Loves Roots. She was crying. Her oily hair hung unbraided and tangled. She clutched at his arm. "Do not go, Little Bird. I am afraid. The Pawnees will kill you. They will torment you at the stake with burning arrows."

He suffered her touch. He looked more beyond her than away from her.

She hung onto his arm. "Remember the fate of Holy Horse. He followed a white ghost horse into a deep cave. There the middle-of-the-earth demons overcame him and he was never seen again."

"I did not dream of a cave.

"Remember also the fate of Wants To Be A Woman. He also was never seen again."

No Name remembered. Wants To Be A Woman had dreamed that a white ghost had come to sit at his side while he lay asleep in bed. Wants To Be A Woman got up and tried to run outdoors, away from it, but the ghost followed him and jumped on his back. Wants To Be A Woman did not feel weight but he knew the white ghost was there anyway. He ran for the river and jumped in, yet the ghost stayed with him. Then he ran to his friend and begged him to destroy the white ghost. His friend saw nothing. He began to laugh at him. "The heat makes your head spin, friend. There is no white ghost." Wants To Be A Woman ran out into the night again, wild with fear. At last he climbed a cliff and got set to jump. At that moment the white ghost spoke to him. It said, "Do not jump, friend. I am not a harmful ghost." But Wants To Be A Woman was very afraid and he jumped off the cliff anyway.

No Name said in young sullen dignity, "What has this to do with me?"

"Did you not dream of a white thing?"

She tried to stroke his arm from the shoulder to the elbow as his mother Star had done, but he pushed her brusquely aside.

"You will not listen?"

"I must go. A certain horse calls from a far place."

She handed him a pair of moccasins. They were packed tight with food.

"What is this?"

"Dried skunk meat. Eat it when you have hunger. It will make you strong because the skunk eats many good roots."

"It is good." He looked down at her bowed head. He looked at the stripe of bright red paint in the parting of her hair. He recalled the night he was tempted to use her. Then he said, "Be kind to my father."

He walked out through the horns of the camp. It was a fresh spring day, the Moon of First Eggs. The sun glowed big and yellow across the river. Mist rose golden off Falling Water.

Next to bid him good-bye were the young braves lounging naked on the red rocks after their morning bath. Among them was a wild youth whom the maidens had nicknamed Bull All The Time. Bull and his rowdy friends had been successful in a horse-stealing raid and since then he had gone around preening himself like a fox with a dead gopher in its jaws. Bull laughed at No Name. "Ho! I see that an old mare in a dream has you chasing a white ghost horse."

Before No Name could retort, a heavy raw voice let go from a large red rock on the other side of the path. "Look who mocks. Is it not the one who only yesterday was begging his mother for more ma-ma?"

It was Circling Hawk speaking and he was referring to something the entire village used to wonder about. Even at eight, Bull had sometimes run after his mother and beseeched her to give him suck.

Bull swelled with sudden hate. His black eyes slowly reddened over.

No Name laughed with the others. Then, with a smile at Circling Hawk, he moved on toward the red ford. "Some day," No Name said to himself, "after I have become a father to my people, I shall make Circling Hawk a chief second only to me."

Another to bid him good-bye was Pretty Walker. The slender virgin stood under a stunted ash. Her easy gestures and the manner in which she held her head to one side reminded him of a shy puppy. She called out, "Have a new song when you return. I will sing it."

He smiled at her. "And I will dance it."

"I did not speak in jest."

"And I did not answer in jest."

"I will wait."

"And I will come."

He took the red stepping stones across the river with easy grace, leaping lightly, sure-footed. Water whorled green at his feet.

He found his father sitting on his heels on the sunny side of a huge boulder some distance out on the prairie. The color of his father's skin was almost exactly the color of the boulder. No Name blinked his eyes at the wonder of it. He saw now how true it was that the Shining People had been formed out of the red bones of the earth.

His father saw him and his face lighted up. He smiled in gentle dignity. "It is a good day to leave on a horse-raiding party, my son. The gods favor you at last."

"It is my helper who does this."

"Have you given your mother a last word?"

No Name smiled. "She spoke of a hill on which I might place my bones so the birds would find them and pick them clean."

Redbird's smile deepened. "Ae. Do not die in a hollow where no one will find you. Also bones will rot in the wet."

No Name looked at his father and again was full of admiration at the manner in which he carried his sixty-one winters. Soon even Loves Roots would appear to have caught up with him in age. No Name said, "I am ready, my father."

For a brief moment a shadow lurked in Redbird's eyes. Then it was gone.

No Name remembered his mother's instruction to speak to his father about something before he left. "My father, what is the way? Can you tell me?"

Redbird took up a stick and leveled a patch of red earth between his knees. He drew some lines on the level patch, a big flowing S for the River of the Double Bend, with a tail which went down until it joined another line, heavier and deeper. The heavy line was the Great Smoky Water. It came out of the northwest, and after joining the River of the Double Bend, went straight south to another line wriggling in from the west.

Redbird pointed at the last line. "Here is the River That Sinks. The Pawnees live four sleeps west of where it joins the Great Smoky Water. In this place."

"Have you seen this river?"

"A long time ago, my son, when a few of us went on a horse-raiding party. The river is very thin and very wide. It flows in some places as after a rain on flat ground. In other places it flows not at all. It is all sand."

"Did you catch many horses?"

"The Pawnees had none to steal that spring. But we saw the tracks of many wild ones."

"It is good." No Name stared intently at the map in the dust. "I see it all. I will remember."

Redbird pointed at a spot on the west side of the Great Smoky Water, below the mouth of the River of the Double Bend. "Here live the Omaha, they who went against the current. The Omaha have come to hate us. They have stories which tell them they were once the keepers of the Place of the Pipestone. Their stories tell them that we defeated them in a great battle and chased them away."

No Name started. He had never heard of this. "Is it true, my father?"

Redbird smiled. "Our old ones did not speak of it. I do not know." He shifted his weight, still squatting on his heels. "Another of their stories tells them it was one of their maidens who found the quarry. Their stories say that she was living with us as the wife of one of our braves. It is said she was digging for prairie turnips when she struck upon the pipe stone."

"Is this true?"

"I do not know. Our old ones did not speak of her either." Redbird mused in reverie. "We have always known it as a place of brothers, where the warclub was put aside and the red pipe smoked in peace. We have never seen it as a place where a battle was fought or where women were captured."

No Name stood back on one leg, considering. He suddenly saw his father very clearly as one of those who could tell much about old things. His father's memory was like a bullhide covered with the pictographs of a long winter count.

"You have your charm, my son?"

"Moon Dreamer gave me a thing to wear. It will be my mystery power until I catch the wild horse. After that there will be another." No Name wondered why his father had not noticed the fetish on him. Late the night before, over a pipe, as the white mare had told them to do, Moon Dreamer had given No Name a piece of horse chestnut to wear in the fat braid behind his left ear. He was to wear this until he returned with the scarlet plume. The grayish black piece of gristle had a powerful odor. No Name decided that his father's sense of smell was failing a little. No Name added, "Also I feel the power of the sun dance in me." No Name touched his shirt where the wounds still stung him when he moved too quickly.

Redbird sighed. His son still had not told him the second part of the vision. Then he stood up and he raised his hands and stroked his son from the shoulder to the wrist four times. "Go, my son. Do not return until you have caught the wild seed stallion."

"I am going." No Name broke away from his father and began to walk south.

The morning continued fair and the vast and blooming prairie was a land of dreams. The grass looked so sweet to him in the broad forenoon sunshine, so fresh, so crisply green, he envied the horses their grazing. He stalked through deep grass. A dew had fallen in the night and soon his moccasins were sopping wet. The sound of wet leather brushing through wet grass was like the vigorous flourishing of horsetails.

The land sloped gently down, leveled off to a bottom through which flowed a slow grass-tressed creek, then sloped gently up toward a wide level rise. From the bottom the country resembled the inside of a cupped hand; from the rise it resembled a rising shoulder. The growth differed too. Ripgut grass grew in the lowlands. If a walker was not careful his moccasins and leggings were soon cut to shreds. Soft green buffalo grasses grew on the upland. The soft carpet made for easy going.

He found a patch of wild honeysuckles growing on a south slope. They belled softly in a gentle breeze, orange petals glowing in sharp contrast to the pale grass. He settled on his heels and picked one and did as he had once done as a boy. He sucked a single drop of clear honey from its throat.

He threaded his way across a meadow of creamy beard-tongue growing as high as his hips. Without having to bend he could peer into individual flowers to see if the wild bees had beaten him to the nectar. The air was so sweet with the smell of the flowers that his eyes watered and his nose became stuffy. He put it down in his memory as a place where he would some day take the new spotted colts.

Birds lifted ahead of him as he went along: settled again

behind him. Bluebirds momentarily deepened the glowing blue of the sky. Tufted redbirds shooting from one wolf-berry bush to another reminded him of bloodied arrows. Redwings chirred at him from the wet lowlands: "Friend! we alone know joy."

He knew when it was almost noon by the way the yellow primroses began to close up. His mother Star had once told him the reason. Their silky blossoms were open all night because they wanted to please the spirits of the dead who lived on the stars. "They of the other world are pleased to see flowers too," she said. "Therefore the primroses bloom best when it is darkest at night." When he protested that he had often seen them open in the morning, she said, "They also bloom in the forenoon for a little while to let us see what we will have to look at when it is our turn to pass on."

When the sun was directly overhead he paused beside a small stream. It was but a step wide and it was clear and trickled musically over round red pebbles. He kneeled beside it and with his palm lapped up a long cool drink. He watched minnows no longer than his little finger come gupping up to lip his hands in play. Their gray bead eyes glowed up at him. As a boy he had once eaten a minnow and found it mushy sweet.

He took off his light pack and made a pillow of it in the deep grass. He lay down, belly up like a lazy puppy resting on the sunny side of a tepee. He watched the birds fly by. He lay so quietly he soon heard mice creeping stealthily through the little shadows in the grass. As long as the birds flew by and the mice moved near him he was safe from ambush.

He got out the dried skunk meat Loves Roots had prepared for him. He was so hungry he emptied both moccasins, even turning them inside out to lick them clean. The skunk meat was excellent. It lay filling and warm in his stomach. It made him think of himself as a sacred snake that had just swallowed a fat gopher. He knew Loves Roots had given him the meat and the moccasins because she hoped he would wive her some day. He remembered the night she crept in with him under his sleeping robe, how she touched him until, become so trembling rigid he thought he would break, he had at last pushed her away.

Thought of Loves Roots reminded him of the Yankton maiden who had performed a feat so great in the old time that men still talked of it, partly in awe and partly in laughter. The maiden's father and mother had been killed in a raid by the Chippewa when she was but a child and so she had been adopted by a chief who had no children. Even as a young girl she had been a daring one, playing boy games with the boldest and roughest of the lads. One fall, after she had grown into a beautiful young woman, to make sure she would get the most manly of all the braves for a husband, she invited forty of the most valiant to a feast. She gave them as much buffalo meat boiled with wild plums as they could hold, then, afterwards, gave each a private treat behind a leather curtain. The young men were all eager to comply. Later, astounded by her generous gift of hospitality, since virginity was highly prized among the Yanktons, all of them courted her eagerly. They thought she was surely of the gods to have given herself to so many men at one time. Otherwise it could not be explained. She finally chose one of the tallest braves and married him. It was told of her subsequently that she had great power over her husband and helped him in the wise rule of the tribe. It also was told of her that she remained his faithful and loving wife until death.

Two goldfinches swirled up. They hovered over and around a columbine bobbing nearby, then together settled on one of its slender purplish stems. They were male and female, the one sun-bright yellow with a black cap and black wings and the other a dull green-yellow with brown wings. The columbine bent under their combined weight and began to undulate gently. The male goldfinch looked at all the red flowers, then cocked a jolly black eye at his mate. "See-see-e!" he sang. "Tic-o-ree, o-ree, ree!" The female took him at his word. She lifted up one of the upside-down red flowers and poked her short beak into it. She found nectar deep within the slender spur. Tipping back her head she beaked it up. The male leaped to the next branch of the flower, again had a look around. "See-see-e!" Once more she took him at his word and had a sip of flower honey. At that, the sun-bright male seemed to tumble over himself for joy and with a blurr of wings mounted the air above her and filled the sky with ecstatic song. "Ter-chic-o-ree!" Chic-o-ree!" She listened a moment, then, taken in, fluttered up beside him and joined him in wild abandon. They hovered above the red flowers for a while like light-hearted butterflies, singing madly, then, in a blurr of sun-bright yellow, winged off.

Watching it all, black eyes so intent they smarted, No Name whispered to himself, "It is a sign. That will be my life with a good wife. Perhaps Pretty Walker."

He sat up. The sun had moved past the middle point overhead. With a guilty start he jumped to his feet and flung his bow and light pack over his shoulder and broke into a swift dog-trot, still heading south. "I have loafed as my mother warned." He ran lightly up the next slow incline. He had almost gained the next rise, when he suddenly began to puff and sweat broke out all over on him. Too late he remembered his father's counsel never to drink more than four palms of water at any one time when out on the trail, especially if he wanted to cover a long distance quickly. Drinking too much water could founder a man as much as it would a horse.

Breath caught, he started in again, jogging steadily. The country gradually leveled off into long flat stretches. It was all upland, the grass was short, in some places dry and crackly. He came across occasional patches of prickly pear cactus. He ran two miles; walked a half mile; ran two miles. He tried to do the running on slowly falling land, the walking on gradually rising land.

Sweat broke out on him again, though this time his breath held. He slipped off his buckskin shirt. His chest gleamed a warm brown. The sweat made the sun dance scabs turn a light purple and softened them so that they lifted a little around the edges.

He delighted in the powers of his body. The longer he ran, then walked, then ran again, the more he saw that he too, like his old father, had a runner's endurance. He would make a fine warrior. Like his father he would travel on foot to the place where the enemy lived, make the raid, and then return riding the enemy's horses.

The sun was almost down, and he had come upon the last rise in the land overlooking the River of the Double Bend, when he spotted brown-black beings moving in the valley below on the other side of the river. Instantly he dropped on his belly in the grass. His heart began to pound and for a moment his vision blurred over.

Inadvertently he had flopped down on the edge of a large ant hill. In a few moments they were swarming all over him, red ones with eager stingers. "Ai!" he cried low to himself, and rolled away from the ants, then brushed them off.

When he looked below again, the black-brown beings had vanished. Pawnees on horseback? Omaha? Had they ducked out of sight when they saw him rolling in the grass?

Then he saw them again, emerging from a fringe of trees on this side of the river, their hides dripping and shiny with water. They were buffalo, some two hundred of them, all males. They were heading into the wind, coming almost straight for him in a long grave procession.

A thought struck him. The buffalo, if they kept heading into the wind, would eventually wind up near the Yankton village. He knew from old woman talk the camp was low in meat. And while bull was tough and not as tasty as cow, it still was meat and would carry them until the hunters found a herd of cows and calves. He looked around, to the right, to the left, for a place to hide himself and his sweat smell. He spotted a small washout in the brow of the rise some dozen steps away. Quickly he crawled on hands and knees through the grass, around another ant hill, across a bare patch of rough gnarly gravel, and dropped out of sight. The washout was about twice the length of his body and a good arm's length deep. He pulled down some of the overhanging grass along both lips to cover himself. And waited.

Presently he heard their measured tread coming up the slope. Grunting shortly, bowels whumpfing strangely on each step, shaggy undersides dripping water, the old bulls trudged past him on both sides. They swung along in stupid dignity. Tongues lolled along the edges of slobbery lips. Little eyeballs glared out at a grassy rolling world through a tangle of long black hair. Short tails switched futilely at clouds of flies. Now and then one of the flies shot up a black nostril, only to be blown out again by a humpfing snort.

At last they were by. As always, behind them ran ghost-gray predators, wolves, jagged mouths laughing, eyes alert to cut off a laggard.

He waited until he could no longer hear their tread through the ground, then sat up, head showing over the lip of the washout. The sun was just setting. Only the tips of the bluffs across the river still glowed in yellow light. Below the valley had already begun to blue over with coming darkness.

After a little thought, he decided to make the washout his camp for the night. The bottom was soft brown earth. It was deep enough to hide him from prowlers. It was also a good lookout.

With a rod fire-drill and a piece of spunk for tinder, he lighted his pipe and had himself a leisurely smoke. He ate a portion of dried meat and some pemmican. He crept down the hill and had a drink in the river.

As he let down his braids, he had a talk with his fetish. "Friend," he said, holding the piece of horse chestnut in his cupped hand, "I have traveled far this day. You have brought me here." Eyes sparkling, he gave it his most winning smile. "My helper, tomorrow I must travel even farther. Will I have a good day? Tell me." He tossed it up, thinking that if the freshly cut end landed right side up it would be a good day, and if the natural end landed right side up it would be a bad day. He caught it and opened his hand. The freshly cut side was up. "Hi-yu-po! it will be a good day. I will travel very far."

He worked his shoulder into the soft brown earth until he felt comfortable. Then, as he was about to drift off into sleep, he whispered, "I want to strike an enemy. If he is to wound me, let the wound be but a slight one. Also I wish to capture a horse."

# 2

Late the next day, running, walking, he approached the flowing together of the River of the Double Bend and the Great Smoky Water. Remembering from his father's dust map that the Omaha lived opposite the mouth of the River of the Double Bend, he decided to cross it and go down the east side of the Great Smoky Water until well past them. He inspected the horizons to all sides for sign, then advanced down a deep wash toward the river. Slough grass grew head-high, its blades sometimes a good two fingers wide, with edges that cut like duck teeth. The damp bottom of the wash gradually became an oily trickle.

The River of the Double Bend flowed silently and green under tall rustling cottonwoods. Its banks were headlong, steep, of black earth with pale gravel showing at the water's edge. He took off his moccasins, leggings, clout, shirt, and holding them in a bundle over his head, stepped naked into the river. The bottom shelved down slowly. Some twenty feet in, gravel gave way to sticky mud.

He remembered his father's counsel about wading in mud bottoms. "Always slide your feet along," Redbird had said, "or a channel catfish will poke out its spines and stick you. Catfish like to live in the mud because that is where the dead bugs drift. The wounds the catfish make are very bad. Sometimes they are poisonous. I have known men to die from them."

He slid his feet along one at a time, big toes down and wary. The river kept deepening. Mud oozed between his toes, whelmed heavily up around his ankles.

He was exactly halfway across, up to his neck in the slid-

ing green water, when his big toe hit something. He knew it
wasn't a log, because it first gave way and then pushed
back, like someone who resented being nudged in sleep.
Catfish. He stood stock still.

He licked his lips. Catfish were good eating. "Ae," he
thought, "there is hardly enough dried meat left for tomorrow. Why not eat the fish?"

Holding his leathers and bow out of the water, taking a
deep breath, he slowly sank under. He groped down with
his free hand, easy. Water flowed between his fingers. At
last he touched the catfish with a forefinger. He could make
out the edge of one of its bony plates. He inched his finger
along, next felt the edge of a fin. At that the sluggish catfish
slowly awakened and slowly a spine in the fin came erect.

A rush of blood exploded in No Name. Suddenly he was
a lurking predator in shadowy waters. His forefinger took
on eyes. He struck. And had it, forefinger deep in the vul-
valike gill. With a powerful lifting lunge, he hauled it up to
the surface. He came up gasping.

The catfish lashed once, twice, like a huge bough snapping in a hard wind. It began to gasp for water. Its long,
gray cat-like feelers bristled in animal rage. Again it shook
itself, mightily, almost unhooking itself from his finger.

He whirled around and around in the water, staying
ahead of its lashing movements. The weight and the power
of the catfish, the resistance of the water almost threw him.
He kept bearing for the opposite shore. The struggle stirred
up mud from the bottom. Gradually boiling brown whirlpools began to stain the softly flowing green current.

When he reached shallow water, he saw what a whopper
he had caught. It was larger even than a grown man's leg,
with a head as wide as his mother's wooden bowl. Grunting, lunging, he heaved it out of the water onto the bank
above. He climbed up after it, threw his bundle aside, and
got a club. Two well-aimed blows on the flat head, hollow,
sodden, and the huge fish lay quivering still.

He leaned on his club, puffing, naked brown body glistening. Never in all his life had he seen a fish like it. His father would have been very proud to see him land such a

monster alone. There was enough meat in it to feed a war party.

He found a tall cottonwood, built a fire of dry sticks under it. He kept the fire small and low. Smoke from it dispersed up through the leaves and vanished before reaching the top.

The catfish, broiled, and eaten with a few stalks of wild onion and some crystals of alkali, was delicious. Eyes watering over, he downed one sweet flake of boneless flesh after another. He sucked and gorged. He wished his rough friend Circling Hawk had come with him. "Ae, it is good, good," he murmured, mouth full. "Not as good as buffalo hump, but good, very good." After eating all he could hold, he jerked a small portion of what was left and hung it over the fire. Smoke would preserve the piece for breakfast.

After a cautious look around to make sure no one had spotted his little fire, he lay down on the grass, brown-naked, tender-skin phallus touching his thigh to one side.

Buffalo had recently passed through the glade and had cropped off the grass, short, and all the leaves of the trees to shoulder height. He could see north and south, either way, to where the river meandered out of sight. East behind him towered wind-honed bluffs, a deep vivid green in the dusk. A soft wind moved down from the north, stirring under the leaves, rippling the silently sliding warm green waters. Occasional pike jumped, sometimes rising out of the waters like rearing colt heads, then fell back with a flat splash, ever widening circles moving across the surface afterwards.

The great meal made him feel sluggish. Half asleep, he watched night swoop down, a vast purple fog. The shadows in the talking cottonwood settled down to where he lay.

Lying on his back, dreaming of home and mother, thinking of bravery and father, he was startled to see a ball of fire come bulging over the near bluff. It took him a moment to realize it was the moon.

He sat up slowly. "Aii," he cried, looking closely at the moon. "Old mother, you are swollen to twice your size with weeping. I see now that my mother is very sorrowful this night. She cries because her son has gone down the bitter path."

He sat awhile, gazing up at the moon. Slowly its hue changed from honeysuckle to sage. Slowly also the valley filled with soft muted light. The cottonwood was given silver leaves. The eddies in the gliding waters winked circles of gold.

He looked down at his fetish. "Will I have a good day tomorrow? Where is the enemy? Is he near? Will I find the path? Tell me."

He tossed it up and caught it. The piece of gray gristle fell with its freshly cut side up. "A good sign."

He put out the fire. He wrapped the smoked fish in green leaves to keep it cool. He put on his buckskins. He found himself a patch of grass under a gooseberry bush, and lying on his full belly, fell sound asleep.

The moon spun silver ovals up the sky. The stars weakened. The White Path Across The Sky vanished. Crickets creaked in the swales. Frogs chorused. The river slid south, a ghostly green. The night became a great silver bell of silence.

They saw him before he saw them. Omaha. They who went against the current.

There were four of them, three grown men and a youth. They were naked except for clout and moccasins, their faces fierce with war paint, their hair done up for action. They were looking directly at him. Then, casually, almost lazily, the tallest Omaha drew an arrow from his quiver and fitted it to his bow and let fly. The arrow came at him with a rush, enlarging, feather streaming, and then, *whinn,* missed him and fell slithering through the cattails behind him.

He dropped flat on his belly. His heart began to jump like a jackrabbit. "Now I will die in a strange place," he thought, "and my mother will never know where my bones lie drying. I will be one of those who went away alone and never returned."

He remembered the bravery of his father and got a grip

on himself. If he was to die he had better die a brave man. The four Omaha were sure to boast of having killed him, a chief's son, and if he let them see he was afraid, word of it was bound to get back to his father.

He turned on his back and looked up at the cattails nodding above him. It occurred to him there had been no redwings hopping about in the cattails. "Ahh, the swamps are always full of happy redwings. I did not see that they had hidden themselves to warn me. My eyes were blind with foolishness."

He couldn't crawl because the Omaha were sure to see where the rushes stirred. He waited.

And waiting, his eye caught a quick, stealthy darting movement nearby, almost in his face. Focusing his eyes, close up, he saw a deer fly circling around and around the tip of his bow. The bow had his smell and the deer fly circled it. There was another stealthy whisk of movement off to one side and then he saw what had really caught his eye: a squat black spider with a yellow dot on its back. It was quickly weaving a web in the path of the circling deer fly, from one cattail stalk to another. He watched amazed as it shuttled back and forth. Line after line of glistening gossamer issued from its tail. Swiftly the net spread between the two cattails.

"It is a sign," he whispered. "If the black spider catches the fly, the Omaha will catch me. If she does not, they will miss me."

He heard the Omaha approaching. Their feet slid through the wet rushes, lifting out of reluctant mud. He guessed they were wading abreast, coming straight for him, combing the narrow patch of cattails. He watched the spider and the circling deer fly at the same time that he listened for the Omaha.

They were almost on him. He was sure that they had already seen him. Yet the deer fly kept circling, circling, each time just barely missing the spider's web.

A foot landed almost in his face. It sank splashing in the mud immediately under his ear. Yet still the deer fly flew around and around.

He held his breath, eyes half closing.

The black spider flung one more strand. The deer fly hit it, struck on it, buzzed fiercely a second, then broke free and flew off.

"Ai! they will miss me."

The next foot came down near his hip, again sinking some in the slime. It lifted slowly with a sucking sound; went on. He was safe. "Ae, I will still be known and return in safety to my mother's pot."

He lay a long time in the same position, waiting for the Omaha to leave the valley.

And waiting, he noticed that the spider's web had a diamond shape. The diamond shape reminded him of a story his father Redbird told. Returning from a hunt, young Redbird had become tired as night came on. Young Redbird had failed to get meat, or make a coup, and was sad about it. So young Redbird lay down in the deep grass on the open prairie and fell asleep. Awakening in the morning, his eyes opened on a spider web woven just above his nose in the tall grass. He looked at it a while. Dew drops glistened on the web in the clear morning light. Marveling at its great beauty, at its neat diamond design, he drifted off to sleep again. And dreamed of the diamond design. A voice told him to use it. The diamond pattern would bring luck to his tribe. When he returned home he told his father Wondering Man about the dream, about the voice, and Wondering Man, overjoyed that his son had returned safe, and full of reverent awe, told the people. Soon everyone was using the diamond pattern in their quillwork.

The cattails whispered overhead, roughly, then softly. No Name's heavy body pressed down into the undergrowth. Soft mud slowly welled between his shoulders. The damp cold came through his buckskins.

Thinking of his own carelessness in being caught by the Omahas, he remembered the story of another foolish youth, named Spider. Spider was out exploring one day and ran across some ripe chokecherries. Spider began stuffing himself with them, until his lips and tongue turned black and his throat almost puckered shut. At last the chokecherry tree decided Spider was making a pig of himself, so she whispered, "Little nephew, do not eat too much of me or your bowels will bind." This made Spider laugh. "Oh, that's all right, little mother tree. I've just had a lot of artichokes and they'll keep me loose." But his bowels did bind, and a few days later he was seen sitting on a hill facing the wind, trying, trying. Suddenly a rabbit ran between his legs. Astounded, he thought he had given birth to a son. Grabbing his clout, he jumped up and ran after it, calling, calling. "My son, my son, wait for me. I'm your father." But the rabbit got away. Muttering, cursing the bad manners of the new generation, Spider went back to his hill and sat down again. Except that this time he wrapped a robe around his legs and seat to make sure nothing could get away. At last it came. He folded his robe carefully over it, then quickly got a stick and began to pound it, crying, "Try to get away from me now, will you? My son you are and my son you will remain."

Thinking about the story again, No Name laughed merrily to himself.

The sun began to shine directly down upon him. It became sticky hot. A few mosquitoes got wind of him and despite the bright sun wisped out of the shadowy undergrowth and sat on him.

"Ae, they have come to tell me something. Perhaps the Omaha have gone."

He reset his wolf cap, then got up on hands and knees and like a skulking fourlegged peered through the cattails to all sides. The Omaha had left. Also, the swamp was suddenly full of singing redwings.

He resumed his running, walking, running routine. His pace was constant more than swift. The little hills and narrow valleys along the east side of the Great Smoky Water unrolled beneath him. He watched the crows and wolves for sign.

At last, sure he was well beyond the country of the Omaha, he turned west and went down to the banks of the great river. He found a dry cotton wood log with two armlike limbs. It was as white as an old licked-over buffalo bone and because it was very dry would float high in the water. He rolled up his clothes and bow inside his light pack, as well as his fetish, and fastened them on top of his head. Then he pushed the cottonwood log down the bank into the coursing waters. Some dozen yards in, the current seized the tree and began carrying him downstream. The two armlike limbs kept the log from turning over in the water. He paddled along easily, aiming his crude craft for a distant high bluff on the west side. The bluff would make a good lookout from which to examine the farther country.

He remembered his grandfather Wondering Man's last request for a drink from the Great Smoky Water. He sipped a few palms of it as he floated along. The tan water was medicine and restored him.

The river came down between two long lines of wind-blown bluffs, swinging back and forth in slow heavy curves. It shoved more than it ran. It threw up innumerable sandbars from its bottoms, then promptly undermined them and dumped them lower down. It undercut its own banks, dropped and overran them, then built them up again. It ripped trees loose from one bank and planted them deep in the opposite bank, sometimes right side up, sometimes upside down. It robbed itself of islands, then promptly created new ones. The great river boiled on, a restless fluid force, driving as well as driven.

Abruptly the current in the main channel caught his log. It was tumultuous, with waves as high as a small tree. It lifted him, dropped him, then spun him around in violent sickening swings. It raced with a low gushing roar. He hugged the old tree with both arms; swallowed water; got dunked; was lifted clear. Then, as suddenly as it had caught him, it let him go.

He steered his log past mushy sandbars and mucky islands and around floating live trees.

He was almost across the old river when it went for him once more. A whirlpool near a sinking collapsing island grabbed his log and ripped it from his grip, taking it from him like a bully taking a stick from a boy. He had just time to take a deep breath, and under he went. The whirlpool sucked him down, down. His head sparked with flying stars. His lungs swelled until he thought he would burst.

Then the airtight pack on his head, tied under his chin with thongs, began to swell up and pull him the other way. The deeper he sank the harder the pack pulled. The tan waters rushed and whelmed and gurgled over him.

"Ae," he thought in the darkness of his skull, "it is my helper. He is hidden in the pack and the great river does not know this. My helper does not wish us to drown."

He began to rise very rapidly, suddenly popped out on the surface. A log lay almost against his face, spinning crazily. He grabbed for it even as he sucked for air. With his hands he stayed the log's wild revolutions, got a leg and an arm over, then his chin. He lay on it, puffing.

At last the rushing stream was through with him and let him drift toward the bank. His feet touched bottom. Spent, he slithered up the muddy bank and collapsed.

When he got his breath, he put on his leathers again, hid his charm in the left braid, ate what was left of the dried meat, and set out. He followed a stream which eventually led up through a brushy ravine. This in turn lifted onto the treeless bluffs. Eyes and ears alert, he kept looking for sign. He saw no tracks, neither of man nor horse. He had struck exactly between the Omaha to the north and the Pawnee to the south.

Ahead to the west lay open prairie. The country rolled some at first, gradually leveled off, became a vast lake of knee-high grass. There were no trees, no bushes, no buffalo, no deer, nothing on which the eye might rest in relief or the spirit fasten in hope. It was all new to him. Yet his helper, hidden in his braid, opened his eyes in such a way that it seemed vaguely familiar. This comforted him.

He followed the sun down the sky. Heat waves danced and glittered on the horizon. Sometimes the burning appearance of the prairie gave him the feeling it was all on fire. He ran. He walked.

Toward dusk he spotted something. It was hard to see against the sun and he could not quite make out what it was or how far away it was. Palm over black glittering eyes, he peered intently. After a while he decided it was some kind of fourlegged. It too seemed to have stopped still, waiting for him to move first. Against the sun there was a curious glowing over its dark back. Ahh. Grizzly. He had once seen a silvertip in the brush along the River of the Double Bend.

He strung his bow and drew an arrow from his quiver. Again he had a vision of himself as dead with his bones whitening in a waste of waving green-gray grass. "Ai, soon someone will weep. I hope it will not be my mother."

He sank slowly out of sight in the grass. He waited. There was no wind. The grass stood still. It also waited.

He raised and looked out again, and was just in time to see the grizzly look back over its shoulder at him and then, shrugging, separate into two parts. Astounded, he watched the two parts become two old crows and fly off. They disappeared into the blue dusk to the south.

When he arrived at where the crows had been sitting, he found a single seedling ash, about hip high, with birdsquit staining the grass at its foot.

Bone-tired, upset by the grizzly apparition, he decided to make a night of it beside the seedling. He poked around through the grass on hands and knees and uncovered a few prairie turnips. Seasoning the spring roots with some brown June bugs, he ate them raw.

The sun sank in a series of color explosions, the one shading off into the other, first bloodstone, then moonstone, last brownstone.

Looking around to all sides, he missed something. He could not think what it was until he took off his wolf cap. "Ahh," he cried out softly, "it is the wolf I miss. Not even the coyote dares to live in this place. It is too wild for even the four leggeds."

Parfleche for a pillow, he stretched out on the grass. Stars came out as thick as mosquitoes. He watched the leaves of the seedling ash stir against the White Path Across The Sky. He counted the leaves and found there were exactly as many as he had lived winters. The tree was his twin brother. He sighed. He missed Circling Hawk. He wished his brother Pretty Rock might have lived so that he could have known him. He lay quietly on the heaving breast of the earth. It turned under him. "My heart is on the ground," he whispered. "I am lonesome."

He slept. He dreamed. A black horse stood on a rise of land. After a while he saw it was Lizard, his black gelding. Two eagles, attracted by the horse's strange raw nose, were attacking it, one from above with enormous sailing wings, the other from the ground. Before he could come up and help, the two eagles had torn open the horse's head so that its eyes hung loosely down its face. He picked up a heavy stick and clubbed the eagles over the head until their brains ran out like curdled milk. Then the two eagles flew off. He bounded on Lizard's back and they were off. After a wild ride they arrived safely in camp. Redbird his father praised him for his bravery. At that, Lizard his horse lifted his long black tail a little and watered on the grass. Then his mother came out of the tepee and took Lizard by the bridle and led him away.

Some of Lizard's water sprinkled on him, and he awoke. Huge drops were hitting the ground all around him. It was raining. The sound of it reminded him of June bugs hitting the taut sides of his mother's leather tepee.

Suddenly, a hundred yards away, a thin streak of fire leaped out of the ground. It speared straight up into the heavens, revealing boiling clouds. Immediately, along the same track, a fat prong of zigzag lightning dazzled down. Thunder smashed into the ground. The earth shook with long heavy undulations. Then a wind sprang up and the sprinkling thickened into a rain, gradually became a heavy downpour.

He slipped out of his buckskins and folded them under his back to keep them dry. The rain pelted his naked body like flicking finger tips. The wind became strong, began to roar. It bent the little tree until finally its wild leaves snapped in his face. The wind became so fierce it drove water under him.

He couldn't keep his buckskins dry, so he decided to use his shirt to catch some of the water. He anchored it down at the corners with his hands and knees. In a few seconds he had more than enough to drink. The water was sweet, as fresh as milk from a mare.

It poured.

After a time, the wind gradually died down, the rain thinned, the shower moved on. He got up and wrung out his leathers. When he put them on they clung clammy to his skin.

A new wind rose, from the south. It was warm and dry. The little tree beside him wrung out its leaves too. Soon both he and the little tree were dry.

Lying down again, he touched the little seedling, gently, just above the roots. And touching it, he fell sound asleep.

The next forenoon found him lost on the gray, green sea.

Shortly after sunup, the sky became overcast. Search the horizons as diligently as he might, he could find no hint of where the sun might be. The sky was all one vast continuous gray cover, with no blue openings or dark thickenings, with no edges or shadows. The prairie also remained flat. It too was one vast continuous piece, with no trees or brush, no rises or valleys. There were just two great sweeps: one overhead, gray; one underfoot, gray-green. Nor could he find in himself any feeling or instinct as to where the four great directions might be. Whether he stood still, or spun around on a toe, it was all the same.

Once he thought he saw a second seedling ash. But when he came up to it, he found flattened grass beside it and knew it to be the same little tree he had slept under. He had wandered in a circle.

He took out his charm and propped it up on a little mound of plucked grass at the foot of the seedling and prayed to it. "Help me, my protector. I am lost. It is the same country where my father was lost. His charm helped him. Help me." He cocked his head this way, that way, waiting to hear.

The piece of horse chestnut gave no sign it had heard.

"Will I perish on the plains, unheard of and unpitied? My mother will soon be crying alone by the River of the Double Bend."

Silence.

At last, angry, he began to scold it. "Have I not been good to you? Have I not carried you far, even tenderly, as though you were my own grandfather? Is this a good way?"

Silence.

He gave the fetish a little flick with his fingers, hard enough to knock it off the mound of grass.

"Ahh, you will not help, I see." And with that he picked it up and put it back in his braid. "Today it wishes to be balky."

He found a few more turnips and ate them raw. He clawed up some of the sod and found a half dozen white or-ange-nosed grubs. He ate them also, found them sweetish.

He heard a gopher whistling off to one side. Hunger still gnawed in him and he looked around cautiously. Finally he spotted the gopher some dozen yards away, yellow-brown, fat, rearing up like a man's stalk out of the grass. He quickly fashioned a snare from his bowstring, then on hands and knees went after it, head and shoulders humped over, black eyes blazing in anticipation. The gopher, still sitting erect on its haunches, cocked first one bright little bulbous eye at him, then the other. It whistled, short. It ducked down into its hole; popped out again. No Name moved stealthily toward it, first on right hand and left knee, then on left hand and right knee, predator eyes half closed. He imagined himself a bobcat. If he went slowly enough, and if the gopher continued daring enough, he might catch it barehanded and not need the string snare. His buttocks lowered as he got set to pounce. At that moment, little slope-jaw chewing rapidly, the gopher gave him a hard look and then, whip! was gone. No Name padded softly to the hole. He studied it a moment, then deftly laid out the loop of his snare. Trip string in hand, he retreated a few feet and lay low in the grass. Holding himself in check, crouch-ing, eyes almost closed, he waited. At last the gopher couldn't resist a quick peek. Then another. Then yet an-other. On its third peek, No Name jerked and zip! had it. He pounced on the struggling gopher and hit it precisely behind the head with his bow. It shivered, its rear legs pumped a few times, and then it stretched out. Before its eyes could glaze over in death No Name skinned and ate it.

The sky continued overcast. It remained very still.

He sat on the ground, bowed, head between his knees. His thoughts were dark. "Alas, why it is that I die? I thought my path would be clear before me and the skies cloudless above me. My thoughts dwelt only on the good. There was no blood in my thoughts. Yet my father the sun has deserted me and my helper will not speak."

He sat still as a stone for a long time.

He had almost fallen into stupefied sleep, when he heard a single low squeak. Looking up, he saw a swallow flying glossy-blue against the gray sky. It was a dirt dauber. He watched it a moment, then realized from the way it flew, low, mouth open, its flight as straight as an arrow's, that it was heading for water. He bounded to his feet and ran after it, hoping to keep it in sight long enough to find where it was heading.

But the swallow flew too swiftly for him and before long it vanished from view. Puffing, eyes stinging with sweat, dejected, he sat down again.

It occurred to him after a while that the ground he sat on felt harder than usual. Getting to his knees, looking, he found two stones half-hidden in the grassy turf. Both were perfectly round, about the size of buffalo testicles. Also, someone had painted them red.

He stared at them. "Ai," he whispered, "sacred stones." He backed away.

Then, even as he stared at them, he saw the stones stir in the tough webbing of grass and shimmer toward him. He wiped stinging sweat from his eyes; stared again.

The stones spoke to him. "My son, hear this. We are round. We have no beginning and no end. We are related to the sun and the moon because they also are round. Therefore we know where the sun and the moon are and where your father lives. We are two. That is why the grizzly became two crows. That is why the black horse was attacked by two eagles." Having spoken, the two stones lay still again in their place in the grass.

"Aii!" He knew then that this was the place where his father had been lost. Full of reverence, of dark awe, he quickly got out his tobacco and placed a pinch of it in sacrifice before the two stones.

He prayed to the stones. "Grandfathers, I thank you. I have been lost, yet you have found me. I thank you. A man as he goes forth makes stops, in one place to eat, in another place to sleep. So also Wakantanka. The sun, which is so high and bright, is one place where Wakantanka has stopped. The moon, which is so soft and beautiful, is another place where he has stopped. The little ash tree, the whistling gopher, the flying swallow, all are places where he has stopped. I think of these places where my god has stopped and I send my prayer to them to help win a blessing."

Again the stones stirred in an oscillating manner, this time as if pointing in a certain direction.

"Ae, they point to where the swallow flew. That way lies water. Thank you, thank you. Now I have found the true path."

# 3

He awoke in the dark. He lay awake on the grass.

Presently he felt something tugging him. A thing warm and strong had a grip on his heart, and it pulled as if to help him to his feet.

Finally the pulling became so insistent he had to get up. He threw quiver and pack over his shoulder.

"I am coming," he said, eyes glowing. He walked quietly. After a while he saw something just ahead in the pre-dawn dark. It curved in a long uneven line before him. "Trees," he said softly, "ae, and a stream." He walked straight for it, unworried that someone might be skulking after him.

The land dipped and the grass deepened. The grass was very wet and soon his leggings and moccasins were soaked. The blades were as sharp as bird teeth. He moved through them slowly to avoid getting cut.

Soon trees lifted over him. From the rustling sound he recognized them as cottonwoods. They were thickly together and were short. He touched them as he moved through them. Some twenty steps further he saw stars twinkling at his feet. He knelt. With his finger tip he touched water. It was a softly flowing stream and it was cool. He had a long drink. The water was gritty with silt and afterward his teeth hurt. He removed his leathers and bathed in the stream. He scrubbed himself harshly with the sandy water. He took down his braids and rinsed them. He combed out his long black hair. He fluffed his hair in the air until it was nearly dry, then he did it up in braids again and bound them tight around his head and put on his wolf cap.

Dawn burst over the horizon. It bloomed over him like an opening lily. It yellowed his buckskins. It yellowed the deep slough grass. It yellowed the undersides of the leaves of the rustling trees.

He danced a short dance in greeting to the oscillating sun. He sang in a low voice:

> "I was lost in a wide place
> Where the wolf did not dare to come.
> Yet you found me, friend.
> I stumbled in a wide place
> Where the coyote slid away.
> Yet you showed me the truth path, friend.
> The world is very wide."

The pulling was still there. It drew hard on his flesh soul. It was as though someone had grabbed up a handful of flesh on his chest and were pulling him forward.

He leaped across the stream. The pulling led him through the young cottonwoods, then south across a swale, then west over a low mound, at last back to the little cottonwoods again where the stream buckled sharply to the south.

He saw a very tall cottonwood. It towered over the smaller cottonwoods like a father over children. The high cottonwood drew him. The pulling was now not as sharp. It drew only a little. Yet he went to the big tree.

Then, level with his eyes, he saw a skull stuck to the cottonwood's gray-edged bark. The skull's eyeholes glowed darkly at him while its glittering teeth smiled a strange welcome. Looking closely, he saw an arrow in its right eyehole. His glance went down. With a gasp, he saw a jumble of bones at the foot of the tree. Sometime, a long time ago, some warrior had been pinned to the tree in battle. Later, wolves had come and ripped body from skull and cleaned off the bones.

Quietly, with sacrificial reverence, he placed a pinch of tobacco beside the bones. Looking around to all sides, then up at the cottonwood leaves overhead, he said, "Stranger, you are gone. You are dead. We will never know what your Name was. Do not turn back. Be happy with your new friends in the other life. My helper and I wish to fare well in this life."

In a half trance, he walked slowly and unhurried toward a low rise. The sun shone warm on his back. The west wind was cool in his face. The wingeds sang softly in the rustling trees along the stream.

When he reached the crest of the rise the pulling was gone. He had come to the place. Dreamily he looked about him. A level meadow covered with pink prairie clover lay between the rise and the twinkling stream. It was the kind of meadow his father would have selected for a camp site. He gazed down at it, looking, half-listening. Then, young face calm, a gentle mask, he stepped toward the stream. Going around a clump of chokecherries, he saw it. A set of bare tepee poles. Also many bare meat racks and rings in the grass where other tepees had stood. And a sweat lodge at the edge of the swamp. And two menstrual lodges standing well back in the grass. His eyes opened. He moved through the grass one slow step after another. The trail from the camp site to the water was fresh. The grass was scuffed but little, with here and there some tan earth showing. The human droppings around the outer ring of the camp were fresh too. Sitting on his heels, he gently brushed away the ashes of one of the camp fires, layer by layer, until he found a few live embers at the bottom. The earth was still hot beneath. The horses, he noted, had been tied close to the lodges. He kicked over their droppings and saw that as yet no colonies of bugs had collected under them. A pile of discarded ribs and cracked leg bones had just begun to stink and collect green blowflies. He found a castoff moccasin and examined it carefully. He noted by the marks made by the pins in the grass that the lodges had been quite small. He also noted that the pins had been hurriedly ripped out of the ground. He came upon a crushed eagle feather with a bit of scarlet plume glued to its tip.

"It is the Pawnee," he said finally, whispering to himself.

"A few of them have been on a hunting party. Also, they have been angry with each other."

His feet moved under him. They took the path to the stream. Bobbing pink polls of prairie clover filled the air with cloying perfume. The perfume was so rich, so sweet, he was dizzy from it. He could almost see the scent wisping up as smoke.

He passed through the fringe of slender cottonwoods and stood upon the sand beside the stream. He saw where someone had scraped the sand back and forth, as if in play, and at first, seeing the brown object lying on the rumpled sand, he thought it a child's buckskin ball left behind in haste. His next thought was that it had a shape similar to the sacred stones he had found the day before, and about as large as the moon when directly overhead. But then he saw the hair falling away on one side of it, black, tangled, and long.

A cry broke from him and with broken knees he ran toward it. "Aii! it is Leaf!" He kelt beside the moon-like head, made a gesture as if to pick it up, then retreated from it. "She who is lost! Yet it cannot be." His hard black eyes became milky with grief. Cold tears blinded him momentarily. "Thy flesh still has its bloom. A day sooner and I would have found thee alive." He tore his hair. "They of the other world let me see two crows and then two eagles and then two sacred stones. Then they began to pull me. But I did not come quickly enough." He shuddered. "They have beheaded you." He made a noise as of one chewing pebbles. "Sister, I have done thee much wrong." He wept. "But I have also suffered much from it."

A sigh broke from the brown head. Then the lips moved and a broken voice said, "I am suffering very much."

He sprang to his feet in astonished terror. A sheet of fear moved under his scalp. His black eyes flashed white.

Again the lips moved. "I am suffering," they said. As the head spoke the round chin touched the sand under it. "I have lived but a little while. Too little."

He leaped back a full step. "Can a head speak without breath?"

For answer a deep sigh broke from the head, then it tilted to one side on the sand.

He stared down at it wild-eyed. His glittering eyes took it all in. The moon-like features seemed fuller than he remembered them, as if they had been bitten by mosquitoes. The wide lips were fat and the pink inner edge was cracked and glazed. There were black bruises over the cheeks and under the ears. The parting in the middle of the hair was crooked, with the usual stripe of vermilion almost worn away.

Then the dark eyes opened. They were bloodshot. A grayish haze lay over them. Rolling, showing pink where they should have been white, they fixed on his feet, then lifted up, lifted until at last they looked him straight in the eye. They looked at him a long time before the haze in them began to clear. Recognition gradually began to shine in them. "Help me," the lips whispered. "They have buried me in the sand."

He stood trembling violently, not knowing whether to fly or to help her.

"The sand is very cold. Yet my body cannot shiver. Help me."

"B-b-but are you not in the other world?"

An infinitely sad smile, yet also an infinitely kind smile, moved over the bruised face. "I have not yet gone to the place so that I might be in it."

"Then you are the daughter of Full Kettle? Your shadow soul and your body soul have not become separated? You are alive? You are not a spirit living in the head of one who has been beheaded?"

Again a deep sad smile came over the brown face. "Dig here with your hands and you will discover my body."

He dropped his bow and fell beside the head on his knees. He began to scrabble furiously. Sand flew in all directions behind him. He was like a dog digging in fury after a retreating squirrel. In a few moments he had dug below the breasts, then down to the waist.

Leaf heaved a huge sigh. "At last. The sand pressed so

tight against me. It was very hard to breathe. Also they jumped on the sand to make it firm."

"Was it the Pawnee?"

"Ae." She rolled and swung her body around from the hips up. Sighs of relief kept rising from her.

When he had dug well below her hips, he saw that she was swollen with child. He repressed a terrible impulse to strike her belly. The child would be a Pawnee's. Already he hated it.

At last he opened a hole wide and deep enough for him to lift her out. He took hold of her under the armpits and gently heaved up and back. She was heavy. The wet sand let go of her feet with a sucking sound. Puffing, he stretched her out on dry sand. Yellowish wet filmed her brown nakedness.

She sighed and sighed. She could not get enough of free breathing. Shudders kept shaking her from head to foot.

He cupped palms of water over her. He washed her until her limbs shone a bright rose-brown. The water was warm but tremors of chills still shook her.

"We must make a fire," he said, looking around, wary. "Yet I dare not."

He remembered the live embers he had found in the deserted Pawnee camp site. The earth under them would still be warm. Quickly he picked her up, one arm under her shoulders and the other under her knees, and staggering under the double burden, carried her tenderly through the fringe of trees and along the path. Her near breast rode soft as a bladder of water against his chest. The nipples were already spreading and he knew then that she would soon be a mother. She kept shuddering against him.

He cleared away the largest pile of white ashes and then placed her on the warm bare ground. He gave her his shirt to wear. He smiled grimly when he saw how it barely covered her hips. He dug out an extra pair of moccasins from his pack and slipped them on her feet. He pulled the thongs out of the pack and opened it to its full width and placed it around her hips.

He kneeled beside her and stroked her arms from the

shoulders to the wrists. He rocked her from side to side, gently, firmly. The fire-heated ground gave off waves of warmth.

She moaned in gratitude. She let her head be rolled from side to side. Presently a rush of dark warmth suffused her bloodied eyes. "Now I see you clearly," she whispered. "I am better."

"The lost one has been found," he said. Beads of sweat rolled off his back. "Sister, my heart is glad."

The sun rose to almost midday before warmth returned to her limbs. It wasn't until she suddenly broke out in a strange slippery sweat that the tremoring chills finally left her.

He helped her sit up. "When have you eaten?"

"Not since they quarreled. It is now two nights."

"I will hunt us some meat." He stood up. "The animals are our friends. The wolves will lead us to the game. They will take care of us."

She clutched him by the leg. "Do not leave me."

He placed his hand on her head as if she were a child. He smiled down at her. "Sister, would you eat?"

She flinched, then sat away from his leg. Her lips quivered, her nostrils flared on each breath. She tried very hard to show fortitude. Then she said, "We are alone in enemy land and we eat out of the same dish. Go. Bring the meat."

He cupped his hand over the fat braid where his charm hung secreted. He listened. He looked within. Gradually a faint bruising sound arose in his cupped hand. Then he looked without, dark predator eyes roving to all sides, searching the pink meadow and the gray-green prairie beyond.

"Ahh," he cried, starting at what he saw. On a low rise south of them two gray prairie wolves were skulking along. "My medicine is working. He is helping me this day. The wolves smell a down buffalo. Perhaps even a young red calf." He strung his bow, got out an arrow, and darted swiftly after the wolves.

Coming over the rise he saw them, a young cow and her red calf. She had a broken front leg and her bunch had left her to die. Already a dozen other wolves sat in the grass around her waiting for her to fall. Occasionally one of the wolves set up a barking to one side while another from the other side sneaked in craftily to slash at her hocks. Despite the dangling front leg, she always managed to get around in time to ward them off with her sharp black horns. The wolves saw him first. Sullenly they gave way, flashing their teeth at him. Coming closer, he saw from the number of her droppings and from the worn circular groove in the trampled grass that she had kept her tormentors at bay for several days.

The brown cow first smelled him, then saw him. She snorted, lowered her head as if to charge. The calf, a male, lifted its bare little tail and circled her once, running wild; then abruptly it stopped, let out a yelp of a bellow. The young cow bawled in answer in a strange flat voice. She turned clumsily, and licked her young.

He approached her on soft feet. He scattered a pinch of tobacco in her direction in sacrifice. He said, "Grandmother, my sister is hungry. She will soon have a child and needs meat. You were made for that. So I must kill you." With one motion he lifted his bow and shot her in the heart, just behind the left front leg at the edge of the long hair. She shuddered, she breathed hard, blood foam formed on her lips, then she fell heavily to the ground. Slowly her eyes glazed over and a gray-black tongue lolled out. Almost immediately flies began to whiz about her fallen head.

The bull calf bellowed at the sound of her fall. He staggered back a few steps, made as if to charge No Name, held. He looked around bewildered. At last he fell to suckling her slack teats, nudging her roughly when the milk did not flow to suit him.

No Name looked at the dozen wolves waiting in the grass around them, looked down at the calf, and said, "Where are your fathers? You will be killed here." Then he looked up at the sky. "Sun, I am doing this for you. May we live until next winter from it. By then we shall be returned to our lodges by the River of the Double Bend." He took a second arrow from his quiver and shot the red calf too.

Swiftly he skinned both mother and calf. He offered a piece of meat to the sky and the earth and the four directions. He withdrew the two arrows and cleaned off the blood with a handful of grass. He cut out the choice meats, the kidneys and liver and hump and leg bones for marrow, and scooped out the brains for tanning purposes. He wrapped up the meat and the calfskin in the cow's brown hide and flung all of it over his shoulder. He spoke to the waiting wolves, saying, "The remainder I give to you because you led me to the game. Take it. I thank you."

When he came back to camp, he was pleased to see that Leaf had been grooming herself. She had washed and combed her hair and it now hung in a long glossy waterfall down her back. The hint of rust he remembered so well glowed in it. She had also salved the bruises on her cheeks and neck with the white juice of milkweed. Except for her swollen body, she was almost the Leaf of old again.

He threw the skinful of meat at her feet. "Sister, let us have a feast in celebration."

She gave him a wonderful smile. Her hands flew over the bundle as she untied the folds of fur. Spotting the calf liver, she tore off a lobe, and with a swift apologetic throw of eyes at him for being so wolfish, spiced the liver with gall squeezings and began to eat it.

He held himself as if he had not seen her ravenous hunger. He got out his tobacco and with his knife chopped up a handful on an old log and filled his pipe. He lit up with a small coal from one of the fire sites. He offered his pipe to the great directions in thanks, then settled back on a stone for a peaceful smoke.

She found a good bed of coals under the largest pile of ashes. Quickly cutting some green sticks from the cottonwoods, she hung some of the hump meat over the coals to broil. Heat soon made the fat drip and the coals burst into low talking flames.

They ate heartily together. The meat was tasty, rich. The bone marrow was especially succulent. They smacked their lips, they licked their fingers.

Much later, after many sighs, she finally told him what

had happened after he had used her and left her on the pink
sand beside the River of the Double Bend. . . .

She lay crying on the sand. She felt so miserable she was
beyond even tearing her hair or gashing her legs. Her
shadow soul shrank until it was very small. And at last, exhausted, she fell asleep in the red willows.

Then something touched her. She rolled over on her back
and opened her eyes. There, ringed around her and staring
down at her, were seven strangers. Six of the strangers were
young and dressed for war; faces garish black and white
and red, each carrying a warclub, and naked except for a
clout. The seventh, older and very tall, was dressed in
buckskins. He had on three redtipped feathers and carried a
war-decorated shield. All seven wore a scalp lock stiffened
with fat and paint and made to stand erect like a curved
horn. It was from the horns that she knew them to be
Pawnees.

One of the youngest made as if to strike her. Deftly,
quickly, the tall older Pawnee held the bow. Then to her
great surprise the older Pawnee spoke to her in good Sioux.
"My daughter, are you alone?"

She remembered her mother sleeping across the river.
Her mother must get away to warn the band. "I have been
swimming alone."

The older Pawnee's brows came together in what seemed
to be an apologetic frown. "Tell me, daughter, are you a
virgin?"

"Ae, I am." She spoke from habit, until that day having
always thought of herself as one.

Eyes glittering, all seven faces looked at each other.
Then the six younger Pawnees looked directly at her naked
thighs, while the chief looked at her face.

She got to her knees and bowed deep at the feet of the
older Pawnee. "You are they who are merciful."

"Come, my daughter," he said, "already we are missed in
our village. Let us hasten." He gave a signal and two of the
burly youths took her by the arm and lifted her to her feet.
The older Pawnee took off his shirt and gave it to her to

cover her nakedness. Then two other youths, using switches, carefully erased all sign of footprints in the sand.

They took her to their horses hidden in the willows. An extra horse stood ready for her. From this she gathered they had come especially to capture some enemy virgin.

They rode hard. In three days they arrived in a Pawnee village beside the River That Sinks.

They were greeted with great rejoicing. A dance was held. She was dressed in flowers. Then after the dance she was bound and confined to the dirt lodge of the tall elderly Pawnee.

After a time she learned enough Pawnee to make out that her tall captor was known as Sounds The Ground As He Walks, that he had pledged to keep her a virgin. He was a warrior priest, and except for one man the entire village held him in awe. The one man who did not fear Sounds The Ground was a sub-chief named Rough Arm.

It quite surprised her to find that the Pawnees guarded her chastity with an almost fierce jealousy. During the day they treated her as a special honored one. Many prayed to her. At night she was bound in hymen cords to prevent rape and placed in a bed between Sounds The Ground and his wife Shifting Wind. She knew rape was the usual fate of captive women. Even those lucky enough to fall into the hands of a kind man had to submit themselves to his lust for the first while. Yet Sounds The Ground never touched her. She wondered if something was wrong with Sounds The Ground as a man. She noted he was very kind, sat brooding much, sang plaintive songs, and often stopped on the prairie alone to contemplate the flowers. These things she associated with those-unable-to-marry or men-touched-by-the-moon-being. Later, when she became better acquainted with his family, his two wives and seven children, and when she learned that as a child he had slept in his slain mother's blood, she saw how wrong she had been. She also learned in time that he had been a captive of her band of Yanktons. This explained why he spoke Sioux so well.

Shortly after arriving among the Pawnees she found she

was with child. She worried about what Sounds The Ground would do when he learned of it. She knew she would soon be suspect if she did not show the usual signs of menstruation, so she secretly cut her hand and pretended that the blood was her menses. Thus always each month, upon the sign of the blood, Shifting Wind, the older of Sounds The Ground's wives, put her alone in a menstrual hut. Five times the stratagem of cutting her hand worked successfully.

It was Shifting Wind who first detected it. Shifting Wind had been given the task of giving her a daily bath in the River That Sinks, to keep her fresh and well-perfumed. Upon emerging from the menstrual hut the sixth time, Shifting Wind took her to the river to cleanse and purify her. There, helping her, rinsing her body with water, she felt the knot in her belly.

There was an immediate hullabaloo. Old Shifting Wind shrieked at the top of her voice, tore her hair, clawed at Leaf with fierce nails. The whole Pawnee village charged the place where they were bathing, Sounds The Ground among them. After Sounds The Ground learned what the trouble was, his face became that of a man who had been grievously betrayed. From him Leaf learned why they had been saving her for all this time. It was their custom to capture a virgin from some enemy tribe, and early in the spring, at corn-planting time, to offer her in sacrifice to the male god, the Morning Star, so that he might be kind to them in the coming year. Sounds The Ground told her that now, learning she was with child, the Pawnee village would demand that she and her unborn child be thrown to the wolves. Sounds The Ground felt very sad about it, yet said he would do what he could to save her.

Leaf wept.

The Pawnee village immediately divided into two camps, Sounds The Ground at the head of one group and Rough Arm of the other. For once Sounds The Ground found himself in the minority. Yet for two months he managed to keep her secure in his dirt lodge. He carefully explained to her that the reason he was saving her life was because the

Yanktons had been kind to him when he had been their captive, always treating him as if he were one of their children. Meanwhile, another virgin was found, from the Kansa to the south, and Rough Arm was momentarily held in check.

Immediately after the sacrifice of the new virgin, however, Rough Arm began drumming up a new campaign to throw Leaf to the wolves. The village finally went into such an uproar about her that Sounds The Ground decided it would be best if he took his group on a short buffalo hunt, hoping that in the meantime the old men of the village could talk some sense into Rough Arm. Sounds The Ground and his group were out on the hunt but a week, when suddenly Rough Arm came with all the braves of his warrior society and surrounded the encampment. They seized her, dragged her to the stream, and buried her in the sand up to her neck. . . .

No Name sat with a stone face. Yet inside he boiled with great astonishment at it all.

A meadowlark whistled from the tip of a wolfberry bush. Slowly the sun sank toward the fringe of young cottonwoods along the curve of the stream. Sweet aroma from the pink prairie clover continued to waft around them. Mingled with it was the stench of the broken bones in the middenheap.

The bad smell of the bones reminded him that danger lurked near. He looked at her. "Sister, let us remove to a place further up the stream. The Pawnees may yet return to see if the wolves have eaten you."

She agreed immediately. "But first we must jerk some of the meat and dry it. Also, I wish to make some clothes for our return to Falling Water. I cannot be wearing a man's shirt when my mother greets me with joy at the edge of the village." Mention of his shirt caused her to look at his muscular chest. And looking, she suddenly clapped hand to mouth.

He caught her look. He had been wondering how long it would take her to catch sight of the sun dance scars on his

bare chest. Yet he disdained to show pleasure at her surprise. He said quietly, "I have been given the vision at last.
I have been sent to catch a certain wild horse. A white stallion."

She looked at him with new respect. "You have come a
long way from home. What is the news?"

He told her that her mother and father were alive and
well, that his grandfather Wondering Man had at last died,
that the Yanktons had lived well on buffalo flesh most of
the winter. Also, almost grudgingly, he told her more of his
vision, first the part given him on the Butte of Thunders
and then some of the second part after the torment of the
sun dance.

This time she could not keep from exclaiming aloud.
"Sounds The Ground has spoken of such a horse. A great
white stallion that no one can catch."

"What! Where?" he exclaimed, jumping up.

Leaf's face closed over instantly. She realized she had
said too much. She shook her head. "It is very far away. I
do not remember."

He was almost beside himself with joy. He recalled the
words of the white mare in his vision. "First, you must take
a long trail alone, on foot. Go to the River That Sinks. It is
to the south where the Pawnees live. There it will be told
you where the white stallion lives." He trembled, thinking
again of that magic day on the Butte of Thunders. The
white mare had also said, "Meat and clothes and a place to
sleep will be given you also. Have courage. Be patient unto
the day." He saw now what the white mare had meant. She
had looked ahead and seen that he would find Leaf in this
place, that it was fated Leaf would tell him about the white
stallion. The white mare had also seen that it would be Leaf
who would provide him with food and clothes and shelter,
as a good woman should, while he went out to catch the sacred horse.

He cried aloud, dancing in the pink prairie clover. "Ai!
now I know that my protector lives. He is helping me. The
vision is coming true. I will become a great man and my

people shall become as numerous as the leaves of the rustling tree."

Leaf bowed her head over her swollen belly.

He stood over her. "Tell me the way. Where does this Sounds The Ground live? Tomorrow I shall go in search of him and make him tell me where the white stallion lives."

She wept. "Rough Arm and his soldiers will kill you."

"I must go," he said. "I have been told all this in a vision and it is fated that I shall do it. It cannot be otherwise."

She shuddered. "The Pawnees call themselves the men of men. They are fierce when they are angry. Rough Arm will kill you." Again she shuddered. "His hands were very rough when he buried me in the sand. This I know."

He stood above her in stiff hauteur. "Woman, it is fated that I should know. Tell me. What is the way?"

She shook her head. Bitter tears fell on her hands. Her face began to swell again.

"My helper will show me the way. I will go without your help."

She clutched him by the leg again. "Do not go. My child was without a father until today. Do not take this from my child again."

He stood very still beside her. Gradually the burning glitter in his eyes subsided and his face resumed the cast of graven stone.

At last, looking down, he touched the painted part in her hair. "Tell me, when will our child come? I have not counted the moons."

She threw him a wild look of joy. "It will be here by the next moon."

He stood considering her. A smile worked his lips. "Ahh, there will be enough time to catch the white horse first." His smile deepened. Then he said winningly, delicately, repeating an old refrain, "I am without a wife. I am naked. Oh, let us run away to my uncle the great white stallion. Let us elope. Come." He tugged in love at a strand of her rust-touched hair. "I have seen a young girl who looks so beautiful to me, I feel sick when I think about her."

Leaf wept.

"Will you be my wife? After I catch the white horse we shall have many horses and I will give more than ten to your father Owl Above."

"I cannot return to the Pawnee. Not even to Sounds The Ground. I cannot."

"I will hide you. I will go alone in the dark and talk to this Sounds The Ground in the privacy of his lodge. With his voice he will tell me where my white horse lives or my knife will be at his throat. So tell me the way! Come. Show me on a dust map."

She held against him.

"Come, let there be no shadow between us. I wish to be a father who has listened to his vision. Will you be the wife of such a one?"

At last, sighing, she consented and drew him the map.

# 4

The next morning he inspected his bow and arrow and knife, put on a new pair of moccasins, and sang a song of self-encouragement in a low private voice. Then, turning his back on Leaf, he resolutely set off in a loping run, south, across the pathless waste of grass.

Late in the afternoon, hungry, he sat down in a swale where the grass was higher than his head. Here he ate the dried meat Leaf had prepared for him. He was thirsty. All sorts of shiny green frogs were hopping about, yet there was no water. Flying above him were some redwing blackbirds, black males with red shoulders, and rust females with whitish undersides. They kept circling low over him, fluttering, scolding, sometimes dipping down as if to peck him in the eye. It came over him that the birds were angry because he sat near their nests. Ahh, eggs. Creeping through the grass, first to one side, then the other, watching to see when the redbirds became the angriest, he finally came upon some grass bent down by stormwind. The moment he crouched over the down grass the female redwings dove at him in desperate fury, wingtips snapping against his wolfcap. Humping over to protect his face, he parted the thick grass carefully. There, well hidden in the center of a tussock, were two nests, each with five speckled greenishwhite eggs. Gravely, with the redwings continuing to strike down at him from on high, he took a pinch of tobacco and scattered it on the wind, saying, "Wingeds, you are my friends. I take these eggs because they were made for this. Tell our grandfather the sun that I do this because there is no water. I am thirsty. I am sorry. But I have been sent to catch the white horse." Carefully he took but two eggs from each nest, leaving three, and withdrew. The eggs were fresh. They quenched his thirst.

He settled back on his heels, knees against his chest. He rocked quietly back and forth in the deep grass.

A single rose bloomed at his feet. Its five pink petals reminded him of baby tongues. A big green-black bee bumbled around and over its powdery yellow stamens, seeking nectar. Off to one side of the prairie rose lay a scab-like patch of prickly pear cactus. The patch glowed with strangely beautiful yellow blossoms.

Slowly he rocked himself to sleep.

He awoke just as the sun was setting. From Leaf's map he knew he was not more than a short run from the Pawnee settlement. At the edge of the swale he lay down in the grass and looked against the sun to see if anyone had passed by in the last day. Shining spider threads vibrated from grass-tip to grass-tip everywhere. Look as he might he couldn't find a single broken thread. Nor could he find any grass bent down or stepped on. Apparently the route Leaf had shown him was one rarely used by the Pawnees.

When darkness finally settled on the vast prairie, he began his approach from the northwest, the wind against him. Presently he came to the brow of a shallow drop-off. Below, not too far away, lay the Pawnee village. He could just make out the irregular pattern of the earth lodges.

He moved reptile-like, humped, slinking through the grass. He kept a bush, then a clump of bunchgrass, then a stone, between himself and the village.

He came upon a field of young corn. He crept through it slowly, going from row to row. From the height of the corn and the crumbly state of the soil, he made out the field had been hoed but once. It meant the men were still home. The Pawnees rarely left their village to go on their summer hunt until at least after the second hoeing. The rustle of the corn leaves was just loud enough to hide the sound of his crawling on the crumbly earth.

Next came a horse corral. One by one the horses lifted their heads as they got wind of him. He recalled Leaf's warning that the Pawnees liked to attract horse thieves by tying a very white horse outside the corral and making it look easy to steal. White could be seen even on the darkest and blackest of nights. He looked carefully to all sides but saw no white horse.

Beyond the corral he felt his fetish working.

"What is it, friend?" he whispered. "I am going so softly not even the mole can hear me."

An owl hooted. Directly ahead. He listened. He stood stooped over with eyes dilated. A moment later another owl hooted. Off to the right. He crouched lower. He listened, mouth open. His heart pulsed in his ears. The first owl hoot sounded true, he thought, but the second not. In rocky land it was easy to tell a true birdcall from a false call by listening to see if there was an echo. If there was an echo it was human and false. On flat ground one had to listen for something else, something almost the opposite, a mumming sound as if someone had held his nose too tight.

Again the owl ahead hooted. Again the owl on the right answered.

"Ho," he whispered to himself. "Both are false. A Pawnee guard has seen me crawling and is whistling to warn his friend. It is perhaps one of Rough Arm's soldiers."

His eyes shone, brilliant. They seemed to be furnished with a light of their own to see things with.

Just ahead was a deep ditch, with a dirt embankment behind about hip high. He decided the first hooting guard was sitting behind it, watching where he lay.

He waited.

At last he saw a bump slowly rising on the embankment. It resembled a skunk coming at him with its tail raised. Gradually it formed into the roach of a Pawnee. He sat tense. He watched the head become a full man. The Pawnee slithered down the embankment, then through the ditch. After a moment the Pawnee came crawling across the bare ground, straight on. No Name waited. He could smell the Pawnee on the wind. He had not been near another man for some time and it surprised him to notice that the Pawnee's smell was like an old wet moccasin held too close to a fire.

He waited until the form was almost on him; then, sudden passionate hate rising out of the dark back of his head, he pounced, driving his knife deep in the Pawnee's back. At the same time he slid his arm around the Pawnee's neck to choke off a cry. There was a low groan, a straining of muscles against him, then the Pawnee lay limp in his arm. He counted coup on him with his bow, then scalped him. "I have overcome this one," he said. It was his third kill and his first coup. He hid the scalp in his shirt.

He waited some more.

Presently the false owl on his right hooted a query.

He pinched his nose very tight and gave a soft low hoot in reply.

Again the false owl hooted a question, wonderingly.

Again he replied, soft, low. With all his mind he willed into his reply the thought that all was well, then willed the thought into the other Pawnee's wondering mind.

There were no more hoots.

He crept on, toe down first, then the heel. His moccasins touched earth with the softness of a velvet paw. He snaked through the ditch, up and over the dirt embankment, and landed behind a dirt lodge. He smelled meat cooking, hides curing, kinnikinick drying. There was also the sacred smell of sage, the delicate incense of sweetgrass, the subtle perfumes of wild flowers. Stronger than them all was the stink of horse dung. The many smells made him homesick.

Leaf had told him that Sounds The Ground's lodge was on the east side of the village. He would be able to tell it from the others by a peculiar vestibule, built higher than usual because Sounds The Ground was such a tall man. Also, Sounds The Ground's war emblem, a stuffed wildcat's tail, was usually flying high on a pole above his lodge.

No Name followed the embankment around the village. Crawling on hands and knees, he kept bumping into all sorts of castoff debris: old clay kettles, broken saddle frames, cracked marrow bones, discarded bows, imperfect arrow points, human dung, worn bone awls.

Twice, dogs smelled him. They growled; came toward him with ruffed necks; then, strangely, retreated.

"Ahh, they smell the scalp of the Pawnee in my shirt," he whispered. "They know the Pawnee's smell and are afraid he will beat them if they come too close."

Just to make sure, when he next came upon some horse dung, he rubbed his clothes with it. The dung smell, along with the strong smell of his horse-gristle fetish, would help throw the dogs off even more.

At last, on the far side of the village, he found an earth lodge with a high vestibule. Looking up, he next spotted a wildcat tail fluffing against the stars. "Ae, I have found the lodge of Sounds The Ground. It is as Leaf told me."

He sat on his heels, very still, wondering what to do next. It was almost midnight. The Pawnees were all asleep. He had left it to chance and a dark night to get himself, somehow, into the presence of Sounds The Ground without being seen by the other Pawnees. He saw now how foolish this was, since a sleepy Sounds The Ground was as apt as any of the guards to kill him. Yet if he waited until morning some rambling nightwalker might spot him outside the high vestibule. Even the dogs, waking as they usually did twice a night to serenade the stars with their strange wild howling, might rove around a bit before settling down and so get wind of him.

Finally he decided to risk entering the lodge anyway. With guards out, and dogs to bark, the tall Pawnee chief would probably be as sound asleep as a beetle in milkweed down.

He was halfway down the dark vestibule, nose and eyes and ears alert, slow knee following cautious hand, when a large dog slowly raised its head and growled at him. He stopped dead in his tracks. With a great effort of will he refrained from gulping, then, after a moment, collecting his wits, he quietly backed out again.

Outside once more, looking up at the wildcat tail fluffing softly in the night breeze, he all of a sudden knew what to do. He scrambled up the roof of the dirt lodge, picking his way carefully through a cover of sparse grass and prickly bushes.

He found the square smokehole at the top and, sliding on

his belly, looked in. Embers still glowed weakly below him in the dark interior. He could just make out the forms of Pawnees sleeping on rush mats: a long gaunt naked man whom he took to be Sounds The Ground, an old woman whom he guessed to be Shifting Wind, a middle-aged woman, and seven naked youngsters. Their heads clustered together resembled a bunch of fat purple grapes.

Again on impulse, boldly, drawing his knife, he slipped over the edge of the smokehole and dropped lightly to the floor below. His feet hit earth so softly beside the firepit that not a single sleeper stirred. He looked at each dusky face carefully, especially the stern sleeping face of Sounds The Ground, toyed with the thought of killing them all in their sleep, in revenge for all they had done to Leaf as well as for a hundred other evil things done to the Yanktons, but then, remembering what he had come for, put the thought away. Instead, seeing some meat curing above him he cut himself a piece and settled down beside the fireplace. Some of the meat wasn't done to suit him, so quite soberly he held it over the embers on a stick a while. Then, having eaten his fill, and taking a long drink from an earthen crock, he stretched himself out on the floor beside Sounds The Ground and calmly fell asleep.

He was the first to stir when dawn began to lighten the smokehole above. He sat up and had a look around at his strange new surroundings. His quick dark eyes took in everything; firepit scooped out of the earth a span wide and a hand deep, stake to one side serving as a crane for cooking, beaten floor dug out below ground level, narrow earth bench all around the wall. Narrowing his eyes, he also made out certain of the objects standing well back in the dusk: a drum, fur robes hung over a wooden frame, strings of red and blue and calico corn hanging from the ceiling, a warclub and spear and bow and quiver and decorated shield dangling from a tripod, pots of food, pestle and mortar, two saddles, fish nets, a bundle of eagle feathers. His roving eye next made out the family altar, an earthen bench projecting out a span or more from the wall directly across from the entrance. On it lay a sun-bleached buffalo skull, a painted ceremonial drum, four dance rattles, a triangular rush mat painted for ceremony, a sacred pipe. Above the altar on a wall of woven willow branches hung a sacred bundle. Sniffling, he noted that the dirt floor smelled different from the dirt floor at home. The Pawnee earth was richer, not unlike the smell of an open blister.

The left side of his face began to tingle. Turning, he found Sounds The Ground awake beside him and looking at him.

They stared at one another. And stared. They looked into each other's eyes so long that wondering inquiry gradually became a contest of will power to see who would give way first. Black hypnotic eye burned into black hypnotic eye.

All the while No Name quietly noted the other's various features: the high noble forehead, the shaven head, the roach running back from the scalp lock, the strong chin, the wide mobile mouth, the handsome broad shoulders and long arms, the sun dance scars across the chest, and the marvelous phallus rivaling even that of a pony stallion. The tall Pawnee's physique reminded No Name of his father's well-preserved body. It came to some men, one here, one there, to keep their youth well into old age.

Light from above opened still more. Then, in the tight silence, a crumble of earth broke off the edge of the smokehole and fell into the firepit in front of them, raising a little puff of white ashes and gray smoke.

Both instantly glanced up at the smokehole, then down at the rising whitish gray puff, then at each other. And looking, both smiled. They understood each other. Sounds The Ground smiled because No Name had been so bold as to enter by way of the smokehole; No Name smiled because he knew Sounds The Ground admired him for it.

Sounds The Ground rose from his sleeping mat. Motioning for No Name to follow, Sounds The Ground crawled over to the firepit and sat down. He got out pipe and tobacco and lighted up with a coal. Again, as they paid their respects to the great directions and as they smoked together, pipe glowing in the gloom, they silently inspected each other, though this time in a more friendly manner.

No Name was privately very much pleased with himself. He had passed a certain test. He could at last look a tough grown man in the eye and hold up to him.

Smoke finished, Sounds The Ground next reached up and cut off two pieces of cured meat. He gave his guest the largest piece, motioned for him to eat up. His manners were exquisite. Only after he made certain his guest had a good start did he begin to eat himself. Solemnly they chewed together, each still with a quiet wondering eye on the other. Halfway through both found the meat not quite to their taste, and both, quite soberly, got a stick and held it over the warm embers for more broiling. Then, having finished their portions exactly at the same time, Sounds The Ground reached in back of him and picked up a small earthen crock of water and held it out to his guest to help himself. No Name was still thirsty, but with fine delicacy took only four swallows, then poured a little over his hands and refreshed his fingers and face and passed the water back.

At last Sounds The Ground spoke up, in Sioux. "My son, what brings you here at this time? Who are you?"

"I am No Name, the son of Redbird, a Yankton Dakotah. I have come to pipe-dance the Pawnees."

The moment they spoke, all the other sleepers in the lodge popped up from their mats, wide awake. The old woman, Shifting Wind, gave a loud gasp of astonishment when she saw No Name. She quickly put a hand to her old wrinkled mouth.

Sounds The Ground looked around mildly at her, said quietly, "Woman, where is my water for the morning washing? Neither my guest nor I have had sufficient with which to start the day. The crock was almost empty."

Eyes wild, Shifting Wind turned to leave by way of the funnel door into the vestibule.

"Hold, woman!" Sounds The Ground said sternly. "There is enough water in the jars under the wall. We will announce that we have a stranger in our midst after we have had some warm soup."

Shifting Wind did as she was told. She gestured for the other wife, somewhat younger and not as withered, to help her. Together the two women brought up more water, then some wood for the fire. They threw some meat in the pot and put out a loaf of cornbread.

The naked children, meanwhile, like a nestful of wildcat kittens, stared at the intruder, their eyes alternately glowing and glittering from under mops of bushy tangled hair.

The meat soup was soon ready and the cornbread heated.

"Here is something warm for you to eat," Sounds The Ground said, giving No Name a horn spoon. "Eat this and may it give you great strength. Loa-ah."

Again, after they had washed themselves, Sounds The Ground asked him, "My son, tell me, what brings you here at this time?"

"I have been told that you know of a great wild stallion who lives on the wide prairies. I have come to catch the stallion."

The eyes of Sounds The Ground opened with astonishment. "How could a Yankton know of the white stallion?"

"Leaf, my wife, told me you knew where he lived."

Sounds The Ground stiffened slowly. "Leaf is your wife?"

"Ho. These many days she has been heavy with my child."

"Leaf is still alive?"

"Ae. I found her buried in the sand beside a stream. She lies now hidden in a certain place waiting for me."

"Ahh," Sounds The Ground said low, "ah."

Again Shifting Wind edged for the door. And once more Sounds The Ground stopped her with a stern word. "Hold, woman, where do you go?"

"But, my husband, he is a Sioux. I will run and tell Rough Arm. Perhaps this Sioux is an advance scout and many more are coming."

"Stay beside me and attend to my wants. He is the son of Redbird who befriended me when I lived with them. I remember this youth well, though he does not remember me. He was a child playing with his father's toes at the time."

Shifting Wind turned on him with the fury of a wildcat. She snarled, "Arrh! I see that my husband has forgotten how the Sioux treated him, how the throat-cutters from the north regarded him as a miserable captive and made him do the work of a slave."

"For a short time only." Sounds The Ground looked at her with firm unbending eye. "Redbird was gentle with me and I have not forgotten it. On a buffalo hunt once, when I was gored by a bull, my shadow soul almost parted from my body soul. But Redbird and his friends stood around me and prayed to their gods, and passed their hands over me, and at length I again breathed regularly."

Shifting Wind's eye blazed. She raged, "You are a soft-hearted woman to welcome this snake of a Sioux into your lodge. That is what comes of smelling pretty flowers when alone, like some silly goose of a girl."

All through the tirade both Sounds The Ground and No Name sat in grave dignity, their faces expressionless. A proud man considered it disgraceful to fight with a woman. Smoke slowly lifted off the firepit and lazily sought the hole in the roof.

Finally, seeing that everything she said to the two men was like rain off a well-greased tepee, Shifting Wind went over and spat No Name in the face. And to make sure she was thoroughly understood, she next spat her husband in the face.

Sounds The Ground jerked back volcanically. His eyes popped open, so wide for a moment he resembled a great gray owl of the north. Then, his eyes snapping down to fierce slits again, he leaped to his feet and grabbed his war-club and gave her a resounding whack over the backbone. He hit her so hard she fell in a heap on the ground.

While she lay groaning, Sounds The Ground quietly lit his pipe again and had another leisurely smoke with No Name.

Sounds The Ground said, "What you have done is a brave thing. I honor you for it. Loa-ah. It is not often that an enemy has crept through the Pawnee village secretly at night and entered the lodge of the head chief without any-one knowing. Also, you could easily have killed us all in our sleep. But you did not. I thank you. Well, my son, now

I must tell you a thing. If the others find you here they will ask for your life."

"I have a helper. He is with me and works for me at all times. Therefore I do not fear any thing or any person. Also it is fated that I will catch a certain wild stallion. A white horse of great fierceness."

"Then no one saw you creep through the village?"

"One did. He called to another as an owl. I had to strike him."

"Ai, now there will be much weeping and wailing by his mother. Rough Arm will be like a mad one." Sounds The Ground shook his head. His plume waggled back and forth like the heavy mane of an old stud. "My son, this wild stallion you wish to catch, did you know of him before you found Leaf?"

"A white mare came to me in a vision. She told me to visit the Pawnees. She said there it would be given to me."

"Were you not late in receiving the vision?"

"Yes, my uncle, it came to me only after the fourth time. The gods were testing me." No Name then told of his various vigils, how the vision finally came to him in two parts, the first half on the Butte of Thunders, the second half in the torment of the sun dance.

"It is a true vision. It is a great vision. Loa-ah." Sounds The Ground nodded. "I see now that you had to come. I am glad. I honor you for it. I will tell you where I have seen the wild stallion. He is white. As you Sioux say, he is wakan. He is very swift and very fierce. He is a killer and will try to destroy you. But I see your vision is also wakan. Therefore I shall show you where he is."

Sounds The Ground put his pipe aside. A green fly came to life at the base of the support pole next to him, and seeing it flex its wings, Sounds The Ground quietly cupped his hand, then snatched at it and caught it. He pinched it so that it popped lightly, dropped it into the firepit. Then he turned and looked at his groaning prostrate wife. "Old woman, get up. There is much work to be done. Prepare more food. Get wood. We shall soon have many visitors." He next fixed his eyes on his oldest son, a lad of ten. "Stiff Twig, my son, call Rough Arm. Tell him a visitor is here from a far place. Tell him we wish to hold a feast for this visitor. Will you do this?"

Stiff Twig nodded and darted out through the door. He went with such reckless speed he woke up all the sleeping dogs in the vestibule. They followed him out and barked after him as he went the rounds.

While the women bustled around the firepit, Sounds The Ground casually prepared himself for company. He combed his roach. He waxed his scalp lock with fresh bear fat and formed it into a neat horn. He put on a deerskin clout, a pair of black leggings fringed with human hair from ankle to thigh, a pair of moccasins, and a buffalo robe thrown casually over the shoulder. He placed a board between his knees and chopped up some fresh tobacco. He got out his best pipe and set it up on a small forked stick before the firepit.

Presently a glittering eye peered in through the dark funnel opening. There was a polite cough. Then the funnel filled with a line of stooping bronze men, all heavily painted, with closely shaven heads, and all wearing the plumage of birds. They filed in in an orderly manner and, sitting, formed a circle around the fire. Each newcomer threw a quick burning look at the guest, then looked at the fire with iron gravity. Behind them poured in a motley array of children and old men and young girls and wondering dogs, all of them looking at No Name with unwavering gaze from the dark part of the lodge.

The men sitting in the council circle were all given to eat, fat ribs roasted, and something to drink, water from The River That Sinks, and then the pipe was lighted and passed, solemnly, in ceremony, moving from right to left around the circle. The ceiling was soon lost in eddying clouds of smoke, both from the firepit and the pipe.

At last Sounds The Ground lifted his eyes. "My children, I have called you here because the son of a benefactor has come to visit me. Redbird his father helped me when the others in his band treated me as a slave. Redbird saved my life. Also, Redbird gave me his best horse and helped me to escape so that I might return alive to my people. Now his

son has come and it is my turn to help." Sounds The
Ground told of No Name's vision, how he had come specif-
ically to him to ask where the great white stallion of the
plains lived. "His dream is wakan and we must honor it. If
we do not, we will invite the wrath of our god, Tirawa, The
One Above, the supreme power."

Rough Arm's savage eyes fixed in hate on No Name.
Rough Arm had painted his face and the shaven portion of
his head with vermilion and the whole of it looked like a
large red potato with a fat sprout still attached to it. In
youth he had been dragged by a horse across stony ground,
bruising his right arm so badly that it left a long scar resembling the rough skin of a muskrat from the elbow to the
wrist.

Rough Arm said to Sounds The Ground, "It has been
told me that this dog of a Sioux is the husband of the
maiden we thought was a virgin."

Sounds The Ground glared at his wife. "I should have
struck thee twice. Once on the back and once on the
mouth."

Shifting Wind's old eyes rolled around wildly. Luckily
for her, some dogs just then began to nose through her
cases of food by the door. Spotting them, she picked up a
club, the same one used on her by her husband, and began
beating and cursing the dogs with all her might. She made
them howl so loud as they shot out through the door that
some of the men had to cover their ears with their hands.
She followed the dogs out.

When the commotion died down, Sounds The Ground
said to Rough Arm, "The Sioux is my guest." His nostrils
dilated. "No one shall touch him."

At that very moment the wild cry of someone singing the
death song sounded in the doorway, and then an old woman
rushed into the lodge, tearing her hair, ripping her leather
clothes. "My son has been murdered!" she cried. "Aii! my
son has been murdered." It was an old mother known as
Woman Who Walks Ahead Of Her Man.

Sounds The Ground flashed a swift look in No Name's
direction. The look did not quite reach No Name, as if at

the last moment Sounds The Ground just barely managed to check himself.

Rough Arm caught the look. He rose to his feet in trembling rage, warclub in hand.

Before he could speak, Woman Who Walks Ahead Of Her Man let out another piercing shriek. For all her wild crying, she had been quick to spot a Sioux warrior sitting beside Sounds The Ground. She fell upon No Name, old claws working. She gave his wolf cap such a jerk it came off and his two braids tumbled down his shoulders. "It is this Sioux, this cutter of throats, who has killed him!" She gave No Name's braids a ferocious pull. "Where is the scalp of my son Sharp Horn? His spirit cannot depart for the other world until we find his scalp! Where is it?"

No Name gave her a dignified shove with his elbow, finally managed to shake off her clawing fingers. He got to his feet and with a look at Rough Arm quietly drew his knife. The scalp of Sharp Horn, which he had secreted in his shirt, began to burn against his skin.

The old dame turned on Sounds The Ground. "Where is the scalp of my son Sharp Horn? His spirit cries for revenge!"

Sounds The Ground got to his feet. He pointed to the door. "Old mother, each thing in its own time. When we have finished with this council, we will listen to what you have to say."

Rough Arm could no longer contain his towering rage. He let go with a great bellow. "Waugh! And I say we shall listen to what she has to tell us! I too wish to know where our brother Sharp Horn has gone! Does anyone see him here? Can we let his mother suffer the torment of his loss without striking in return? No! Death to the Sioux!" Rough Arm gave an explosive downward gesture with his hand, the sign for death. "I have said."

The crowd in the shadows began to cry loudly for the death of the Sioux intruder. Meanwhile the warriors around the circle sat in stiff dignity. Only their eyes showed interest. They burned like winking coals.

No Name understood what was wanted. He waited. He was ready.

Sounds The Ground raised his hand. He spoke slowly, with quiet even composure, his eye lingering on each face in turn. "My children, I am a mild man. You know this. For fifteen winters I have herded you like a band of horses. In the winter I have defended you here in the village against the enemy. In the summer I have led you over the wide plains and found buffalo for you. My tongue has been worn thin and my teeth have been loosened in giving you advice. Listen. Listen well. My advice to you now is that we honor this guest who has come to your chief to ask where the great white stallion lives. The dream of this Sioux is wakan. It is fated that he will catch the fierce white horse of whom we have often talked. We cannot oppose the will of his god. No one was there to see who killed Sharp Horn. Has our guest waved Sharp Horn's scalp in our faces to taunt us with it? No. It is thus my advice that we should help him in his quest." Again he looked at each warrior in the eye. "We are known as the men of men. Loa-ah. Let each now speak what is in his heart. Whatever is decided upon let it be manly. I will listen. I have said."

Rough Arm gave No Name yet another venomous look. Then, glancing down at the pipe where it lay resting in its forked stick in front of the firepit, he said to Sounds The Ground, "Father, your tobacco stinks. If I smoke more of it I will taste the blood of our brother Sharp Horn. I wish to kill this dog of a Sioux. It will please me to see the white skull of this young Sioux upon the ground. The teeth in the skull of a young man are sound and beautiful. When one sees the white skull of a young man, such a skull appears to say, 'I have died when I should and have not waited at home until my teeth were worn to the gums eating dried meat.' Therefore let us kill this young Sioux because it is a good thing to do. I have said."

No Name caught the meaning of the exchange of Pawnee words. He stood very straight, defiant, and cried, "Pawnee, listen! This I have to say. I want to die here! Come, kill me! You are many, I am one. You are in your own village, I am in a strange place. I want to die here! Come, strike! My heart was made to beat so that it might be stopped by my enemies. My lips were made to move so that they might be stilled by those who hate me. My scalp lock was braided long so that it might be taken with ease from my skull. Strike! I want my father to know that I have done this. It is what he wanted when he had me born."

Sounds The Ground translated No Name's words into Pawnee.

A gasp went around the circle. The motley crowd behind moved back into the shadows under the wall. All, including Rough Arm, marveled at this show of bravery.

Again Sounds The Ground looked at the faces around the circle. "You see? You asked for his life because an old woman comes crying into my lodge saying that her son has been killed. Yet no one has seen him killed. What can I do? This Sioux has been told by his god to visit me. Also he has eaten of my food. I cannot kill a man who has eaten with me in my lodge, who has smoked the pipe with me, who has drunk of my family water. Are the Pawnees to be known as treacherous hosts?" The eyes of Sounds The Ground searched each face around the circle. "What do my friends say? Shall he live? He is brave. He has a sacred quest."

"Let him live!" cried certain of the braves as with one voice.

A murmur of assent went around the firepit and through the crowd behind in the shadows.

Rough Arm saw the drift of the meeting. He stood stiffly a moment; then, with a final throw of bitter eyes at No Name, stalked from the circle and stooped out through the door.

Sounds The Ground turned to the old mother. "Woman, go bury your son. After my guest has departed we will consider your trouble. Each thing in its own time."

When the warriors and the crowd had dispersed, Sounds The Ground turned to No Name and said, "By your bravery you have saved your life. Also the life of Leaf your wife. I shall make white the road to where the wakan stallion lives. There will not be one blood spot on it."

"Ai! my father, my mind is big when I look at you."

"My son, I do this because of your father Redbird. When you were a child at his feet he was kind to me. Where he stepped I stepped. I trod where his feet were placed in the grass. Though he was of the enemy I had one mind with him. Also, my heart is sad because of what has happened to Leaf. I was chosen to catch an enemy virgin. I had to go. My heart is sad."

"My father, I shall tell my father Redbird all the things I have seen."

"Loa-ah. It is good. I will give you two horses. We will get Leaf from her hiding place. Then we will ride with you to the brink of the River That Sinks to make certain that Rough Arm and his young braves do not attack you until you are safely across."

# 5

Riding a prancing blood bay, Sounds The Ground pointed out the true way. Sounds The Ground held his mount tightly reined in, so that its chin lay almost on its chest. Beside him rode No Name on a sorrel gelding, with Leaf following behind on a dun mare. A mounted guard of honor accompanied them, four fierce warriors ahead on white horses, four on the right on red horses, four on the left with blue horses, and four behind on black horses. The tail and mane of every horse was bedecked with bright eagle feathers. Each bridle bore several enemy scalps.

They rode across a vast expanse of grass, waving in the early morning wind, rising and falling. The eye ached to make out the end of it. In the swales the grass sometimes rose as high as a horse's ears. Where the wind and rain had blown it down it clogged the way. Every now and then large flocks of green parroquets whirled past, screaming harshly, joyous with morning euphoria. Wild turkeys rose from a growth of chokecherries, first crying "quit, quit," and then scolding "quawk, quawk!" Further along buzzards sat perched on the naked red skeletons of buffalo.

They trotted gently down a low slope, crossed a meadow yellow with sunflowers, stepped down a low bench, walked through a fringe of fluttering little cottonwoods, finally stood on the banks of the River That Sinks. Ahead was the ford.

No Name saw that the river was as his father had said, flowing in some places as after a rain on flat ground, in other places not flowing at all, and all of it sand. The river looked more like a lacework of many streams than one stream.

The four guards on the white horses ahead splashed in. Sounds The Ground, No Name, and Leaf followed. Sometimes the water was knee deep, sometimes hoof deep. The water flowed in a rising gush one moment, in a sinking gush the next. It played out in a dozen sheets, vanished into gold sand, reappeared as a weak spring a dozen yards further down. A thick desert of fine sand seemed to be always blocking its way, yet always the river kept pushing east toward the Great Smoky Water. The river had padded up its bed so that it seemed higher than the meadows to either side.

Sounds The Ground pointed to some lighter mush sand to one side. "My son, it is in such a place that the sand sucks. It will swallow a horse and a man before another can gallop away to get help."

"I will remember, my father."

"Should your horse fall into it in the night, remember to lie flat." Sounds The Ground pointed to an old weathered white cottonwood lying half submerged in the quicksand. "That old friend has slept a dozen winters in the same place because he lies flat. So fall flat, my son, and lie on your back until help comes."

"I have it painted on my mind, my father."

Little green willows fringed the edge of one of the larger islands in the middle. The island was covered with a thick mulch of fermenting leaves. At its far end stood a single bull willow, horse-high, its thin feathery arms bent by wind and tortured by high water. Debris still hung caught in its highest fork, marking the passing of a boiling flood long ago.

They moved quietly, gently, in deference to Leaf. Water and frogs sprayed ahead of the throwing hooves.

Further along they scared up a flock of great white cranes. The cranes were as tall as a man. They were so heavy that they had to jump off the ground before they could become air borne. They floated away across the silver river, gradually mounting the skies, to rise at last to such a great height they seemed no larger than mosquitoes.

The horsebackers reached the farther bank and climbed it. They climbed the first bench and then the higher slope. Ahead to the south lay another vast sweep of short-grass country. They rode on, bobbing lightly. The only sounds were the pock-pock-pock of hooves and the gingling of rattles and the whistling of tails.

An hour later they reached the top of the first divide. Beyond, sliding slowly away, spread another sweep of land, ending finally in a wide valley. Through the center of the valley ran a fringe of willows.

Sounds The Ground signaled for all to stop. He pointed toward the fringe of willows. "My son, there you see a stream. It is known to us as the River of Blue Mud. It runs thinly and it is not very wide. Pass through the opening you see there in the willows and you will be safe from the sucking sand. Do not stop, but go on. Soon, beyond another lift in the land, you will find a second shallow stream. We call this stream the River of Little Ducks. It is not as wide as the River That Sinks. On the other side of this river you will see a cliff of the color of old pemmican. Cross it there. To the east of the cliff you will see three very high hills. There you will find the drinking place of the great white stallion. He comes there with his mares and colts. He may graze very far away, sometimes far up the river, sometimes far down the river, yet he drinks only at this place. At noon. This I saw."

"I will remember."

"Beyond this river live the Kansa. They once were great killers." A strange look passed over Sounds The Ground's face, as if what he had to say next distressed him. "They will not come this summer. They have had much sickness. Many have died from the spots. It is a sickness that comes with a fat fly whose bite burns. The fly lays a sweetness like maple sap with its tail and then eats it. It is a very strange fly and it has caused many deaths. I do not like it. It is a pet of men who are born with white paint on their faces and who come from the east."

"I hear, my father."

Sounds The Ground sniffed the sky, then looked at the grass underfoot. "It is now the Moon of Fat Horses, the time when the white stallion likes to eat blue-eyed grass in low places. Because he is a great leader he loves the smell of flowers. This is something you may well remember."

"My ear is open, father."

"Once he tried to kill me. He will try to kill you. Once he took away my mare. He will try to take away Leaf's mare. He hates all men."

"It is fated that I shall catch him. I am ready."

"May you live to see your vision come true. Loa-ah."

Then without further word, No Name and Leaf rode on. The warriors on the four white horses ahead slowly separated into pairs, leaving them a clear path to the south. The warriors looked away so that No Name would not have to say the going-away word.

When they had ridden well out of sight, No Name at last looked at Leaf. His eyes were stern. "Woman, much time will go by before I catch the white horse."

"I will be waiting each day with warm soup."

"The child may come before I catch him."

"My mother Full Kettle has told me how it is with a woman at such a time."

Her quick answers made him smile. "Well, then, my wife, I see that we are both ready. It is good. Tomorrow we shall see the great wild stallion."

She smiled back, an impish look in her willow-leaf eyes. "I have already seen him."

"Ho," he cried, "and when was this?"

"He was very winning. He likes to catch young maidens who bathe alone in rivers."

"I see the gods have given me a wife who likes to jest."

"It is sometimes a good thing to laugh."

He took the lead. They rode across the barrens, a hard gray-yellow land sparsely covered with buffalo grass. Occasionally they came upon patches of foxgrass, headed out silky silver, waving, bending at the least touch of wind, swaying even to the air currents stirred up by the walking horses. The high country was so dry in places that the prickly pear cactus had coiled in upon itself. Occasionally the horses nosed down to smell the hardpan soil, then jerked up and plodded on. The burning appearance of the prairie hurt the eyes.

It was almost sundown when No Name finally reined in and held up his hand. He leaned forward from the hips, palm over his eyes, peering over the sorrel's ears. The sorrel's ears worked, first one fuzzy earhole ahead, then the other. They had ridden just far enough for No Name to see clearly down the slope of a shallow valley ahead. The valley was almost as wide as that of the River That Sinks. But the stream running through it was smaller. He studied the trees and was surprised to see they were very tall, as high as the cottonwoods at home beside Falling Water. The stream ran in slow doubling turns, coming out of a brilliant yellow sunset in the west and disappearing into a blue-green haze in the east. He let his eye run along the ridge of bluffs across the river, at last spotted the cliff of the color of old pemmican, and then the three high hills. Staring hard, he saw no sign of horses.

After sitting patiently for some time behind him, Leaf spoke up. "Do you see him?"

"It is past his drinking time. He drinks at noon."

"Then why do we wait here, my husband?" She was uncomfortable on the horse and stirred as if longing to step down. "Also, you will soon want supper."

He continued to look.

"My husband—"

"—patience, woman."

She sighed, fell silent. Her head tipped forward.

He wanted a safe hiding place not too far from the three bluffs. Again he studied the cliff, especially along the base, to see if he could find the opening of a cave.

A shadow from on high gradually edged over them.

She spoke up again. "It will soon rain, my husband. How much longer must we wait?"

He glanced around. A thunderhead hung high in the northwest. It resembled an eagle standing on tall slim legs, its wings outspread, ready to take off. A spear of lightning zigzagged to earth. A moment later the two thin sheets of rain under the thunderhead thickened. "It will be a quiet rain," he said. "I do not see any wind clouds."

She sighed, fell silent.

"Come," he said at last, "we will try the cliff and hope to find a cave."

"We will not build a tepee?"

"Woman, we do not have the hide to build one. Also, it is easily seen. We will live in a cave if there is one."

She began to half-croon, half-wail to herself. "My life is sad. My lover leaves me. The Pawnees take me and bury me in the sand. And now my baby is to be born in a cave."

"Woman, a man does not wish to hear much said on the same thing."

"A dark wet cave for my child."

"I wish a safe place."

"It is told of the Old Ones that they lived in caves. Must we go back to live as they did?"

He held up his hand for silence. "Shh, my helper is telling me a thing. I am listening." He cupped his hand over his fat braid. He listened, gravely. Finally he said, "Come, there will be a place."

They descended into the shallow valley. The grass underfoot thickened. It lay tangled on the ground in some places, brushed the undersides of the bellies in others. The horses bent down to eat, tearing off large mouthfuls as they went along. The scent of the cropped grass was sweet in the nostril.

"The grass is so thick that some has died," he mused, looking straight down.

"There are snakes," she said.

"They will not hurt us. They are wakan and our friends."

"They make two holes in the skin and then the leg swells up like a bowel roasted over a fire. Sometimes the holes bring death."

"Such a thing is fated."

They found a stony ford, crossed over pale ocher waters, and rode to the base of the chalk cliff.

While she held the horses, he went on foot and searched the entire length of the cliff. Bank swallows cut across the sky like flying arrows. He poked through all the bushes, found only short cutback ravines. He next climbed to the top of the cliff, going up the slope. The land above spread south in a long level plateau. He walked all along the irregular edge of the cliff, carefully going around each ravine. Still he found no place for them to hide.

He was beginning to wonder if his medicine had lost its power, when he happened to notice a cottonwood lying across the bottom of one of the deepest ravines. Its roots still had a good hold on the falling wall and it was very much alive. It was a fat tree and its shiny, glittering green leaves completely filled the floor of the ravine. Examining the tree more closely, he saw a small stream trickling out from under it. The stream ran shallow across shale for a ways, then ran deep through a narrow meadow, at last broke through the fringe of cottonwoods along the river.

"Ha-ho! this is the place my helper told me I would find."

He descended to the base of the cliff, took off his moccasins, and, barefooted, followed the stream to its source under the fallen tree. And there, under the tree, he found a cave. It augered back into the cliff a good dozen yards. It was high enough to be dry and yet was but a couple of steps from running water. Once he and Leaf had enough meat and pemmican stored away, they could live in it for weeks without having to show themselves. Better yet, the fallen tree was thick enough to disperse the smoke of any small fire they might make.

He went back to her. He showed her how to hide their trail by walking the horses up the stream where it flowed across the shale.

"The water will also carry away our smells so the stallion will not become suspicious."

Leaf got down heavily from her horse. She stooped and cupped a palm of water. Then she cried out. "It is sweet water, my husband. It is like fresh rain water out of a rock."

He restrained a smile. "It is as the Old Ones had it. But

perhaps now it is not good enough for a woman of this day."

"Let us make a good smell in our cave by burning cedar leaves. I saw some cedars growing between the hills."

"Have you meat?"

"There is some dried left."

"It is good. Care for the horses." He looked up at the on-coming thunderhead. "There is yet time."

"Where is my husband going?"

"I go to lie in wait for a deer. Before the rain comes to make my bow useless. There will be deer in such a fat valley."

She too looked up. "Do not be gone long."

There was a flash of lightning. A moment later thunder crashed, then rattled slowly down the valley. As he strung his bow, a doe stepped out from behind some gooseberry bushes under the tall cottonwoods along the river. The doe came forward a few steps, head up, ears erect, bulb-eyes shining in the dusk. Casually No Name reached for an arrow, fitted it, let fly. The arrow speared ahead in a low arch, leveled, caught the doe behind the shoulder. She sprang up, at the same time gave a single mouse-like squeak, then fell dead.

Leaf said quietly, "I see that my husband has become a great hunter. It is good. We will have plenty of meat and many new shirts."

He carried the deer inside the cave just as the rain began to fall on the cottonwood leaves outside.

The next morning, awakening, he quietly slipped from Leaf's side and stepped out of the cave. A vague gray light came filtering down through the leaves of the fallen cotton-wood. It was still out. The leaves barely turned. Occasionally a star twinkled through.

He took a long drink from the trickling stream, then purged himself with his goose feather. He bathed. Then, slipped into his clothes, he followed the stream out from under the fallen tree and across the meadow. He found the sorrel gelding and the dun mare secure in the brush. He petted them, and blew into their nostrils, and scratched them behind their ears. He led them out to the meadow and reset their stakes.

Alert to all sounds, he followed the trickling stream into the fringe of cottonwoods along the river. A jackrabbit jumped up. For a moment it was so confused it butted into a tree; then getting its bearings, it crashed away through the underbrush. An owl next awakened. It gave him a great round eye, grumped at him in a melancholy way, then, resettling its feathers, sank back into sleep.

He reached the river just as light began to open a filmy pink over the cliff. The river lay before him like polished slate. He looked up and down the running water, finally spotted what he was seeking, a patch of tall reeds growing in a still place. He approached silently. It wasn't until he was almost in the middle of the reeds that he saw them, ducklings, eyes winking in the half-dark, sitting very still, bobbing like gourds upon the water, all of them still too weak to fly. Suddenly the mother ducks quacked loud and angry. The mothers couldn't rise out of the reeds. A month before they had plucked their wing feathers for nest-making. Chasing the little ones down, splashing through the quiet waters, he soon had a dozen in hand. He snapped off their heads, one by one, then picked them up by their slim orange legs and carried them back to the cave.

He found Leaf up. Her sleep-swollen eyes widened, then glowed, at the sight of the fat little ducklings.

He explained, "Sounds The Ground told us the Name of this place was the River of Little Ducks. Ha-ho, I said to myself, it has been many moons since I brought home some ducklings for the pot. I will get some for my wife."

"I will soon have them picked and roasted."

"Good, my wife. I will sit and smoke until they are ready."

After they had eaten heartily together, he picked up his bow and quiver. "I am going to look for the place where the wild stallion comes down to drink. Wait here."

"There is much to do, my husband. Do not fear."

To kill his scent, he went down to the river again and

rinsed his hair thoroughly, and washed out his clout and moccasins in a harsh fashion, and then daubed himself from head to foot with smelly mud.

Satisfied that not even a wolf could have told the difference between him and a clod of earth, he waded downstream until he came upon another little trickle of water running down from the high ground on the south side. Following it with his eye, he saw that it issued from a cedar-filled ravine between the first and second bluff.

Then he saw it, a wide much-used trail in the grass next to the trickle of water. "Ho! Here are his tracks. I have come to the place at last."

He studied the tracks a while from where he stood in the water. He tried to make out the trail beyond the cedars on the bluffs above, but couldn't quite decide if it was hoof marks he saw or a strip of flowers.

He waded further downstream, well past the horse trail, then swung in and climbed the bank. He found some rag-weeds with leaves as big as floppy dog ears. To make doubly sure of hiding his scent, he wrapped the leaves around his feet.

He climbed the steep incline of the third bluff. He went slowly, stopping every now and then to catch his breath and have a look around for a sign. As he climbed, the other two bluffs lifted with him, while the valley behind fell away.

He reached the top just as the sun exploded over the east horizon. The tops of the three fat bluffs shone a luminant green in its yellow light.

He stood very still for a time, admiring it all, examining it point for point. Turkeyfoot grass flourished underfoot. Occasional gopher holes opened into gray-yellow clay. A bumblebee crawled clumsily over a red-centered hard little daisy. A tall bull thistle stood nearby, pricked out like a tri-pod covered with spears. A brilliant green hummingbird hovered a beating moment over an orange globe mallow, then a silver cactus, then a blue spiderwort, then, in a blurr and a blink, was gone. Over it all whistled the cheery meadowlark, singing in what seemed perfect Sioux.

His eye caught sight of something ahead. Stepping up, he

found where the grass was trampled down by a horse. Some of the hoof marks were fresh, made but the day before. He followed the tracks back a ways, finally made out that a single horse often came to the spot, stopped for a look around, then after stomping a bit, turned and went back. There were no droppings, no places where the horse had staled. It puzzled him.

He walked on, following the trail east.

Presently he began to see the three bluffs and the land around them in a slightly different light. The three bluffs were actually a part of a long undulating hogback.

The ragweed leaves on his left foot worked loose and he stopped to rewind them.

Looking east again, he was startled to see the edge of the horizon, to the right just under the sun, unraveling off toward the south. At first he thought it a prairie fire racing before a wind. Yellow smoke seemed to be lofting high above. It took him a moment to realize that after the rain last night the prairie was hardly dry enough to burn.

Palm over his eyes, he tried to fix the edge of the horizon firmly in sight. The edge still shimmered unnaturally with seeming flame and smoke. He blinked. Cleared his eyes. Stared.

Gradually his eyes began to pick the racing edge apart, to see it in segments. It was a herd of some sort. Horses. The waving flamelike motion could come only from manes and tails flowing in the sunlight. Something had spooked the horses and they were running away in the morning sun. What had looked like smoke was actually dust rising from their beating hooves.

He leaped straight up in exultation. "It is the white stallion and his mares!"

He watched them go. They raced off far to the south like slowly vanishing heat waves. Yellow dust lingered high behind them.

He went back down the bluff. He removed the cocoon of ragweed leaves from his feet, also the moccasins, and waded into the river. He had a long drink, then climbed the north bank.

He found what he was looking for, a towering cotton-wood standing directly across from the horse trail. The tree was an embattled old veteran, with one side dead and riven-white by lightning, and the other side thick with glittering green leaves. The tree would make a good lookout from which to watch the horses when they came down to drink. Also scent rarely sank to the ground.

With a run he climbed up its rough bark and caught hold of the first branch. He heaved himself up. He scrambled up as high as the top branches would bear him. Near the top he found an arm-thick limb with some side branches. He flat-tened himself along it.

He waited.

Presently a gentle wind came out of the southeast. It streamed down off the bluffs and rippled across the river and tinkled the leaves around him. He thought this a good omen. Wind from that quarter would make it all the harder for the stallion to get scent of him.

The gentle wind rocked his limb. He rested. And resting, he fell asleep.

The sound of trampling thunder awoke him. He came to with such a start he almost fell out of the tree.

Peering through the leaves, he saw them, single white horses on each of the three fat bluffs, in bold relief against a pale blue sky. Behind them, farther back on the plateau, was the slow melee of manes and tails of still more horses.

His eye fastened on the dancing blur on the middle bluff. He blinked. The horse's coat of hair was so dazzling white it hurt his eyes. "It is the sacred white stallion," he whis-pered. He closed his eyes a moment, rubbing them. He broke out into a heavy sweat.

He looked again. The whiteness of the stallion still hurt his eyes. It was like staring at a glinting mound of pure white alkali under a pitiless desert sun. The whiteness of the stallion was exactly as radiant as the whiteness of his dream mare. And the stallion's movements, like the dream mare's, spread upon the immediate air a halo of glittering white motes.

The more he looked at the magnificent shining appearance on the middle bluff, the more he began to wonder if the gods had not made a mistake. The horse on the middle bluff was too wakan for him to catch. "He is not a true horse, but a ghost horse," he whispered. "Perhaps he is a great mysterious one from the world above, one of those grandfather Wondering Man sometimes spoke of."

Trembling in awe, No Name touched his fetish. He tried to recall clearly the sweet winning talk of his dream mare. Surely she could not have meant this great, wild white one. This wild white one was too fearful and too terrible a being for a Yankton boy to catch. This white being could be Wakantanka himself. And who would be so foolish as to try and catch Wakantanka with a rawhide rope?

He lay trembling on the fat limb high in the cottonwood tree.

Then a winning voice spoke in his ear. "Do not be afraid. He is the one you seek. Hey-hey-hey. Are you not the one who overcame the flaming sky-horse beside the River of the Double Bend? Remember the little children who wait for you to return in glory!"

"It is my helper!" he whispered, touching his braid. "Now I know."

Gradually, hardening himself to it, he overcame the weakness in his limbs. His hands steadied on the branches. His vision cleared. And by looking a little below and to one side of the stallion, he began to pick out its various points.

The white stallion stood with his pink ears shot forward. His mane and tail were as scarlet as the down of a woodpecker. When he moved, his mane flowed like a flame. His mane was very long, reaching almost to his knees, completely hiding one side of his high proud neck. His tail trailed over the grass like a leaping prairie fire.

No Name considered. If his dream mare spoke true, he would soon cut himself a new fetish from the red mane hanging down from the stallion's broad forehead, that place of great thought. Ae, and the new protector would help make him a great leader of his people, would help him grow old without becoming feeble or racked with the pains of age, would enable him to desire maidens until the day he died.

The white stallion pranced on the bluff, tail an arching red comet, mane a flashing cascade. The white stallion turned his wide brow first to the west, then to the east, then to where No Name lay hidden in the cottonwood.

Presently the stallion left his post and ran down the trail in the ravine and came toward the river. He ran with a scornful lofty mien, strongly, a fearless monarch. He smelled and tested the ground as he came on. He snuffed the river. He looked west. He looked north. He looked east. Then he turned and looked up the trail. He whinnied at the young white sentinel mare on the east bluff, received a certain neigh in reply. He whinnied in query at the young sentinel on the west bluff, again received a certain neigh in reply. Then he reared, high, pawing the air, mane and tail toothy saws of fire. He wheeled completely around and bugled a loud command. Instantly the melee of manes and tails further back on the bluffs parted and half of the bunch ran at an easy trot toward the cedar-filled ravine. A wise old buckskin mare loped at their head.

A couple of playful colts broke away. They whirled off to the right and climbed to the white stallion's lookout. The white stallion spotted them instantly. In a flash he beat up the draw. With great pumping buttocks he mounted the middle bluff. He was suddenly upon the usurpers, showing vicious teeth to one, bumping the other with his bluff chest, driving them down to the rest of the band.

The lead mare trotted quietly on, leading the way under the cedars and then across the hard shale. In a moment the horses were all in the river, drinking, splashing, whinnying with joy.

No Name peered down at them. They were immediately below the old cottonwood. He counted twenty mares and fourteen colts. He was pleased to see the fine alert heads, the well-shaped bellies, the bluff shoulders and solid hips. He saw too the fine-boned yet strong legs, the quick small feet. But what pleased him especially was their coloring. Most were creams and paints. The special whiteness of the stallion was in every one of them. Ae, the white horse was truly a strong stud. He would breed many fine spotted horses for the Yankton people. With his wakan blood in them, the Sioux horses would soon be invulnerable in battle.

Occasionally one or another of the horses would toss up his head with a wild and startled look. Mane erect, eyes blazing, nostrils distended, the horse would look to all sides for a time as if scenting danger. Then, reluctantly sure all was safe, the horse would go back to sipping water.

No Name lay enraptured on his high perch. He exulted in the wild free motions of the horses. Their whistling tails filled the air with sparks of light. Waves of glossy brilliance shimmered across their sleek coats.

At last they left off drinking and began to nip each other in play, splashing and squealing in the water. At that the old buckskin mare, having had her fill too, drove them out of the river and up the trail.

The white master stood above them on the middle bluff, watching them go by, one by one, as if reviewing a parade held especially for his benefit. When all were safely back on top of the plateau, he lifted himself on two feet and for a second time shrilled a signal. Another mare, a light gray with white feet, and heavy with foal, came out leading the second half of the bunch. The white stallion dashed up to her full of play, made as if to nip her in love. She accepted this token of affection placidly. White feet twinkling, she trotted dutifully down the shadowed ravine, the others following.

No Name decided the light gray mare was the stallion's favorite wife, while the old wise buckskin was probably his mother and the two white sentinel mares his sisters. "Ae, with his many wives and relatives, he is like a true Yankton father."

When the horses in the second group began to squeal and play in the water, they also were driven up the trail to the plateau above.

The white stallion whistled a third time. The white sentinels whistled a reply and ran back to where their bluffs joined the hogback and then, passing below the master, proceeded down the trail and into the water. They quickly drank their fill, played a moment, then promptly returned to their positions on the bluffs. Only then, after all had been watered, did the white monarch trot down to get his drink.

Parting the leaves carefully, No Name stared down at the great horse directly below him. The whiteness of the horse, in contrast to the pale ocher waters of the river, now glowed more than it glinted. Head arched down, mane afire in the sunlight, tail slowly whistling back and forth at flies, the stallion drank in easy measured draughts. Water wrinkled in little eddies around each of his legs.

The sister on the east bluff whistled sharply. Up came the stallion's head, with a jerk, tossing high in wondering query.

For a moment No Name was afraid the sister had spotted him moving in the cottonwood.

The stallion stared up at her, then stared and snuffed around to all sides. Finally, finding nothing amiss, he fluttered his pink nostrils in irritation, then went back to drinking. No Name decided she hadn't called him so much in warning as to show her impatience that her lord and master, and brother, presumed to take so much time.

Presently, tossing his mane, arching his tail, the stallion walked out of the river and trotted slowly up the hill and mounted the middle bluff. With a rolling snort, he dismissed his sister sentinels. He had a last regal look around. Then, bugling suddenly, in a flash of white, he charged his bunch. The old wise mare jumped into the lead, the white sisters took up positions on the flanks, and soon the bunch was gone.

No Name was still trembling with excitement when he returned to his cave.

Leaf saw it. "You have seen him?"

"Ae, and I am afraid of him. Were it not fated that he is to be mine, I would not try to catch him. He is wakan."

"Is he not but a horse, my husband?"

"His mane and tail are like the rays of the sun. His white

body is like the center of the sun. To look at him one must look a little below him."

"I have cooked some meat. I have gathered sweet tipsinna from the meadow nearby. I have found some wild potatoes from the bottom across the river." Moving heavily, she set the food before him.

"Well, I must eat to be strong so that I may catch him." Suddenly he shivered. "But my belly is not very hungry."

"Then he is a very good horse, my husband?"

"He is greatly wakan. He goes too fast for a horse that is only walking. He moves like a ghost horse, covering much ground with but a few steps."

Only then did she catch what he was trying to tell her. She clapped hand to mouth. Her eyes swung from side to side as if she could not bear to look at the thing he told of.

"Even when he stands very still he seems to be dancing." Then No Name added, "I shall call him Dancing Sun. It is a good Name for so great a stallion."

# 6

During the next days, No Name made a close study of Dancing Sun. Packing food, he managed to walk completely around the stallion's range. Hiding in tall trees, he observed him early in the morning, at high noon, and late at night.

One thing soon became apparent. Dancing Sun never galloped. Dancing Sun was a gaited horse. No matter how fast the others in the bunch might run, Dancing Sun never broke out of his pacing gait. Always he ran along easy, serene, head up, legs stroking lightly. He took twice the stride of the best pacing mare in his band. As he ran, his long red tail brushed along the tops of the grass. From a distance he seemed to skim over the ground like a low-flying white eagle.

In all, Dancing Sun had a band of some forty mares and some thirty colts. Rare was the male colt over a year and a half old. Twice No Name saw Dancing Sun drive a two-year-old stud from the band, cutting one of them, the more reluctant of the two, to ribbons with his hooves so that he died. The two young studs had been caught in the act of trying to corner themselves a bunch of mares. Only he, Dancing Sun, was going to be king of the females.

Dancing Sun could be merciless. Once a tall noisy whirlwind came racing toward them. Dancing Sun, ever on the alert, saw it coming. He whistled a warning and set the whole bunch in motion at right angles to the whirlwind. He circled his bunch at full speed, nipping laggards here, charging drifters there. Then a mare dropped back because her freshly born colt had trouble keeping up. Instantly

Dancing Sun dashed for the colt, seizing it by the neck with his teeth, and smashing it to the ground. The mare whinnied shrilly in anguish. In a fit of frenzy she lay down beside her broken colt. Ears laid back, Dancing Sun drove at her, bit her cruelly over the back and neck. Finally, when she still would not get up, he ran off a short ways, then whirled and made for her, teeth bared, head so low he resembled an enraged wolf. So fierce was his aspect that the mare leaped to her feet in panic and raced off to join the rest of the flying bunch. Looking back over his shoulder, Dancing Sun saw that the whirlwind had not only gathered in size and speed but had changed direction. He shot swiftly after his band, pacing up one side and racing down the other, ramming his bluff chest into the ribcase of one mare, whirling around in full fight and kicking another, raking still another with his bared teeth, biting into the flesh of still another. Gradually, squealing his commands, he turned them in the direction he wanted them to go, at last drove them out of sight of the whirlwind where all was safe.

One day No Name discovered a male colt more than two years old in the band. The male was brown and quite fat. This surprised No Name and after watching a while he decided it was because the brown one was not much of a stud. The mother of the fat son indulged him much, often neighing him over to where she had found some specially luscious sweetgrass, and letting him get the first drink while the water was still clear, and shielding him from the sharp teeth of jealous mares. Mother and son were always together, often standing side by side, head to tail, switching flies off each other. Sometimes they leaned across each other's necks, nuzzling each other affectionately. Dancing Sun had his eye on them as they roamed and grazed together but did nothing about it. But then one fine morning the brown one found himself a stud at last, and after some nuzzling together with his mother, mounted her and made connection. The white master spotted them almost immediately and with a great scream of jealous rage was upon them. He drove at them so hard he bowled them both over. He sent the mare off galloping for dear life, then leaped for the slow stud. He fastened his teeth into the slow stud's withers and with one great jerk ripped off a piece of hide all the way to the rump. The brown stud rolled over backwards from the force of the jerk and hit the ground so hard his neck broke. He was left alone, gasping in death.

Dancing Sun controlled a range some twenty miles across. To make certain that interloper stallions understood just where his empire lay, Dancing Sun made it a practice to leave cones of droppings at each of the four corners. Every few days he made the circuit, checking his pyramids of dung to see if visitors had left notices around. Occasionally he would find one and then would carefully smell it over. Usually what he found did not disturb his regal calm much.

The great white stallion also had private staling spots along his run. When some of the young male colts tried to approach these hallowed grounds, Dancing Sun chased them off. From these spots No Name saw more evidence that the stallion was wakan. The white one's stalings caused deep green rings to jump up in the grass. It was as if his watering of the earth prompted springs to burst forth, even on high dry ground. His whitish-yellow stream was of Wakantanka himself, a supernatural fluid.

Occasionally Dancing Sun was stand-offish, moody. When a fresh wind came out of the north, bringing with it the cool sweet scent of the snow country, or when the prairie was all aflower with pink peas, or when the wild clover made the air thick with its lush aroma, Dancing Sun would run off by himself. He would take his stance on the highest point of land, head lifted into the wind, inhaling with great gusto. Sometimes he would point his nose at the blue sky and grimace as if about to break out into godlike song. And sometimes he would even whinny to himself, his lonesome cry floating on the wind as pure and clear as the morning call of the cardinal, full of elation and joy at being alive in the midst of the flowering plains. The white one reminded No Name of Sounds The Ground and his lonesome pondering of flowers.

Later, breaking out of the pensive mood, Dancing Sun

would round up his band and bunch them up into a tight knot, so tight there seemed to be nothing but raised heads and whistling tails. With a fierce and terrible mien he would pace around and around them, close-herding them harshly, and would keep at it until he had worn a trail in the grass. Every mare and colt betrayed the greatest fear of him during these times. Not one would dare to stray out so much as the length of a neck or the breadth of a rump. Then, having kept them standing right together in fear and trembling for an hour or more, the harsh disciplinarian would suddenly lift up on two legs, whirl completely around, then cut through the middle of them, squealing fearfully, scattering them all over the prairie.

No Name wondered about the stallion's strange whim of close-herding, until the morning he witnessed an attack by a pack of lobo wolves. Some forty of them came streaking out of a ravine, gray sliding shadows. No Name was sitting high in a tree on the edge of a lookout at the time, so missed being hunted down himself. The moment Dancing Sun spotted the wolves, he let go with a deep full-chested roar. To No Name he suddenly sounded like a combination mad bull and raging lion. Without even looking around, or wondering what it was all about, the mares called in their colts, "Euee! agh-agh-agh," and immediately formed a circle around them. The mares stood facing out, teeth bared. Meanwhile the white master paced around and around his bunch, mane lifted, teeth bared too, heels carefully kept away from the wolves to keep from being hamstrung.

The wolves were somewhat startled to run into a stallion with such a defense, and they withdrew to a prairie knoll to reconsider. They sat on their haunches, tails whisking, every now and then glancing over at the dancing stallion and his tight knot of fierce mares.

After a short wait, two of the wolves approached the stallion in a playful manner, as frolicsome as puppy dogs, rolling on the ground in front of him. They frisked about as if they had always been his friends and meant him no harm.

Dancing Sun resorted to a stratagem of his own. First whickering a low warning to his band to keep tight, Danc-

ing Sun pretended to be taken in by the playing wolves.
Slowly he grazed toward them, cropping grass one moment, rearing his head in inquiry the next. Finally, just as
the two wolves had maneuvered themselves into position,
one at his head and the other at his heels, just as they were
about to spring, Dancing Sun made a great leap for the
nearest wolf. With snarling teeth he caught the wolf by its
ruffled neck and tossed it high in the air. The moment the
wolf hit ground, Dancing Sun leaped on it with both front
hooves, crushing its skull. Then, before the other wolf
could collect its wits, he seized it too with his teeth and
trampled it to death.

Howling at the skies in disgust, the rest of the lobo
wolves gave up. Toothy jaws flashing a last time, they
drifted off one by one, over the edge of the ravine.

Two mornings later, No Name saw for a second time
why Dancing Sun trained his bunch in close-herding.
Perched in the same tree on the edge of the lookout, No
Name saw Dancing Sun lift his head and look off to the
southwest. No Name looked too. Over a rise came a small
band of horses, running straight for Dancing Sun and his
bunch. What surprised No Name was to see that the small
band was all male. They were bachelors who had been driven out when colts. They were of almost every color: blood
bays and dark bays, light chestnuts and dark chestnuts, rust
roans and strawberry roans. At their head ran a powerful
black. His mane and tail glowed like the shine of a black
grackle. Bluish streaks kept racing over his coat as he
turned and wheeled in the sun. There wasn't a mark on
him. He too had the swift gait of the pacer. He and his male
chums came on with a rush, manes raised, ears shot forward, tails arched high.

Dancing Sun trumpeted piercingly. The glory of his nostrils was terrible to behold. His neck seemed clothed in
thunder. A chill of terror shot through his mares and colts
and instantly they bunched up into a tight knot. Head held
low like a predator, snarling, Dancing Sun began to circle
his herd around and around. His growl was like that of a
monster wolf, deep, primordial. Then, sure they understood

that he was their mighty king and dominator, that he would permit no dallying with any of the visitor bachelors, he turned and went for the intruders. He had made up his mind to fight them all, to the death. He went straight for their leader, the black one.

The big black had watched Dancing Sun close-herding his bunch, had seen him whistle his mares and colts into submission, had even seen how half of his own bunch of odds and ends had backed off a way. But for himself, the black one was not afraid.

Black One bared his vivid white teeth, laughing scorn both at Dancing Sun and at the craven cowardice of his comrades. He reared, whistled a shrilling challenge. Then he dug his forefeet into the hard ground as far out in front of him as he could reach, waggled his head furiously, stopping only to see what effect his mad antics had on Dancing Sun, then jumped gracefully around in the air, swapping ends like a frisky dog snapping at flies.

Black One's show of haughty defiance enraged Dancing Sun. He raised on his hind legs too. Eyes flashing blue lightning, teeth glinting like a grizzly's, ears laid back tight to his head, he shrilled and shrilled. His gray forefeet cut the air as if he were a dog digging a hole. Rampant, thighs stretched like massive white birches, he closed on the other in towering majesty.

Black One shrilled loud too, came on terrible and black, his blackness making him seem almost taller than Dancing Sun. They squealed at each other until white foam ran dripping from their jaws. Their started eyes blazed with primal hate and rage.

Suddenly they lunged for each other, lunged with all their force. They hit with the sound of colliding cottonwoods. They raked each other with slashing hooves, from front to rear. Their hooves beat a tattoo on each other's barrels. Teeth caught hold of skin and ripped until flesh bled black. Sometimes, when their bite slipped off, their teeth clicked together with the sound of hammers hit on rocks. They went after each other like mad lions. Once they got a good grip with their teeth, they hung on until flesh pulled away. They rolled on the ground like wrestlers, over and over. They screamed. Mouths open, teeth glittering, they dove for each other's throats. They whirled around as quick as cats. Kicking at each other, rear to rear, their flint-hard hooves hit together with the sound of crackling chain lightning.

Raw patches began to show on the Black One's glossy hide, on the rump, over the shoulder, along the belly. Streaks of blood began to show on Dancing Sun's immaculate white coat. One moment both puffed exhausted, the next they went at it again with snarls of rage. Flecks of blood and froth flew in all directions.

Finally Dancing Sun managed to catch Black One's nose between his jaws. He bit in and shook him with all his might. He growled. He backed around and around, shaking and mangling him. Black One suffered it for a few moments. Then, rousing himself with great effort, Black One gave a desperate jerk—and broke free, with half of his nose gone.

They backed off. They let fly another ear-splitting piercing challenge. Then, rampant, they flew at each other yet once again, throwing their whole weight into it. They hit. The ground shuddered under them. Dust puffed up. For a moment they hung balanced against each other. Then, slowly, Black One tottered over on his back. Dancing Sun pounced on him in a flash, stunning him with his sharp forefeet, cracking open his skull. Again and again Dancing Sun struck, cutting him to ribbons with his hammering hooves. With his teeth he stripped off Black One's ears, flung them across the prairie. He struck until Black One's brains began to run out.

Sure that Black One was dead at last, Dancing Sun suddenly set out after the other ambitious lovers, scattering them pell-mell, chasing them until they were out of sight.

When Dancing Sun came back, head high, he appeared to disdain the loving attention of his mares and colts.

During all this time, Leaf worked like a muskrat mother, preparing her nest. She made a cradle by weaving a flat platform out of willow withes and covering it with buckskin. She scraped and tanned hides for a small tepee to be used on the way home. She dried many cases of meat. She made her husband a dozen pair of tough moccasins. She also tanned him a new buffalo robe, a new pair of leggings, and a new fetish case.

For herself she made a dress, a loose supple piece of doeskin which she worked until it shone like fresh snow. She covered it with beautiful quillwork, blue and yellow and white and red. Even the lift strings, used to tie up the dress when the grass was wet with dew, were placed in pleasing symmetry all around the bottom. Every now and then she held up the dress against her body, smiling and tittering to herself, as if surrounded by a circle of admiring women friends.

Sometimes No Name caught her sitting silent by herself in the entrance of the cave, her black eyes on him but not seeing him, absorbed in herself. Her look caused him to recall what his mother had once remarked about pregnant women. "Before her child is born, a good Yankton mother always fixes her mind on a certain hero. This is done so that when the child grows up he will desire to do great things and become a great hero himself." He wondered if Leaf had him in mind, or her father Owl Above, or her brother Burnt Thigh. Though tempted, he dared not intrude upon her thoughts and ask her.

For some odd reason, another of his mother's warnings came to him, that a woman should not look too hard at an animal before her child was born. "There was once a woman," Star said, "who found a rabbit hiding in some wild plums. The rabbit was gentle and soft. She took it in her arms and petted it and held it close to her face. When her time came, her child was born with a split nose. This man is still alive." No Name hoped that some evil spirit had not placed the thought in his mind. They of the other world often knew beforehand what was to come to pass.

Eyes averted, yet studying Leaf closely, he soon came to see that he was one of those who had been fortunate in the choice of a wife. Leaf rarely complained about her lot in life. She accepted what came. She did not long for tomorrow that it should bring her some great and wondrous surprise. The great thing was now, it was happening now, and she lived it to the full. When she ate juicy broiled hump, she enjoyed the hump, fully, at that moment. When she sucked marrow from a warm bone, running her tongue deep into it, she lived in the tip of her tongue, for that moment. When she looked into the fire, she enjoyed the warmth and color and the mystery of the flames, fully, at that moment, then. When she crooned a hero song to herself for the coming boy, she lived in her throat, in the song, for the moment even becoming the hero.

One evening No Name came home to wife and cave bone-tired, exhausted, dispirited. He hardly noted that Leaf took off his moccasins and rubbed his feet as usual.

He got out his pipe. He lit up with a coal from the fire, much in the manner of his father. He blew up a big puff of smoke. It hit one of the broad leaves of the fallen cottonwood above, baffled around it, streamed up in finer wisps, and vanished.

He inclined his head to the left, still waiting, as he had waited all week, for his helper to speak to him.

Presently Leaf served him supper. He ate slowly, with little relish. When he finished his first helping of boiled meat, he turned his dish over to signify he no longer had hunger.

Leaf retreated into the shadows. She sat watching him.

Again he lighted his pipe. He brooded. This time the pipe had an unpleasant taste. And he finished his smoke only because it was bad luck not to do so.

"You have not told of today, my husband," Leaf said finally from the shadows.

A frown drew his brows together. He did not like it when she began the talk. "Nothing of importance happened today."

"When will you catch the stallion, my husband?"

He swallowed back a sharp word.

"My husband?"

"It is for the gods to decide."

"This cave is a dark place even in the day. Well, I am afraid for our child. The cave will cast a shadow over its life."

He put his pipe away. "Now you speak as one touched by the moon being." He sat staring at the graying embers along the edge of the fire.

She waited an interval, then said again, "You have not told of today, my husband."

Suddenly he said it all in a rush. "Today I saw Dancing Sun walk along the horizon. I became afraid. He walked, yet he looked like a ghost horse going very swiftly. He walked, yet his mares and colts had to run very swiftly to keep up with him. Ai, sometimes I think it is the same horse that Holy Horse saw. One day this white stallion will take me to the middle-of-the-earth too where the demons will overcome me and I will not be heard of again."

"What does your helper say?"

He started. How had she known it had fallen silent? "Ai, woman, I am still waiting for him to speak."

"Have you offended him that he does not speak?"

"I have thought of this. Yet I can not remember anything."

Again, after a silence, she asked, "My husband, this Dancing Sun, is he as all male horses?"

"I do not understand, my wife."

"Does he torment his sons?"

He fell silent. After a moment he shuddered. He remembered what Dancing Sun had done to the slow brown stud.

Leaf persisted. "What do the mothers say to this?"

"They submit," he said shortly.

She sighed. "Ae, so it is with the Yanktons also. The fathers permit us to hold the sons for a short time. After that they take them away and send them to a high hill where they must seek a vision."

"I love my father very much and do not wish to hurt him. He has always been very tender with me his son."

"Thus it seems," she said quietly, eyes downcast, hand

on her swollen belly. "Yet did not your father require that you torment yourself?"

"My father wished for me to show my bravery that I might be ready to replace him as chief when the time came for him to join those of the other world."

"A mother's heart is always large for her son. She will always weep when it is time for him to leave on his trail."

"It is not the way of all Yankton mothers," he said patiently. "My mother told me a great thing when I was about to depart. 'Son, the thing you seek lives in a far place. It is good. Go to it. Do not turn around after you have gone part way, but go as far as you were going and then come back.'"

Leaf sighed from the depths of her belly. Her breasts stirred under her leather dress. At last she said, "When I am old, may it be given me to say such a great thing to my son."


He had been careful to keep their horses, the sorrel gelding and the dun mare, well hidden from the white stallion, either in the brush under the cottonwoods when the wind was north, or in the back of the cave when it was south.

But one evening the white stallion surprised him by coming along to the meadow just west of the cliff. The white stallion walked out to where a patch of blue-eyed grass grew deep and lush. After sniffing around at it some, the white one began eating with relish.

"Haho!" No Name exclaimed softly to himself, watching from behind a thick cottonwood. "It is as Sounds The Ground said. He likes to go into the low places and eat the flowering grass. I well remember him saying this."

No Name stole softly out of the brush to get the mare and the sorrel before Dancing Sun got wind of them. The mare, whom they had named Black Stripe because of a thin band of dark hair running down her spine, was in heat. She stalled frequently. Dancing Sun was certain to scent her before very long and come and steal her.

But as luck would have it, the wind changed before he could get Black Stripe into the cave, and in a few moments

Dancing Sun's shrill inquiring neigh cut through the evening silence. No Name tried to hurry the mare inside, but the stallion's call had roused her and she hung back on the rope.

Dancing Sun shrilled another high piercing call of desire. This time Black Stripe let up on the rope long enough to whinny loudly in answer.

There was a sudden crashing in the brush and the next moment the green leaves parted and out paced Dancing Sun, noble head high, long mane flowing in two scarlet waves. He came on swiftly, smoothly.

He spotted No Name pulling at the rawhide rope. Instantly his whole demeanor as a lover changed. He became the warrior. His head came down, his teeth flashed, his ears shot forward. His tail pointed straight back like a cat's, jerking spasmodically. Then, with a resounding snort, he made straight for No Name as if he no longer saw the mare, but saw only the man.

No Name dropped the mare's rope and leaped to one side just as Dancing Sun, dazzling and white and huge, lunged for him. Dancing Sun missed him by no more than a hair.

Then, as Dancing Sun stopped short to wheel around for another charge, No Name, on a sudden impulse, born as much out of fear as out of inspiration, leaped astride the great stallion's back. No Name grabbed hold of the flashing scarlet mane with both hands, gripped the horse's belly hard with both legs.

Dancing Sun reacted volcanically. He went straight up on all fours. No Name felt him rising under him like a wave on the Great Smoky Water. At the top of his jump, Dancing Sun broke four ways, and when he came down, as each leg hit ground one after another, there were four separate jolts. Then, shrieking outrage at finding something still latched to his back, Dancing Sun began a strange twisting run on the meadow. No Name felt the great muscles of the horse squirming and bulging and undulating powerfully under him. It was like riding an enormous snake which had just had its head chopped off.

Dancing Sun stopped dead. He seemed to reflect to himself a moment. Then, snorting, he turned his head and snapped at No Name. His face was so close, No Name could see red inflamed arteries pulsing furiously in the backs of his blazing eyes. No Name ducked to one side to avoid the terrible snapping teeth. Again Dancing Sun rose wonderfully under him, very high. And at the top of the jump, because of the awkward way he sat on the stallion, No Name lost his hold. He arched into the air in a tumbling somersault and landed on his back.

It took a moment for No Name to collect his wits. Then he sprang to his feet, fully expecting to find the mad stallion on top of him. But to his surprise, the stallion did not come on. The stallion was still snorting and shrilling with rage, but he was being held at bay by Leaf. Leaf had fire and smoke in her hand and was waving it in the stallion's face.

No Name stared. Then he understood. Leaf had heard, then seen, the stallion come for the mare Black Stripe too. When No Name dropped the lead rope, Leaf had quickly secured the mare with the gelding, who was already in the cave, and then seized a burning brand from the fire and had rushed out to help her man. Instinctively she had known what to do. Fight fire with fire. In the rust-tinted dusk the smoke from the burning brand was almost exactly the color of the stallion's coat.

No Name saw how Leaf strained to be quick despite her heavy oblong belly, saw how ferocious her eyes were. He leaped to help her and took the burning brand from her.

Dancing Sun seemed to understand that the hot brand had changed hands, from female to male, and once again charged, mouth and head down like a raging predator lizard. No Name thrust the burning brand into his face. Dancing Sun shrieked, reared, struck out with both forefeet, almost knocking the brand from No Name's hand.

Again Dancing Sun charged. Again No Name jabbed the brand into his face.

The furious action roused No Name, and fear in him changed to anger. He too suddenly became enraged, completely forgetting that he had ever thought the horse wakan.

He began to roar. "Back, you white devil! Hehan, so you wish to make my heart hot this day? Good, eat this! Fire you are and fire you shall have!"

Behind him Leaf had become infuriated too. "Kill him, my husband!" she cried. "Burn his eyes! Do not be afraid. Rush him, he is afraid of fire!"

Still the white fury came on. Dancing Sun reared and struck out at them with his glittering gray hooves. He whistled piercingly.

Then, from behind No Name and Leaf, the mare Black Stripe in the back of the cave whinnied, high, wonderingly.

The stallion seemed to go blind at that. He drove so fiercely at No Name and Leaf that both had to retreat under the fallen cottonwood. Teeth bared, froth flying in flakes, Dancing Sun made a final snap at No Name. He caught the burning brand with the side of his mouth and knocked it sailing into the stream at their feet. The brand went out with a quick whistling sizzle.

No Name jumped back, so hard, he knocked himself and Leaf backwards into the cave, falling past the embers of the fire in the entrance. No Name was sure the stallion, gone crazy, was coming into the cave with them.

There was a loud cry behind them, and suddenly the mare in the dark back of the cave lunged and tore loose her rope and made a break for it. She shot past them both, rawhide rope trailing for a second through the fire, and joined the stallion outside.

The stallion reared, suddenly whickered in a very low guttural voice, and then, the fierce heat of desire coming over him again, forgot about the man enemy and his wife. With a great frolicsome leap, and a snort, he ran off with the mare into the dusk over the meadow.

The next afternoon, sitting high in his lookout cottonwood on the north side of the river, No Name watched the horses come down to drink again. The white one and his sister sentinels stood guard as usual on the bluffs.

He spotted the dun mare Black Stripe with the first bunch, submissive, no different from the other wild ones except for what was left of her lead rope trailing in the dust. Dancing Sun paid her no more attention when she went past than he did any of the other mares.

Later, when the second bunch came down, No Name once more saw Dancing Sun run over and nip his favorite, the light-gray mare with the twinkling feet, in love and play. She was leading the second bunch with slow heavy dignity and as before accepted his show of affection placidly.

It was while he was looking at the pregnant mare, and also thinking of his heavy Leaf, that his helper finally told him something. "Take the sorrel gelding and ride slowly after the light-gray mare with the twinkling feet. Go mostly at a walking pace. Twinkling Feet cannot run very fast very long. Pretend to chase no one but her, not the white one. The white one loves Twinkling Feet and will always stay near her. Keep chasing her. The stallion will give the commands to the old buckskin his mother where they are to go. He will keep them circling and have them come back to this watering place. When they return to this place, do not let him or the mares drink, but keep them moving. Chase him until he is very thirsty and very tired. Even four days and four nights. Otherwise he will kill you. After he is very tired, make a loop in your rope and throw it and catch him."

No Name thought to himself, "Four days and four nights without sleep? That is a very long time. Well, I must be brave. The time has come for me to be valiant."

That night he made himself a short heavy whip from a leg bone and some extra thick bullhide. He added a thin piece of buckskin at the tip for the popper. The white one would never again catch him unarmed.

# 7

In the morning he told her.

"Today it begins. Listen carefully. The stallion drives his band slowly because the one he loves will soon have a colt. I will trail after them on our sorrel. Because of the one he loves, he will not run very far ahead of me. Well, after a time he will get used to me. Then it will be given me how to catch him."

"But, my husband—"

"Woman, listen carefully. Each day he will try to come to his watering place under the bluffs. But I will not let him. I will chase him on. After he has gone by, I will come quickly to water the sorrel. Woman, have a parfleche of food and a heartskin of fresh water ready for me at that time. I will eat and drink quickly and then go on."

"But, my husband—"

"Today it begins."

"My husband, I am afraid. My time is very near. Perhaps I cannot always have the food ready."

"The birth of our son must wait. The fulfillment of the vision comes first." His black eyes glittered.

She bowed her head. Her hands strayed over her belly. "I hear you, my husband."

"Haho! In four days I will return in triumph with a painted face."

"I will wait."

"Hang the provisions each day in a certain tree that I will show you. Do it before the stallion comes. Do not try to meet me. The stallion will get used to my smell after a time and accept it. But the smell of another will scare him off. Do as I command and it will go well with us. This I know."

"I hear you, my husband."

He ate heartily and drank long and deep. He readied his lariat, his whip, his war bridle with its long rein, his parfleche of dried meat, and his new white buffalo robe. He filled a heartskin with fresh water from their stream. He placed a skin pad stuffed with hair on the sorrel for a saddle. He showed Leaf the tree, a green cedar growing on the near side of the west bluff, where he wanted her to hang fresh provisions each day. He gathered driftwood from the river and piled it on the horse trail where it emerged out of the ravine on top of the bluffs. He scattered sacrificial pinches of tobacco along the trail in the ravine and across the tops of the bluffs. Then, ready, he waited on the middle bluff, sitting on the hard ground, holding the long rein of his sorrel in hand as it grazed.

It was well past noon before he saw them coming. He waited until he could make out individual horses, then went over and set fire to a pile of driftwood. Soon white smoke rose in a high billowing plume, straight up, like an enormous ghost tree. The fire made such a crackling noise he had trouble keeping the sorrel quiet. He jumped on his horse and waited in the shadow of the cedar tree, whip dangling from his wrist. He watched the band come on.

Presently Dancing Sun came pacing from behind, where he usually ran, and took over the lead from the old buckskin mare. Dancing Sun called up his white sister sentinels. It was only then, as he wheeled them all for the bluffs, that he spotted the bonfire and its high floating plume of smoke. He let go a warning snort. Instantly the band stopped dead in its tracks. All stood with raised heads, ears shot forward, wild and roused, looking more like alert deer than horses. Dancing Sun whistled again and they quickly bunched into a tight knot. He approached alone. He came up to within a hundred yards of the fire before he saw No Name on his sorrel under the green cedar. Again Dancing Sun trumpeted a command. The knot of mares and colts tightened even more. Dancing Sun looked from the fire to No Name and back again. He moved around to his left, then around to his right, trying to get No Name's scent. But the wind was northeast and he couldn't quite get around far enough to pick it up. He snuffed. He clapped his tail in irritation. He stamped. The band behind waited in a close profusion of raised heads and whistling tails.

No Name watched him. He sang a song of self-encouragement in a low private voice:

> "Friend, you are like the sun.
> You are a begetter of many fine children.
> The white mare said you would be fierce.
> Friend, a Yankton has come to get you.
> Friend, it has been said. Epelo."

Then, strong in the knowledge that the gods had nothing but good in mind for him, No Name touched heel to flank and he and the sorrel moved out of the shadow of the green cedar.

Dancing Sun snorted. Haughty head up, snuffing loudly, he ran forward a few steps. He sniffed. He pawed the earth like a bull. He took a few more steps. Then, at last getting wind of the man enemy's scent, with a scream of rage, he charged.

No Name waited until Dancing Sun was almost on top of him, until the sorrel under him tried to double away, then suddenly he sat up very straight and with a quick hard sweep of his arm snapped his new whip in the stallion's face. The buckskin popper at the end cracked, loud, directly in front of the stallion's eyes. Astonished, Dancing Sun skated to a stop on all four legs. He reared, staggered backwards. Then, before Dancing Sun could collect himself, No Name raised his big white robe and snapped it vigorously around and around, yelling "Oh-ow-ow-ow!" at the top of his voice. He dug his heels hard into the sorrel's flanks, forcing him toward the stallion. The sorrel bucked, again tried to shy off. No Name brought his whip hard across the sorrel's flanks, both sides, again reined him toward the stallion. Dancing Sun staggered back some more. Then of a sudden, abruptly, he spooked. He raced off toward his band. With a blood-curdling yell, No Name followed them.

Dancing Sun bugled piercingly. Instantly the whole bunch ahead of him wheeled and broke into a wild thundering run, stampeding west. Up front, galloping as wild as the wildest of them, ran Black Stripe, Leaf's dun mare, her dragging line raising a little snake of racing yellow dust.

No Name went after them furiously for a short way, still howling, still snapping his white robe around and around. The white one and his bunch and their following dust were soon out of sight. No Name reined in his sorrel and let them run, content to go along at a slower pace, certain that the stallion would not let Twinkling Feet run very far.

No Name found it easy to track the bunch. Dancing Sun ran his band from the rear, and as a pacer, not as a galloper, left a characteristic track that was always easy to pick out. No Name followed the fresh tracks for an hour, then headed his horse almost straight south, quartering across the stallion's run.

He rode naked except for a clout. The sun sank down a brassy sky. In its raw light his body glowed a blackish brown. The air on the high barrens was so dry it made the nostrils crack. To keep breathing he sometimes had to lick the inside of his mouth. The sorrel's hooves kicked up minute dust storms. The little puffs of light-gray lingered in the air behind them for a long time. Every now and then he checked to see that the long rein of his war bridle was securely tucked in folds under his belt. He had long ago learned that, somehow thrown from his horse, he could always catch hold of the rope as it payed out along the ground. On the prairies a man was no man at all unless he had four feet.

He saw the horses again just as the sun set, far to the south, circling out of the west. They were grazing quietly along. He had cut across at exactly the right angle, and thus had saved his sorrel miles of running. He reined in. He let the sorrel graze quietly toward them. He guided him toward the pregnant Twinkling Feet.

After a while Dancing Sun saw them. He came racing

up, snorting a challenge, then checked himself as if remembering the buckskin popper. He wheeled, and with a single high whistle set his band in motion, this time at a good walking pace.

No Name smiled. He urged the sorrel up and followed them.

The sun set. A coppery light slowly suffused all things, the sparse grass, the prickly pear cactus, the occasional tufts of gray-green bunchgrass. The grazing wild horses with their prevailing cream colors resembled rolling balls of pounded copper. The brassy sky changed to gold, then to gold and purple, at last to purple and pink. There was no wind. Raised dust, after hovering a while, fell back into place again.

The moon rose before dark. It came up round and full, a globe mallow, flowering huge and orange out of the horizon. It came up turning, and for a little time it seemed to be rolling toward them. Dancing Sun wondered about its strange rising too, and challenged it with a sharp rolling snort. Then gradually the great globe mallow parted from its stalk, floating free of the earth, and became the moon proper.

No Name pushed the band along at a steady gait. The band sometimes trotted, sometimes galloped, while he kept his sorrel to a good walk. He quartered across the stallion's run at every opportunity. Dancing Sun hated the pushing and often bugled his displeasure. His snorts kept the bunch in a jittery state. Every now and then his imperious neighs sent them dashing ahead, going hard, with thundering sound.

"Are you angry, great white one? I am happy. It is good. You are twice the horse that my sorrel is. Therefore I want you to cover twice the ground. We will tire together. Perhaps after that I will get off and walk. I will be fresh, you will be tired."

The moon lifted. It became smaller, became silver. It cast a smoky ghostly light over the dry barrens. Dust became yellow smoke. The occasional tufts of bunchgrass resembled the gray feelers of a catfish. The white stallion became a silver stallion. His scarlet tail became a pink tail.

After one of their spurts ahead, No Name found the bunch standing in sleep. Even the white one slept. In the silver night they reminded No Name of immobile snow-men.

No Name became sly. He readied his lariat, setting the loop, tying one end to the belly band of his pad saddle. He gave his horse the heel.

One of the white sisters on the flank awoke. She looked around, saw them, whistled sharply in warning. Dancing Sun awoke with a jump. He too looked around, then trumpeted loudly. He gave his head a certain shake to one side and sent his mares and colts crashing away in the soft delicate night.

No Name rewound his lariat. "Wise white ones, I will wait until you are very tired and very thirsty. Also I shall try to keep you from some of your sleep. It will be the worry and loss of sleep that will make you mine."

Horses, both tame and wild, usually napped three times a night: shortly after sunset, at midnight, and just before dawn. The final nap was the soundest, the most refreshing. No Name decided that he might let them have one of the earlier naps, if it meant he himself could get some sleep, but he would never let them have that last nap.

They moved on, gradually circling around to the east, then to the northeast. Dancing Sun ran behind his bunch, keeping himself between them and the man enemy. The old buckskin mother and the two white sisters remained alert to his every command. If he lifted his head higher than usual, they hurried the band along. If he lowered it, they slowed the horses down. If he ran sideways, head to the left, they turned the bunch to the left. If he ran with his head to the right, they turned the bunch right. Occasionally one or another of the mares or colts would drop out of place, on the right, or left, or behind, and Dancing Sun would promptly move up, showing his teeth, bugling, to put them back in place. Occasionally too he would run beside his favorite,

Twinkling Feet, and nip her in love, and seem to whisper to her that all was well.

A high white haze began to move across the moon. Soon a bluish circle appeared around it. Later the same kind of haze, a mist, began to slide across the land close to the ground.

No Name nodded. He slept. He awoke. With a start, looking, he saw them still ahead. "Ae, my sorrel has learned the game and now follows them without instruction." He petted his sorrel over the withers. "Friend, you are my helper. After we have caught him, I will take you to my father's meadow beside Falling Water where the grass grows very sweet. I will give you a long rest in reward. I give you the Name of One Who Follows."

He nodded. He slept. He awoke. And waking, he saw them all as white shadows, white silences, of the other world. Both he and his sorrel and the white one and his bunch were spirit ghosts. They were all gods together in the night. They had now no need of either life or death. They had need now only of song, of vision, of long white wings.

They drifted on. The bluish mist thickened. He slept again.

Waking, he saw a strange thing. Objects were continually changing before his very eyes. Sometimes Dancing Sun and his band stalked along as tall as a grove of rustling trees. Sometimes they slid along the ground as lowly as a family of mud turtles. Sometimes they walked above the blue mist. Sometimes they walked under it. When the land dipped and the mist lifted a few feet he could see nothing but horse legs, many legs, like walking birches. When the land raised he could see nothing but flowing manes and alert ears. The horses seemed to be swimming across a lake of milk.

He slept. And waking, he saw that the horses had vanished.

Well, he did not care. The night was wakan and he was very tired. Besides, he now trusted One Who Follows.

He slept. And waking, he saw that the horses had reappeared. He smiled. He had known One Who Follows would never lose them. One Who Follows was a wise one and would keep quartering after them.

Two hours before dawn, he suddenly felt rested and wide awake.

"Ha-ho!" he said aloud. "It is good. It is as I planned. And now I must make sure that Dancing Sun and his band do not rest. I will keep them snorty, even a little wild, during their best hour of sleep."

He pushed them hard. After an hour of it, Dancing Sun turned and came snarling at him. The horse resented being kept from his golden nap time.

No Name rose against him. He kicked up his sorrel and went after him in cool fury, cracking his buckskin popper in the stallion's broad white face to remind him that man enemy now had the overhand.

Of a sudden, almost between steps, the moon vanished behind a silky web in the west. Then, the next moment, the sun was up. The sun came up as red as a blood clot from a slain buffalo's lungs. It swelled, became huge. It too seemed to roll straight for them for a time. Then, rising, oscillating, it ascended the skies.

No Name opened his parfleche and gawed on some dried meat as he jogged along. He washed the meat down with a drink from his heartskin. He also gave his faithful sorrel a drink.

A light wind drifted in from the southeast, touching him on the right cheek. The wind had in it the smell of a robe freshly washed in rain water. Both horse and man snuffed it in pleasure.

No Name studied the western sky. A blue haze hugging the horizon made him wonder if rain was on the way. "Helper, it is not rain we want. Tell it to stay beyond the river. We wish to keep the ground hard and thus give the horses sore feet. Also, a rain will fill the little hollows with water and give the wild ones to drink."

He kept them going, cutting across the inside of the stallion's run, sometimes walking.

At mid-forenoon, Twinkling Feet the pregnant mare began to lag behind. Dancing Sun spotted it. Tail glowing like a down-flowing flame, he ran up and inquired with a wondering whinny. When she didn't respond, he urged her up. Still she lagged. Finally, half in love, half in anger, he nipped her at the root of her tail. She turned heavily and snapped at him. He snorted, then nipped her again, this time hard. At last she gathered her huge belly into a rolling trot and rejoined the bunch, taking her place in the center again with the jolting yearlings.

At noon, hot, the earth shimmering under a white glaring light, No Name happened to throw a look up at the sun. As he did so, one of the rays of the sun broke away and became a winged one. Astounded, No Name watched it slowly form into the shape of a hawk.

"Ai!" he whispered, "the sun is sending a messenger. He wishes to tell me something. I will watch the shape closely to see where it will fly."

Slowly, silently, in ever larger ovals, like a maple leaf drifting down, the hawk settled toward him. Presently No Name could see its rust-red tail, then make out the ribs in the individual feathers of its wavering wings. Its claws worked spasmodically. Its eyes blinked down at him. At last it opened its beak and cried, "Kee-er-r-r!"

No Name looked up in awe. "Take care? Will the fierce white one attack me again?"

"Kee-er-r-r!"

Then the hawk, dipping its wings, lifted up, up, finally blended off into the sun, becoming one of its rays again.

He leaned forward and whispered in the hairy earhole of his horse One Who Follows. "Something is coming. Get ready."

One Who Follows twitched his ear, then shook his head, trying to get rid of the tickling words.

"I am ready," No Name said. "My helper is near me." He placed his hand over the charm hidden in his braid. "It is good to know the gods approve and are willing to warn me."

Out of the shimmering heat waves along the northeast

horizon a faint line gradually appeared. No Name stared at it a while, then recognized it as the valley of the River of Little Ducks. Presently the tops of the cottonwoods began to show. The stallion's watering place was at hand.

Just as he was beginning to wonder how he should spook the wild ones past the place, Black Stripe the dun mare accidentally helped him out. Tiring the last while, she had taken to jogging along at the rear. All of a sudden her lead rope, still trailing from her neck, got caught on the stump of an old wolfberry bush. It tightened, stretched, abruptly hauled her up short. She reared. There was a loud snap and the rawhide broke, with what was left of it coiling up and lashing after her. The snakelike lashing of the rope scared her. She bolted. The faster she ran the faster the trailing rope raced after her. With a scream of terror she charged straight through the bunch, scattering them in all directions.

Dancing Sun was instantly on the job. Trumpeting loudly, he raced back and forth, up one side and down the other, trying to turn them into a compact unit again. By hard running, and vicious biting, he did manage to get them bunched. But not until they had all run well past the watering place. They headed west, starting around the circle a second time.

No Name waited until they were almost out of sight, then turned his sorrel for the cedar tree on the near side of the first bluff. He found the provisions hanging from a limb just as he had ordered, with Leaf herself nowhere in sight. Using some big leaves from wild hemp as gloves, he transferred the dried meat and fresh spring water to his own parfleche and heartskin, very carefully so as not to pick up her scent.

He headed his sorrel for the river. One Who Follows instantly picked up his head and trotted down the trail between the two bluffs. One Who Follows was so happy at seeing the water again he ran halfway into the river and stuck his head under all the way to the eyes. In his eagerness to drink he almost drowned himself.

No Name laughed. "My brother, you behave like a foolish colt." No Name removed his moccasins and slid off into the water, stumbling stiff. He gave the bridle a jerk and held the sorrel's head out of the water for a few moments. "Friend, patience. Drink little by little or we will never catch the white one."

One Who Follows nuzzled against No Name's belly as if he understood, then lowered his head again and drank slowly and steadily. Soft swallows chased up the underside of his neck one after another. The hollow between his belly and hips slowly filled out again.

No Name was overjoyed at seeing the water too. He bathed his limbs, he splashed his chest, he refreshed his face and neck. He drank long and deep from the ocher waters.

The sun was almost down when he picked up the trail on the barrens again. The white one and his band were completely out of sight, even their dust. No Name set his course straight south, knowing for certain this time that he would run into them again on the far side of the circle.

Long after the round red ball of the sun had halved itself out of sight, a glory of scarlets and golds continued to reach far across the skies. The colors suffused the land, transforming it into a vast plain of rich reddish earth covered by golden grass. The sorrel became a red-gold horse and he himself a red-gold god. For a little while he forgot his quest, and where he was, and where Leaf might be. The scarlet and gold flowed into him and he conceived himself as having a scarlet soul and golden blood. Later, in turn, the moon rose out of the east. In the gradually thickening haze, it came up a deep red, almost like a morning sun. It remained red until halfway up the heavens, then slowly turned into a flying yellow pumpkin.

"The sun is my father. He shines upon me. The moon is my mother. She shines upon me. I am strong when they look upon me in love. I am happy. Hoppo! May this continue for the rest of my life. The earth hears me."

He let the sorrel take its own gait. Hoofbeats falling into the soft dust were the only sounds in the dreamy yellow light. He hooked his foot under the belly band. He looked heavy-eyed at the flat and endless world for a while. Then gradually he drifted off, rocked to sleep by the swaying walk of the sorrel. He dreamed of a white sun with a scarlet mane.

A terrible squealing awoke him. He came to with a start, one hand instinctively seeking his bow and the other an arrow over his shoulder. Directly in front of him, rampant, teeth flashing, stood Dancing Sun. Behind the stallion stood his mares and colts, alert, in the posture of the hunted, ears shot forward. For a moment No Name could not understand it. Hair raised on his scalp. "Is this a nightmare, my helper?" Then the sorrel under him shied, almost unseating him, jerking the leg he had caught under the belly band. "Ai, it is a true thing. Also I have hit upon them again as I planned. But I have done so in my sleep. Well, that Dancing Sun was a smart one to see that his enemy was off guard."

No Name let go his bow, instead grabbed for his bone-handled whip. He swung with all his might. This time, instead of cracking loudly, the buckskin popper hit flesh, cutting the white one over the nostrils. Dancing Sun screamed. He reared higher; struck. His flashing hoof hit the sorrel a glancing blow high on the withers, just missing No Name's thigh. Then No Name raised in wrath himself. Again he lashed out, this time with redoubled might. His whip caught the stallion squarely across the broad forehead, cutting him over the eyes.

Dancing Sun wheeled. Bugling, falling into his ceaseless swinging pace again, he sent his bunch roaring away, their manes flying, tails popping, dust following in a high slow-moving cloud.

No Name watched them go, curving off to the east. He set his course accordingly. He hooked his foot under the belly band again and relaxed.

He slept. He dreamed. He was in a canoe riding across choppy waves. He dreamed a second time. A hawk swooped down to lift him from his horse. He dreamed a third time. His father Redbird came to take a red bull-baby away from Leaf.

Near dawn he awoke. Ahead of him walked the bunch.

"My brother," he said to One Who Follows, "twice now you have followed them while I slept. When we return to Falling Water, I shall give you a year without labor on its sweetest meadows."

He ate a little of the dried meat. He refreshed both the sorrel and himself with spring water.

The sun came up an ugly red, resembling a buffalo cow that had not cleaned well after a birthing.

He rubbed dust out of his eyes with a knuckle. He examined the band ahead. It seemed to him they somehow looked different. Most of them hoofed it along dead tired. Somehow too there did not seem to be as many. He counted them. "Ho! a third is missing." He turned sideways in his saddle and looked back. There, against the red horizon, stood some twenty horses, heads down, exhausted, motionless. All would soon be wolf bait.

"They lack the water. Soon even the strongest will drop out. Then it will be given me what to do."

It came to him then, like a blow on the head, as he studied the bunch in front of him, that Dancing Sun was not among them. Twinkling Feet the light-gray mare heavy with young was still there but not the white one. Then he understood why the horses had been drifting along in such a hangdog manner. Dancing Sun was not there to keep them bunched up and on the alert.

Again he turned sideways in his saddle and looked back. He could see those that had dropped out clearly against the horizon, head down, motionless. Some were mares, some were colts. But Dancing Sun was not among them.

"Horse," he cried down at One Who Follows, "what have you done? I trusted you to follow him while I slept. Yet now I awake and find him gone."

The sorrel under him stopped dead, as if in disgust, and began to crop at dry spears of buffalo grass. One Who Follows did not even bother to flick his ears at the words.

No Name's eyes filled with wonder. Was One Who Follows trying to tell him a thing? No Name looked at the grass underfoot. He could not imagine a horse enjoying it, much less eat it. It was thin, as sparse as the solitary hairs on an old dog's nose.

His eye happened to catch sight of some fresh droppings. He saw immediately they were hard and dry, not shiny and ripe as they usually were when a horse had enough to drink. Ha-ho, the hard droppings meant the band was about dried out.

The dry droppings next reminded him that Dancing Sun had his own private places for dunging, four of them, marking the corners of his empire. No Name remembered that one of these corners was nearby, beside a deep washout. He turned his sorrel toward it. To his surprise, the sorrel readily gave up his grazing.

They were almost within sight of the curious pyramids of dung, when of a sudden from behind them came a rolling snort and then the furious oncoming beat of horse hooves. No Name jerked viciously on the reins, wheeling his horse around.

It was the white one, just emerged from a yellow ravine, head held low like a rabid lobo wolf, teeth flashing. He came straight for them.

No Name grabbed his heavy whip, sat high on his horse. When Dancing Sun's head came up below him, he lashed down at him with all his force. Dancing Sun took the blow across his ears just as his teeth sank into the skin over No Name's thigh. Dancing Sun gave a vicious rip and a small slab of flesh came away. No Name was too startled to scream. There was no pain. Only a sudden numbness shot all up and down his leg.

Dancing Sun reared directly in front of him, looming over him. Holding the bloody tatter of skin and flesh between his teeth, snarling, Dancing Sun shook his head, snapping it back and forth like a dog trying to shred a grass doll to pieces.

"Friend," No Name cried, "it is very plain you will breed wakan warhorses. The enemy arrow will never touch them. Friend, you are a great horse. Become my friend. I have said."

Dancing Sun still shook his head like a mad dog. He

waggled his head so hard back and forth the flap of flesh at last flew out of his mouth and sailed across the dry land, landing in a patch of prickly pear. Then, still rearing, whirling completely around on two dancing legs, Dancing Sun jumped away. He raced across the plains, tail flowing, head up, looking this way and that.

No Name followed him slowly. He bathed his oozing wound with spring water from the heartskin. He bound it with a piece of rawhide. "Friend," he said, shooting the words after the white one with a pursing of lips, "friend, at last you have tasted the blood of a Yankton warrior. Do you like it? Well, there is much more. Be careful that a Yankton does not taste your blood. I have said."

Dancing Sun flew at his band. With a single loud trumpeting snort, ears laid back, shaking his head vigorously at the old buckskin mare up in the lead and the white sisters on the flanks, he sent them beating across the barrens once more.

There was no wind. The dust they raised lofted high into the blue-gray haze. No Name rode first on one side of his buttocks, then the other.

It was Leaf who spooked them when they approached the watering place the next time. She was standing under the cedar tree. The lead buckskin mare got a whiff of her, shied, popped her tail, and before Dancing Sun could stop them the bunch was off and running.

No Name watched them go, smiling grimly. Yet he could not refrain from scolding Leaf when he rode up to her. "Well, I see now I have a wife who disobeys."

Leaf looked meekly down at her hands. She was trembling. "I heard coughing in the night, my husband."

"Ai-ye!"

"Perhaps it was Rough Arm and his killers."

No Name was instantly all eyes and ears. He flicked a swift fierce look to all sides. "What was the cough, one that could not be helped? Or one done in warning to say that a stranger approached?"

"I was sleeping, my husband, and did not hear it clearly. Yet I heard it."

No Name looked down at her. He recalled that a woman heavy with young often imagined strange things the last days. He decided to indulge her. "Woman, you were wise to come and tell me. After I have given the horse some water and grass, I will look for sign. Return quietly. If I find they have been here, I will come to help you hide in some other place. Otherwise I will go on. The white one is tiring."

"How soon will it be?"

"I can not tell. It has not been given me when to catch him. Have patience. Great things come slowly and after much bravery. I have said."

She saw the bloody bandage on his thigh. "Ai, he has bitten you. He will kill you." She came up to touch him.

He kicked the sorrel in the flank, making it shy away from her. "Woman, have I not told you not to touch me? Go back. The white one knows my smell and has become used to it. If I come with yet another smell he will not let me come close. Return to the cave."

"It will end sadly," she said in a low voice. "Already the wild one has taken a bite from my husband."

"Return, woman."

"The cave is dark, my husband. The place where you sleep is cold. In the night I hear spirit ghosts. The Old Ones who lived in the cave in the old days come and wake me. I am very lonesome."

He pretended not to hear her. He looked at the fresh provisions hanging in the cedar. He noticed she had hung up a new shirt beside them. "Woman," he cried angrily, "have I not told you I cannot even change clothes or he will take fright at the new smell and run away to some other range? I do not wish to begin the circling all over again. Take it with you."

She hid her face. Then she began to cry. Turning heavily, she pulled the new shirt from the tree and started for their cave.

He watched her walk down the face of the bluff, going

with heavy falling step, her back stiff, her small buttocks taut, her swollen belly swinging from side to side in front.

Dark face stern, he turned his back on her. He moved the fresh provisions to his own parfleche and heartskin, then rode down to the river to refresh his horse and wash his wound.

He found Dancing Sun just before dusk. The white one and what was left of his bunch, some thirty head, plus the gravid light-gray mare, had given up grazing and instead were slowly dozing along. Only the stallion still showed grace in his carriage.

The sky hazed over. The haze became so thick the sun vanished before it set. At last a bad thing was on the way. Rain.

Then, just after dark, he saw it, a low line of smoldering lights all along the northwest horizon. It resembled an advancing enemy carrying torches. He stopped his horse and watched it with narrowed eyes.

Finally he made it out. Fire, prairie fire. Ai-ye! so that was what the sun hawk had tried to warn him about. Leaf was perhaps right that Rough Arm had been skulking along their river. Rough Arm, to get revenge, had fired the prairie grass. Rough Arm hoped to spoil his vision of catching the great white stallion. Luckily there was but little wind. It would be a while yet before it overran them.

Dancing Sun also spotted the prairie fire. With a single snort he rounded up the remnant of his band and bunched them into a tight waiting knot, then ran a short distance toward the advancing line of flames, nostrils fluttering loudly, trying to get scent of it. He ran close to where No Name sat on his horse, for the moment ignoring his man enemy.

The fire came on. As it advanced it also slowly spread toward the north.

"Rough Arm has fired the grass all along the River of Little Ducks. He has cut off our retreat. He knows there is no water at all to the south."

As No Name and Dancing Sun watched, a puff of wind,

hot and dry, hit them. Then another wafted past, stronger, drier. Again, another. Finally a gale of hot wind began to blow past them.

"Now an evil god is helping Rough Arm. He has sent him a strong wind. The grass is short and thin. Yet it burns as if it were tall and thick. Even the earth is burning."

Dancing Sun abruptly wheeled. He bugled piercingly. He gave a certain vigorous waggling motion of his head and faced his bunch around into the fierce wind.

Then No Name saw a thing that made him marvel. The stallion whistled again and all his mares and colts began to trot straight for the advancing ring of fire. Hehan! What a great chief the stallion was. Such control of the spirit souls of others was of the gods, was wakan.

Yet even so the mares, especially the gravid light-gray one, showed reluctance to buck the fire. They held their heads sideways as they advanced. Some tried to shy off to the left, others tried to dodge around to the right, but Dancing Sun was always there with fierce teeth, his blunt chest, his striking flashing forefeet, to force them back into place. And as always, swift feet flickering, he glided smoothly along.

"Will he never tire, my helper?"

But Dancing Sun had not reckoned with other wild creatures. Suddenly the barrens were full of streaking four-leggeds, yowling wolves and coyotes, bounding deer and jackrabbits; of flying wingeds, numbed meadowlarks and owls, dumbfounded ducks and quail. Dancing Sun screamed, and wheeled, trying desperately to keep his mares and colts from being stampeded by the terrorized creatures. But finally another band of wild horses, led by a roan stallion, came pounding by, tails and manes whipping like the flames of the prairie fire itself, and he lost control. What had been dead-tired dozing laggards were now suddenly breakneck racers.

Dancing Sun shook his great mane with a final shrug of despair, and let them all go. But one. That one was his favorite, Twinkling Feet. He ran along beside the light-gray gravid mare neighing winningly, commandingly. She wanted desperately to fly along with the rest, but he kept bearing in on her, turned her each time she dodged, nipping her, biting her, bumping her first on one side, then on the other. And finally she gave in. Nose down, she turned and headed into the advancing fire with him.

By that time the wind was howling around No Name and his sorrel. Smoke wafted toward them in enormous streams of gray. No Name coughed. One Who Follows coughed. So did Dancing Sun and his mate immediately up front. The whole sky ahead and the earth beneath raged with mounting manes of fire. No Name found it difficult to make out Dancing Sun and his mare against the flames. They seemed to have become orange flames themselves, dancing, snapping, rushing. In the weird snapping hellish light, No Name's face glowed a stone red, while the sorrel's coat glowed a clay yellow. Heat surged toward them in jumps. The air became so searing hot No Name had to cover his mouth to breathe.

A burning rabbit bounded toward them. With every leap it started up a new little fire. It ran crazed. It screamed. It ran veering from right to left to right. Finally, blind, it circled back into the oncoming fire, and, squeaking, fell dead.

It seemed inconceivable to No Name that so little grass could cause such a raging fire. It could only be that, beside the powerful wind, the earth itself, truly, was burning up.

Head to one side, looking past his hand, coughing, No Name saw the fire dance toward them but a couple of dozen jumps away. The grass immediately ahead of it seemed to ignite of itself, here, then there, then everywhere. Then before the ignited little spots could themselves become racing prairie fires, the main line of the flames was upon them, engulfing them.

A slow-moving badger, running desperately, and yet for all its desperation waddling along hardly faster than a turtle, came straight for them. The sorrel shied, almost unseating No Name. Then, not a dozen yards away, the badger burst into a single searing yellow flame, its fat body exploding with a snap like the crack of a buckskin popper.

Dancing Sun shrilled. Then he bit his heavy stumbling

mate one last time, and charged. He leaped high over the line of fire. His leap seemed miraculously high to No Name. And he cleared it. A split second later the mare went up and over too, for all her weight lifting high and graceful. Then with the white one she vanished into the wall of exploding smoke.

No Name was next. He whipped his sorrel, hard, across the flanks. Head to one side, coughing heavily, One Who Follows understood what was wanted of him. At precisely the right moment, just as a bunch of grass underfoot burst into flames, he leaped, high, soaring aloft. The main fire raced under them. It stung the soles of No Name's feet. Instantly a great blast of hot wind hit them, almost doubling them up. Then they landed, hard, stumbling on the other side in smoking darkness.

"Hi-ye!" No Name cried. In a frenzy he whipped his horse, viciously. They galloped. They raced through popping plumes of pink smoke. No Name held his breath. They pounded. At last the smoke cleared some. Then, up ahead, in the weak light reflecting from the fire behind them, he saw Dancing Sun, noble head still up, scarlet tail glowing like a swamp ghost, phosphorescent, pacing gracefully beside his favorite mare.

"He is of the spirit of fire itself, truly," No Name whispered. "Fire can not touch him. He knows this. He will make a great warhorse for the Yanktons."

They walked through a waste of black. Thin columns of smoke twisted off still burning horseballs and thick whorls of grass and seared cactus. Underfoot a half-fried meadowlark craked mournfully. A seared lobo, looking very skinny without its hair, sighed a last rasping breath out of a gaping mouth. A baked rabbit stroked its feet spasmodically, kicking up black soot. The smells of the burning waste shut the nose.

They moved on.

The wind let up, at last died out altogether. Behind them raced the fire, rushing south across the farther prairies, gradually sinking out of sight beyond the curve of the earth.

The heavy mare lagged. The white one lagged with her.

Gradually the sorrel caught up with them. Soon they were as one band, the stallion and the mare and the sorrel with the man enemy aboard walking side by side. They headed north, going straight for the watering place.

On the morning of the fourth day, the sun came up a gold ball out of a black horizon. It rose into an orange sky. Ocher smoke and gray haze drifted low in the farther reaches.

No Name touched the piece of horse chestnut in his braid. "Were it not for my helper we would now be in the other world."

They came across occasional, smoldering half-burnt bodies of gophers. They skirted fire-blackened coils of rattlesnakes. They rode past a prairie dog town where surviving inhabitants sat beside their blackened honeycomb of holes discussing the past night's disaster. They turned aside to avoid the burnt gaunt body of a colt from the roan stallion's wild bunch. The smell of fried flesh and burnt hair was nauseating.

Then his helper spoke to him, clearly. "Let the white one drink. Also the mare if she wishes."

"But, helper, the white one still seems fresh. See, he walks with his head high. A drink now and he will be again as he once was."

"He is brave. He is a warrior. He is very tired and sleepy yet he hides his inner torment from the watching eye. Let him drink. He is so thirsty, so crazy for water, he will drink too much. A sudden heavy drink will stiffen his legs and shorten his wind. It will founder him. While he is in the river prepare to meet him on the trail halfway up between the third and second bluff. Have both your loops ready."

"Will he attack?"

"Perhaps. But this time it will be given you to capture him."

"Yelo."

Against the black earth and in the orange sunlight, the whiteness of the white stallion seemed more dazzling than ever. No Name had to shield his eyes to look at him. Dancing Sun seemed to scatter a whiteness like floating snowflakes on the air.

The valley of the River of Little Ducks at last appeared. Except for the taller cottonwoods and the deeper green meadows, everything south of the river was burned off. Only the north side remained strangely green.

No Name reined in his sorrel. He let the stallion and the mare go on by themselves. The white one did not stop to investigate from the height of the middle bluff as he usually did, but walked quietly, stolidly, down the trail into the ravine. The mare followed him. Despite her gravid state, there were wide hunger hollows between her hipbones and her belly. She stumbled along, almost as one blind. Looking at her closely No Name saw that her dugs were waxy and had dropped.

While the two drank below, No Name slipped to the ground and let the sorrel have the last few swallows of spring water in his heartskin. The small amount would not founder the sorrel; if anything would freshen him greatly for the struggle ahead. Having drunk, the sorrel lowered his head and snuffed at the ashen grass on the fire-shaven earth. Every spear of growth had been seared off at the roots. No Name petted the sorrel. For the first time he saw how gaunt his faithful mount had become. He considered taking the sorrel across the river for a few bites of grass. Instead he went over and plucked a handful of green leaves from a dying cottonwood sapling in the ravine. The sorrel ate the dryish green leaves with relish.

No Name looked down at the white stallion below in the river. "Truly, he is wakan. He went without water for four days and yet has remained a lusty one."

He watched Dancing Sun stalk out of the river and enter a small patch of green grass on the north side. Dancing Sun was so ravenously hungry, ate with such fury, that he tore up the grass, roots and all, even chunks of earth, as he grazed along.

No Name glanced west toward the cliff. To his surprise he saw that the fallen cottonwood still showed green where it lay across the opening to their cave. The prairie fire had missed it. "Ho, Leaf still lies hidden in our underground lodge."

No Name rode halfway down the ravine. He got off his horse and spread the loop of his longest and toughest lariat across the narrow part of the trail. He did not bother to hide it. Dancing Sun was now familiar with his smell. He tied the end of the lariat to the sorrel's belly band. He also readied the loop of his second lariat.

While the sorrel chewed the last of the dry cottonwood leaves, No Name sat on his heels in the black dust. In mimicry, a boy again with a small stick-horse and two buckskin thongs, he pretended to be catching a stallion. To his satisfaction, the white one was roped and thrown and tamed.

He looked down at where Dancing Sun still tore angrily at the grass. He sang in a low private voice. "Friend, you are strong. Friend, you are fierce. But a certain Yankton brave has come to get you. Get ready. Something you will see." He looked up at the strange orange morning sun. "Thank you for coming. Thank you. I can do anything when you are shining. I seem to have more power when you my father shine on me." He turned to the southwest where the moon hung almost obscured by a thick haze. "Thank you. I see that it will all happen as the white mare promised. Soon I will tell this to your friend, Moon Dreamer."

His bitten thigh began to throb under the rawhide bandage. He set his face against it. It was not a good thing to look at. It might weaken him for the struggle.

Dancing Sun left off grazing and re-entered the ocher river. He drank long and deep, nose under, bubbles rising. Once he lifted his head and trumpeted a short winning neigh at his wife Twinkling Feet.

No Name waited. He scanned the green horizon to the north, looking out as far as the enveloping purple haze would permit. He saw no sign of Rough Arm and his wild men.

He almost fell asleep. Clopping steps jerked him wide awake. Looking down, he saw Twinkling Feet and Dancing Sun come stepping up the trail. They came heavily, waterlogged, stiffened. Quickly No Name positioned the sorrel so the pull on the ground loop would not throw him. He held the rope in hand, ready to jerk.

His pulse beat painfully in his wound. His head came up. He sniffed in anticipation. His fierce black eyes glittered. Red passion glowed in his brain. A cold-blooded green-eyed predator writhed in old darkness in his belly. He licked his lips, once, already wildly happy that he had seized the white one.

The heavy mare stepped over the waiting loop. Her hoof touched the edge of it. She paid no attention to it. She waddled heavily on.

Then the white stallion stepped into it with his forefeet. He also paid it no mind.

In that instant No Name moved. He gave the lariat a flip. The flip undulated down the lariat and lifted the loop off the ground under the stallion. Again No Name moved, this time giving the lariat a powerful jerk at the same time that he quirted the sorrel under him. Just as he had planned in mimicry, the rope jerked high and the loop caught the white one well up on the forefeet. It threw him. The stallion hit the ground with a loud whumpfing grunt. Black dust puffed up. The mare ahead heard the crash of bones behind her and with a startled snort came up out of her self-absorption. She lumbered heavily up the bluff and out of sight.

Dancing Sun lay stunned a moment; then, with a scream of astonishment, of outrage, at the great indignity suffered, tried to rise. His head arched gracefully up, his forefeet came part way up, even his belly rolled.

No Name quirted the sorrel again, viciously. The sorrel leaned until the quivering rawhide threatened to snap.

Once more No Name quirted the sorrel. This time the rope rolled Dancing Sun completely over. The sorrel kept digging, began to drag the white one across the ground.

"Hehan!" No Name leaped to the ground, second lariat in hand. He gave the sorrel another whack on the rump to make sure he understood he was to keep the rope taut, then went hand over hand down the rope. He approached the wild one carefully, going in from the side. He placed his knee on the great arched neck, tried to catch up the stallion's near back leg. Dancing Sun felt the knee, kicked violently, and No Name missed his grab.

"Hold him!" No Name cried back at the sorrel. "Hold him tight!"

One Who Follows understood. He leaned back so far he looked like a great dog sitting down.

Again No Name reached for the back leg. Dancing Sun shuddered. Suddenly he came around at No Name with his head and tried to bite him. His eyes were blazing. Mysterious sounds gurgled in his belly.

"Ho, I have a horse who likes to bite Yanktons! Well, all you shall have for your teeth is empty air."

At last No Name got the other loop around the back leg. He pulled it tight. Then, as the stallion once more tried to bite him, he also caught the lower jaw in a half loop. This too he pulled up tight. Then he flipped another loop around the head and had him bridled as well as lashed down. He pushed the rawhide down the nose until it lay exactly in the right place, so that the slightest pull would put painful pressure on certain nerves.

Dancing Sun tried to move; couldn't. He groaned; lay still. Slowly the look of a trapped eagle came over his bluish eyes.

No Name stood up. "I have you, mighty white one!" he cried, exultant. "Wait until my father hears of this. I shall be known. Hey-hey-hey! I feel the power of it in me all the time."

There was a great clap of thunder behind them, then a cracking echo off the cliff. He looked up and around. There, all along the horizon behind them, from the southwest all the way to the northwest, almost on the ground, lay a low, angry green cloud. He had been so busy catching the wild one he had not noticed the sky suddenly becoming overcast.

Ahead of the low green cloud were still other wild clouds, raggy, boiling, darting. The wild gray shrouds seemed to be rushing toward a common center above him. Listening, he heard a sullen roar descending.

Dancing Sun and One Who Follows heard it too. Both horses whickered strangely, brokenly. They understood some sort of disaster was impending.

"Helper," No Name said in a low voice, "what, are you deserting me this time? I have the white horse. Let us keep him. He is a good one. Send the storm along some other path."

There was another crackle of lightning. It hit the ground higher up the trail. Pinkish blue light dazzled all around them; stunned them. A tremendous boom of thunder exploded against the earth. The valley seemed to crack apart.

No Name threw another look around behind them. The low green cloud came on, rolling down the valley. Even while he watched, it engulfed the yellow cliff, then the first fat bluff, then his grizzled lookout cottonwood across the river. Meanwhile above them the boiling gray shrouds concentrated into a churning black mass. A great droning roar as of some tremendous spinning top came pressing down upon them. His ears began to hurt with it. He could feel the blood beating in his dogteeth.

A few hailstones the size of robin eggs struck around them. A moment more, then the swirling blast of a great wind whelmed over them. Hailstones and black smut and grayish water churned as one. He covered his head with his free hand against the striking hail. He could feel the sorrel tugging through the white horse. He looked around but could not see the sorrel. Hailstones the size of eagle eggs began to hammer around them. Then a hailstone the size of a baby's skull plunked him squarely on the brow and arm. He saw fire. The arm over his head became numb. He changed arms. It too was hit, became numb. The roaring of the wind deepened. It began to whine hoarsely, like the terrible and continuous and reverberating roar of a lion. Under the pounding balls of hail the stallion beneath him struggled with wild frenzy.

"Ai-ye!" No Name cried, coughing under the pummeling hail. "He will hurt himself."

He took his knife and boldly cut the rope from the white one's forefeet. The sorrel, suddenly released, fell over. No

Name next cut the rope from the wild one's rear leg. Then suddenly, before the wild one could realize he was free to rise, No Name jumped on his back, clamping his slim legs tight.

The stallion rose under him like a canoe overcoming two successive waves. No Name could feel the warm muscles gathering under him for a jump. Again he was struck how much it felt like riding a massive writhing snake. Then, risen, ducking his head to one side away from the falling hail, the stallion bolted heavily up the trail for the barren above. Once he slipped. Quickly he regained his step and beat on. Hailstones splattered around them in the mud. Dancing Sun squealed every time a hailstone hit him over the ears.

"Run, great one," No Name cried. "You are my god. I will take care of you."

Slipping, regathering himself, quartering away from the storm, Dancing Sun bounded up the trail.

"Run, let us escape the Thunders who want to kill us. Would that my father Redbird were here. He would appease them with a powerful prayer of supplication."

When they reached the level prairie above, the stallion began to buck, sunfishing, trying to stand on his head. No Name was ready for him at every turn, at every twist. When the stallion dropped to the ground and rolled to get rid of him. No Name stepped to one side. When Dancing Sun got to his feet again, No Name quickly remounted him.

Howling winds pressed down from the skies. Green hail thickened. The big stones raised blood blisters on both man and horse. Sheets of water rose over the ground, first hoof-deep then ankle-deep. Soon islands of hailstones were floating to all sides.

"A cloud has burst," No Name cried. "My father once spoke of having seen such a thing. There will be a flood in the valley and it will be fearful."

Then, abruptly, hail and wind slackened off. And the stallion quit his pitching.

They drifted with the storm. It rained, rained. No Name did not dare to open his eyes except under a protective palm. The rain came down so sheeting thick he could scarcely make out the stallion's white ears. No Name's head and the backs of his arms felt like one solid bruise.

Presently the rain let up too. Horse and man stopped. Both lifted their heads and looked wonderingly around. Ahead of them a solid gray wall of slanting driving rain moved swiftly on.

There was no land to be seen. Even the black ashes of the prairie fire had vanished. The whole flat top of the hogback was covered with bubbling ice and water, all of it beginning to sheet off toward the low places to either side. It went with a slowly gathering rush. It had rained so hard so fast the water had not had time to run off.

"It is my father's friends, the Thunders. They sent the hailing rain to help me subdue the wild one. Thank you, thank you. I am happy."

He sat at ease.

At that moment Dancing Sun exploded beneath him. Despite the mud, the wild one managed to rise almost twice his height in the air. At the top of the jump, his head and rump went down, his back up.

No Name grabbed desperately for the scarlet mane, hung on.

Dancing Sun hit the muddy ground on a slant, came down with such a jolt No Name's head snapped like the head of a floppy grass doll.

"Helper!" No Name cried, "what is this? He still thinks to be free?"

A new and even stronger voice seemed to speak to him. "Take courage. This is a good day to die. Think of the children and the helpless at home who expect you to be valiant. Do not fear. What is to come has already been foreseen."

In anger No Name gave the bridle rope a hard jerk. The jerk pinched the wild one's nose. He squealed. He rose off the ground like a great fish leaping free of water and standing on its tail. Again they came down, hard, both grunting.

Red rage rose in the dark back of No Name's head. "Cursed one, do you not know the gods have already foreseen what is to happen?" He whipped the stallion across the flanks with the end of his raw-hide rope, hard, on both sides, raising welts.

Dancing Sun screamed. A whipping he had never had before. He lowered his head and bolted straight ahead.

Slops of mud and drifts of gray-green hail still lay everywhere on the hogback. It made heavy going. Yet Dancing Sun sped over the ground as if it were hard and dry. He ran as sure-footed as a bighorn. He paced so smoothly, so swiftly, No Name had a vision of himself riding a white bird flying low along the ground in a gray-green dream. It was the same as having a nightmare while wide awake.

The smoothness of the flight enraged No Name still more. He whipped the stallion again.

Dancing Sun shivered, shuddered, let go a deep rasping roar, broke into a gallop.

"He-han!" No Name cried. "I have won! I have broken you. You have galloped at last. You are now as all other mortal horses. Run, run, run! Ah, that my father could see this great thing! I feel like a man. I can feel the power of it with me all the time."

They leaped about on the hogback. They went in circles. The stallion was a great white crane trying to get rid of a weasel on its back.

Between jumps, catching sight of the land below the three bluffs, No Name was startled to see that the whole valley had filled with a racing sheet of yellow water. Uprooted trees, ripped up bushes, dead bodies of half-burned deer, scuds of loose leaves and sticks, floated swiftly east.

"Ei-ye! another Great Smoky Water has entered the valley."

Then he recalled something. When just thirteen, he had once helped his father tame a balky pinto. They had driven it into the River of the Double Bend at flood time. In deep water the pinto was helpless. The pinto hated getting its ears wet, had to swim for its life, had no time for fancy curvetting. By the time the pinto reached shore, it was docile. No Name remembered the time very well. What great sport it had been to sit on the pinto's back in the racing water. He had thrilled to the warm feeling of the horse's body between his legs, bunching and humping its big muscles under him, desperate, vigorous, yet always easy to control.

No Name jerked on the bridle rope, pulling the white stallion around. Then, by slapping him over the eyes, first one side, then the other, smartly, he headed him for the trail.

In his frenzy the wild one did not seem to mind. He galloped in long mud-slopping strides straight for the river. Pellmell they went over the edge of the bluff and down the ravine past the green cedar, and then, with a spring, jumped into the roaring flood. They went completely under. After a moment they popped up, spilling water. And still the stallion wanted to gallop. He humped along in the water like a stumbler in a sticky dream, up and under, down and up. Like the balky pinto, the white stallion also hated getting his ears wet. All the while he humped and galloped in the flood, he somehow managed to keep them above water.

The mad bobbing, the driving current, gradually made No Name lose his grip. Feeling himself sliding off, he decided to take to the water. To keep from getting kicked by Dancing Sun's stroking hooves, No Name grabbed hold of the horse's tail and swam along behind. Dancing Sun took the full shove of the current while No Name swam in gentled waters.

Yet still Dancing Sun wanted to gallop in the water. He could not break out of it.

"Helper!" No Name cried, gulping in the moiling waters, "what must I do? He is as one gone crazy. They of the underworld are stirring his brains with a stick."

Dancing Sun seemed to have heard. He let out a great sigh; sank; came up sputtering. Then, calmer, he began to swim in a horse's usual manner.

No Name let go a great sigh, too. Taking a firm hold of the horse's tail, he began to steer him through the sliding sudsing water. They turned in a slow circle and headed for shore.

They drifted a long way down river before the stallion touched solid ground. It was at a place where the prairies sloped gently into the valley. As they emerged, No Name quickly slipped up on Dancing Sun's back again. Both dripped muddy water. Froth hung from the corners of their mouths. The stallion's dazzling white coat was now a soppy placked-down gray, almost the white-gray look of death; the red flame in his mane and tail was dowsed.

They went slowly up the greasy rise. Standing water had by now mostly run off the plateau. Only irregular drifts of hail still lay over the ground.

No Name guided Dancing Sun toward the bluffs. The horse went meekly, seemingly subdued at last.

When they reached the middle bluff again, where the footing was fairly firm, Dancing Sun groaned and suddenly lay down. No Name had just time to jump to one side to keep from being crushed.

Great head lying stretched out in the mud, worn out, covered with blood-tinged sweat, sobbing convulsively, the stallion lay as if about to die. Drops of blood gathering in the corners of his delicate bluish eyes ran down his long white face. A trickle of blood also ran out of his pink nostrils and stained the hail-studded sod.

No Name's heart melted within him. He let go of the bridle rein and knelt beside him. He caressed him, shushed him tenderly. He ran his hands gently over his ears and nose. He marveled to see the breadth of the great white forehead, that part where the horse knows all, marveled to see the deep arch of the neck, that part which shows the horse to be of noble birth.

He massaged Dancing Sun's neck and shoulders and back, working slowly. He grunted to him in gruff friendly tones. "Hroh. Hroh. Hroh." He stroked the horse's flanks, his legs. There was not one part of the horse's body he did not touch. He worked into the horse his man smell, his touch, his spirit.

He took the stallion's head in his arms and exchanged breaths with each nostril. He took some of the blood dripping from his own nose and mingled it with the blood in the stallion's nose. He also took some of the stallion's blood and mingled it with the blood in his own nose.

"Horse, now you have my breath and blood and I have yours. We belong to each other. You are now my brother and I am your brother. We are brothers forever. We have lived through a great thing. We will return known to all as great ones. Let us have peace between us."

Dancing Sun suddenly snorted, shooting a spray of blood and froth all over No Name. His eyes blazed red hate. With a last supreme effort, his head came off the ground, then his forefeet.

"Ho, what is this? What does my brother wish now?"

Quickly, just as the horse got up on all fours, No Name leaped aboard again.

Dancing Sun shuddered. Then a mad spirit seized him, and sobbing he ran in a pacing gait west down off the slope of the bluffs. Straight across a meadow he flew, then up to the top of the cliff. No Name hung on, grimly.

A dozen leaps and they passed where the cottonwood lay fallen across the ravine. Looking over the horse's scarlet mane, No Name saw the valley ahead and below approaching with sudden swiftness. No Name's eyes bugged out in horror. He barely had time to realize that the flash flood had subsided some, that should the horse leap off the cliff there would not be enough water to break their long fall. Instead they would splatter onto the hard rock where the spring flowed past Leaf's cave. With each rolling throw of his hooves, Dancing Sun gathered speed. No Name reached ahead and slapped the horse across the eyes, on the right side, again and again, trying to head him off to the left. Dancing Sun ignored the slapping. Obsessed, he drove on.

Seeing it hopeless, that in the next couple of jumps they would both sail over the precipice, No Name let go of the scarlet mane and, sliding, bouncing, fell to the ground. He just had time to look up to see Dancing Sun take a final jump and then go soaring off, noble head up, neck arched, long scarlet mane snapping, lifted tail fluttering. Then, descending like a statue, Dancing Sun passed from view. A moment later there was a shrill scream, triumphant, derisive, and then came the crash of bulk and bones on rock.

No Name hurried down. He arrived in time to see the great mystery slowly die out of the white one's soft delicate bluish eyes.

He looked down at the broken white king, and then, impulsively, knelt beside him and threw his arms around his neck. "I love you, my brother," he cried. "Why must you leave me? You are scarred on my heart forever. I shall never forget you."

He stood up and sang the stallion's death song. His voice, lamenting, echoed clearly, word for word, off the cliff. "My brother, you are gone. Go then. Depart. Tell them of the other world that I loved you. You were my god. But now you are dead. Why did you die? You have broken my dream. You have destroyed my vision. You have confounded my helper. Now I am nothing. I have said."

He wept.

After he had wept a sufficient time, he arose and took his knife and cut off part of the scarlet mane between the ears as the white mare of his vision had commanded him to do. As he cut, he noted that under the coat of white hair a strip of black skin ran down the stallion's back. It reached all the way to his tail.

"Ae, the sign of the First One. Now I see. Now I know. It tells why he was the father of so many spotted ones, perhaps even of brave Black One."

Next he slit open the belly of the stallion and took away the heart. It was still filled with blood and he drank therefrom. Then he cut a few slices off the heart and ate them.

"This I do to bring our spirits together. Now I can die a brave one."

Again he looked down at the broken white one. Slowly a glittering white-gray look of death stole up the horse's muzzle. Watching it, a feeling of revulsion passed over No Name. He shuddered.

"Horse, I give you to Wakantanka. I shall let you lie upon the rocks. I do this that the elements may take you back: the spirits your white coat, the air your lungs, the earth your blood, the rocks your bones, the worms your flesh. It was from all these that you were formed and it is to all these that you must return. Life is a circle. The power of the world works always in circles. All things try to be round. Life is all one. It begins in one place, it flows for a time, it returns to one place. The earth is all that lasts. I have said. Yelo."

# PART
## FOUR

# The Fathers

# 1

He stood up, listening in the evening air.

A new voice spoke to him. It seemed to come from the piece of scarlet mane he held in his hand. The voice spoke in the manner of his father Redbird, quietly, with a sweet gentle air. "Where is your wife Leaf?"

"I have lost the white horse that was promised me. My heart is on the ground."

"Find your wife Leaf and it will be given you."

"The white mare of my vision said I was to catch the great stallion. Yet he is dead."

"Obey the voice."

"The white mare of the silver tail has tricked me. Perhaps she means to trick me again in the second part of the vision. Perhaps my father need not die at last."

"Live inward. Grow inward. Pass into that place where there is nothing but joy which makes life good. Do this and it will be given you."

"I love my father dearly and do not wish to kill him. What shall I do?"

"Obey the voice. Where is your wife Leaf?"

"It is fated. I cannot weep. I must do that which is asked of me. Yelo."

He made a circlet of the piece of scarlet mane and thrust it under the belt of his clout. Then, rolling up his war bridle, he crossed the sticky ground and went in under the fallen cottonwood and entered their cave.

The cave was empty. He stood stunned for a time.

At last his eyes moved and he began to see. The dirt floor underfoot was slimy with mud. The fire was out. The store of dried meat was gone. Only the new clothes which Leaf had made were left, hanging from a peg driven high into the wall.

"The flood has driven her out."

He looked for her footprints in the entrance. There were none. The waters had washed them away.

He stepped outside. "Surely she would not have gone down into the flood. She would have gone in the other direction." He got down on hands and knees and crawled further under the cottonwood and worked his way up the ravine. In a few moments he climbed above the high-water mark. Searching, eyes glittering, he found her footprints. He followed them to where they led to a sheer wall. Glancing up, he saw where she had scrabbled to the top. Bushes hung down, half-torn out by the roots. A swallow hole had been ruptured open by a handhold. A snake hole had been widened raw by a toe.

He hurried back down the ravine, and going around, climbed to the top of the cliff. He found the place where she had gained the precipice. It was almost the same place from where the stallion had taken his final leap. Rain had nearly obscured her moccasin prints in the wet ashy soil. "Ah, the flood forced her out before the storm was over."

He followed the footprints down through the meadow and up over the tops of the three bluffs. They ended in a cut where the fire had missed some green grass.

He was about to part the leaves of a gooseberry bush, when he heard the cry of a baby. It was a cry strong with protest.

"It is a man child," he whispered. "Already he knows there is much to overcome."

He peered through the three-eared leaves.

Leaf was handling a pink infant in a loving manner, washing it with the palm of one hand while holding it with the other. The baby had fat arms and legs, and it wriggled and kicked rhythmically as it cried. Its black hair lay slicked back, and where she had not yet washed its body the skin had a glazed shine. Its navel cord had been neatly tied back with a buckskin thong. Plainly to be seen too was the spot of the Ancient Ones, a purple darkening in the skin at the base of the spine which always denoted the true Yankton. Beside Leaf on the grass lay the afterbirth, a puddle of silken flesh. The baby had just been born.

With delicate regard for her privacy, he withdrew a few paces. Then, to let her know someone had come, he coughed lightly.

The cry of the baby was instantly shut off.

Afraid that she might harm the baby, he quickly cried out, "It is your husband. I am coming."

The moment she removed her hand from the baby's mouth it began to bellow again. "Wait, my husband."

Over the baby's howling he heard rustling behind the gooseberry bush, then heavy breathing.

"I am ready, my husband. Come see your son. Our first-born has arrived."

He stepped into the enclosure. The afterbirth had vanished, buried in the earth. The infant was covered with a robe and lay in her arms. The moment No Name loomed over it, a shadow, the infant fell silent. It stared up blinking, unseeing, its bluish-black eyes slowly sliding off to one side. Leaf looked down at it, then smiled a wide white smile up at No Name. The skin over her high cheekbones shone a healthy rose-brown. Her eyes were milky with mother love.

He examined the infant point for point. "The skin of the child is like the inside of a lip. Pink."

"The skin will darken in a few days in the proper manner. It is the way of all fresh-born."

"Its hair also has some red in it."

"Have you forgotten, my husband, that we are related to the buffalo? They also are born red into the world and then turn brown after a certain time."

"His nose seems fallen."

She glanced down at the nubbin nose with its two small holes. Smiling, she gave it a tug. "All Yankton mothers know that a child's nose must be given a pull every morning until it has passed four winters. By then it will begin to rise."

"Its eyes have a strange color."

She pretended to be dismayed at his remarks. "Does he not please you, my husband?"

"Have you presented him to the great directions?"

"Even unto the earth and the sky."

"Remove the robe. I wish to see if he is perfectly formed."

She slipped the robe aside, shyly. The baby lay a moment with its fat arms and fat legs outspread. Its tiny phallus stood up like the opening curl of a wild turnip. She saw the risen flesh and after a moment modestly covered it. "Is he not a whole child?"

"He will make a fine son." No Name toyed with his rolled up war bridle. "I am glad he has come. You are well?"

"When I finish clothing the child I shall be ready to leave for our home beside Falling Water." She gave him a most winning look, her face flushed with love and trust. "Does he not please you, my husband?"

He reached down and touched the child's plump belly with a forefinger. "When we return to our home I will bring a horse to my uncle Moon Dreamer and ask him to give our firstborn his name."

Her face filled with joy. "I am glad, my husband. Thank you, thank you."

Then shyly, quietly, she began to dress the baby. She laid him in a soft calfskin clout, hair against the skin, and poured fresh sand under his feet to catch the excess urine. Next she wrapped the fur robe tightly around him, placed him on a cradle board, and, pulling the halves of the quilled cover snugly together, laced up the thongs. When she finished, all that could be seen of him were his luminous liquid-blue eyes and a shiny ruddy face. The baby remained quiet. He seemed to like the touch of soft fur on his skin.

No Name watched in pride. There was nothing his mother Star could have found to criticize. Leaf had learned her lessons well from Full Kettle.

Her eyes were on him. "Is the white horse ready to ride?"

His face clouded over. "I have a sad thing to tell." He

dropped his rolled up war bridle to the ground to show he had no further use for it. "The white one did not want to live with his red brother. His spirit soul would not let him wear the Yankton war bridle." No Name told her all that had happened. "Thus we have no horses. We will have to go on foot. It will be a long weary journey. Will you be strong enough to carry both the papoose and the parfleches?"

"Do not worry, my husband. I am not one to complain."

"It is not manly for a husband to bear burdens. A man must lead the way with his weapons and be ready to defend his family at all times."

She laughed merrily at him. "How strangely you talk, my husband. Even after I have given our baby suck, neither he nor I will be any heavier than when I climbed the cliff to come here. Even with all the parfleches on my back." She stood up and bound a wide leather belt tightly around her middle. "I am ready."

"On foot we shall be at the mercy of those who have horses."

"My husband, look behind you. Is that not our sorrel feeding on tree leaves?"

He turned slowly.

Looking down at them from the rim of the cut stood One Who Follows. A spray of hackberry leaves was in his mouth, while the cut lariat, still tied to his pad saddle, hung to the ground. The sorrel was so sharply outlined against the clear blue evening sky that No Name could see big humps over his back and shoulders where hailstones had struck him. The sorrel nickered at them. The nicker had in it quiet mild protest at being neglected so long.

No Name laughed, showing glittering white teeth. "Well, well, One Who Follows. I see your Name still fits you. It is good. My wife and I were speaking of a horse we might use." No Name whistled low, coaxingly. "Come."

Lowering his head, pebbles rattling at his heels, the sorrel slid down the side of the cut and walked obediently toward him.

No Name removed the sorrel's pad saddle and scratched his hide. He also stroked him under the flowing yellow mane. With tender fingers he soothed the lumps over his back. No Name said over his shoulder, "Wife, never have I had a more faithful friend in trouble or battle. Neither fire nor flood could tear him from me. He is a true Yankton."

Leaf smiled a slow side smile. "Perhaps it is as my father Owl Above has said. A castrated horse is no longer loved by either the female or the male fourlegged and thus seeks the companionship of the twolegged."

No Name sobered. He petted the sorrel some more. "Horse, when we arrive at my father's lodge I will tell him about you. He will have an extra eagle feather to put in your mane."

A low pathetic nicker sounded behind them.

No Name snapped around. So did Leaf. There above them, on the rim of the cut, exactly where the sorrel had appeared a moment before, stood Black Stripe, Leaf's dun mare. Black Stripe stood with her head down, ears flopped forward, nose turned slightly to one side, as if trying to understand what was going on between the sorrel and the man. She was gaunt from the long ordeal of running.

The sorrel lifted his head with a jerk. He whinnied, loud and joyful, then broke away from No Name and ran for the mare. The mare in turn, at last sure she had seen right, that the sorrel was her lost chum, whinnied loud in reply. She slid down the embankment on all fours. The two met with a rough butting of bluff chests. They crossed their necks in affectionate greeting, began to nip at each other in love.

Tears came into No Name's eyes as he watched them.

But Leaf laughed. "Ha-ha! so the silly one has returned, has she? See how she nearly falls down from thirst and hunger. It is good. It is what the old fool mare deserves. A maid of good sense never elopes. I have said."

No Name then had a different thought. "Hi-e, perhaps the mare already carries the great white one's child. Perhaps that will be the horse the white mare told of." He cupped his hand to his left braid and set himself to listen to his charm.

Leaf broke in on his musing. "We will have to let the mare graze a few days before we can use her. Also, let us hope she will not have a white colt with a scarlet mane when she foals. We have had enough of the wild wakan one."

"Ha!" No Name cried. "I have forgotten." Quickly he got out the circlet of scarlet mane that he had hidden under his belt. He held it to his ear. "I have a new helper. It is from the wakan one himself. It will tell me if she carries a colt by him." He listened closely.

Practical Leaf, however, picked up the war bridle from the ground where No Name had dropped it and quietly went over and secured the joyful sorrel and mare. She tied both of them to a sapling hackberry. Some tufts of green grass grew at the foot of it.

No Name continued to listen closely.

A heavy groan of a female in labor came from below them in the cut. The groan was profound, dolorous, sounding as if coming out of the last extremity of flesh.

No Name looked at Leaf, black eyes opening in big wondering circles.

Leaf also stood as one transfixed.

"Woman, it was not you?" he finally asked.

"Foolish man, our child has already come." Then she added, her willow-leaf eyes narrowing in scorn, "Unless there is to be twins."

His eyes wicked from side to side. "Perhaps it is someone caught by those of the underworld and calling for help."

Leaf clapped hand to mouth. "I have forgotten. Only now I remember. When our son was about to break into the world, and I lay calling for help from the moon being, I heard a sad groan behind me. I thought it was my guardian spirit who had come to help me groan. But now I know."

"What do you know?"

"My husband, I know it now as the groan of a mare giving birth."

"Where do you see such a mare?" he demanded, looking around.

She flashed him a mischievous smile. "Has my husband

suddenly become bashful that he cannot look upon a female giving birth alone? Look in the plum bushes below."

He gave her a fierce look; then, head proud, started for the brush below. He moved on tiptoe, soundlessly, choosing the larger stones to step on.

Parting the branches of the plum thicket, narrow eyes glittering, he saw flesh shining on grass. He couldn't quite see what it was, so he pushed farther through the stiff prickly twigs. Leaning down for a closer look, he finally made out a sack of pale diaphanous skin. Inside lay a curled-up colt. It was a bag of waters, unbroken, and the colt inside was dead. "Ahh-h-h," he said, and sank to his heels.

After a moment, collecting himself, he picked up a stick and poked into the silken envelope. The envelope broke and syrupy fluid spilled across the grass. With his fingers he widened the rent for a better look at the baby horse. It was a female. He drew out one of its rear legs. The leg was already cold, stiff. When he let go of it, it snapped back into place. He lifted the colt's short plume of a tail. It was reddish. He opened the rent farther and saw that the colt's hair was a light gray. Except for a somewhat thin rump the colt was perfectly formed.

"I do not understand, my helper."

He looked up. Some ten steps away stood the white stallion's favorite mare, the light-gray with the white hooves. Twinkling Feet looked even more gaunt and bony than Black Stripe. She stood trembling, as if about to collapse. Her flanks were spotted with shiny film and blood.

She heard him move and turned her head, nickering weakly.

Thinking she might be an easy catch in her weakened state, he approached a few steps, holding out his hand.

She let him come to within an arm's length, then up came her head and her tail lashed twice against him.

He stood. He shook his head. "I can see you are not happy, favorite one. Well, I know another who is not happy. It is a sad thing to lose so fine a colt. It is all from the running. It was not good. Yet the gods told me to catch your master."

He withdrew from the plum thicket and called back to tell Leaf that he had found another horse.

Leaf stepped out from the gooseberry bushes. "Twinkling Feet was one of the wild ones?"

"She was his favorite wife."

"Can you catch her?"

"She is not worth catching. She will die by morning."

"It would be a good thing to arrive at the door of your father's lodge with three horses."

"What would you have me do?"

She went back into the gooseberries and searched her parfleches. After a bit she found what she was looking for, a small leather case and a rawhide strap, and brought them to him. "Sounds The Ground gave me a small gift of corn against an evil day on the trail. Here is also a strap I made while you were seeking the stallion."

"Ho, now I see I have a wife who is full of pleasant surprise. What else have you hidden?"

"Cup your hands."

"I hold them open before you."

She poured out half of the multi-colored corn. "See if the mare likes it. It may give her strength to live." She hung the rawhide strap over his shoulder. "Try to catch her while she eats."

He suppressed a smile. He turned and again pushed through the plum bushes.

The gray mare stood in the same place, switching her wet tail. He held out the corn to her. She got the smell of it, nickered weakly, but made no move to come for it. He stepped closer, reaching as far as he could, at last got the corn under her nose. She lipped up a few kernels, rolled them around loosely in her mouth, then let them dribble to the ground.

Moving still closer, he stepped on something soft and giving. He looked down. There, barely hidden under old leaves, lay a second colt. "Ahh-h-h," he said. Looking around, he spotted another bag of waters, this one broken, and next to it the afterbirth. "Twins," he whispered softly. He poured the corn to one side on the ground and knelt softly. Gently he scratched away the leaves.

The second colt was alive. Barely. The mare had cleaned it thoroughly. She had bitten the cord off neatly, close to the navel. Examining the earth behind them, he saw she had picked it up by the neck and carried it to dry ground and then had covered it with leaves to keep it warm. He lifted its rear leg. "Ai-ye!" he cried aloud. "It is a stud colt."

Leaf heard his cry and came hurrying through the plum thicket. "What is it, my husband? What have you seen?"

He jumped up for joy. "It is yet another colt, my wife. The white stallion's favorite has had twins. A wonderful thing. Truly a sign from the gods."

"Ahh-h-h," Leaf said, low.

He knelt beside the colt again. "See, it is a white colt with a reddish mane and tail. A true son of his father."

"Ahh-h-h," Leaf said again, low.

He looked across to where the sun was setting. A flare of red gleamed on the winking river. "My father, you have given me what my vision desired. Thank you, thank you."

He lifted the colt's pulpy head. Its half-closed bluish eyes were glazed over. A film of dust covered its under eye. Its mouth, already pursed for suckling, weakly drew air instead. The colt smiled a strange ludicrous smile, lower lip hanging, fuzzy nose lifted.

"It is dying," Leaf said.

No Name knew it. But it enraged him to hear her say it. He lashed out, snarling, "Woman, why do you hate the white ones? Are they not holy and wakan? Woman, perhaps this is the horse the white mare told about in my vision. Would you destroy my vision?"

Meekly she bowed her head, "I hear you, my husband."

He picked up the colt tenderly in his arms. "You are my god," he cried, looking down at it. "Live! I will take care of you as if you were my own son. You shall see."

Holding its slender slippery body close, he felt its heart beating against his bare chest. "Aii," he cried, "it will live. Already I feel my power entering its heart." Gently he laid it down again. He cupped his hands around its soft protruding lips and breathed into its mouth, deep, long; breathed until the colt's chest began to lift and fall on its own a little. His breath and the breath of the colt became one. The breath of the colt had a flesh-sweet taste.

Leaf said behind him, "It was born too weak to stand. It could not get the milk."

He let go of the colt's mouth. "Ha," he snapped around at her, "at last you speak with the wisdom of a Yankton breeder. Woman, it is well known a colt must drink milk immediately after it is born or it will die." He picked up the slack body in his arms again, with its head in the palm of his hand, and moved toward Twinkling Feet.

But Twinkling Feet, though weak, and interested in what was happening to her colt, was suspicious and moved away.

"Wait a moment, my husband." Leaf scooped up the corn No Name had thrown to one side. Carefully she held it to the mare's lips. Twinkling Feet, with some reluctance, at last took a mouthful and began chewing.

Leaf waited until the mare had chewed the corn some, then took the rawhide strap from No Name's shoulder and secured the mare. Twinkling Feet, never touched before, was at last too beaten down to care.

Again No Name approached Twinkling Feet, holding the mouth of the colt to her bag. The mare stood. Her black dugs were dripping full. With a prying finger, No Name opened the colt's mouth and pushed its lips around the near dug. The colt lay inert.

Leaf said quietly, "Milk a little in the colt's mouth, my husband. So it gets the taste."

No Name gave her a scorching look. "Count my hands, woman, and then tell me which one is not busy."

"I hear you, my husband." Holding the strap with one hand, she reached her other hand under the mare and milked the dug into the colt's mouth a few times.

The colt's lips moved loosely, milk ran out of the corners of its mouth, its glazed eyes rolled once.

"When my father still had horses," Leaf said, "he often

said twin colts were not a good thing. Neither the one nor the other was ever born strong enough to stand. The mother could not sustain both of them in her belly at the same time and yet give them full hindquarters with which to stand."

"Ho, no doubt that is another bit of wisdom your father unearthed alone, which my father Redbird as a horse breeder never knew."

"Nevertheless, my husband, what my father said remains a true thing."

"Milk the mare again, woman."

Leaf stripped the dug a half-dozen times. Again milk ran out of the corners of the colt's mouth and down its slippery white hide. The mare shuddered, and almost collapsed.

Leaf withdrew her hand as if to suggest it was no longer any use.

"Again!" No Name ordered harshly. "It is the wakan white horse of my vision that I hold in my hands. Would you destroy my vision?"

Once more Leaf milked into the little one's mouth, a series of good steady streams.

All of a sudden the colt gathered itself up and coughed, exploding milk over No Name's face and Leaf's arm and the underside of Twinkling Feet. All three jumped a little.

"Look," Leaf said, matter-of-fact, "it coughs."

"See," No Name cried, joyfully, "it lives!"

The colt licked its lips and swallowed. It rolled its eyes. Some of the glaze and dust on its pupils washed off under its long pink lashes.

"Drink, my son," No Name urged coaxingly, cuddling the colt against his chest. "Drink, all the Yanktons wish it." He held the colt's mouth to the mare's dripping dug again.

This time the touch of the fat dug awakened the colt and it suckled a few moments. Its throat pulsed twice.

"Ahh," Leaf whispered.

"Hi-ye," No Name cried.

Twinkling Feet looked around and nickered at her colt. She smelled its thin rump where it lay over No Name's arm. She seemed to understand that the thing being done was good.

"It is well, mother," No Name murmured. "He has my breath and I have his. Also my wife has the smell of your milk on her. We belong to you."

The colt sagged again, and quit breathing.

No Name whispered fiercely, "Woman, quickly, milk the mare a little."

Milk ran out of the corner of the colt's mouth again before it exploded a cough. Then, abruptly, it began to breathe in an even steady rhythm. Gradually too what was left of the glaze vanished from its eyes. It seemed to awaken to the world. At last it began to push its nose around against the mare's bag. It found the dug by itself.

The colt suckled for some time. No Name counted some thirty swallows before the colt quit, exhausted.

Happy, No Name carried the colt back to the nest of dry leaves. He laid it down gently. It lay breathing to itself, slowly.

"Woman, fetch us a robe. The colt must be kept warm while the milk works."

She brought the robe quickly. No Name lay down beside the colt and took it in his arms while she covered them both. He stroked the colt under the robe, down its back, down its leg, over its head. He loved it. Gradually, after what seemed a very long time, warmth seemed to return to the colt's slender white body.

He saw Twinkling Feet pulling against the strap, desiring to be near her colt.

"Let her come," he said. "Tie her to this bush close by."

Leaf led the mare over and tied her securely.

He looked up at Leaf again from under the robe. "I have almost forgotten our son. Where is he? He is well?"

"He hangs sleeping in his cradle from a tree."

"Care for him while I care for this one."

Lying patiently in the nest of dry leaves, under the warm buffalo robe, he held the white colt in his arms. He lay holding it in love the whole night through.

Early in the morning he fed the colt again, holding it up to the mare's other dug. It fed well. When he put it back on the dry leaves under the robe, he saw that its eyes finally shone bright with life. Its white ears and short reddish plume of a tail flopped occasionally at the buzzing flies. Sometimes its legs trembled as if in a phantom gallop.

He waited until the sun had risen some, then uncovered the colt and began to work it. He rubbed its legs, stretching all the ligaments and muscles, and shaped its slender ears with his fingers, and combed out its lovely baby tail with a brush of sticks. He lighted a fire of dry sage and hardened the colt's slippery cartilaginous hooves in the smoke and heat. He collected certain aromatic leaves, chewed them thoroughly, then perfumed the colt by blowing and spitting the particles into the reddish mane and tail.

At noon, at the same time that Leaf gave breast to their son, he again held the colt up to Twinkling Feet's bag. This time the colt drank eagerly.

Later that evening, when he held it up to drink once more, it struggled to break free of his arms. When he let it rest lightly on its feet, it took hold and stood alone. And alone it punched its nose into the bag and found the dugs. It drank until the mare was dry.


The next day, try as they might, they could not get Twinkling Feet to eat. They brought her more corn. They coaxed her with fresh grass gathered from the unburnt meadow across the river. They brought her fresh prairie clover from the unburnt meadow across the river and from farther down the valley. They rubbed her down. They lavished love upon her. Yet she would not let her teeth be parted. She had resigned herself to dying.

"She wishes to follow her husband Dancing Sun," No Name said. "She has been wild too long."

"Perhaps we should let mother and son go free," Leaf suggested.

"The white colt? Woman, why do you hate the white ones?"

"If the mare dies the colt dies."

"I will get the mare some water," he said. "If she drinks she will eat."

But Twinkling Feet refused the water too. She did not even bother to lip it.

And that evening, Twinkling Feet went down. She died as the sun set, her eyes glazing over even as the colt emptied her bag for the last time.


The following evening they were back in their cave, sitting by the fire. The baby hung in its cradle from a peg in the wall, the colt slept curled up at No Name's feet. Earlier in the day, to make sure the colt would stay close, No Name had cut a belt from the hide over Twinkling Feet's back and belly, including the dugs, and he wore it around his middle.

No Name felt bad. At supper the colt had refused to drink a gruel made of cornmeal and water. No Name had begun to wonder how he was to keep the colt alive.

No Name and Leaf sat watching the fire die away. They sat a long time, wordless.

Finally Leaf, knowing his thoughts, had a suggestion to make. "My husband, I have a thing to give to the colt. Yet I am afraid to speak of it."

He said nothing.

"It is because I am afraid you will scorn me."

He sighed, then said, "Speak, woman, my ears hear you."

"My husband, well, our son does not need all there is to drink. I have too much milk. Therefore let me give the colt suck. I have seen that his mouth is very tender."

No Name stared at her.

"Once my mother told me she did not have enough milk for me when I was born. Therefore she gave me some milk to drink from a mare. It is time that I repay horsekind. Why cannot this colt be raised on a mother's milk? Yankton mothers are often known to give little puppies to suck."

He continued to stare at her with large black fixed eyes.

"I wish that my husband may be happy. He has had a great vision for his scarlet people. He has overcome many difficulties. He has an enemy scalp to show. Soon he will be wearing an honor feather. Thus perhaps it is right and good for him to cling to the little white stud. The stud colt will no doubt help the Yanktons become a rich and proud people. I have said."

He still could not speak. He looked down at the sunken fire. Presently he picked up a twig and without thinking scratched pictures in the dust of the cave floor.

"Has my husband lost his tongue?"

He coughed; then looked into the darkness outside the cave. "Do as your heart tells you. But do not let me see it."

"My mother also told of another thing she gave me. She cooked some cornmeal in marrow soup and then strained it and gave it to me to drink through a leather teat."

"Ahh."

"Also, the colt will soon be able to drink water and eat of the tender grasses by itself. It will not take long."

He nodded. "When we arrive at my father's lodge he will find us a milch mare and let the colt feed from her."

She reached a hand around the side of the fire. "Give it to me."

"Give you what?" he cried wonderingly.

"The gray belt. That the colt may smell its old mother when it abides with its new mother."

Slowly, gravely, he unstrapped the gray hide belt from around his middle and handed it across to her.

In the next days, during the Moon of Black Cherries, while the white colt filled out and became strong, they prepared for the long trip home.

He hunted buffalo; she dried meat and cured hides. He cut thirteen short tepee poles; she patched together a skin cover. He made a high saddle for her; she got ready a travois on which to carry their possessions. He shot a porcupine; she made combs from its tail and dyed the quills. He made himself a new quiver; she decorated it tastefully with quillwork. He made himself a new sinew-backed bow from second-growth ash; she embossed it beautifully with more quillwork.

He made himself a good warclub out of maple knurl and a thick shield out of tough bullhide, and painted the main elements of his vision on both to make them sacred. She made leather cases for them so they might always be covered except in time of battle. She also made him a heavy buckskin shirt, with fringes of varying lengths on his right arm, the varying lengths indicating the kinds of trails he had taken. With quills he embossed the small leather charm case she had made for him and placed in it, reverently, the circlet of scarlet mane he had cut from Dancing Sun. Out of deer shinbones she made charms and hung them on the cradle to protect the baby from evil spirits.

To vary the diet, he went to the river and caught fish. He found the channel catfish fat and lazy. Sometimes they were so sluggish he could charm them to the surface by gently tickling them under the belly with a willow twig and then throw them out onto the shore. He gathered twists of kinnikinick and wild tobacco and cured them in the sun and then put the twists in parfleches.

She gathered cherries, sometimes serving them raw and sometimes stewing them with meat. Some of them she pounded to a fine pulp—skin, flesh, pit—to make soap.

He took the colt to the river and gentled it into the deeper waters, teaching it to swim and to accept his handling. He delighted in swimming with the colt under his arm.

She hung the child from the peg in the wall near the fire. She rocked it to sleep, singing a lullaby in a low, whispering drawling manner:

> "A-wu-wu-wu
> Be still my baby
> Sleep sleep
> A-hu-hu-hu.
>
> "A-wu-wu-wu
> My baby be still
> Sleep sleep
> A-hu-hu-hu.

When the baby would not sleep, she sang songs to strengthen its man soul:

"My son, it is a sad thing.
A day will soon come
When you must leave your mother.
Your father will call,
The drums will call,

   The warriors will call,
   Crying loud:
   'They are coming, the chargers!
   It is good to die young!'

"My son, be strong, do not fear.
Remember the old ones.
Remember the hungry children."

Over the days the white colt became vexingly domestic.
They could not make a move but what it was in the way,
bumping into them around the fire, gamboling against them
when they went for water, even insisting on lying next to
them when they went to bed.

Yet, for all the colt's affectionate playing, No Name still
brooded on occasion. Haunting images tormented him.
Sometimes, memory of his mother telling of his older
brother Pretty Rock became confused with a picture of Circling Hawk kneeling over him on the grit sand beside the
Great Smoky Water. Sometimes memory of his father sitting in noble repose beside his fire got mixed up with
Dancing Sun in rampant battle with Black One on the burning prairie. Sometimes memory of the love between the
slow brown stud and its mother became mixed up with
scenes from his childhood. And sometimes, when he con-
templated the healing wound on his thigh where Dancing
Sun had bitten him, he thought of himself as Leaf's brother
Burnt Thigh.

Once Leaf broke across his brooding with a question.
She was sitting across the fire from him, giving suck to the
baby. "My husband, I see that you look often into the darkness."

He jerked erect. Ahh, her spirit soul had been visiting

with his spirit soul and he had not known it. He permitted a silence to widen between them, then said, "It is nothing."

"What is it that you see in the darkness?"

"It is nothing."

"You have not told me much of your vision, my husband. Is there more?"

"What can a woman know of a man's vision?"

"I have seen you thinking about your father. Do you not remember your mother?"

He watched her narrowly. He wasn't sure if it was the shadow of a sinking flame passing over her moon-round face or a brief knowing smile. He said shortly, "A son always remembers his mother."

She looked down in love at her suckling son. "Does he think of her when he is being very brave?"

"When he is brave he remembers how his father stood up to the enemy and overcame him."

"Does he ever think of his mother's brother?"

"I think mostly of my father. Moon Dreamer is sometimes my preceptor but my father is my father."

She sat very still. A complete awareness of his troubles seemed to emanate from her stolid silence.

"Ae," he said then, sighing, "sometimes it is difficult to know when a memory is not a vision."

"My husband, what has your vision to do with your father?" Upon her question, the baby quit suckling. It gradually let her nipple slip from its lips. Slowly, after a moment, a white drop of milk formed over the dark nipple and then ran down the underside of her rose-brown breast.

"Woman, the question you ask is as dark as its answer."

She threw a brief look up at the leather case containing his warclub. "I have seen your warclub. On one side I see painted a white mare and the Butte of Thunders and a Yankton capturing a white stallion. On the other side I see painted a white stud colt and a young warrior returning to his father's lodge and the figure of an old one rising in the sky."

He held himself severely erect. "You see well, woman."

"Why should the father have to die?"

"Woman, the answer to your question is a thing that sometimes does not let me sleep at night."

"Tell me the full vision, my husband. Perhaps a wife can help her husband understand it."

Slowly, reluctantly, in the briefest of words, he told her all that had been revealed to him in the sun dance.

Her eyes showed rings of white by the time he finished. Then slowly her eyes fell and she looked down at her baby. She shivered. "Let us hope our son will never be tormented by so terrible a vision."

"Aii," No Name cried. "Yet I would never deny it him. It is not a good thing to deny the vision. Worse misfortune always befalls those who do."

"What will you do?"

"My helper will tell me."

"How can a son destroy his father?"

"My helper will tell me what to do when the time comes."

"It is a terrible thing when a son is asked to do such a thing to his father."

"A man must obey the voice within."

There was a long pause, then she asked, as she gazed in sad love upon her smiling baby, "When will you make the divination for our return?"

"Tomorrow, after the sun sets. I will then offer sacrifices and seek instruction from those of the other world."

"It will be a good thing to show our son to my mother and father. Yet I shall be sad on our return. I have come to love your father."

The next day at dusk he made the divination. He went to a lonely place beside the river and built a small stick fire. He sprinkled a handful of tobacco in the flames as a token offering to the sun. He hung some dried meat in the brush for the four-leggeds to eat so they might tell those of the other world that his heart was good. He threw a few kernels of precious corn upon the grass so the wingeds would tell Wakantanka that his hand was always open.

Last he poured some badger blood over a buffalo chip and stirred the two together with a stick. When he had mixed them sufficiently, so that the wisdom-giving power of those who live underground had become one with the truth-telling power of those who live above the ground, he peered into the blood-and-dung pie long and anxiously. Gradually, as the evening light faded, lines and swirls began to form into a picture. Only when it was almost dark did he see it clearly: a man on a sorrel horse leading the way, with a woman following on a dun mare, a baby and some household goods riding in a basket on two travois poles, while around them a white colt galloped, making a circle like a burning corona around a sun.

"Thank you, thank you. Now I fear only what must be done to my father. I love my father dearly and do not wish to kill him."

# 2

First the ears of a sorrel horse showed over the low rise, then the tufts of a wolf-cap, then the bronze face of a man. Slowly the whole of the man and the horse came to view. It was late in the afternoon and the sinking sun hit the high cheeks of the man and the bluff chest of the horse full on. The man was stripped for action: quiver bristling with arrows, bow strung, knife ready in the belt, warclub dangling from the wrist.

Behind the man came a woman on a dun mare. The woman sat with her legs straddled over the thin ends of travois poles. Behind her on the travois, on top of a basket of goods, rode a baby nodding in its cradle. Farther behind ran a white colt, sometimes skimming over the grass, sometimes stumbling in buck brush.

The man held up his hand. They stopped. Leaning forward, eyes glittering, the man searched the horizon ahead.

The woman looked back and smiled tiredly at the sleeping baby and the gamboling colt.

The man sat as high as he could on his horse and looked once more along the entire length of the horizon before them. At last the man said, "They are not in their accustomed place beside Falling Water."

"Perhaps they have not returned from the Place of the Pipestone."

"It is now the Moon of Ripe Corn, woman. It is already long past the time for the making of the pipe."

The woman waited patiently.

The man said, "Perhaps they have removed to a new place along the river."

"Perhaps the buffalo did not come to the valley this summer and they have gone for a summer hunt from which they have not yet returned."

"Woman, you have forgotten the power of Moon Dreamer's buffalo medicine. When he dances and sings for the buffalo to come, they come. His dancing and their coming is one and the same. His medicine has never failed the Yanktons."

The woman waited patiently.

Again the man rose to his full height on the horse. Finally, staring intently at the wide valley ahead, he made out what looked like a circle of sharp wolf teeth.

"Do you see them, my husband?"

"It is as I have said. They have removed to a new place. I see the Yankton tepees on the east side of the river. It is where the grass is deep for the horses."

"Ahh, the new encampment will have a sweet smell."

As the man watched, a puff of smoke rose off the bluffs above the camp, white against a yellow sunset. "They have seen us," he cried. "They ask what is the news."

Quickly he put his horse through a series of zigzag maneuvers, telling the guards on the bluffs that he brought much that was good. He watched until he saw small specks run down toward camp, then said, "Let us rest the horses. I wish to prepare for the welcome home."

He slid to the ground and settled to one side in the green grass. From a small leather case he dug out some black paint, the symbol of joy, and smeared a wide band across his face from nose to ear. He next decorated the sorrel, painting white circles on its flanks and hanging brilliant red feathers in its tail. He also caught the white colt and hung a beautiful necklace of red quills around its neck. And last he fastened the scalp of the Pawnee, as well as a portion of Dancing Sun's scarlet mane, on the necklace, in such a way that they dangled noticeably every time the colt moved.

The woman waited until he had finished, then asked, "Will my husband carry his warclub?"

He caught what she meant. He looked down at the figures he had painted on it. "Perhaps my father Redbird will not see them if I swing the warclub swiftly about to show my joy."

"You will forget and he will see." She sighed. "It is a sad thing."

He remounted the sorrel. "Woman, the gods have decided what is to be done. Let us not speak of it any more."

They rode in dignity toward the camp. The white stud colt gamboled around them, its necklace gingling on each leap.

When they were yet some distance away, the people began to stream out toward them, first the children, then the young maidens, then the stalking guards. The old men, smoking on the nearby red rocks, slowly got to their feet, while the old women, looking wonderingly, gathered in the doorways of their tepees.

No Name held his head high, looking from side to side in triumph. The golden sunset struck his high cheekbones a warm glancing blow. Leaf rode demurely behind him, with an occasional flash of eye to either side to see if the people properly appreciated their miraculous return.

The maidens and the guards laughed and cried. They sang songs. They danced. They cried out the names of No Name and Leaf again and again. The children raced around the two walking horses and the pacing white colt like swift swallows. There was a great tumult of shouting and rejoicing and a rising of thick red dust. All held out their hands to No Name and Leaf. Yet no one touched them. The people were full of marveling and, in awe, kept a proper distance.

The triumphant procession had hardly passed in through the horns of the camp, when the maiden named Pretty Walker came weeping around the side of a tepee. She had seen both Leaf and the baby and knew what their coming meant. She cried out at No Name in a piercing voice, "I have waited! Let me hear your new song!"

No Name's eyes slowly hardened over.

"I have waited," Pretty Walker cried again. "Where is he who said he would come?"

No Name guided his horse over to where she stood. He looked down at her sternly. "Are you angry that a Yankton woman who was once lost is now found? Also, the day will soon come when I shall become known as a great chief and a lucky hunter. My lodge shall be known as one belonging to a generous feastmaker, who has mercy on the hungry and the helpless. I shall have need of more than one wife. Therefore, woman, wait as before. I shall come. Do not always act as one who resembles a hurt puppy."

Pretty Walker hid her face in her hands. Then with a quick, almost violent motion, she whirled around and disappeared into her mother's tepee.

When No Name looked back, he caught Leaf looking at him with angry flashing eyes. He stiffened, almost haughtily, and said, "Woman, put away your jealousy. I spoke to Pretty Walker the day I left, when it was thought by all that you were dead."

The people continued to rejoice and dance around them, singing, calling out their names. Some of the young men came running with a belly drum and began to beat out impromptu songs.

The loud drumming frightened the colt. It ran close against Leaf and the dun mare, stepping high and quick, its blue eyes dilated, its little red plume of a tail lifted.

Out of a further tepee popped first an old woman, then an old man. Both looked as if awakened from a long sleep. Their eyes fell upon the triumphant figure of No Name, then upon Leaf behind him, then upon the baby in its cradle on the travois. Slowly their eyes widened to large white circles. Then both clapped hand to mouth.

Leaf saw them. "My father, my mother," she cried, "look, I return!" Then Leaf's face broke and her eyes closed over. Her lips twisted.

Owl Above and Full Kettle came running on old knees. They touched the hem of their daughter's tunic, weeping, laughing.

Between gasps, Leaf cried, "See my son, see my husband!"

"We see them, our daughter, we see them," they cried, and fell against her leg.

No Name held himself in check. It was not a good thing

for a son-in-law to look too closely upon the faces of his in-laws.

Then Circling Hawk stepped out of the soldiers' lodge in the middle of the camp. He came stalking toward No Name, a large hearty smile on his rough face. "Ho, I see you return with a blackened face, friend."

"Ho, and I see that you have kept camp well, brother. There is not a face missing."

"Have you a song for us to sing?" the maidens around them cried.

No Name smiled. "I will sing it at the proper time."

"Give it to us now. We wish to sing."

No Name smiled again. "I have not thought much upon it."

"Sing us a song," they cried. "Have you not done a great thing?"

Still smiling, he reined in some and sang in step with his horse. He began each stanza on a high note and slowly let the melody drift down.

> "Friends, behold my horse.
> It is a seed colt,
> Son of a great white one.
> There is much to say.

> "Friends, behold my wife.
> She is a brave one.
> The Pawnees could not destroy her.
> There is much to say.

> "Friends, behold us.
> I went away one,
> I return five and one.
> There is much to say."

The young singers at the belly drum, holding a hand to the side of the mouth, repeated it after him loud and full. The young braves bounded, the maidens hop-danced, the children swirled underfoot, the old men shuffled stiffly beside the red rocks, and the old women sang in falling quavering accents. Again the rising dust of wild tumult filled the center of the village.

No Name looked ahead to Moon Dreamer's lodge. The door was lashed shut. No Name's face fell. The closed door meant that his uncle was not going to rejoice on his safe return until after all of the vision had been fulfilled.

No Name next looked ahead to his father's tepee. His heart leaped up. His father and mother were waiting at the door. No Name's face slowly became grave with duty. And forgetting, he let his warclub dangle from his wrist in full view of his father.

His father looked at him, then at Leaf, then at the two horses, finally at the skittish white colt.

No Name saw that his father had aged greatly. The nipples of his chest hung slack, his arms hung crooked, and a wrinkled gathering of old skin puffed out at the elbows.

No Name reined in his horse and stepped down. Before he could defend himself, his old mother Star That Does Not Move rushed up and, crying, ran her fingers over his face as one who was blind. Tears coursed down her old smoked cheeks.

No Name suffered her. He stood very still.

At last his mother broke off, and still crying, without saying anything, she took the reins from his hand and led his sorrel away.

Loves Roots next stepped out of the tepee. Loves Roots looked at No Name, choked back a cry, made a move as if to touch him, then went to help Leaf with the baby and the dun mare and the white colt.

Left alone, father and son looked at each other with eyes full of delicate questioning. Then, just as their dark faces were about to break, they fell upon each other's shoulder in love and embraced each other.

No Name was the first to withdraw. He held his father fondly by the elbows a moment, then let him go and stepped into the tepee.

Son and father sat by the fire, the son in the place of the guest of honor, the father against his willow back-rest. Both began to pick up tiny twigs and one by one to throw them into the fire. The flames brightened, and lighted their faces clearly, the son's blackened one and the father's gray-tinged one.

Star bustled in. She took off No Name's moccasins, rubbed the soles of his feet, then slipped on a new pair of moccasins. She set a pot of meat and dried plums to warm near the fire. A moment later Leaf and the baby and Loves Roots came in. The two women made themselves busy on the woman's side.

Presently the food was warm enough and Star filled two wooden bowls and handed them to father and son. Redbird waited politely until his son was almost finished before he began.

After the bowls were removed, Redbird prepared some tobacco on his cutting board. He filled his red pipe in quiet ceremony. After he had it going properly, and had held it out to the great directions, he handed the pipe across to No Name. Calmly, wordless, the two men took turns puffing. Star and Loves Roots and Leaf rustled in the shadows behind them. The women waited.

Redbird puffed the pipe a last time, then clapped out the ball of dead ashes in the palm of his hand and threw it in the fire. Looking No Name clearly in the eye, he said, "My son, I see you have returned with a blackened face."

No Name could not quite hold up to his father. "My father, I have been to a great distance. I have worn out many moccasins."

"Tell me, at what place have you stood and seen the good?"

"In all the places you told me of before I left. Beside the River That Sinks. Beside the River of Little Ducks. Also, I saw the sacred stones. They were two and they were painted red."

"Ai," his father cried, starting back, "did they show you the true path?"

"Ae, they did. I was very happy."

No Name then told of his long journey in detail. His father listened with parted mouth, lips moving as if he already knew the words before No Name spoke them.

As he talked, No Name was keenly aware of Leaf listening behind him with the other two women. Leaf would be wondering if he would again withhold from his father the last part of the vision. Well, now that he was home again, sitting before his father face to face, he found he still loved his father too much to hurt him in his old age. So yet again he would withhold it.

When No Name finished the telling, there was a long silence, broken only by the sighs of Star and Loves Roots.

No Name dropped another little stick into the fire. After a moment the heat of the fire caught hold of the stick and it burst into flame. He watched the new flame for a time, then threw a quick look at his father to see how he had taken it.

His father sat impassive, also musing at the new flame. There was no hint, neither in the expression around his eyes nor on his wide lips, that he did not accept the recital as the full truth.

No Name just barely managed to keep the trembles out of his fingers.

The door flap parted and an old man known as Shakes His Spear pushed in, his brown wrinkled face covered with a fawning smile. Shakes His Spear shuffled up to No Name, nudged him, and in a low whisper urged him to let him announce his deed of valor to the village.

No Name shook his head gently yet firmly. He felt sorry for the old man. Shakes His Spear had outlived his usefulness as warrior and provider, and now in his old age tried to get returning warriors to let him tell the news. Everyone knew that in return for the telling the old man expected the present of some food or a new blanket.

"The people wait," Shakes His Spear said. "They wish to hear the news of the great things you have done. Also, they wish to dance the victory."

"Later," No Name said. "My father and I still have much to talk about."

Shakes His Spear still tugged at him, filling his ear with flattery. "You have overcome a great enemy. You have been a very brave one. The people wish to know of this. They wish to know how and where each wound was given and received."

"My father and I still wish to talk. Go. Later we will call the herald."

"The people wish to celebrate the glory. It is theirs to know. What you have done belongs to them."

No Name shook off the old man's touch again. "Later. Go."

"Already some of the young braves laugh and say that you have chased a ghost stallion seen in a boy's dream."

"Go."

"They also laugh and wonder at this white colt you have brought home. They wonder why he should be considered a great horse."

"Ho, would they mock at the wishes of the gods?"

"Ahh, it is only a manner of saying by the young men."

Redbird finally raised his eyes. "When my son and I have finished talking together, I will call Thunder Close By to tell of it." Then Redbird smiled, and added kindly, "It is a chief's son who has returned. Therefore it must fall to the camp herald to tell of it. But do not fear. There will be many gifts and you will be among those who shall receive. I have heard your words of praise for my son, and they are good. Tell the people a feast is being prepared. Let everybody paint up, cook meat, cut tobacco, and get ready for a big dance."

"Thank you, thank you," old Shakes His Spear cried.

"Also, inform the old men and the chiefs of the warrior societies to gather in the soldiers' lodge that they may examine my son closely as to his deed of valor as well as to the second part of his vision. This is to be done before the feast and the dance. It is time that my son wore an honor feather. Also that he be given a new name."

"Hi-ye, thank you, thank you." Shakes His Spear placed his hands on No Name's head and shed tears over him a moment. Then he scuttled for the door and disappeared.

There was a whispering outside in the dusk, then gradually a hum of excited voices rose on the evening air.

Redbird listened to the happy sounds outside, then, again lifting his old eyes, looked across the lodge at Star. "Woman," he said gently, "where is the meat for the feast? My son has returned in glory."

Without a word, Star and Loves Roots stepped outdoors. They called up the dogs. There was some scuffling, then some cringing and whimpering, then some crushing blows on skulls. Soon four fat dogs were in the pot and cooking.

Smiling gently, yet carefully avoiding a direct look at Leaf, Redbird said, "My son, I am glad that you have brought home a good wife. Where is my grandson? I wish to see him."

There was a low cry of pleasure from Leaf. She took the baby from its cradle and handed it over to No Name. Leaf had been waiting for this moment ever since their arrival and had cleaned the baby carefully, repacking its buttocks with fresh milkweed down and scenting it with the juice of the orange lily. No Name fondled the baby a moment, smiled at it, and then handed it around the fire to Redbird.

Redbird looked down at the baby a long time. The baby in turn blinked up at him, its black eyes for once holding steady on one spot.

At last Redbird smiled. With his thumb and forefinger, playfully, he gave the baby's nose a tweak. "Little one, this is done so that your nose may be made to grow long before it is hard."

The boy was not in the least frightened at Redbird's touch. To both No Name's and Leaf's surprise, he suddenly smiled up at his grandfather.

Everyone in the tepee, including Star and Loves Roots, laughed happily.

Redbird gave No Name a gently inquiring look.

No Name instantly caught what his father wanted. "He is well formed, my father."

"Hi-e. It is well." Redbird gave the baby back to No Name for him to give back to Leaf. Then with a hand on his knee, groaning some, Redbird rose from his back-rest. "My son, let us go to the council lodge where the elders and warriors await us. It is time."

At that very moment, the herald Thunder Close By coughed outside the door, then stepped inside.

"Ae, what is it?" Redbird inquired mildly.

"Circling Hawk sends to say that the elders and the warriors have spoken together." Thunder Close By saw the baby and lowered his voice to a whisper. But even his whispering was so penetrating it scared the baby and caused it to cry in fear. "With one voice they say it would be a good thing if Redbird's son were to tell of his great deed and also the second part of his vision to all of the people at once, the women and children at the same time with the council of elders and warriors. The people cry to hear it. The elders and warriors already know that Redbird's son deserves an honor feather and a new name. What Redbird's son has dreamed and done belongs to all of the people immediately."

Redbird grunted. He waited until Leaf had quieted the child, then said, "I hear you. It is good. Tell the keeper of the sacred fire to build a large camp fire. Tell the elders and the warriors and all the people to assemble in one place." Redbird shook his head a little. "It is not the customary thing. But the people wish it and thus it shall be done."

Thunder Close By grunted, then turned and left.

No Name sat very still. Tears filled his eyes. "My helper, they wish to know. How can I tell them that a true son has been commanded to kill so loving and so old a father?"

Silence.

"Also, my helper, if I withhold the white mare's words from my father and all the people, will it not be considered an evil thing? The wrath of the gods are certain to fall upon the Yanktons if I tell a partial truth." No Name wept within. "Helper, I have come to a fork in the trail. I am not a twin spirit that I can travel down two paths at the same time. Which is the true path?"

Silence.

Thunder Close By began to bellow outside, going the rounds, calling up the people, telling them No Name would soon appear with his father to tell of great things, telling them to dress for the scalp dance, calling up the singers and drummers.

A deep murmur of approbation spread from tepee to tepee. The little children cried gleefully that now they could stay up late and play. The warriors began to hold kill talks in groups all over the village common.

Redbird looked wonderingly at No Name still sitting by the fire. "My son, why do you not get up and paint yourself for the telling and the dance?"

No Name got to his feet slowly. "My face is already blackened, my father."

"What? Is this not an occasion for your best ceremonial painting? The people demand it, my son."

With a heavy heart, No Name began to prepare himself. He let his father step outside unknowing.

When all the people had assembled around the big fire in the center of the camp, Circling Hawk brought out the white skull of a dog and placed it on a piece of ground cleared of all grass and sticks and insects. The moment the skull touched earth the voices of the singers fell low and the drummers tapped lightly. Children sat on the ground on the inner circle, while ring upon ring of grownups stood behind them, the nearest faces lighted a bright red-brown, the farther faces a dark brown. Teeth flashed in dusky faces; eyes sparkled under slanted brows.

The drummers paused. One of them gave the drum a thump. Then the herald began to clear a way for Redbird and No Name. Redbird walked in quiet dignity, holding his copper-tipped spear before him. No Name walked with face averted.

Redbird held up his copper-tipped spear. "My children, you see me now an old man." Firelight glinted on his bear-claw necklace. "I have waited many winters for this day. At last it is here. My son has returned in glory. He wishes to tell you of his deed of valor. He also wishes to tell you the second part of the vision which was withheld from you at the sun dance. This is so that the Yanktons may know how great a nation they are." Redbird let his spear sink to the earth, slowly. "I have said."

The drummers beat up a short resounding song. The old women lifted their voices in trills of hope.

Leaf came next carrying Sharp Horn's scalp tied to the tip of a pole. The scalp pole had been daubed with bright vermilion. She had on her best dress, a loose supple doeskin tunic, and had painted her cheeks and the parting in her hair a deep red. She looked up at the dangling Pawnee scalp, her eyes suddenly full of feverish hate, her face expressing terrible revulsion. She shook the pole frenziedly, whipping the scalp about so hard it snapped like a small whip, as if she believed it to be still alive and capable of suffering. A murmuring, then a loud cry of hate, swept over the assembly. Leaf accepted the cry of the people eagerly. She began to revile the enemy scalp, then revile all of the Pawnee people. The Pawnees were dogs of dogs, not men of men as they bragged. Pawnee sons were rapers and killers of their mothers. Pawnee daughters were vampires and murderers of their fathers. Then, suddenly breaking off, violent passions abruptly passing away, Leaf set the pole in a hole beside the dog skull and stepped back.

The drummers beat up a short measured chant, then followed it with a quick loud yell.

No Name stepped forward. Because of his father's remark, he had taken some pains to dress for the occasion. A scarlet plume bobbed in his hair, red woodpecker feathers shimmered down the front and back of his clout, and a pair of shell anklets clashed every time he took a step. Circling Hawk had helped him paint on his sun dance markings again, a red sun on his chest and a black crescent moon on his back, with twenty-eight stripes of white radiating from the sun and coming together again on the moon.

The people recognized the sun dance markings and a low cry moved through the assembly. "Ahh-h-h."

No Name felt all eyes on him. The close attention of the people lifted him despite his melancholy. The moment had come for him to exalt them. His heart began to beat high in his throat. His chest swelled. Memory of all the difficulties he had overcome during the past year rushed over him as a great wind. His eyes glittered like a panther's in his blackened face, darting this way and that. His limbs shuddered with power. He lifted his warclub flashing in the light of the glowing bonfire. Then quickly, with a show of authority, he struck the dog skull.

All fell silent.

Lifting his voice, with swift gestures, he recited the details of his adventure. He told of eluding the Omaha beyond the River of the Double Bend, told of finding two sacred painted stones which pointed the way for him, told of finding Leaf buried in the sand.

He turned completely around to take a look into all the ranked black eyes a moment. "When I listened for the voice within, I found the true path. Wakantanka, he who lives behind the sun, also wants you to listen for the voice within. It is when all do this, all rocks and earth and sand, all growing things, all fourleggeds, all twoleggeds, all wingeds, all spirits great and small, even Wakantanka himself, that all are happy together."

A single boom sounded on the drum.

The red flames of the bonfire subtly became gray smoke, and the gray smoke in turn subtly became a purple plume rising against the black sky of night.

He told next how he killed a Pawnee and counted coup on him. He pointed to the scalp on the pole in proof. Instantly the people let go with a mighty roar. He then told, point for point, of entering the lodge of the Pawnee chief Sounds The Ground As He Walks and of all that happened therein. He told of Sounds The Ground's eventual kindness to them and how he and Leaf were given two horses and safe conduct toward the River of Little Ducks.

"Even among the hated there are sometimes good men."

Boom!

Voice low, yet vibrant with power, he told of finding at last the great white stallion himself, with a family of many spotted horses, of how he watched Dancing Sun for days to learn his ways, watering and feeding and herding, of how he finally set out after him, going around and around in a circling drive on the wide lonesome barrens. As proof of it all, he held up his dark leg to show them the light-brown scar where Dancing Sun had bitten him.

He paused for a breath.

The eyes of all, young as well as old, stared at him in fixed unwavering gaze. Blushes of light from the rose-pink fire moved across their faces.

He began to shake with emotion. His voice sank, he almost choked, when he told them of leaping astride Dancing Sun and of the wonderful ride that followed. In vivid pantomime he showed them how he and the horse ducked and dodged the great hail, how they swam in the raging flood, how the great white one finally took his own life by leaping off a cliff. He staggered, sobbed, shrieked, as he recounted his sorrow in that awful hour of loss.

"He died as a noble Yankton would die. As one of those who cannot be conquered!"

The people listened as with one heart and one mind. The drummers and singers sat stunned. The wise old men sat with their mouths open, little boys again being told a marvelous fable from another time. The maidens and the children sat with their breaths held and their eyes dilated. For one long beating moment of time, the people were as one being with No Name.

Then he told of how he found immediately after, first, Leaf his wife washing a newborn infant, second, Twinkling Feet the stallion's favorite mare giving birth to twin colts.

"Twins!" Redbird ejaculated. "Such a thing happens only when the gods intervene. Ai, it is wakan."

"Wakan!" all the people murmured.

"One was alive!" No Name cried. He pointed to someone standing beyond the rim of the firelight. "You see how now!"

All faces turned to look.

Looking proudly from side to side, stepping with pompous straddled legs, Circling Hawk came in leading the little white stud colt.

No Name pointed again. "See him! There he is. The son of Dancing Sun. Soon he will be as great as his father. He will make a noble seed-father for all our mares. All the Yankton breeders shall use him. He will give us many spotted horses and will make our nation a great one."

A roar of joy exploded from the assembled host. The drummers and singers beat up an ecstatic chant. The old women ululated a high wild chorus.

No Name held up his hand for silence, again beckoned for someone beyond the rim of light to come forward.

This time it was his old friend Strikes Twice, leading the sorrel One Who Follows and the dun mare Black Stripe.

"See them," No Name cried. "They became our faithful friend in the land of the enemy. There is no fault in them. I give them both to Owl Above. The Pawnees took from Owl Above's herd and now the Pawnees give back to Owl Above's herd. Hi-e! I have said."

The people broke out with cries of approval.

Then it was Redbird's turn to hold up his hand for silence. He stepped forward gravely. He looked at the individual faces of the elders and warriors around the circle, his slow gaze picking them out one by one. "You have heard my son tell of great things. You have seen the white seed colt. What is your wish? Does our son deserve the honor feather at last? Shall we give him a new name? What is your wish?"

Without hesitation, with one voice, the elders and warriors and all the people shouted, "The son of Redbird has done a great thing! Give him the feather of the golden eagle! Give him his name!"

Silence. Full. Intent. Black eyes glittered in the jumping firelight. Bronze forms stood as statues in the red dust.

"No one steps forward to deny it. It is good."

Redbird turned to Speaks Once the father of Strikes Twice, standing at the edge of the crowd. He beckoned for him to come forward. "Friend," Redbird said, "we ask this. Our son needs a new name. Will you give it?"

Speaks Once strutted up. Thick lips proud, deerbone breastpiece gingling, he drew a single eagle feather from his belt. He held it up to the light for all to see. He turned it slowly. The tip of the feather was fluffed out with the red down of a woodpecker.

"My son," Speaks Once said, and he tapped No Name lightly on the shoulder with the point of the feather.

No Name knelt in the red dust at the foot of the scalp pole.

"My son," Speaks Once said, "this day you have made the Yankton people a great nation."

"Houw, houw!"

"It is because of what you have done that we give you this." Speaks Once thrust the long tail feather into No Name's hair, at the back so that the tip stuck straight up.

No Name shivered at the touch.

Speaks Once turned slowly, solemnly, and faced toward the tepee of Moon Dreamer. He said aloud, "It has been told us that the gods have given our intercessor a new Name for our son. Let our holy man now come forward and tell it so that it may be given."

All eyes turned to look at Moon Dreamer's lodge. Even as they looked, an old hand reached out of the lodge and pulled the door flap shut and lashed it down tight.

A gasp went up.

No Name shuddered. Looking to one side as he knelt, past his left cheek, he caught his father looking at him with glittering probing eyes. No Name groaned. His father still expected him to tell the remainder of the vision. In the excitement of the moment, the people had forgotten about it, but not his father. Moon Dreamer knew this and that was why he would not join them in the naming.

All stood stunned for some moments. All feared what the gods might do. Some even looked up to see if the Thunders might not be coming.

Then Redbird, his eyes almost closing over, pointed to the herald Thunder Close By and said, "Friend, approach the lodge of our holy man. Ask him if he will not at least give us the name. We wish this. Though there is yet much to know, our son deserves a Name at this time." Redbird slowly looked down at his son in love. "Hi-ye! far better this son than his father."

Thunder Close By walked across the space toward Moon Dreamer's painted tepee. He coughed. He said aloud, "Our father, what have we done wrong? Give us the name."

A silence followed, a silence so deep hearts began to beat like wild running horses. All listened as Thunder Close By leaned forward to hear what Moon Dreamer might have to say.

There was a low harsh whispering between Thunder Close By standing without the lodge and Moon Dreamer sitting within.

At last Thunder Close By nodded. He returned to the circle. He whispered clearly and closely into the ear of Speaks Once. Again the people stilled and tried to catch what was said.

Speaks Once turned and looked down at the kneeling No Name again. "My son, take courage. All is well. Moon Dreamer withholds himself only because a certain thing is yet to come. But he sends to say that you have earned the honor feather and the new name." Speaks Once faced the people. He lifted his hand and proclaimed to all. "Ha-ho! let the people know this. Our son was valiant and dared to face the great wild stallion. He rode after him and caught him. He rode him over the cliff and almost into the skies. Also he returned with the great one's white colt. Therefore know our son at last as He Comes From Conquering A Horse." Speaks Once placed his hands on No Name's head and wept over him. "My son, take courage. Your name is now Conquering Horse. Arise. Stand on your feet. I have said. Yelo."

Bearing the burden of his new name, Conquering Horse rose slowly to his feet.

Redbird held up his copper-tipped spear. "My children, you have seen my son give all his horse wealth to Owl Above, who once had a fine herd. It is good." Redbird turned his stiff body slowly around, looking at the people every one. "Tomorrow, before the sun reaches the midday point, many more gifts will be distributed to the needy and to those who were valiant in the summer hunt." Redbird's old hawk face became gentle with indulgence. "But now it is time for dancing and feasting. Sing, my children. Dance, my children. Be happy. A great thing has come to our nation. This day we are the fortunate ones under the sun."

"Houw, houw!"

The drum boomed, once, twice, thrice, and on the fourth stroke, boom! the singers began to cry the scalp dance song. Men dancers shot out into the circles of light and began to bounce and leap about in wild abandon. They gesticulated. Agitated feathers snapped and sunflower bustles bobbed. The men cried, they howled, they bellowed. Some became as crows, some as hawks, some as eagles, some as fox, some as wolves, some as buffalo bulls. Feet danced up on the beat. Red dust swirled overhead.

At last, not able to resist it, young maidens along the outside of the dancing area began to dance too. They stood facing the scalp pole, hopping, fringes flouncing in unison, dancing in one place.

The men cried, "U-hu-hu-hu-hu!"

The women cried, "U-wu-wu-wu!"

Gradually the drumming and the singing and the dancing rose to a tremendous pitch. The dancers churned up the red earth like the striking down of a great whirlwind. The bluffs across the valley resounded with the roar of it.

Suddenly a widow named Her Thighs Are Scarlet, and known as one of the ones who could perform magic tricks, flew in among the men dancers. She heaped up a small mound of dust on the ground, then fixed a small wooden effigy of a man on top of it. Moving with a quick back-slip step, eyes pinched shut, braids flopping, leaping and jumping, she contorted herself into such a mad whirling dance around the effigy that her dress revolved up around her neck. Her face ran with the sweat of terrible concentration. With all the power of her flesh soul she was willing a shadow soul into the man effigy.

Presently all saw the magic thing she had for them. Slowly but surely the little wooden man began to jiggle on the dust mound, then to dance on it. The little wooden man continued to dance with her until she fell to the ground exhausted and unconscious. Then it too fell and lay still.

It was a great and wakan trick, and the people cried in admiration.

In the morning, as he had promised, Redbird gave away all of his horses to his people, sharing them equally among the poor as well as the valiant.

Conquering Horse received four mares, each of them to be mated some day with his white seed colt. Among them was Swift As Wind, Redbird's favorite.

# 3

It was just after dark. Conquering Horse and Leaf lay side by side on fur bedding in their own tepee. He lay naked, she had on a doeskin nightdress. The fire, sunk to embers, cast a soft rosy light against the slanting leather sides. The sleeping baby hung in its cradle from a tepee pole. The white stud colt, curled up like a dog, slept on a pile of grass at their feet. Conquering Horse's war gear hung on a tripod just inside the door.

They lay in silence. Except for an occasional whoop from the council lodge in the center of the village and the distant murmur of Falling Water, the camp too lay in silence.

Presently Conquering Horse placed a hand of love on Leaf.

Leaf stirred, then slowly rolled away from him, on her right side. His hand slipped off her belly.

Conquering Horse considered this. What? Wasn't life already enough of a sorrow without the added burden of living with a wife who did not love one? He rolled toward her and tried again, this time placing his hand on the soft curve of her hip.

She lay stiff under it.

"Ho," he thought to himself, his eyes opening slightly. "What is this? Does she hate my touch? Have I taken unto myself a disobedient woman for a wife?" He shook her, a bit roughly, to let her know what he thought.

She continued to lay stiff under his hand.

"Woman," he said finally, taking one of her braids in his

hand and giving it a playful tug, "what would you have me do, obey the dream, or obey the love I have for my father?"

Gently, yet firmly, she pulled the braid out of his hand.

He continued this too for a while. Then he asked, in what he thought was the same sweet gentle air his father might have used, "Woman, have you turned against me?"

She moved her shoulder as if to shrug off his question.

Outside, a young brave began to blow his flute, singing a courting song to some maiden. The young brave was signaling his love to come out, that he had something to tell her. Conquering Horse's eyes filmed over in memory. Not thirteen moons ago he himself had sung such a song to Leaf. And remembering, he smiled to himself, and placed his hand on Leaf's round hip again. Gently, with soft tact, he rolled her toward him. Then he lay upon her so that her eyes were directly under his.

"Woman," he asked yet once again, "have you turned against me?"

Her eyes opened momentarily. They were hardened against him. They glittered in the soft rose light, shining in the black fixed manner of a reptile. Also she placed her elbows against him.

"Woman," he said, startled, "I see that you have turned away from your husband."

Her eyes at last softened, though she continued to hold her elbows against him.

He looked a long time into her eyes, trying to melt her with a longing look of love. He pressed his risen ardor against her.

At last, heaving a deep sigh, she said, "Foolish husband, have you forgotten to count the days? It is not fitting that we mate at this time. We must wait until after two moons have passed."

He rolled away from her. His mind hauled up short. He went back in time. He counted the days on his fingers, beginning with the little finger of his left hand, shutting it down forcibly with the thumb of his right, and when the five fingers were shut down, starting on the thumb of his right hand, shutting it down in turn with his left fist.

It was true. Four and forty nights had passed since the baby was born. Taboo required that five and forty nights should pass before man and wife could make love again.

He hated to give it up. He was aroused, and was a man, and disliked thwarting. He rolled toward her again. He slid his hands under her soft doeskin nightdress. He stroked her across the soft tufts of her pubes.

She closed her eyes and crossed her legs. She held herself rigid against him.

He tried to pry her limbs open with a knee.

She tightened harder against him. The months of carrying the baby, of lifting tepee poles and leather covering, of handling horses, had made her, in defense, more than his match.

He rubbed his nose against hers. He stroked her shoulders, downward, in love.

Yet she did not relent. Eyes held fiercely shut against him, muscles of her crossed legs hard, she continued to refuse him his pleasure.

It was then, lying hard on her, that he noticed something. She had not perfumed herself in the usual way. The smell of her was like the smell of ordinary moccasin leather. When a woman desired a man to caress her she invariably sweetened herself with one of the scents of the prairie flowers. With a grunt of anger he pushed her away.

He lay breathing hard for a few moments, then abruptly got up. He slipped into his buckskin garments. Picking up the square case in which he kept the circlet of scarlet horsehair, taking with him also a new buffalo robe, he swept out into the black night.

He stopped beside his father's lodge a moment, listening. Star's fire had fallen so low no illumination showed through the leather walls. Conquering Horse fancied he could hear his father snoring lightly, could make out his mother's occasional sighs. As for Loves Roots, he did not want to think of what she might be doing.

A thickness took hold of him. His arms felt stone heavy.

His nose was almost closed. It was in him to rage and weep at the same time.

He placed his hand over the charm behind his ear. He whispered, "I love my father very much. Must it still be done?"

Silence.

He looked down at the square case in his hand and spoke to the scarlet plume inside it. "I see you are displeased. Let us seek out Moon Dreamer that he may perform the proper ceremony. It is time."

He moved cautiously across the center of the camp, letting his toes drag across the grass to keep from tripping over ropes and stakes. He was also careful not to stumble over those who might be sleeping outside. It was not a pleasant thing to step on a soft belly in the dark and then hear a sudden gasp from the ground.

The young nightwalker still blew his flute, asking his love to come out and join him under his robe. The center campfire, collapsed to a low mound of pink coals, gave off a small aura of light. Above, a silver net of stars drifted slowly across the sky.

When he came to Moon Dreamer's lodge, he saw that a small fire still burned within the tepee. The tepee glowed softly like a huge pointed lantern. There was just enough light within to make the white decoration painted high on the outside glow like a bloody moon. As he stood before the door, he saw the shadow of someone passing the fire within moving upon the semi-transparent walls. Ahh, his uncle was still up.

Conquering Horse coughed lightly to let his uncle know a visitor stood without. Then he lifted the flap, stooped inside, and, moving around the fire, seated himself on the guest robe. He waited a decent interval; then, with modest demeanor, looked around.

Moon Dreamer sat across the lodge from him, legs crossed, looking at his small stick fire, unmoving, stiff, as if someone had carved him out of dark redwood. Except for a clout, he was naked.

Conquering Horse was startled to see the change in his

uncle. Like his father, Moon Dreamer had aged greatly the past summer. Pus ran in the corner of his left eye and the marks of the woman on his chest hung even lower than his father's.

"Ae," Conquering Horse thought, "soon I alone will have the burden of watching over my people. My uncle will also soon join those of the other world. Hi-e! And I have not yet seen the end of my torment."

After a further silence, Conquering Horse held up the new white robe he had brought with him, folded it, and placed it to one side of Moon Dreamer's doubled knees. "My uncle," he said, "see, I have brought you a present. It is from a buffalo that was slain so that Leaf my wife and I might eat while I chased the great white stallion. It is the best of all the robes that my wife has yet made. She prays that you will find it warm in the winter moons to come. I have said."

Moon Dreamer sat as if he had not heard a word. He neither inclined his head up or down, nor moved it to the right or the left. Only the drop of pus in the corner of his eye moved. It rolled halfway down the side of his high hawk nose.

"My father," Conquering Horse said, "you did not step out of your door to see me return in glory. You did not come to visit my lodge to see your new grandnephew. You did not attend the ceremony of my naming. Therefore, my father, I have come with the scarlet plume. It is that which the white mare spoke of, from that place where all can be seen by a horse." Conquering Horse placed the leather case containing the circlet of scarlet mane before Moon Dreamer. "My father, I have come. Bless my fetish that I may do that which has been bidden me. Remember, I have chosen you as my intercessor."

Moon Dreamer cracked out of his stiff pose. He picked up the white robe, hefted it once in his gray-edged hands, grunted, set it to one side behind him. He reached back and picked up his black buffalo mask and slipped it on. Its two curved horns gleamed like ebony. Next he picked up his red ceremonial pipe from its resting place, filled it, lighted it. After saluting the six great powers, he offered it to Conquering Horse. They smoked the pipe by turns until all the tobacco was burned away.

Then Moon Dreamer lifted his old eyes and fixed them glittering on Conquering Horse. "Are you ready to fulfill the vision that was given you?"

Conquering Horse groaned. He bowed his head. "I am ready. I must try to be a brave man and take things as they come. I cannot weep."

"You are ready to see your father die at last?" A mysterious black lurked in the eyeholes of Moon Dreamer's buffalo mask.

"I am ready."

"Even if it must be by your own hand?"

"I cannot weep."

"Ai, now the gods know that you fear them, seeing that you are willing to give up your true father to them. It is good."

Conquering Horse shuddered.

Moon Dreamer brushed clean a small square of earth before the fireplace. Then he took up the leather case and opened it and removed the circlet of scarlet mane. Very carefully he divided the mane into two equal parts, making a smooth round twist of each. He placed the two twists and the square case on the clean place of earth. He passed his hands over them, murmuring to himself, then let his hands fall to his doubled knees.

"My nephew, where is the piece of horse chestnut that was given you?"

Conquering Horse removed the bit of chestnut from the braid behind his left ear and gave it to Moon Dreamer. The chestnut had become cracked with age. It no longer had much odor.

Moon Dreamer looked at it, then, passing it from his left hand to his right hand, dropped it into the fire. It smoldered for a moment, then flared up brightly. A thin plume of gray smoke rose toward the smokehole. As the horse chestnut burned Moon Dreamer said, "The new has come, let the old go." Next Moon Dreamer picked up the two twists of mane and the square case and passed them from right to left and held them up over his head. "Wakantanka," he said, looking up at the smokehole, "you see these. The two scarlet twists were taken from a wakan white one, one of yours, the leather case was taken from the buffalo, also one of yours. It was done as you commanded. Let your power enter them." He waited a moment.

Of a sudden a breath of wind puffed down through the smokehole. The thin plume of smoke broke and turned aside. The fire itself darkened a moment, then quickly brightened.

Moon Dreamer looked at Conquering Horse. "My son, the power of Wakantanka has come. It has entered these things you have brought me. Treat them with the same veneration that is due Wakantanka." Moon Dreamer picked up the red pipe again, filled it, lighted it, once more offered the stem to each of the six powers. He and Conquering Horse smoked until they had finished all of the tobacco.

Moon Dreamer folded one of the red twists into the square case. Then he handed the case and the other twist to Conquering Horse. "Take these. You know what they are. The square case is your medicine bag. The twist in it is your medicine. The second twist is your fetish. When you wish to call on your medicine or on your fetish for help, remember to speak in the following manner: 'Helper, you are my god. I am in trouble. Tell me the true way. My ears are open and my heart waits. I wish to be one with you.' My son, always call on them in this manner and with these words. Now, my son, repeat the words after me."

Conquering Horse repeated the words, slowly, distinctly.

"It is good." Moon Dreamer got to his feet and reached into the dark back of his lodge and picked up a long horsetail. The horsetail had been dyed red. Moon Dreamer stood behind Conquering Horse and held the horsetail over his head. "My nephew, I have given you a fetish to hide in your hair. I have also given you a medicine to take to your lodge. The white mare told me how to prepare this fetish and this medicine. The white mare says that you should let yourself be controlled by their power. If you do this, she says it will go well with you in the life to come. You will provide for the women and children. You will be brave and truthful. The people will listen to you. You will never have to cut off the nose of your woman because of adultery."

"I hear you, my father."

"If you are lazy or a coward, the white mare says you will sleep with coyotes. Also no woman will gash her flesh for you when you die. If you tell lies the buffalo will laugh at you. Your women will suffer and your babes will have great pains in their bowels. But she says that if you listen to your holy man, the warm south wind will stay with you. I now wave the horsetail over you." Moon Dreamer slowly flourished the red horsetail over Conquering Horse's head, back and forth, four times, sharply, so that it whistled. "Go, my son. Take your new fetish and put it in your braid. Take your new medicine and hang it beside the armor that hangs on your tripod by the door. Do this so that all may see you have gone down the long road of torment."

"But, my uncle, when must I kill my father?"

Moon Dreamer looked gently down at Conquering Horse. Carefully he reached a finger under his buffalo mask and wiped away a sliding tear of yellow matter. "My son, tomorrow, at dusk, it will be given to you."

"My father is greater than I. Yet I hear you, my uncle."

"My son, do you feel the power of the white mare?"

"It is entering me."

"My son, do you feel the power of the white mare?"

"Ai, it is warming my belly."

"My son, do you feel the power of the white mare?"

"Aii! it is making me a mighty man."

Yet a fourth time Moon Dreamer asked it. "My son, do you feel the power of the white mare?"

"Hi-ye! Yes, yes, I am a great man! I am happy! Thank you, thank you."

"Return to your wife. It is now past the middle of the night. She awaits you."

He stole into his tepee. Quickly he lashed down the door flap. He stepped out of his buckskins and slipped naked into bed beside Leaf.

He trembled with exultation. He quivered from head to foot. Little shivers stirred in the muscles all over and inside his body. He could still feel the power of the white mare throbbing in him. He now saw all life as one huge flow, with himself a streaming part of it. And being a part of it he felt the whole of it. The huge flow included the lives of the wingeds and the fourleggeds and the twoleggeds, and also his life and the life of his father. One part of the flow was exactly like any other part of it. It was all one and the same. Therefore he no longer needed to think about how his father's life would end.

Leaf said suddenly beside him, "My husband, you tremble as one who has been seized with a madness."

"I have at last become one with the great flow."

"Did Moon Dreamer speak of what you must do with your father?"

"Ae, woman, he did. Tomorrow is the day. I await it. I am ready."

She lay silent a moment, then said, "My husband, I have something to ask you. Yet I am afraid to ask it."

"Speak, my wife. Are we not alone in our lodge? Neither the child nor the colt yet have ears of understanding."

She paused again, then in a hesitant voice asked, "Has your uncle ever shown jealousy of your father?"

Conquering Horse popped straight up in bed. "Woman, why should he?"

"I do not know. Though I have seen that both your father and your uncle loved your mother very much."

"Woman, why should they not love my mother?"

"I do not know. Though I have often heard my mother wonder why it was that your uncle never took a wife."

Conquering Horse's ire rose. "Woman, you have been married but a year and already gossip like a common magpie, chattering of little things."

"Is it a little thing when a great man does not take a wife to himself?"

Conquering Horse's mouth hung open in the dark. He puffed oddly. This wife of his, this Leaf woman, what a gift she had for speaking of troublesome things. Just when he had become reconciled with what had happened so far and with what was yet to happen, she came to him with a question that chilled him to the bone. He drew in a great breath, let it out again. Then he lay down.

The fire at his feet was almost out. It no longer smoked. Only in one place did a pink ember show. It peeked at him like the partly opened eye of a sleepy gray dog.

Leaf seemed to guess that her husband's sense of well-being had been disturbed. She placed a firm calloused hand on his belly, then after a moment stroked him, from the arch of his chest to his groin. Her stroking was like running fire.

Conquering Horse almost leaped off the fur bedding. "Woman," he said, trembling, "why was this done?"

For answer, she took his hand and placed it on her belly.

Moving his finger tips a little, he discovered that she too lay naked, that she had removed her doeskin nightdress. Sniffing, he also discovered that while he had been with his uncle she had perfumed herself with the juice of the purple smartweed. "Woman," he said, "when we went to bed, did you not tell me it was but the forty-fourth day?"

"Husband, it is long past the middle of the night. The morning of a new day is almost here."

He cried aloud in surprise. "Ho, I have forgotten."

"Can you now forgive me for denying you?"

"Ai," he cried.

And like clouds, his anger passed off and once again power surged through him. He found himself suddenly throbbing with love. Mating with a woman had been denied him a long time, almost another lifetime ago. An ardor like the sweet, sweet honey of the bumblebee moved through his veins.

He rolled on his side. He thrust his right hand under her head and with his left hand made love. He touched her. Her breasts were like well-fed puppies curled in sleep. He touched her. The cleft of her thighs was like a red melon split with ripeness.

"Woman, let me lie between thy breasts."

She moved eagerly under his hand. "It will be as you wish when you will it, my great one."

"Woman, do you feel the power of it?"

"Husband, your power is as the head of an eagle and I await it." She took hold of him. "It is also as the turtledove. Has not the time for the singing of birds come?"

"Open to me, my sister, my dove."

"My husband, ravish me. Love me as you once loved me by the river long ago. I have dreamed of it many times since."

"You have sweetened your breath with the juice of rose hips."

"Your head is sprinkled over with the drops of night."

"I have seen a maiden who is very beautiful. I feel sick when I think about her."

"O, my husband!" she cried, leaping under his hand, "feed among the river lilies. Be as terrible as a war party with flying pennons!"

"You have used sorcery on me, woman. I cannot help myself."

"Oh, that you were as my brother Burnt Thigh, who was lost, who sucked the breasts of my mother with me. If I should find you standing without, I would lead you inside and give you to eat of our valley, even unto the scarlet plums."

"Woman, you have eaten a part of me and now I desire to have myself back."

"Make haste, my beloved, be as the young male deer are. Come leaping upon me."

He rose as one riding a horse. With his right hand he held her head and with his left hand he caressed her hips. He thrust down at her. She thrust up at him. She clasped him around the small of his back and drew him closer and deeper. Their hips danced together. Soon his toes curled in the fur. Her heels touched behind his back. They cried in joy together. Power flowed from him and he strengthened her. She accepted it eagerly. All life flowed as one.

# 4

Conquering Horse sat on a red rock just inside the village circle.

As evening came on, a fall chill moved in from the northeast and all the tepees began to spume slow pennants of smoke. The smoke, drifting across the river, gradually formed into a low veil of fog. Most of the little children had been put to bed, though a few of the older ones still played on the tumble of red rocks beside Falling Water. A mother at the far end scolded a son to come in, telling him that if he did not hurry she would send the Owl Man after him. Two guards armed with society spears sat on their heels before the door of the council lodge warming their hands over a small stick fire. Frogs grumped beneath some cattails in a nearby swale. While off in the southwest a scattering of puffy clouds gathered slowly into a thunderhead.

Conquering Horse sighed. He crossed his legs and closed his eyes. It had been a day of waiting. Dusk was upon them and yet it had not been shown him what was to be done about his father.

Then, as he sat musing to himself, he heard a tepee door flap open.

Looking, he saw his father Redbird step outside, first stooping, then slowly straightening up. His father had on his ceremonial clothes as chief: headdress of eagle feathers falling in a beautiful crest down his back, a black glistening Buffalo bull horn set on either side of his forehead, braids long and fur-wrapped, leather shirt covered with intricate quillwork, leggings trimmed with dried scalps, a pictured robe thrown gracefully over his shoulder, and his treasured copper-tipped lance in hand.

Conquering Horse sat up. The moment had come at last.

Redbird turned toward the southwest where dusk lay like a band of rusty gold under the thunderhead. The evening light gave his lined face a momentary look of glowing youth. He stood looking fixedly at the long dark cloud.

The thundercloud began to gather in size against the wind. The already sunken sun caught it for a last time, fringing its jet-black deeps with a lace of silver. It threw a huge shadow toward the village. The sky to the north took on an eerie green cast.

Redbird's lips moved, shaping some private prayer. The expression on the whispering lips revealed neither sorrow nor happiness. Only the eyes gleamed, lighted up as if by an inward fire. A ghost sun seemed to have risen in them.

Gradually the soft northeast wind fell away. Almost at the same moment the plumes of smoke from the tepees veered and began to rise straight up, each remaining single and inviolate until they vanished into the high-thrown shadow overhead. Then, imperceptibly, the wind swung around until it came out of the southwest. At the same time the thunderhead began to move in. Its sides widened, spreading off to the north and the south. Its silver fringes slowly changed to bloody edges. The wind became warm, became soft and caressing. Shadows rustled across the green grass.

Just as the thunderhead's edges became a watery red, a vivid forked tongue zigzagged out of the ground. It hit the underside of the cloud, quivered once, then exploded into a great flash of bright blue lightning. The dazzling stroke hit a distant tree on the brown horizon. The tree seemed to vanish before the eyes. A few moments later a boom of thunder raced across the plains.

Redbird slowly straightened. His hand lifted. "Hi-e!" he cried. "Thunders, you have come for me too late. The white mare has decreed otherwise."

Again the thunderhead shot down a stroke, this time a claw of fire that caught at the highest bluff west of the river and stirred up a puff of dust. Thunder boomed deep and long as it raced east.

"Friends, I hear your war whoop!" Redbird cried. "But you have come for me too late."

Redbird's eyes burned. Holding the lance with its burnished copper tip straight up, he advanced toward the center of the village. He walked in stately dignity, erect, knees thrown forward turn by turn from the hips, slowly. When he came to the scalp pole from which the Pawnee's scalp still dangled, he stopped. He stood still a moment. Again his lips moved in inward prayer. Then, turning slowly around, he called to all sides. "Ha-ho! listen to me, my children. Now will I speak out among the Yanktons, tamers of horses." He set the heel of his lance on the ground. "Hey-a-hey, hey-a-hey, hey-a-hey, hey-a-hey! The thunder beings who have been like relations to me say they are coming to visit me again. You hear them. Well, they have come too late."

Deep silence fell over the camp. The mother calling her son stopped dead in her tracks and bowed her head. The two guards in front of the council lodge sat listening raptly. Warriors in the doorway behind the guards sat motionless. The people sitting just inside their tepees, the old as well as the young, also listened closely.

Redbird turned completely around once more, surveying all the village. As he did so, his roving eyes caught sight of Conquering Horse sitting on a red rock. Redbird fixed his gaze on his son a moment, eyes gleaming with the ghostly brightness of a sundog, then moved on.

Redbird threw back his head and again spoke loudly and clearly. "I am killed. The white mare says I must die at last. I am no longer needed. Now, my children, I am sad that I must leave you so poor. I am sad that I leave the Yankton nation not yet a great nation. I am sad that you are not rich with many spotted horses. I am sad that the Pawnees still come and steal our horses and rape our maidens and kill our young men. Therefore, that I should die is good, that I should live is bad. Old age is an evil thing when one is no longer needed."

A soft puff of smoke bloomed out of the top of Moon Dreamer's tepee.

"My children, we all come from the same mother and the same father, the earth and the sun. This was true of my father. It is true of me. It is true of my son. It is true of my grandson. As the days go by, like the breaths we take, one father must give way to another so that the great flow of life may remain unbroken and one."

Softly overhead the cloud moved up. Its wings touched the far south horizon and the far north horizon. It hovered over the tiny tepees like a huge eagle brood-mother. Its tail of rain trailed along the earth. First it flashed lightning out of its left eye, then out of its right eye.

"See the great thunderbird!" Redbird cried. "Hehan! he comes too late."

A second puff blossomed out of Moon Dreamer's smokehole.

"My people, listen to me. I have looked ahead to this day many times. In the night on my sleeping robe I have thought of how it might be. Once the nightmare came to me and said, 'You have heard of those who in some sacred way died alone and never were seen again. Listen, old one, and I will show you how it is done.' When I listened carefully and saw that the nightmare meant for me to throw my life away, by letting myself fall into the Great Smoky Water, I cast her words aside. A Yankton chief belongs to his people. Therefore to throw his life away is to throw away the life of his people." Redbird turned slowly with little steps, looking above the pointed tops of the tepees, eyes fixed on the lifting veils of smoke. "Still another time a spirit demon whispered in my ear and said, 'Take your son to a high place and offer him in sacrifice to Wakantanka. Wakantanka will then see that you love him very much and will give you a second youth.' Again I saw this could not be done. Even as the chief belongs to his people, so the son of a chief belongs to his people. Thus I cast these words aside also."

It began to sprinkle. A scattering of heavy raindrops

smacked onto the leather lodges. Dark sodden spots began to show on Redbird's buckskins.

"My children, listen to me. At last, after many sleepless nights, the white mare of my son's vision came to me in dream." Redbird pointed his lance at Conquering Horse. "My children, look upon a noble son." A spark seemed to leap from the copper tip, darting straight for Conquering Horse. "My children, the white mare gave me the same dream she gave my son, both the dream he saw on the Butte of Thunders and the dream he saw in the sun dance beside Falling Water. Then I saw. Then I knew. I was happy. I accepted it."

Conquering Horse jumped to his feet. He clapped hand to mouth. His eyes rolled from side to side as if he could not bear to listen to the thing his father told of. Then he cried aloud, "My father, my father, let it not be!"

"Do not weep, my son. A Yankton never throws away his tears. It is well. They of the other world have decided."

A third puff of smoke bloomed out of the top of Moon Dreamer's lodge.

"My children, your new chief will have a good heart. This I know. On the Butte of Thunders the white mare told my son to catch a white seed horse. My son told you of this when he returned. It was a good thing. In the sun dance beside our river the white mare told my son that his true father must die at last. Hi-e. Well, my son did not wish to accept this part of the vision. He wept. He loved his father very much. He wished to keep the knowledge of what had been told him from his father. Yet it had to be."

The only sounds in camp were the soft cracklings of the hearth fires.

"My son had a heavy heart, thinking that on his return from capturing the seed horse the white mare would require him to kill his true father. This was a dark vision. My son carried this knowledge with him when he took the trail alone. Yet he persevered. He counted coup on the Pawnee. He found his wife Leaf. He found the white stallion. He did all the things required of him and returned with a son and a seed colt. My children, I tell you these things so that you may know how great the Yankton nation is with such a new chief at its head."

A drum sounded in the council lodge, once, deep.

"Then the white mare came to me in a dream again. She waved her red tail over me and spoke to me. She said, "You have lived long and done well, but now it is time for you to go to the country of the spirits where your grandfather Scarlet Whirlwind and your father Wondering Man await you, as well as the Old Ones. You have the courage of the Old Ones and deserve this. Listen carefully. After your son has returned this is what you must do. Put on your vestments as chief and walk to the scalp pole. There you must tell the people in a loud voice that the white mare has told you to declare yourself their enemy. You will remember that your grandfather Scarlet Whirlwind often spoke of a custom in which the very aged were disposed of in a certain way, a custom called "making enemies of the old fathers." The old fathers were armed and allowed to defend themselves as best they could, while the young braves killed them with clubs. This was done so that the old fathers could die honorably in battle and thus glorify the greatness of the Yanktons. Therefore, on the last day of the Moon of Scarlet Plums, at dusk, after the sun sinks, call up the young braves in Circling Hawk's war society, as well as your son who will be chosen as chief, and command them to attack you in the red rocks across the river. Fight well. Do not fight in a mocking manner. We will be watching. There in the red rocks, it will be given you as well as your son!' "

A fourth puff billowed up from Moon Dreamer's lodge.

Conquering Horse slid forward to his knees. He lifted his arms in supplication. "My father, my father, is this a true thing? Did the white mare tell you this thing in truth? My father, how can this be, when we love you very much and do not wish to see you killed?"

"My son, do not cry. I go to a place of peace. My shadow soul goes to the south where it will no longer be troubled by the pains of life. My shadow soul will not visit you nor frighten you in this life. Remember this, my son. While you still remain here in misery, I will be happy in death."

Lightning, then thunder, smashed into the tumble of red rocks across the river. Almost immediately after, the sprinkling thickened into a heavy rain. It drenched the tepees and those standing without.

"My son, it does not matter where the body lies, for it is as grass. But where the spirit is, there it will be a good place to be. My son, be not like a woman. Do not kneel, but stand on your feet. Come, call up Circling Hawk and his braves and prepare for the battle."

Conquering Horse got up as one commanded in a trance.

Buckskins soaking wet, holding his lance high, Redbird walked in a stately manner out of the village circle. He took the stepping stones across the red cataracts and climbed into the tumble of red rocks above Falling Water. Then, having set himself, he lifted his voice and began to sing his death chant in an eerie high-pitched voice:

> "Friend, my sorrow would be great
> Were I to be given a long life.
> Therefore, I wish to die."

Redbird pointed his lance at the black belly of the thunderhead, gazing upward in ecstasy, crying:

> "See, my grandfather is dangerous!
> When he brandishes his warclub
> Death flies about like many crows.
> Yet my friends the Thunders come too late.
> The white mare of my son's vision is very powerful.
> The young men come and rise against me.
> I am no longer of use to my people.
> Therefore, I have become their enemy. Epelo!"

Redbird looked across the river toward the camp. When he saw that his son and the young braves still had not followed him, he cried aloud, "What, have I been a father to cowards? The white mare commands, my son. Even the Thunders obey her. She is your god. She is your vision. Come. Attack. It is fated."

At that moment Moon Dreamer emerged from his lodge. He waggled his buffalo head back and forth and up and down. Fixing his eyes on Conquering Horse, he cried, "What, and have I been a holy man to dogs? Advance, my sons, the gods wish it."

Conquering Horse stiffened under the lashing words. His face flushed black. His eyes hardened and became fixed in the manner of a reptile. He looked at the guards sitting before the door of the council lodge, then gave an explosive gesture downward, the sign for death.

Immediately Circling Hawk and a dozen braves came bursting out of the council lodge, all of them bristling with honor feathers and armed with warclubs.

Conquering Horse gestured again, first to the left, then to the right. "Charge!" he cried. "Hokay-hey! you see the enemy. Surround him."

Quickly the braves ran for the river, leaping across, and began to surround the tumble of red rocks. They shrilled cupped yells. "Oh-ow-ow-ow!"

Star and Loves Roots and Leaf, and all the people, came out of their tepees. They stood in the heavy rain and watched. Star and Loves Roots and Leaf lifted their voices, chanting, their voices wild and haunting. Others of the women fell to their knees and wept. Some tore their clothes. Some held a hand over their eyes. All cried as with one voice, "Father, father, why are you fighting us?"

Redbird lifted his copper-tipped lance four times and cried down at the advancing braves. "Ho-hech-e-tu! It is a good day to die. Come, defend yourselves."

Then, just as Conquering Horse and the young warriors climbed into the tumble of red rocks and were about to fall on Redbird, the Thunders spoke. A long pink tongue of fire licked down out of the churning black cloud above and ticked the copper tip of Redbird's lance. There was a dazzling explosion, completely enveloping Redbird. The explosion was so great it hurled Conquering Horse and the young braves entirely out of the tumble of red rocks and threw them backward upon the ground.

When the people looked again, after the lightning spots had cleared from their eyes, Redbird was gone.

Conquering Horse and the braves slowly picked themselves off the ground.

The old men stood in numb wordlessness.

The little children ran cowering to their grandmothers.

Star and Loves Roots and Leaf, and all the women, began to wail dismally beside their tepees in the pelting rain, slowly scarifying their breasts and legs.

Conquering Horse surveyed the red rocks and the river and the camp beyond, then lifted his hand and cried in a great voice, "He-han! It has at last been given us. Now we see. Now we know. Wakantanka has tested us all and found us worthy. Therefore, he told the Thunders to come for our father as they had promised him. Because of this the white mare could also give the son of the father all that she had promised him. The prophecy has been fulfilled. Hi-ye!"

Conquering Horse took his knife and, slicing, ran it around his left forefinger. "My father, this I do in memory of you. Take this finger and keep it until I come for it in the afterlife." Conquering Horse snapped the finger off at the knuckle and threw it at the skies in the direction his father had gone.

# Glossary

Butte of Thunders. Thunder Butte in South Dakota.

Falling Water. The falls on the Big Sioux River in Sioux Falls, South Dakota.

Great Smoky Water. The Missouri River.

Increasing Moon. First quarter.

Moon of Black Cherries. July.

Moon of Fat Horses. June.

Moon of First Eggs. May.

Moon of New Grass. April.

Moon of Ripe Corn. August.

Moon of Scarlet Plums. September.

Nibbled Moon. Second quarter.

Place of the Pipestone. Pipestone quarry in the Pipestone National Monument, Pipestone, Minnesota.

Place of Six Strange Boulders. The Two Maidens in the Pipestone National Monument, Pipestone, Minnesota.

River of Blue Mud. Blue River in Nebraska.

River of Little Ducks. Republican River in Nebraska.

River of Milky Water. Minnesota River.

River of the Double Bend. The Big Sioux River which drains Siouxland.

River That Sinks. The Platte River in Nebraska.

River With Red Blood. The Red River which forms the boundary between Minnesota and the two Dakotas.